IMAGINE LOVE

KATHERINE STONE

FAWCETT COLUMBINE
New York

A Fawcett Columbine Book
Published by Ballantine Books

Copyright © 1996 by Katherine Stone

All rights reserved under
International and Pan-American Copyright Conventions. Published in the
United States by Ballantine Books,
a division of Random House, Inc., New York,
and simultaneously in Canada by Random House of Canada Limited,
Toronto.

Library of Congress Cataloging-in-Publication Data
Stone, Katherine, 1949-
Imagine love / by Katherine Stone. — 1st ed.
p.   cm.
ISBN 0-449-90830-5
1. Friendship—United States—Fiction.   2. Family—United States—Fiction.
3. Women—United States—Fiction.   I. Title.
PS3569.T64134I5   1996
813'.54—dc20   95-44277
CIP

Designed by Ruth Kolbert

Manufactured in the United States of America

First Edition: April 1996

10   9   8   7   6   5   4   3   2   1

Prologue

West Texas
December Eighteenth
Twenty-seven Years Ago

I T WAS AFTER MIDNIGHT WHEN THE TWO BOYS
began their journey. The younger one had been sleeping, but
he was awakened so gently by his older brother that he uttered
not a sound.

Only the older boy knew the importance of absolute silence.
He alone knew the purpose of their journey, where it would
take them and what it would mean.

The boys' parents were asleep in the adjacent room. If experience meant anything, they wouldn't awaken until morning. After an evening of terror for their sons, they always fell
into the deepest of sleep. Never, not once in the older boy's
memory, had sounds in the night disturbed their slumber, not
even when those sounds had been the anguished cries of their
children.

Still, as he awakened his little brother, he whispered the need
for silence. It was a gentle command, obeyed without question—and with such trust. Somehow, despite his shock and his
pain, the little boy's faith in his older brother had not been
shattered. He understood, somehow, that even though the valiant effort had failed, his brother had tried, as always, to protect him.

But tonight, for the first time, the older boy's effort had

failed. Tonight, for the first time, their father had struck his youngest son.

For the first time . . . and for the last.

Their destination was a truck stop on the interstate. The older boy didn't know the distance in miles. But he knew with absolute certainty that it was far too great a distance for his little brother to walk—and too far as well for him to carry the beloved bundle. They would travel as they had traveled so many times before, the younger one in the wagon, the older one pulling.

The wagon had once been shiny and red. But that was long before it had become theirs, a discard—but a gift—from a neighbor. The wagon was rusty now, and it squeaked, a shrill protest from wheels that were no longer aligned. But to the boys it was a treasure, a magic carpet on which they could fly far away. In Breaux Bridge, Louisiana, their home until a month ago, they journeyed along the banks of the bayou, becoming lost in its languid blue splendor; and during this past month in Texas, they wandered along the river, marveling at the drama of its racing white waters.

Tonight the older boy carried the rusty wagon until they were well away from the riverside cabin that had become their new home. His little brother walked beside him, a toddling yet determined gait, and he clutched in his small arms their other special treasure. The patchwork quilt was as battered as the wagon, but as beloved. Crafted for a baby's crib, it had been rescued from a trash heap. One entire edge was badly damaged, enthusiastically chewed, perhaps, by a puppy, and there were dark stains that would never come out, and its patches were faded from a thousand washings. But to the brothers the embroidered images of happiness were dazzlingly bright. The smiling sun shone a brilliant gold, the tulips bloomed in a vivid bouquet of purple and pink, the caboose of the gingham train gleamed a deep, dark red, and the rippling ocean on which the tiny sailboat danced could not have been more blue.

Once they were a safe distance from the cabin, the older boy put the wagon on the ground and gestured for his brother to climb aboard. The little boy did so willingly, deferring as always to his older brother—and acceding as well to the cries of pain from his own injured body. Both his brother and his damaged body wanted him to sleep. But on this night, the little boy rebelled, riding as he always did, seated upright, alert and eager, ready for whatever adventure lay ahead.

He didn't want to sleep, didn't want to miss a moment of this mysterious midnight voyage. But soon his eyelids began to flutter and his bruised head began to droop. His brother stopped pulling the wagon then, curled his arms around the sleepy little boy, and began to sing.

He sang their favorite song, a happy memory from their life in Breaux Bridge. Its lyrics urged a beloved brother to awaken, not to fall asleep, but for them it had always been a lullaby, a carol of love that seduced the little one into the downy cloak of sleep and sent the solemn promise that his older brother would be there, loving him, protecting him, the moment he awoke.

But that solemn promise was no longer true. It had been replaced by an even more important vow: Our father will never hurt you again, *never*.

As the little boy drifted off to sleep, his brother softly kissed his temple, a caress so gentle that even though the young flesh was badly bruised, it caused no pain. And as he carefully swaddled the slumbering body in their tattered quilt, he whispered, in their own secret language, "I love you."

The moon bathed the earth in a pale yellow mist. It was a winter moon, and in a week would be a Christmas one, full then, and bright and golden.

The older boy trudged across the fields, guided by moonglow as he pulled his precious sleeping cargo. He needed to stop sometimes, a brief rest for his aching arms and gasping lungs, and when he did he gazed up at the moon.

They might have become allies then, the winter moon and the determined boy, conspirators in this most bold act of love. The boy might have implored the heavenly body to report back to him from time to time, shining to him brilliant gold messages of reassurance: how happy his little brother was, how safe, how loved.

But the boy made no such request of the moon. There was no point. He knew without question that he would not be alive to receive even the first moonlit report.

The winter dawn was still several hours away when they reached the interstate. The truck stop bustled with activity, however, just as it had a month ago, on their middle-of-the-night arrival in West Texas. It had seemed so festive to him then, a place of bright light amid the darkness, and his young heart had filled with hope. Perhaps, in this new home, there would be happiness and peace. Perhaps, here, the violence would end.

But it had been worse. He knew only vaguely why they had been forced to flee their Breaux Bridge home. Something about his father's job, an argument with a superior. The argument festered within his father still, a fury that fueled even greater violence than before. Someday they would return to Louisiana, his father vowed. But until that return could be a triumphant one, they would live here, in this place his father loathed, and his sons would pay for his rage.

The truck stop was as alive as it had been on that November night. But now it felt more menacing than cheerful. The truckers who were outside the restaurant, filling their mammoth vehicles with gallons of diesel, stared openly at the boy pulling the rusty red wagon. Some laughed, some even jeered, and there might have been even more taunts had any of them realized that beneath the tattered quilt lay an even younger, slumbering child.

Were all men as cruel as his father? Something deep within the boy, a bold leap of faith, had made him believe that they were not. But now he wondered. Had he been destined to live—were he not just about to die—would he, too, have become a man who enjoyed mocking those weaker than himself?

Would there have come a time when he, too, struck his own sons with vicious pleasure?

And what of his precious little brother? Despite his own brave plan, would that innocent young life mature into a monster?

And what of women? Were they all silent accomplices to the crimes of men? Did they watch, as his own mother did, her eyes oddly dull—yet ominously approving—as her sons were brutally indoctrinated into what it meant to be male?

Had it been pure foolishness to believe that there must be something more, something better? Was it sheer folly to imagine in others a gentleness to match what had been born within him the moment he had first seen his infant brother—and which had grown with each passing day?

No, he told himself. It had not been foolishness. There had to be kindness, gentleness, *somewhere* . . . for his brother.

Perhaps he wouldn't find it here, on this night, when the moon's pale yellow beams had lighted his way to cruel taunts and mocking laughter. He glared heavenward now, wanting to shout his anger at the false gold of that celestial light. But the traitorous moon had vanished from the black winter sky.

I won't give up! he cried silently to the blackness where once the moon had shone. I *can't*. I have to keep searching, believing. . . .

"Hello, there."

It was a man's voice, as deep as his father's, but it held a softness that he had never heard from a grownup. And the face that was now directly before him, because the man had crouched to be level with his eyes, was smiling and kind.

"My name is Sam." And you, Sam thought, must be a runaway. He guessed that it was an impulsive flight, perhaps precipitated by a dispute with his parents regarding a Christmas present that wasn't to be. In the fury of the moment the boy had probably heaped his belongings onto the battered wagon and defiantly marched into the night. The young face was solemn, and exhausted, but now Sam saw a flicker of hope—as if the boy instinctively understood that he was a friend, not foe. "What's your name?"

The boy answered with a decisive shake of his head. But his hopeful expression did not fade. "I need your help."

"Okay."

"Does one of these trucks belong to you?"

"Not one of the big ones. That one, over there, the pickup."

"But you're not from around here."

"No, just driving through. But if you need a ride somewhere, anywhere, I'd be happy to give you a lift."

Again the young head shook a decisive no. "Could we walk over to your truck and talk?"

"Sure."

Sam's pickup was in the shadows, away from the bright lights of the fueling area and the interested eyes of the truckers. Once in the sanctuary of those concealing shadows, the boy revealed to Sam what lay sleeping beneath the quilt.

"Will you take him?"

"Take him?"

"Home with you? Will you be his father?"

"*What?*"

"His real father is very mean. He hit him. See?"

Even in the shadows Sam could see the huge purple bruise on the small sleeping face. The idea of striking a child was so foreign to Sam, so unimaginable, that for a moment he simply stared, willing the bruise—and its violence—to be merely a mirage. But the purple mark only became more vivid, more clear. As did his own anger.

"Yes, I see," he answered finally. "I think I should take him to the police."

"*No!* You can't do that."

"Why not?"

Because his father is a cop, was a cop. "His father's friends are police officers. They would never believe that he did this. They'd give him back, and he'd be even more angry, and . . ." The image of violence halted his voice for a moment, then filled it with renewed urgency. "Take him with you, *please.* He'll die if you don't. He's so young, too young to fight back."

"And what about you?"

"Me?" This hadn't occurred to him, the idea of his own rescue, the astonishing possibility that he, too, might escape. *Be-cause it wasn't a possibility.* He had to return to the cabin, to tell his parents that he had pulled the red wagon too close to the river and that his brother had climbed out and been swept away. He would lead them to the river, to the place where the wagon would be overturned on the steep slope, a rusty grave-stone, silent now, squealing no more. His parents would believe his story, and they would blame him . . . and his father would kill him.

But his little brother would be safe.

"Won't your father hurt you, too?"

The boy was an expert liar, but now he had to pause, to steel his dying heart, before uttering the most important lie of all. "We're not brothers. I'm his neighbor, his friend. *My* father is gentle and kind."

"Where is your father now?"

"Just down the road, waiting for me. He couldn't come with me because people here might know him." As he spoke, the boy gestured vaguely toward the darkness beyond the truck stop, to the imaginary place where his imaginary father waited. Then he resumed his urgent plea. "We need to hurry. You need to take him *now*."

"I can't take him," Sam said gently. "No one can. I can't simply—"

"Yes you can! His father will never know. He'll never even *look* for him!"

"Why not?"

"Because he'll believe he's dead. I'll leave the wagon by the river, and when he finds it, he'll think he drowned. He *will* drown one day, because no one watches him—except me. He'll drown, or his father will hit him too hard. He's going to die, don't you see? Just like his brother did."

"His brother?"

"He had an older brother." He was speaking of himself now, of his own death, and even though that death was still hours away, he saw it clearly—and his words conveyed a chillingly authentic recounting of the murder of a son. "But one day their father got very angry with him. He hit him until he died—and then he hit him even more, even *after* he was dead. He told the police that it was an accident, that his son had fallen from a tree, and they believed him."

The boy shivered, as if his body was already being claimed by death, and for the first time he felt fear of the icy black emptiness in which, so soon, he would forever dwell. Refocusing quickly on the only thing that mattered, he asked, "Will you hold him now? He's probably cold."

"Yes. Okay. I'll hold him." *Just for a few moments, just while I decide what to do.* But as he cradled the entire bundle— tattered quilt and battered boy—and gazed at the small bruised face, Sam knew the truth. He was holding his son. He could make no other choice for this innocent little life.

Sam wasn't entirely convinced of everything the older boy had told him. Indeed, he seriously doubted that the boy's own father was a silent—and nearby—accomplice. But Sam did not question the boy's two most important assertions: that this defenseless child had been brutally struck by his father . . . and that that same father had already killed another son.

And if he was wrong? If, in fact, those assertions were false? Sam would find out. The frantic search for a missing child by his loving parents would be headlines in local papers, perhaps even nationwide. And if that was the case, Sam would return to accept full responsibility for his actions on this night.

But I won't be returning, Sam thought as he looked from the violent purple bruise to the earnest face of the neighbor boy. *I am holding my son.*

"How old is he?" Sam asked softly.

"He just turned two, in November."

"And his name?"

Something stopped the boy before speaking his little brother's name. Was it a deep instinct, warning him that revealing that truth amid all the lies would be far too dangerous? Or was it merely that he could no longer speak?

His heart had been torn from his chest the moment the stranger had cradled his brother in his arms. He was suffocating now, dying now. How long could he survive, a creature without a heart? Not long . . . just long enough . . . because if he died here, all would be lost.

He had to go—now—but first he had to touch his brother one last time, *had to*, a caress to sustain him for the rest of his journey, the final hours of his own life. His trembling fingers touched the small cheek. He knew of the touch, *saw* it. But he could not feel it. His fingers were numb, nearly dead. With the realization he almost seized the beloved bundle, needing to clutch him close, a life buoy that would save him from his own gasping, drowning death.

He withdrew his fingers swiftly, as if they were numb no more and had just felt fire. Then he ran. The wagon squealed behind him, so light now—and yet, in its emptiness, so very heavy.

In just a few seconds he was swallowed by the moonless darkness. But he sensed that the man was following him, guided by the screech of the rusted wheels. He picked up the wagon and ran soundlessly across the field, and when he finally stopped running, he was alone.

He had escaped.

Escaped? Yes. He had fled from a man who might have rescued him, and now he was going home, to the place where he would die.

But he did not die.

Not quite.

He merely spent his childhood wishing that he had.

*C*hapter One

Harlanville, Terrebonne Parish, Louisiana
Friday, December Twenty-third
Present Day

T WELVE YEARS AGO, ON THIS SAME DATE, he had left Harlanville. He had returned once before—six years later—only to leave again. And today, once more, he had come back.

And why was he here, on this twelve-year anniversary of the event that had driven him from his dreams, from her? Had he come to reclaim those wondrous dreams? Of course not. He knew the truth of those dreams—impossible—and the truth of those shattering moments of violence.

Those moments had freed her *from him*; freed her to fall in love with someone who could promise her all that he could not. And she *had* fallen in love with such a man . . . and she had married him.

And now, as Cole neared Belle Rêve, the home, the mansion, of Mr. and Mrs. Andrew Harlan, he fought a piercing ache with the most powerful truth of all. *This* was where Claire belonged. Here. With Andrew. At a place named Beautiful Dream. Not with him. Not anywhere. Not ever.

So why, if not in pursuit of his own beautiful dream, was he driving along the cypress-sheltered lane of snow-white cobblestones that was the grand entrance to Belle Rêve? Because of a nightmare, not a dream, a haunting image of cinnamon and crimson and snow—of Claire, stabbed, bleeding, calling to him, pleading with him not to leave.

The nightmare had been with him for twelve years, sometimes silent, sometimes screaming, never far away, and not fading even with the passage of time. Indeed, during this past year, it had become more vivid than before, and more relentless, tormenting him even in the light of day.

All the hours of Cole's life, either waking or asleep, could be tormented forever. It couldn't matter less. He deserved nightmares, just as Claire deserved dreams. It wasn't to rid himself of his nightmare that Cole had returned to Harlanville, but for Claire, because of Claire—because the newly vivid images came with the persistent worry that she was in trouble, needing help, needing *him*.

Once before, six years ago today, Cole had returned. He had believed, then, that he was answering the silent call of her heart. But that day had been Claire's wedding day. He had been wrong, as he would be wrong now.

Claire would be fine, happy, a wife now, perhaps a mother. And dreaming still?

Yes. The bright blue eyes that had sparkled with joy as she envisioned *their* glorious future would doubtless be aglow with bold imaginings still. Claire had been so confident of her dreams for them. And if the lives of Cole Taylor and Claire Chamberlain were taken together, entwined as one—as once they had planned to do—then all of Claire's grand visions had indeed come true.

She was married, and perhaps there were already daughters and sons, and Cole was a singer of love songs. Those were Claire's dreams.

But . . . her children were supposed to have been his.

And . . . his songs of love were supposed to have been theirs, duets sung only and always together.

Would Claire even remember she had once imagined that they would dazzle the world with songs of love? If so, the memory would come without a flicker of regret. She would know, as he did, as they both had known even then, that the dream she was living, of family and of love, was the only dream that mattered.

The mansion came into view then, imposing and familiar. Belle Rêve had belonged to Andrew Harlan's great-grandfather, the man who founded the town and gave it his name. Joshua Harlan's fortune had come from white gold, the sugar that flourished in the fertile soil. But forty years ago Andrew's father and his partner, Lamont Prentice, began mining black gold, the oil hidden beneath the warm waters of the gulf. By the time the price of oil began to waver, Harlan-Prentice had long since diversified, and the two families prospered still.

Belle Rêve had been built after the Civil War, but the style was antebellum, a celebration not of that era in history, but merely of its architectural grace. The stately structure looked exactly as it had twelve years ago, impeccably maintained, shimmering like a lustrous pearl beneath the gray December sky.

As Cole ascended the stairs to the front door, he wondered about the gazebo around back. Was it, too, impeccably maintained? Did the mistress of the mansion make certain that it was given a new coat of paint every year?

Or had Mrs. Andrew Harlan insisted that the gazebo be removed?

Neither, Cole told himself as he touched the doorbell. Claire will have neither enshrined that place of dreams, nor destroyed it. Either gesture would bespeak too strong a bond with the past. She has forgotten. She *needs* to have forgotten.

That's what I want for her. The nightmares are only for me.

Cole imagined that it would take a while for Claire to respond to the doorbell. The house was vast, and she was probably in the music room, singing to her children.

But the huge door swung open almost immediately, answered not by Claire but by a uniformed maid.

"I was hoping that I might see Mrs. Harlan. I'm an old friend of hers. My name is—"

"I *know* who you are!" the maid replied, her eyes wide and bright, her cheeks dimpled and rosy.

Cole was somewhat relieved by the sudden transformation from the staid formality of a servant to the exuberance of a teenaged girl. Claire would undoubtedly need a housekeeper, because the mansion was so big. But a maid? That didn't seem like Claire—and it *wasn't*, because now Cole saw the maid for who she truly was: a teenager, employed by Claire because she needed the work, money for college perhaps, or to buy *Remembrance*, Cole Taylor's latest CD of love.

Claire's teenage helper was staring at him now, beaming with pure, youthful adoration. Such moments never failed to amaze—and trouble—Cole. He sang songs of love, emotional, evocative, lyrical; but, with one recent notable exception, none of the songs was ever written by him. He sang other people's words of love, transporting them to lofty celebrity by a voice that promised breathtaking passion and never-ending love. As if he were an authority on the subject. Instead of an impostor.

"Is Mrs. Harlan at home?" Cole asked, wanting the uneasy moment to end.

"Oh! Yes, she is. Please follow me."

The journey from the white marble foyer was a festive one. The mansion's usual decor was cheerful enough, walls abloom with hand-painted lilacs, but on this day before Christmas Eve there was seasonal cheer as well: garlands of holly and pine, wreaths of eucalyptus and winter roses, scented candles encased by prisms of crystal, shining silver bells suspended by ribbons of gold.

Claire had always loved Christmas. And Cole? For him, until Claire, it had been a time of sadness, of loss. But bravely—oh, she had been so brave!—the intrepid angel had determined to convince the fierce infidel that Christmas was a time of magic, of wonder, of joy.

And at last she *had* convinced him, on that moonlit night in the gazebo ... and the following day, twelve years ago today, they had both been harshly punished for his foolishness.

The journey through the mansion halted abruptly beneath the living room's arched entrance, perilously close to a beribboned sprig of mistletoe. Cole assumed that it was a temporary stop along the way, to enable him to admire the tree. It didn't seem like a room in which Claire would spend much time, and he seriously doubted that the rosy-cheeked girl had the temerity to demand the ritual of mistletoe.

The tree stood at the far end of the formal living room. A twelve-foot noble fir, it was adorned with Waterford crystal ornaments, rose-pink glass balls, and silver lights. It was magnificent, of course. But it couldn't compare to the small trees that had spent their Christmases in Claire's modest girlhood home. The trees themselves were often scraggly, rescued—and loved—by Claire and Aunt Augusta because they knew that no one else would want them.

Sometimes their bedraggled trees were dressed in shimmering evening gowns of silvery tinsel, and on other Christmases in less glittering fare—braided strands of popcorn and garlands of cranberries. Despite the dress, however, the accessories were always the same, freshly baked cookies, handmade ornaments, and lights of many colors that bubbled, twinkled, and glowed.

Had Claire's children helped decorate *this* magnificently haute couture tree? No, Cole decided. But there would be another tree, fragrant with cookies, in the music room, with the children and Claire.

"Mrs. Harlan? You have a visitor."

The girl's words caught Cole by surprise. Claire was here? Behind the tree, perhaps, or in one of the several alcoves in this vast, coldly formal room? He should have sensed her presence. But he hadn't. And now, even knowing that she was here, he didn't know where to look, couldn't anticipate from which shadow she would emerge. It seemed impossible that the woman who lived so vividly in his heart could be a phantom now, when she was this close.

But Mrs. Andrew Harlan was most definitely in Belle Rêve's formal living room. She was walking toward him, a stylish flow of crimson satin, a Parisian designer's creation of trousers and tunic encircled with gold at her slender waist. Her nails matched the satin, and a trio of spectacular diamonds sparkled on her left hand. Clusters of smaller gems glittered at her ears and throat, and her hair, as black as his, shined with a lustrous inner light.

Most brilliant of all, however, were her eyes. They fairly shimmered their surprise, and their happiness, to see him.

There was absolutely no doubt that the ravishingly beautiful Mrs. Andrew Harlan was delighted to welcome home Harlanville's famous—and infamous—singer of love songs.

But . . . the ravishingly beautiful Mrs. Andrew Harlan was not Claire.

"Annabelle."

"Hello, Cole," she replied, moving gracefully toward him, her eyes never leaving his even as she issued an imperious dismissal to her maid. "Thank you, Susannah. That will be all."

Cole saw the roses leave the dimpled cheeks of his teenaged escort. But they bloomed anew when he smiled. "It was nice to have met you, Susannah."

"Oh, Mr. Taylor, it was nice to have met *you*, too."

Then Susannah was gone, and Cole and Annabelle were alone, and even had he not been standing beneath the mistletoe, Annabelle would have greeted him precisely as she did, with long crimson nails that caressed his cheeks as she tiptoed to touch her lips to his.

"My hero," she whispered.

Cole responded by encircling both of her slender wrists with the strong lean fingers of his left hand. Then, after removing her caressing touch from his face, and holding her handcuffed at arm's length, he said, "I'm not your hero."

"But you *are*! It's always bothered me that you left town before I could thank you properly. But now you're back. And now I can."

"I came to see Claire. I thought that she and Andrew were married."

Had his hand not imprisoned her still, Annabelle would have answered with a dismissive wave of crimson and diamonds. As it was, she shrugged her red satin shoulders.

"They *were* married. Very briefly." She frowned, as if debating whether to say more. Then, the decision apparently made, a decision to remain silent, her frown vanished, replaced by a petulant and seductive pout. "Let go of me, Cole. I won't attack you again, I promise. Not until you're ready, that is. Come have a martini with me. I've just finished making an entire pitcher."

Cole released her. "No, thank you."

"Oh, Cole! Come *on*. Just one drink, for old times' sake."

There had been no old times with Annabelle, not the kind that her provocative expression implied. True, heiress Annabelle Prentice and bad boy Cole Taylor had done some drinking together. But Annabelle had been his father's lover, not his.

Cole did have one vivid memory of Annabelle—on that December day, when blood as bright as the crimson satin she now wore had flowed so freely, drenching him in death and drowning all his dreams.

Annabelle had been there that day. Indeed, had it not been for Annabelle . . .

"Where's Claire?"

"How should I know?"

"Does she still live in Harlanville?"

"Yes. She lives in Aunt Augusta's house and teaches music at the school."

"And Aunt Augusta?"

"Oh." Annabelle's expression became thoughtful. "You obviously don't know. She died about six months ago, in her sleep. She was almost eighty, and it happened the way everyone would wish, very peacefully, but it was still a huge loss. You know what Augusta Chamberlain was. A town legend. Just like you." She smiled seductively, but Cole's chilling glare warned her away. "Oh, all *right*, Cole! I remember you as being a little more fun."

"You remember wrong. I can find my way out."

"If you're really abandoning me to search for Claire, I have a suggestion. Try the school. She's probably there, getting ready for the pageant."

"The pageant is always held on the twenty-second." It was a quiet statement, but it held a note of protest. Harlanville's traditional Christmas pageant should have already taken place, last night, *as always*. That was why Cole had returned today, on the twelfth anniversary of the most devastating day of his life, not yesterday, the anniversary of the one that had been the most wondrous.

"Always before," Annabelle clarified. "Actually, the change is because of us, Andrew and me. We're giving a gift to the school, perpetual funding for the music program and its faculty, an enduring endowment no matter what the legislators decide about the value of music in public schools. Anyway, since Andrew had to be in New Orleans last night, the pageant was scheduled for this evening." Her smile returned. "It's really rather perfect, isn't it? Who better to be here on the night of the pageant than Harlanville's living proof of just how valuable a music program can be?"

Chapter Two

COMPELLED BY A NIGHTMARE THAT WOULD not fade, Cole had returned to Harlanville to make certain that Claire was all right, joyously happy, living her dream. He'd had no doubt that that was what he would find, and when he left this time it would truly be forever.

Adieu, not *au revoir.*

And now? Nothing had changed except the venue in which he would see her again. And, he thought, it was a venue that virtually assured her happiness. The image of her as mistress of the mansion had always been a little out of focus. But as Cole drove toward the school, the image of Claire teaching music became brilliantly clear.

His mind's eye saw her delicate hands dancing in air as she led her students in song. Claire's hands were bare—except for the band of gold, the simple yet eloquent symbol of her wedding vows, far more glittering than the most flawless of diamonds. And now her hands were abandoning their midair dance and floating downward, to her lower abdomen, and now they were touching with reverent wonder the almost imperceptible swelling.

Cole had to stop the image. It was too clear, too painful, a glaringly bright reminder of the life of love that he and Claire had planned. The image receded, but the void was quickly filled with more aching remembrance—to which, finally, he surrendered.

It was necessary, he realized. He must remember *everything*, must permit the smoldering ember of every memory to flame brightly one last time.

Before he could truly say good-bye, he had to once again live their hello. . . .

It was late June. Cole and his father had moved to Harlanville two weeks before, two weeks—for Cole—of sheer torment. The town was far too close to the bayou. Even from their small house, almost two miles away, Cole could feel it beckoning to him, evoking emotions that were so anguished . . . and so sweet.

Come to me, the bayou whispered, its enticing message carried by a steamy breeze that was fragrant with intoxicating scents and alive with a symphony of sounds. Cole could hear the cicadas hum, and the birds trill, and even from this distance he believed that he could hear the rhythmic splashing as the pirogues glided by. Come to me, Cole. *Come.*

For two weeks Cole had resisted the sultry call, the aching enchantment. Instead, he prowled the sizzling-hot sidewalks of his new home, glowering his contemptuous reply to the disapproving stares that greeted him.

This boy was going to be trouble, the townspeople agreed. This boy, this angry stranger with the long black hair and hostile gray eyes and the body that, despite its youth, roamed the scorching pavement without buoyancy. He stood tall, arrogant and proud. But an immense heaviness seemed to ride upon his young shoulders, a formidable burden against which he must struggle always.

Cole Taylor had turned eleven in February. But those who watched him prowl concluded that he was thirteen at least, perhaps older, and he was undoubtedly experienced in things unknown to the children of Harlanville. It was the early seventies, a decade still reeling from the aftershocks of the one that had come before, that wanton era of sex, drugs, and rock 'n' roll.

But not here. Not in Harlanville. LSD and marijuana and free love might still taint other parts of the country, but not this sleepy bayou town in Terrebonne Parish.

Except that now their pristine town had been invaded, and even the adults saw that there was something compelling about Cole Taylor, a sinister, sensual magnetism. As he walked by the Cypress Café, the town's coffee shop and unofficial meeting place, they saw the truth of his gait: graceful yet predatory, a panther in search of his prey. He was going to sell drugs to their sons, and corrupt in unspeakable ways the virtue of their daughters, and—

But he wouldn't *dare*, they tried to tell themselves. Not given his father's job. He couldn't, wouldn't . . . would he?

On that June day, as they watched his restless weighted gait carry him toward the bayou, the good townspeople of Harlanville shared an unspoken thought. Perhaps he would venture too far into the brooding forest that lined its banks, lost in that enchantment. Lost forever. It could happen.

Even to a panther.

Cole had known that he would eventually submit to the sultry whispers of the bayou, its scented invitation to magic, to pain, to memories of another bayou and that long-ago time when there had been such love—and such loss.

He chose this day, when the sky was bright turquoise and the blazing sun sent searing punishment to all human flesh. But it was a different day in the lush woods that enveloped the languid blue waters. A different world. Cooler, softer, shaded. A place where a gossamer veil of Spanish moss splintered the sky into tiny turquoise shards and muted the sun's angry glare to the soothing glow of candles.

The bayou sang to him once again, a bittersweet serenade, touching his heart, reopening his wounds, killing him softly. It was then, as his heart flooded with grief and his soul was nearly drowned, that he heard the other sound. New. Unfamiliar. Wondrous.

A human voice—or was it? The tone was so clear, so pure, and even the lyrics came from another realm.

"Amazing Grace, how sweet the sound . . ."

Cole Taylor did not believe in heaven, despite his abiding belief in its evil twin. Hell he knew firsthand, an old friend, a constant companion. But heaven? It was a place beyond imagination—for him—even in death.

"That saved a wretch like me . . ."

But now, as the balmy air filled with this song, this joy, he began to believe. He was in heaven, and in a few more steps, just around that next eucalyptus tree, he would meet an angel. Cole realized then what had happened. His wounds had wept such grief that he had drowned in their tears. He was dead, and she had come for him.

And if he was wrong? If she was here on another mission of mercy? Then he would implore her to let him die, to take him with her.

"I once was lost, but now am found . . ."

In another moment he would see his angel. Her hair would be golden, as would the aura that haloed her entire being. The enveloping luminescence would not, however, be merely the consequence of sunlight filtered through a mossy veil. It would be something else, something more—a truly celestial glow. Her gown would be flowing white silk, and yes, she would have wings, and . . .

. . . and Cole was right about one thing: she was caressed by shafts of light that seemed otherworldly. But his angel's hair was the color of cinnamon, and she wore a gingham blouse and blue jeans, and she had no wings.

She was facing away from him still, and her song had not faltered, but Cole believed that she knew he was there, that she had somehow sensed his presence. And she had—because just before the final lyric, she turned to him, to sing the words to his stone-gray eyes.

"Was blind, but now I see."

And then Cole's angel, who was in fact an eight-year-old girl, shined upon him. He was a stranger, and even to the adults of Harlanville, he was a fearsome, menacing force. But the innocent little girl with whom he was now alone was absolutely unafraid. Her freckled face glowed with welcome, and her bright blue eyes sparkled, and when she spoke her voice was musical still.

"Hi." It was a single syllable, a solitary note, but it danced around them in the steamy air, an entire ballet of joy. She smiled then, an angel's smile, except that it was missing at least one tooth, more proof of her age . . . and of her humanity. "Who are you?"

"Cole."

"I'm Claire."

It began on that day, the magical friendship of the lost boy and the innocent girl. They were children then, bonded by that wonder, that sameness—and blissfully unaware of the differences that, too soon, would drive them apart.

Cole's new little friend wanted to know everything about him. He shared with her what truths he could. There weren't many. He couldn't even tell her what grade he would enter in the fall. His schooling had been sporadic. No one compelled him to go. No one cared.

Until now.

"Who do you think you are? Peter Pan?" Claire demanded when Cole told her that he might not bother to enroll at all. She shook a young finger at him and implored earnestly, "You *have* to go to school, Cole. It's very important. Your entire future depends on it."

But I don't have a future. It was a silent yet confident protest, and it came even as Claire was taking him to see her aunt Augusta.

Augusta Chamberlain had taught fifth grade at Harlanville's only school for almost forty years. The beloved and revered schoolmarm was a legend—and a mystery. She had forsaken her family in Lafayette, and the inheritance that would have been hers, and moved to Harlanville. That was remarkable enough. But why had this elegant woman, whose physical beauty had only become more regal with age, always been alone? Why had she, of all people, remained a spinster? Why had she never been wanted, desired, loved?

The truth was that Augusta Chamberlain *had* been loved, desperately, passionately, and forever. Theirs had been a secret love, the southern belle and the Cajun boy. She was educated, and he was not. Her family was prosperous, and his barely survived. But his nobility, his sense of honor, knew no bounds. He went to war and died for his country.

Augusta spent every day of her life being grateful that she had given herself to him, all of herself, defying even that most sacred of societal mandates. And she spent every day regretting that their clandestine love had not left her with his child.

Augusta was fifty-four when two-year-old Claire's parents perished in a blaze in their home near Baton Rouge and Augusta became the toddler's legal guardian. In truth, because Claire's father had been Augusta's nephew, Augusta was Claire's great-aunt. But even before her parents' death, Claire had called her Aunt Augusta, and it was a contagious name, because within a year of little Claire's arrival in Harlanville, *everyone*—except pupils who were actually in her class—abandoned the austere "Miss Chamberlain" for the affectionate "Aunt Augusta."

The orphaned girl and her lonely great-aunt loved each other, nurtured each other; and Claire and Augusta nurtured Harlanville as well, infusing into the town a new sense of community, of *family*.

Claire was always bringing home strays, fellow orphans who needed love, and Aunt Augusta always welcomed them all. Which was precisely how she greeted Cole Taylor.

But as she looked at the hard lines of sadness that etched his young face, Augusta found herself wondering if this stray of Claire's could truly be saved. Or was it already far too late?

Cole could read, and was obviously terribly bright, and even though there were huge gaps in what he knew, Augusta made the decision that, come fall, he would be enrolled in her fifth-grade class. That way she could help him, and it seemed unfair to place him in any lower grade. As it was, at eleven, he would be her oldest pupil.

"I can teach him everything he needs to know through second grade," Claire volunteered. "And—"

"Oh no you don't," Augusta interjected, correctly anticipating Claire's next words. "You can teach him through second grade, young lady, but not one lesson beyond. I won't have you being bored in your classes for the next two years. Cole, you must promise me that you won't let Claire work on any of the assignments I give you for third and fourth grades."

"I promise," he vowed, stunned that the girl-angel and her elegant great-aunt had taken him on, deeming him a worthwhile summertime project. *I'm not worth it. I have no future. Don't you see?*

But they didn't see. Neither did they become bored or impatient. Every Monday morning Aunt Augusta would provide him with the lessons for the week, and within an hour he and Claire would be in the forest, hard at work in their cathedral of lacy moss and whispering leaves.

Claire took her role very seriously, this all-important education of Peter Pan. She quizzed him relentlessly, and was so proud of him when he knew the answers, and, oddly, she seemed equally proud of him even when he didn't know. Indeed, the only heavy sighs from Cole's freckle-faced teacher came when he was studying subjects that were forbidden to her.

Claire would read her own books then, ones that Aunt Augusta allowed, and she would wander restlessly, but never completely out of sight, dancing across fallen logs while she waited for him to take his next break, sometimes humming to herself, sometimes singing aloud to her audience of snow-white egrets.

"I still haven't heard *you* sing, Cole," she announced one day.

"You never will."

"Why not?"

"Maybe I can't sing."

"*Everyone* can sing."

"Everyone can carry a tune?"

"No, but that's not really what singing is about, is it?"

"Isn't it?"

Claire gave him a look of pure exasperation, and the hands that had been planted firmly on her narrow hips began to wave in the humid air. "Of course not! People need to sing. *All* people. It's like sleeping or eating or *breathing*." The exasperation vanished then, replaced by an expression that was wise beyond her years. "You'll feel better if you sing, Cole. I know you will."

Her words stunned him. What else did this wise little elf know? That his soul had long since died? But that once, long ago, it had been alive with happiness—and with song?

"Besides, you'll *have* to sing in school. In addition to teaching fifth grade, Aunt Augusta is the music teacher for the entire school. There are several pageants each year, and people come from throughout the parish, and sometimes even from New Orleans, just to hear them. Everyone in Harlanville sings, Cole. I'll teach you how. It's really very easy. Won't you try?" Cole didn't know if she saw some signal in his eyes—a flicker, perhaps, of hope—or if she simply made a decision. But as he watched, the determined expression he had come to know settled firmly on her lovely face and she took his hands from the textbook he was studying and held them in hers. "Now pay attention, Cole, and sing with me."

Sing with me. How they had sung, filling the forest with sounds as pure as birdsong and as clear as the summer air. Theirs were the high, sweet voices of children, the girl who feared nothing and believed in all dreams . . . and the boy, fearless, too, who believed in nothing—except these moments of paradise with her.

They sang a cappella in their emerald chapel. They needed no instruments beyond their own voices, no orchestral support beyond the symphony of the bayou. Still, one day, Claire arrived with a guitar. It was hers, a gift from Aunt Augusta, and now, she told him, it was his.

"It's too big for me," she explained. "And besides, it hurts my fingers too much to try to play. You have to press the strings very hard against the frets. Eventually, *supposedly*, you develop calluses. But I've decided I'm just going to stick with the piano. So it's yours, if you want it."

Cole wanted the guitar, this gift from his generous, joyful little friend. He didn't mind the pain to his fingertips, he played right through it, familiar melodies and new ones, haunting strains of his own creation, for which, together, they often added words.

The magical—and so innocent—friendship of Cole and Claire lasted almost two years. But during the year when he turned thirteen, Cole stopped coming to their enchanted forest. He was changing, a boy becoming a man, and she was still a girl. Even before he stopped choosing to be with her, his singing voice forewarned the impending separation. The pure, clear, glorious harmony they had known as children vanished as his voice began its descent to the deep, sensual richness that one day would enthrall the world.

For the next six years, Cole and Claire passed each other almost daily in the hallways at school, seeing but not acknowledging, and truly looking only when it was safe. And when they *did* look? They saw the changes, and ached for the lost innocence . . . until the day when Claire, too, began the journey toward adulthood.

It was then that Cole had to stop looking altogether. And he did. His longings were far too dangerous—and far too selfish.

The little girl who had been his friend was becoming a young woman, blossoming before his eyes, a brave flower opening joyously toward the sun. For her sake, *for her sake*, Claire must remain a stranger to him.

But Claire had not remained a stranger. The harsh thought came to Cole now, as he slowed his rental car to a stop in front of the school. He should have stayed far away from her, and they most certainly should never have sung together again.

But twelve years ago, when she was sixteen and he was nineteen, their voices had joined anew, blending in a harmony more perfect than the sweetness of children—the magnificent duet of love between a woman and a man, a song sung by two voices, but with a single heart.

Cole and Claire had sung together on that December evening, strangers no more, and later that moonlit night there had been even greater magic—and wondrous dreams.

But the following day the magic was shattered by violence . . . and all the dreams were drowned in blood.

Chapter Three

EVEN FROM THE MAIN FOYER OF THE SCHOOL, Cole heard the carols. They came from the auditorium and drifted along the empty corridors like haunting echoes from that long-ago night.

Cole followed the sound, past Claire's steel locker and his, on linoleum scuffed, still, from the shoes they once had worn. There was Aunt Augusta's classroom, much smaller now than it had seemed then, and the principal's office he knew so well, and the cafeteria where all twelve classes ate lunch together and where he and Claire had looked at each other without looking.

Twelve years was not even a blink in the history of mankind, and in this place, nestled near the primeval Acadian forest of *Evangeline*, it seemed as if no time had passed at all.

Until he reached the auditorium. Here time had moved forward, progress had been made. Totally renovated, the auditorium now boasted cushiony seats, where once there had been only wood, and its once barren walls were freshly painted and adorned with murals. There had been acoustical improvements as well, an invisible change that the talented musician instantly detected and appreciated.

As if in answer to the question that was forming in his

mind—how this modern-day auditorium had found itself here—
Cole noticed the gleaming bronze plaque. *Augusta Chamberlain
Theatre*, it read. *Donated by Andrew and Annabelle Harlan.*

Cole hoped that the theater had been completed before Aunt
Augusta's death, that she had been able to stand in this precise
spot where he stood now and marvel at the enveloping sound
as she gazed at the newly varnished stage and beheld her grandniece leading her students in song.

Cole had almost forgotten, had forbidden himself to remember, the grace of Claire's arms. But on that December night he
had known their exquisiteness. And they had been graceful still,
a desperate grace, the following day, when she had reached for
him, touching him, loving him—until he pushed her away.

Her arms were pale now, snow-white and womanly. But
once they had been deeply tanned, and constantly swinging,
as the elf-angel marched to the silent rhythms that pulsed
within.

Cole could see only the floating of Claire's white arms and
the thoughtful tilt of her cinnamon-colored head. But he imagined her face. Her lips would be quietly mouthing the familiar
carols, and smiling, and her bright blue eyes would shimmer
like a summer sky aglow with sunlight.

Soon he would see that face. Would Claire smile, still, when
she saw him? Or would the sky, that glowing happiness, become cloudy with sadness?

Cole wouldn't know until the rehearsal was through. At once
eager for that moment—and dreading it—he was quite content
to wait, watching her, listening to the carols, and remembering.

Quite suddenly, and without direction from the graceful
arms, the singing stopped, replaced by whispers, hushed yet
clear in this vast place of acoustical perfection.

"It's *him*."

"It can't be."

"But it is! It's—"

Even before Claire heard the echoing whispers of his name, she
knew. Hadn't she, in fact, felt his presence before the very first

whisper? Hadn't an icy chill trembled through her entire being? Hadn't she sensed the sudden appearance of a ghost?

He was here. Again. At last. Too late.

Why? Did he know? Had Aunt Augusta broken her solemn promise after all? In the final days of her life had her beloved great-aunt written to Cole despite Claire's own fervent pleas? Was that—Aunt Augusta's revelation of the truth—the reason Cole had returned to Harlanville after all these years?

Or would it come as a surprise to him, a shock? *And how would she know?*

"It's Cole Taylor, Miss Chamberlain. Cole Taylor!" The students were imploring her now, wanting her permission to abandon their posts on the varnished stage and approach the school's most famous student. "Miss Chamberlain? It's really *him*. Can we—"

Claire gave permission with a nod, and her slender white arms, suspended still in midair, fell slowly to the podium. Her hands clutched the polished wood, and she bowed her head as she listened to the thunder of eager footsteps rushing past her, to him.

Cole hadn't wanted this to happen. He had made a conscious decision to remain in the shadows, hidden until the rehearsal was over and the students were gone. But the sight of Claire had beckoned to him, not to the superstar he had become but to the nineteen-year-old he once had been, and without thought he had followed that invisible command, moving closer to her—out of the shadows and into the light.

Claire's choir of students surrounded him now, far too shy to touch but brave enough to ask for his autograph on the sheets of music that they held. Cole complied, murmuring the right words, the polite ones, focused on the ardent young faces but so very aware of the face he could not see.

She stood at the podium, and still she had not turned toward him, and her body was stiff, and her head was bent as if in shame, *or in fear.*

It was obvious that Claire was waiting for him, *would* wait until he was through and they could be alone. But even from this distance, Cole sensed that it was a decision of resignation, not of joy. She *would* see him, but she didn't want to. He was a stranger now . . . and that was how she wanted him to remain.

Finally the last sheets of music had been signed, and there was no possibility that the rehearsal would continue. The students were too eager to spread the word that Harlanville's notorious celebrity had returned. But before disbanding, someone asked, "You'll be here tonight, won't you, Mr. Taylor? You'll sing at the pageant?"

No, because the pageant should have been last night, and today is the solemn anniversary of the day that shattered all dreams, and it's so very clear that she doesn't want me here, not even, at last, to truly say good-bye.

"I . . . don't know."

The new theater, built in honor of Aunt Augusta, was a celebration of sound, of music, of song. It was not meant to be silent.

But it was silent now, and the structure that had been designed to exalt every note, to worship even the faintest hum, captured the soundlessness, amplifying it to a near-deafening roar. The air quivered, as if a live thing with its own racing heart, and the footfalls that approached her fairly thundered, as if he were an executioner of sorts, an assassin of dreams.

Then there was a voice, a hoarse whisper, soft yet harsh. The softness was for her, the harshness for himself.

"Claire?"

"Cole."

Her voice drifted through the thick veil of her shining auburn hair as once it had drifted through thick garlands of Spanish moss. On that long-ago June day, when he had first beheld his angel in blue jeans, Claire had been facing away from him, as she was now. But on that day, she had turned to him, to sing to him the final lyric of her joyous song.

Was blind, but now I . . .

She was turning now, at last, and slowly, the pirouette of a condemned ballerina, resigned to twirl, destined to do so, but fearful, as if this were the final dance . . . the end of all dancing.

Then she was facing him, and as she tipped her head to look up, the cinnamon veil parted, revealing skin that was startlingly white, strikingly pale. Claire had, it seemed, forsaken the sun. But no matter, Cole thought vaguely. She had always had her own sun, her own private star, glowing brightly within.

He searched now for proof of that private golden sun. It was there still, in her magnificent eyes, amber flecks aglow amid the shimmering blue. But the flecks of starshine were darker than Cole remembered, a deeper, burnished gold—like the gold of a wedding band, richer, deeper, more lustrous with wear.

Cole's gaze fell to the snowy whiteness of her hands. They were fisted at her sides, their knuckles translucent, their fingers quite ringless.

You're supposed to be married, Claire. Married, happy, living your dream—without me.

As he stared at her ringless hands, Cole realized that Claire must be witnessing his curious glance and wondering what it meant. *It means nothing, Claire. Nothing has changed.* I want what I've always wanted—your happiness . . . without me.

The presumptuousness of his thought struck him then, and still staring at her hands, he imagined her reply. You're too *late*, Cole! We're not married yet, but I've met someone, a wonderful man. I'm in love, and now I truly know what love means, what it's *supposed* to mean. I've learned that from him, not from you. Your specialty was cruelty, wasn't it? Cruelty, not love. Oh, I'm so *lucky* that you left!

Cruelty was his specialty, not Claire's. And, Cole realized, no matter how lucky she feels to have escaped my love, she will never be cruel in return.

As he lifted his gaze from her bloodless, ringless hands, Cole anticipated the thoughtful expression that would greet his obvious search for a wedding ring. But what greeted him caused a stab of pain, a sharp, piercing slash that far surpassed all previous assaults his heart had been compelled to endure.

Claire was looking up at him still, her eyes aglow with welcome—and with fear. She had not followed his gaze to her
hands, nor did she follow it now as he found the snow-white
symbol of the truth that lay, neatly compressed, beside her on
the floor. She merely waited, expectant and apprehensive, as he
made the discovery.

The private sun that lived in Claire Chamberlain's lovely
heart was shining still. Indeed, its glow seemed brighter than
ever, brilliantly illuminating even the darkest of golden flecks.
It was a glorious sun, but a small one. Its mission was to light
all the shadows of her heart, and in that task the tiny star succeeded splendidly.

But there were things Claire's little sun could not do.

It could not, for example, enable her glowing blue eyes to see.

Nor could it cast its golden beams beyond her heart, to illuminate the world of blackness in which Claire Chamberlain
was now destined to dwell.

He hadn't known. Claire could feel his shock, could sense its
power filling the air between them.

"I guess Aunt Augusta didn't write to you."

"No."

Not once in her six years of blindness had Claire prayed for
sight, needing it so desperately that any trade—her heart, her
very soul—was a fair price. But now . . . oh, how she needed to
see the face of this man. His face. His eyes. Were they smoky
now, ablaze with anger at the twist of fate that had condemned
her to darkness?

Or were they wintry, his rage pure ice?

And was his greatest fury directed not toward fate but toward her, the once bold nymph who had betrayed them both
by becoming—to his glacial eyes—a figure of pity?

"What happened, Claire?"

I need to see him, please! His voice sounds gentle, but . . .

He was shadow and stone, this man she had loved, a formidable fortress of night-dark secrets. Fierce. Hard. Impenetrable.

Unreadable. But Claire *could* read him, sometimes, when she could see the strong muscles that rippled in his jaw, and the pace and power of the pulse in his throat, and the set of his lips, and the glint of steel in his silvery eyes.

Claire had none of those guideposts now. She had only the voice of the man whose songs of love had seduced the world. And from him, this darkest of all shadows, this man who believed that his heart was carved from stone, even the gentlest whisper could mean nothing at all.

"Why are you here, Cole?"

"To see you."

"But you didn't know."

"No. I assumed that you and Andrew were still married."

"You knew about our marriage?"

"I was here, on that evening. There were signs everywhere—in store windows and even on the theater marquee—announcing your wedding and wishing you and Andrew the best. Did you know that?"

Claire nodded, unable to speak. *You were in Harlanville on my wedding night? Why, Cole? Why? Were you coming back to me at last? Should I have waited one more day? Should I have told my heart to endure just a little longer before I numbed forever the place that missed you, cried for you, loved you so much?*

Her eyes could not see, but they could speak. And now Cole saw pure anguish. "Claire?"

"I knew about the signs. I saw them." *I could* see *then, Cole! I could still see.* And if I had seen you, your eyes, the muscles of your jaw, the heartbeat in your throat . . . "The accident happened just a few hours after we were married. There was a rainstorm that night. The roads were very wet, slippery."

"I remember," Cole said quietly. He would never forget the thunder of that night, the storm that raged in the world outside—and the more ferocious one that swirled within.

He had left Harlanville within minutes of learning that she was to marry. He'd hitched the first ride that came along, willing to go wherever the driver was headed. When he was a few hours away, he felt a sudden chill, bone-deep, ominous, and then demanding. *Go to her*, the icy quivers whispered. *She needs you.*

No, he had countered firmly, harshly. *It's my need I'm feeling. My need, my despair—not hers.*

But what if that was wrong? What if Claire *had* cried out for him on that long-ago stormy night?

"What happened, Claire?"

"We were driving to New Orleans."

"After the reception?"

"Yes."

"Andrew was driving? In a rainstorm? After a few bottles of champagne?"

"I . . . no. The reception was at Belle Rêve. He drove only until we were out of sight of the mansion, then I took over."

Because you hadn't had anything to drink, not even on your wedding night.

There had been times during those years when they were wary strangers that Claire had bravely crossed the invisible line that kept them apart. In the beginning, such times had been to share a bit of news, as if they were still friends, the boy and girl in the forest beside their bayou. She would impart her news, some cheerful little tidbit that she believed her friend would want to know, and her eyes would be so bright, so hopeful as she awaited his reply. Cole would answer with a mocking glare; and finally, bewildered—and so hurt!—she would dash away.

As Claire began to grow up, to catch up, the invisible line became a deep and dangerous abyss. But still, when she had to—for him—she braved it. Cole remembered now the night of her greatest courage. She was fourteen, awakening, blossoming, on the very verge of shedding her little-girl chrysalis, and he was seventeen, old for his age, far more man than boy, and already notorious for relationships that were fleeting, volatile, intensely sexual.

On that night, the sultry eroticism that Cole was enjoying with his current girlfriend was abundantly clear. They were in public, talking with friends, but their bodies were touching with an explicitness that Claire did not fully comprehend. It was intimacy, she knew that, and seeing him like that made her ache with a longing she had yet to understand. But still she approached him . . . them.

Cole had been drinking, was drinking still, as were his friends. The others were becoming raucous, boisterous and loud. But Cole, who had consumed the most, was silent. It was that eerie silence that compelled Claire to approach him. That silence—and his eyes. She had never seen the gray look so empty, so *remote*. It was as if Cole had died and was watching his ghost.

But as he listened to her valiant challenge, the detachment vanished, replaced by a stone-gray gaze that was infinitely cruel.

"I *dare* you never to drink again, Cole Taylor." Her voice was as brave as it had been during their halcyon days beside the bayou. She was constantly daring him then. Close your eyes, Cole, and *then* walk across the log! Claire's challenges were always for both of them, always shared; and now as then she offered to meet the challenge with him. "I'm never going to drink, Cole. Not ever."

"You shouldn't drink, Claire. You're far too young. Go away, little girl."

Cole could not accept her dare, not then. He could only hurt her, somehow needing to do that—a need as strong as his own need to drink. He couldn't imagine a time when he wouldn't drink. But that time had come, on the rain-drenched night when Claire Chamberlain had wed. His abstinence became a different kind of punishment, far more severe than the self-destructive urges that once compelled him to drink. With abstinence, Cole condemned himself to a life that was blurred no more, a world in which he was forced to face the sharp, blinding brightness of truth.

Six years ago, on Claire's wedding night, Cole had accepted her dare. But was it a shared challenge still? Or had Claire long since learned the intoxicating pleasures of champagne?

"Had you been drinking?"

"Oh, no. I don't . . ." She shrugged. "I was quite sober, but I must have been driving carelessly, too fast for the slickness of the road. Fortunately, no one else was involved."

Fast, careless driving didn't sound like Claire. Had she been so desperate to get to New Orleans? To begin her wedding night with Andrew Harlan?

"Must have been?" Cole echoed. "Don't you remember the accident?"

"No. I had a fairly serious head injury. It left me with permanent amnesia for the accident—and for several hours before. I remember getting dressed for the wedding." *And I remember Aunt Augusta asking me one last time if I was really certain that I wanted to marry Andrew, to stop waiting for you—at last.* "Then nothing until I awakened two days later."

You have no memory of your wedding? That lacy, romantic dream? "Are you sure you were driving?"

She hesitated briefly, then confessed, "No, I'm not sure. But it doesn't matter," she added with haste. "Andrew plans to run for public office someday."

And what of *your* plans, Claire? Your dreams? The questions came unbidden from his heart, screaming into the silence . . . into her darkness.

Claire couldn't hear Cole's thoughts. But she sensed their power, their rage, and she ached anew, her own silent anguished scream, at her helplessness.

"The doctors talked about operating," she said, needing to finish her story, *needing him to leave.* "To try to reverse the blindness. There was only a chance that the surgery would succeed, and the procedure itself was quite risky, and because of my other injuries, I was already a very poor surgical candidate."

"So Andrew wouldn't let them operate."

Claire seemed surprised by the confidence of his assertion, and oddly confused.

"No," she answered finally. "It was my decision. If something happened to me, something more than what already had, it would have been too much for Aunt Augusta."

It would have killed her. The words were unspoken, but Cole knew that they were true. Claire's decision had been an unselfish choice of love, made for Aunt Augusta. And if there hadn't been an Aunt Augusta? Wouldn't Claire have made the same choice for herself, choosing blindness over death? She was a bride, after all, beginning her life with the man she loved.

Her blue eyes had glowed at the mention of Aunt Augusta's name, but now the glow was fading, and even the lustrous flecks of gold were becoming dull, tarnished—as if they weren't truly gold at all, not truly precious, just mere impostors.

There had never been anything false about Claire, no pretenses—or pretensions—whatsoever. But now the expression on her pale lovely face looked almost like shame, as if she had been caught in a masquerade.

"Claire?"

"Claire?"

She heard her name, floating on a cloud far above her. Aunt Augusta was in that fleecy cloud, calling to her, as was Andrew. Claire wanted to answer, but she couldn't. Her limbs were weighted, and even her eyelids were too heavy to open.

I'm sleeping. But I'll awaken soon. Don't leave me, Aunt Augusta! Andrew? *Please.* I'm going to wake up. Even now my lids are feeling lighter, and now they're beginning to flutter, and in another moment I'll see you, and you'll see that I'm fine, and the worry from your voices—oh, Aunt Augusta, especially from yours!—will disappear, and—

Why can't I see you? My eyes are open, I know they are, and I'm awake. Why is everything so dark? This is a dream, it has to be. But soon, *soon,* I'll truly wake up.

But Claire was never to wake up, not from the dense curtain of blackness. In the days that followed, there *were* awakenings, however, ones that were almost as devastating as her blindness. For it was during those days that Claire learned about Andrew. From the vantage point of her eternal darkness, she saw the man she had married—at last.

For six years Andrew had pursued her, a courtship that commenced shortly after Cole vanished from Harlanville. It was far too soon for her then—and for most of the ensuing years. But

Andrew understood, and he was infinitely patient, and infinitely charming, and finally Claire surrendered to his persistent—and so confident—persuasion. She would never love Andrew as she had loved Cole. But that had been a dangerous, destructive passion. With Andrew, her heart would be safe.

Claire was scrupulously honest with Andrew, from the confession that yes, she had cared deeply for Cole, to her surprise that the town's golden heir would really want *her* as his wife. She was a minor celebrity, of course, the great-niece of the beloved Aunt Augusta. But still . . .

I want you, Claire. And I promise you that in time, with me, you will forget all about Cole Taylor.

Andrew Harlan wanted Claire Chamberlain as his wife, and the mother of his children, and the woman who would stand beside him during his campaigns for political office, successful campaigns that would take him to the governor's mansion and perhaps beyond.

Andrew was accustomed to getting what he wanted. *Always.* And from her new darkness, from that ebony world in which all her other senses were heightened, painfully acute, Claire heard what Andrew Harlan wanted now: a wife who could see. No matter what.

Why? Because the sympathy votes to be garnered weren't enough to outweigh the nuisance of her disability? Or because Andrew, whose world had always been so perfect, felt extreme discomfort with an imperfection such as hers? Or was it something else, something even more personal?

Someday, Claire, you'll look at me exactly as you used to look at Cole.

Claire didn't know, would never know, what made Andrew so resolute in his determination that she undergo the risky surgery. The man she had married, and truly came to know only from her darkness, would not tell her. Claire knew only that Andrew's fervent wish that her sight be restored was for *him*, not for *her*. Never once, during those days of darkness— when the newlyweds should have been honeymooning aboard the *Queen Elizabeth 2*—did Andrew Harlan say to his new bride, *I want you to be able to see the moon again, Claire, and the garlands of moss in the forest you love, and our children, Claire, our babies. I want you to see that joy.*

"Claire?"

She heard her name, soft and clear in the acoustical perfection of the Augusta Chamberlain Theatre. There *was* perfection here, Andrew Harlan style. The theater had been a gift to Aunt Augusta, and an expensive offering to Claire as well, the bride—and then the ex-wife—who had refused even a cent of his fortune at the time of their divorce.

The voice that now spoke her name with such exquisite clarity—and breathtaking concern—belonged to Cole. He had assumed that Andrew wouldn't let the doctors operate, and she had already confessed that the decision had been hers.

But Cole had obviously guessed that there was something else, something more . . . and he needed to know the entire truth, she needed to tell him . . . and for an astonishing moment Claire was truly glad that she could not see.

"Andrew wanted me to have the surgery."

Her quiet confession said it all: as a woman who was loved deeply, unconditionally, she *was* an impostor. Her marriage had not survived even the first test of the wedding vows she and Andrew had made. For better, for worse. Andrew had not *wanted* her to die, of course. Indeed, he was prepared to marshal the full force of his vast fortune to ensure that she had the most skillful surgeons money could buy.

But the fact remained. Her husband, her bridegroom, the man who had in all likelihood been driving the car, preferred a dead wife to a sightless one.

The rage that swept through Cole was dangerously familiar. A killing rage. A rage that could kill. Such violent fury *had* killed once, swiftly . . . and it had been killing him slowly, ever since.

As Claire sensed his anger, sparking like wildfire in the darkness between them, she felt her fists begin to uncurl, and in another moment they would be reaching to touch him, to love him, as they had on that day twelve years ago.

But she had been an impostor on that day, too! Her love had not been enough. *She* had not been enough.

Claire's hands remained at her side, prickling and tingling as they recovered from their bloodlessness.

"It doesn't matter, Cole." *Nothing has mattered, not really, not since the day you left.*

Until now. Now what mattered most to Claire was that he leave. She was so safe in Harlanville, had been so safe. And she would be safe again when Cole was gone. Eventually her heart would cease this dangerous fluttering, and she would be able once again to truly breathe, and somehow she would forbid her mind to replay forever these moments. She would not, could not, torment herself with questions she could never answer. Why had he returned, six years ago and now? What truths might she have seen had she not been blind? What words might she herself have uttered had she been able to see their impact? *I loved you, and then I hated you.*

"It was so nice of you to come, Cole."

Claire wanted him to leave. Cole heard the wish in her gracious yet dismissive words and saw its urgency in the tautness of her slender body. She stood before him, a delicate soldier, steeling herself against an enemy she perceived but could not see.

He was that invisible enemy, that marauding invader who had so brutally ravaged her heart and her dreams. He needed to leave, for her. And for his own heart.

But it was that very heart—his own—that spoke. "I'd like to sing in the pageant."

"Oh! Well, that would be lovely. Everyone would be thrilled."

"I want you to sing with me, Claire."

Just like twelve years ago, on that night of magic, that eve of tragedy. It had been Aunt Augusta's idea then, a last-minute suggestion made to Cole during the intermission. He was alone, standing in a shadowed corner of the auditorium. But Aunt Augusta had found him. *Just one song, Cole. The finale—"Silent Night"—with Claire.*

"I couldn't," Claire murmured now. "I can't. People will want to hear you, not us."

Cole heard her words, and more—her unspoken plea. Don't do this! Don't make me journey into the past.

He almost heeded her silent plea, almost bid her the final adieu. But as his own mind journeyed even further into their past, he saw again the girl-angel, that bold weaver of dreams. "I'm going to be a *songstress*," she had proclaimed. "I'm going to tour the world, and make lots of albums, and you can come with me, Cole. You can be my backup singer!" Her expression had become solemn, and then radiant with joy as, so generously, she wove *him*, the lost, angry, lonely boy, into *her* magnificent dreams. "No. We'll get someone else to sing backup for us. You and I will sing duets." And then earnestly, urgently, she had implored, "Let's make a promise, Cole. Let's promise never to sing duets with anyone else, not ever. Okay? *Promise?*"

Eleven-year-old Cole had made that promise to eight-year-old Claire.

And it was a promise he had kept.

"I won't sing without you, Claire," Cole told the woman who, as a girl, had possessed the confidence to demand such a promise. Be that girl again, Claire. Be that gloriously, confident elf-angel.

Claire's heart had been fluttering dangerously, and now that frantic soaring thing threatened to shatter in midair—as its wounds, scarred with only the most fragile of gossamer, ripped wide open and began to weep, to scream, anew.

How could she sing with him again?

How could she not?

Chapter Four

London, England
Friday, December Twenty-third

S HE HAD TO GET RID OF HIM, THIS EARNEST young man who had been assigned to guard her, to protect her from an evil so unspeakable that Scotland Yard was importing an American, a consultant to the FBI, to explain it to her. Not for the first time, Sarah wished that she had never shown the letter to the authorities.

Had she known then that its ominous message was merely a personal one, she would have kept it to herself. But she hadn't known, and had felt obliged to pass it along. This was the era of televised war, a time in which the journalists who provided the color commentary for that blood sport sometimes became part of the game. Indeed, the killing of war correspondents had become a rite of passage for the youngest of soldiers, warriors who were no more than boys.

For the most part, the murders seemed random, acts of violence committed by children. Recently, however, there had been speculation that the elimination of specific journalists might be part of some global terrorist agenda. Thus, Sarah had promptly forwarded the letter to Scotland Yard.

Within hours electronic reproductions had been sent to intelligence organizations around the world and computers had begun to whir in reply, searching their vast memory banks for the elegant yet sinister symbol. It was found, finally, not by Interpol or the CIA, but at Quantico, in the Behavioral Science Unit computers at the FBI.

The black heart was personal, not political, a message from a lone killer, a private monster, not an organized unit of assassins. The ominous message of death was a warning to Sarah only, not to her colleagues.

Had she known, she would have tossed the letter in the trash.

But now it was too late. Scotland Yard was engaged. Indeed, it was the commissioner himself who had contacted her, who had announced with polite apology that she was in grave danger. The FBI consultant, an expert in murder, would be arriving tomorrow, Christmas Eve, at which time they would meet to discuss the logical next step. In the interim, she would be provided with her very own policeman.

The constable had been with her all day, standing at attention outside her office while she worked, shadowing her whenever she emerged, and now, at day's end, escorting her to the front entrance of her condominium building in Mayfair.

Her *security* building, she reminded him now. "No one can get in without both the building code and a personal one."

"Unless they're let in by mistake, or slip inside when the door is opened for someone else."

"Neither of those possibilities apply," Sarah countered decisively. "It is of paramount importance to every resident of this building that strangers do not get in. We're all extremely careful. We never permit entrance to people we don't know, and when we have guests, we watch the closed-circuit screen until that visitor is inside and the door has closed shut. No one slips in, not in this building. So you needn't escort me upstairs, neither do you need to spend the evening posted here. I'm not expecting anyone, and since I'm not on call for the network, I won't be going out." Sarah forced a smile. "Look, it's two days before Christmas. Have you finished all your shopping?"

"Well . . ."

"Neither have I. Why don't you start tonight, and tomorrow we'll finish up together, at Harrod's."

Was she flirting? No. Sarah didn't know how. She was manipulating, using her celebrity, pressing to her advantage the fact that this man, surely only a few years younger than she, was more than slightly dazzled by his famous charge.

Her voice was as calm as the voice with which she told the world about war. Sarah *felt* calm then, when gunfire crackled in the air and the earth on which she walked was warm with blood. But now, as she stood outside her London home and tried to convince this bedazzled officer that she didn't need his protection, what Sarah felt was pure fear.

She could not be watched, protected, guarded. *Could not.* Not ever again.

"Are we agreed?" Sarah asked.

"I have a pager," he said. "If you decide to go out tonight after all, or if anyone comes to visit—"

"I shall page you straightaway."

"All right then. What time should I come by tomorrow?"

Sarah concealed her surprise. She wouldn't be here tomorrow. She would be leaving London tonight, to make her yearly pilgrimage of love to the tiny grave in the churchyard in Norfolk, and by morning she would be in Paris. But this earnest policeman had believed her lies, that they would go shopping at Harrod's, as if she actually had gifts to buy . . . as if Sarah Pembroke actually had family or friends with whom to share Christmas.

"Why don't we say noon?" she suggested. "I think I shall sleep late, indulge myself. Today's been a bit of a grind, what with the mysterious menace of the black heart."

"Will that give you enough time to shop? The meeting with the FBI chap is at three."

But I won't be meeting with the FBI chap, Sarah mused. At least not tomorrow. "Yes, it's enough time. I know exactly what I'm going to buy."

The few items for her trip to Paris were already neatly packed in a small bag. Sarah's only task before leaving was to write the

letter to Scotland Yard's commissioner of police. She explained
the situation with succinct candor.

> I'm afraid that I have quite deliberately deceived Consta-
> ble Hewitt. Please don't blame him. I was most determined.
> I am, of course, appreciative of your willingness to address
> this issue with such urgency. But tomorrow is Christmas Eve,
> and I have holiday plans; I'm sure we all do—including the con-
> sultant from America. Unless he's planning to take the morn-
> ing Concorde from D.C., I fear that this letter won't arrive in
> time to stop him. The enclosed check, however, is meant to
> cover the cost of his return flight to the States and back.
> I shall be in London as of noon on the twenty-sixth and
> am at your disposal any time thereafter.

Sarah concluded the letter with yet another apology, a final
plea that Constable Hewitt not be blamed, and the promise
that she would be careful. She did not add the reminder that,
despite today's sudden flurry of activity and concern, this was
not truly an emergency. The letter had languished, unopened in
her office, for almost a week while she was still in Moscow,
and it had taken the world's most sophisticated computers
nearly two days to conclude their search. Nor did Sarah add
the other truth: since it had now been established that the menace was only a personal one, there was really no urgency at all.

Sarah called a courier, who met her at the corner of Upper
Brook and North Audley in Grosvenor Square. She gave him
the letter, with the instruction that it be delivered to Scotland
Yard first thing in the morning. Then she walked into the darkness of the December night.

Sarah had promised to be careful. But she was not. She took
the most direct route to King's Cross Station, oblivious to any
and all dangers that might be lurking in the shadows.

Her mind was far away, already on her destination, the late-
night rendezvous with her heart.

Jack Dalton had in fact been planning to take British Airways'
morning Concorde to London. But when he cleared the wait list

for United's evening 747 from Dulles, he gladly altered his plans. The seat that became available happened to be in first class, thus affording him space and privacy in which to study the sensitive documents in his briefcase, but Jack would have happily flown coach. He was restless to get to London, to *her*. This way, perhaps, the meeting that had been scheduled for three o'clock tomorrow afternoon could take place even sooner.

The documents in Jack's briefcase needed to be read with great discretion. Despite the spacious luxury of the first-class cabin, he would have to be careful. The crime-scene photographs were too disturbing, too ghastly, to be observed even from afar.

The Los Angeles Police Department files on the "Valentine Murders" arrived shortly before Jack left for the airport. He had already spoken at length with the homicide detectives involved, but was eager to study the actual photographs and read the original files. That was, after all, Jack's forte. Some even called it his gift.

Even before speaking with the police, Jack was familiar with what the press—and therefore the public—had been told about the celebrated murders. The stabbing deaths of two of Hollywood's premier actresses had been major news. The fact that the slayings had been particularly brutal had leaked to the press, but that was all. The more specific and revealing details, the signature knife wounds and the ominous black heart, had remained carefully guarded. The police wanted no copycat killings. The two unsolved murders were gruesome enough, and they feared there would be more.

But the twin killings, committed within hours of each other and by the same monster, did not mark the beginning of a reign of terror. They remained isolated, contained, a bizarre double homicide. Still, in the event that the monster had struck elsewhere, LAPD had transmitted a copy of the distinctive imprint of the heart to the Behavioral Science Unit at Quantico. The sinister symbol was unfamiliar to the murder mavens at the FBI, unlinked to previous crimes, but it was entered into the BSU's vast computer data bank in the event that the murderer ever resurfaced.

And now he had. In London. At least the symbol that was his calling card, his engraved invitation to murder, was there—along with his next victim. And the monster himself? The letter to Lady Sarah Pembroke had been postmarked in Los Angeles, in Beverly Hills, on December eighth. But the murderer might not have yet made the transatlantic voyage. He might be waiting to appear until the date of death, Valentine's Day, was perilously near.

The killer would need *some* lead time in London, of course, to meet the famous journalist, befriend her, seduce her—assuming that he and Sarah Pembroke weren't already friends.

As the powerful 747 lifted off the tarmac, Jack felt anew the powerful sense of urgency that had been taunting him for the past twenty-four hours, a compelling urgency that defied all logic. The Valentine's Day killer was *not* about to strike. There was plenty of time, more than six weeks, in which to figure out who he was—and stop him.

Which was precisely what Jack Dalton was going to do. That was his specialty. There was nothing mystical about what Jack did, no inexplicable psychic connection with either killer or victim. Nor, in Jack's estimation, was his ability either a talent or a gift. It was problem solving, pure and simple, disciplined attention to detail combined with dispassionate application of logic.

Still, the fact remained: In case after case, Jack saw the clue that no one else could see, made the all-important connection that no one else would ever think to make.

Nothing would have pleased Jack more than to share his crime-solving technique with every FBI agent and homicide detective on earth. Indeed, he'd spent endless hours attempting to do just that. But Jack's aptitude could not be taught, either by relentless repetition of the mantra *disciplined, dispassionate attention to detail*, or by example.

Whenever Jack presented actual case studies, the response was amazement, not comprehension. It would never, not ever, have occurred to any of his students that the library books were critical to solving the murders in Boston. And as for the notes sent to the police in San Francisco? No matter how many times his pupils read them, they never saw the killer's hidden code that had been so obvious to Jack.

Jack presented the case studies without arrogance. He could not, after all, take any credit for his "gift." He had been born with it, an inheritance as inevitable as his sable brown hair and dark blue eyes. Jack's ability to solve puzzles—of all sorts—had proven immensely valuable, *profitable*. Indeed, it permitted him to be what he was now, an unpaid consultant whose specialty was murder.

Jack didn't need money, more money, but he did need to help find murderers. It was his gift to himself, an abiding sense of purpose, and there was something else. This was the way that Jack Dalton was meant to make his contribution to the planet. This was his destiny.

Jack smiled wryly at the fanciful notion of destiny. The master at solving murders, the man who found even the most clever of killers through simple—yet resolute—adherence to logic, was *not* a great believer in destiny.

Jack's wry smile vanished as another powerful rush of restlessness swept through him. Where was the logic to the urgency he felt about this case? Admittedly, there was reason for *some* uneasiness. Before leaving Quantico, he had glanced briefly at the crime-scene photographs; and he had found himself wanting to see images that hadn't been included in the shots. What foreshadowing of the impending carnage might have been found in the remote corners of the two blood-splattered living rooms? What hints to the identity of the killer, and to the nature of the victim's relationship to him? Had the doomed actresses compulsively removed all traces of personal clutter? Had they, like the murderer himself, set the mood for romance?

Was that why he felt such misgivings about this case? Because already he sensed that there were clues, perhaps critical ones, that he would never see?

Jack's gift had failed him only once, in the most important puzzle of his life—a puzzle for which dispassion had been impossible . . . and for which the application of ice-cold logic had been as fanciful then as the notion of destiny was now.

There had been no corpse, that other time. Only hope had

died. And this time? If his gift failed yet again? There would be no corpse, either. Lady Sarah Pembroke would be safe, as she was even now, protected by Scotland Yard's finest.

So why did Jack feel this urgency? As if, somehow, it was already too late to save her? As if, somehow, Sarah Pembroke was already dying?

Jack had no answers, only the ominous restlessness that pulsed within him still. Forcing control, forcing dispassion, he abandoned his plan to study the police files on the two women who had died and concentrated instead on the one who was not dying—and who, because she had correctly interpreted the sinister significance of the black heart, would not die.

Lady Sarah Pembroke had, in essence, already saved herself. It wasn't surprising, of course, that the woman who had been to war would perceive covert messages of death. Nor was Jack truly surprised when Scotland Yard's police commissioner reported her reaction to the news that she had been targeted for murder as "dismissive."

Jack remembered with vivid clarity the first time he became aware of the now famous war correspondent. She had been in Baghdad, at the Al-Rashid Hotel, the night the Gulf War began. For many hours all Jack had known was her voice, its elegance—and its total lack of fear. Even in the midst of madness, she was calm, cool, controlled.

Jack stayed up all night—with Sarah, for Sarah, keeping vigil, hoping for her safety, far more fearful, he decided, than she. At last daylight came, and the skies overhead became quiet, and the camera finally turned to her. Her face matched her voice: startlingly elegant, stunningly serene, achingly serious.

Jack had seen that face many times since, as Sarah Pembroke shared with the watching world the terror and tragedy that plagued its fellow citizens. She always looked the same, solemn and austere. She never wore makeup, or jewelry, and her raven-black hair was always pulled tightly off her face, restrained in a single long braid. In the heat of the desert, she wore shades of sand, long-sleeved ivory silk blouses and khaki slacks. And in the bitter cold of wintertime wars, her clothes matched her hair: black shirt, black jeans, black cowboy boots, black parka.

She looked like a warrior. She *was* a warrior. A warrior. An aristocrat. A widow. And a cover girl. Magazine publishers could not resist putting her image on their covers. Sarah never posed for the shots. But it didn't matter. Portraits of her appeared nonetheless. She was a photographer's dream—stark yet striking from every angle.

Jack wondered what Lady Sarah Pembroke looked like when she smiled, *if* she smiled. A smile was an adornment the journalist never wore, an accessory as useless—and as inappropriate—as jewelry would have been in the places where she chose to spend her life.

The most desperate—and dangerous—places on earth *were* where Sarah chose to spend her life, despite a never-ending stream of safer, and ever more lucrative, offers. Every news organization on the planet wanted her. She could cover the White House, if she liked, or Parliament; and she could host her own weekly news magazine; and if she wanted to be the sole anchor for a nightly newscast, well, that could easily be arranged. . . .

But Sarah chose to remain in London, with Global News Network, ever loyal to her country, her city, and to Timothy Asquith, the media mogul who had discovered her. And, until now, she had always chosen to go to war.

As of January second, however, Sarah Pembroke would become the weeknight anchor of Global's *International News Hour*, a broadcast carried live to over two hundred countries. According to Scotland Yard's commissioner, Sarah's new role as anchor was a command performance, ordered by Timothy Asquith himself. The dangers for Sarah on the battlefields of the world had, in his estimation, finally become too great. Her fame, as well as her gender, made her a coveted target, a prized trophy, marked for kidnapping—or death.

Sarah's new position had been announced by the network on December sixth. Two days later the black heart had been mailed from Los Angeles. Had Sarah merely been one of several possible names on the murderer's hit list for this February's carnage? Had his hand simply been tipped by the news that she would be in London on Valentine's Day? Or was the killer as intrepid as she? Would he have followed her anywhere, to Tu-zla, perhaps, or Sarajevo, Kigali, or Port-au-Prince?

They would never know. Sarah Pembroke would be in London, safe from the assailants of war, and safe as well from the madman who murdered women on the most romantic day of the year.

She was safe, protected, an unnecessary precaution now, with February still so many weeks away. And, Jack thought, perhaps an unnecessary precaution at any time. Because, he mused, Lady Sarah Pembroke seemed quite capable of saving herself.

So why was he hurtling through space to get to her? Why did he feel such fear *for her*?

And why did he feel this restlessness, this urgency, this *inevitability* . . . as if somehow, astonishingly, *this* was his destiny?

Chapter Five

O N   T H A T   N I G H T ,   T W E L V E   Y E A R S   A G O ,   C O L E
and Claire's duet of "Silent Night" marked the finale of
the pageant. When they finished, when the last echoes of their
perfect harmony disappeared in the darkness, there had been
reverent silence, not thunderous applause.

There never was applause that night. There was only a faint
rustling, a resigned sigh as the audience reluctantly accepted the
fact that the performance was over and it was time to leave.
They moved as one, slowly, quietly, as if trying to take the
magic with them, a Christmas gift to last the entire season.

For decades, beginning with the first Christmas pageant—
Augusta Chamberlain's own Christmas present to her new
home—a reception following the pageant was held at Belle
Rêve. The student performers were all invited, as were their
parents, teachers, and an elite group of prominent Louisianians
from as far away as New Orleans.

Jed Taylor did not watch his nineteen-year-old son sing
"Silent Night" with the sixteen-year-old grandniece of Har-
lanville's beloved schoolmarm. Nor did he attend the reception.
Jed's lover, however, attended both events. But in sharp con-
trast to the decidedly wanton hours spent with Jed, tonight
Annabelle Prentice was not slumming.

Indeed, the young woman who would one day inherit her parents' half of Harlan-Prentice Oil was behaving precisely as she had been bred to behave, like a lady—and the future mistress of Belle Rêve. That Andrew Harlan and Annabelle Prentice would one day wed had been inevitable since their births, one month apart, twenty-two years before. It was a fate that Annabelle and Andrew alternately rejected and embraced.

For the moment they had a private pact. At social times, such as the traditional Christmas reception, they would be together. But beyond that they were free to do whatever they liked with whomever they chose—discreetly, of course. For most of the year, Andrew and Annabelle inhabited different parts of the globe. He was in his final year at Princeton, and in the fall he would begin law school at Tulane; whereas, since age nineteen, after announcing that she was *finished* with finishing school, Annabelle had enjoyed the lavish pleasures of Saint-Tropez, Paris, and Gstaad.

Annabelle had not imagined such sultry pleasures in little old Harlanville. But during a visit home over the summer she had discovered Jed Taylor, and sensual delights beyond compare. And Annabelle Prentice had discovered something else—her own almost insatiable passion for danger.

Her affair with Jed Taylor was risky enough, but there were times when Annabelle chose to raise the stakes even higher by attempting to seduce his son. Jed would be due home at any moment, and Cole would be drinking with her, keeping her company until Jed arrived, and she would wonder aloud who was the better lover, father or son. She would reach for him then, her slender fingers weaving through his coal-black hair. But Cole would always pull away, his gray eyes as cold, as hard, as granite.

Cole's rejections infuriated her, and tonight, as she stood with Andrew greeting Belle Rêve's Christmastime guests, Annabelle Prentice looked at Cole Taylor with imperious disdain. He was so *far* beneath her, her look said, so *unworthy* that the very idea of his rough hands on her delicate flesh conjured an image of pure torture.

Andrew's appraisal of Cole held comparable disdain. But all traces of contempt promptly vanished when his gaze found

Claire. Andrew had been captivated by her singing voice, and now, at close range, he saw quite clearly that the girl he remembered vaguely as a freckle-faced waif had blossomed into a creature of uncommon beauty.

It wasn't a cultivated southern-belle prettiness, the immaculate perfection of an Annabelle Prentice. Claire's beauty was quite different, quite distinct. Unaffected, and lush and untamed, it was like the bayou forest where she had frolicked as a child. Yet unlike that place of enchantment, that sultry and arrogant mistress, Claire seemed oblivious to her allure, unaware of the rich gleam of her coppery hair, or the deep luster of her bright blue eyes, or the lips that were so pink, so full.

I want you, Claire Chamberlain. It was a surprising thought, stunning really. And it came with astonishing conviction. I want you to look at me just as you looked at Cole during your duet, shy—and adoring.

Claire was looking at Cole that way still. Shimmering adoration. Luminous love.

Someday, Claire, I want your brilliant blue eyes to glow precisely that way—for me.

The words of greeting exchanged with Andrew and Annabelle in the mansion's marble foyer were the first words either Claire or Cole had spoken since the musical wish that had been the final lyric of their duet—"Sleep in heavenly peace." The reverent silence that had fallen over the audience had touched the singers as well, as had the reluctance to relinquish the magic.

They had left the stage together, strangely bonded, invisibly joined, and it was only as they were walking to his car that Claire realized with a start what she was doing. She had never been in Cole's car, he had never invited her to be. But she knew about it. Battered but functional, it had been purchased with money earned doing manual labor beneath the scorching summertime sun.

And what functions did Cole's battered car perform? There were two, and they were vaguely related. The first was to transport him to parts of Terrebonne Parish where he wasn't known, and where it was assumed that he was at least twenty-one, and thus legally entitled to buy all the alcohol he desired.

The car's second function had to do with desire as well.

Claire slowed as she approached the vehicle in which many, many girls had spent many, many hours alone with Cole. What was she doing? How dare she? Her questions seemed mirrored on the face that turned to her now, a harsh expression that seemed at once angry and surprised. But without a word, Cole opened the car door for her . . . and when she was safely inside, he closed it, very gently, behind her.

The magnet that compelled them to stay close would not release its powerful pull. After exchanging greetings with Annabelle and Andrew, they wandered together amid the festive crowd.

And did their young bodies, drawn so close and yet not touching, move in a graceful duet? Did they celebrate with motion the same wondrous harmony that was present in their voices when they sang?

Yes . . . and no. The air shared by their lungs was heated, shimmering and fierce; and although they murmured quiet acknowledgments to those awed by their performance, to each other, Cole and Claire did not speak; and it was only when they were offered something to drink that Cole finally even looked at her.

The offer was made by a white-gloved butler carrying a shining silver tray laden with frosted crystal flutes. There was a choice of honey-colored liquids—vintage champagne or Louisiana's best sparkling cider. The butler's role was to serve, not to censure. He would not have arched a skeptical eyebrow had the young couple chosen champagne.

On any other night, the alcoholic beverage would most certainly have been Cole's choice. But tonight, with Claire, because he knew how much it mattered to her, he chose sparkling cider for them both. It was then, as he handed her one of the crystal flutes, that Cole saw her eyes.

They were bright blue, brilliant blue, and their inner light was so radiant that now it was illuminating even the darkest shadows of his heart, filling that vast blackness with glowing gold, making him smile, making him want, making him believe. Until he remembered who he was.

He scowled, casting her joy in shadows as black as his heart, and the air between them sparked and seared, threatening to flame, to explode—and pleading to be set free.

But the invisible chains that bound them would not break. Indeed they seemed to wrap ever tighter, twining them ever closer. . . .

Finally, harshly, Cole commanded, "Let's go outside."

"Do you think it's going to snow?"

The question was Claire's, posed just as they reached the secluded gazebo. She was trembling inside, a quiver of hope and fear that had commenced the moment Aunt Augusta told her that she and Cole were going to sing "Silent Night" and had been crescendoing ever since. There were questions trembling in her mind as well, fearsome and hopeful, yet *this* was the question that sprung to her lips.

It was not a new question, but an ancient one, a Christmas-time tradition between the boy and girl who had been such good friends. Beginning in early December Claire would begin wondering about the possibility of snow. It *had* snowed in Harlanville, she would remind him. Years ago, on Aunt Augusta's very first Christmas in her new home, a plush layer of whiteness had blanketed the earth.

It could snow again, Claire maintained. In fact, it *would*, someday. *Someday* there would be another white Christmas in their bayou town.

As a girl, Claire had wished for snow, had dreamed of it, and it was obvious that she hoped for that pristine enchantment still. And now as then, Cole considered her question very seriously, staring skyward before answering.

The heavens had never been more clear, the winter moon more full or bright.

And Cole Taylor's voice had never been more gentle.

"No snow this year, Claire."

"Oh, well."

Her moonlit eyes met his, not disappointed, merely glowing, and in the dazzling luminescence Cole saw new dreams, womanly ones. Claire wanted him, *wanted* him, in the same forbidden, dangerous, glorious way that he wanted her.

Forbidden. Dangerous. Glorious. *Impossible.* His mind screamed the silent warning. But the strident sound went unheard, drowned by the powerful music of his heart.

I will give you snow, Claire. Someday I will give you all your dreams.

It was a foolish promise, a future that could never be. But Claire wasn't focused on some faraway dream of snow. She was looking at him, and she was telling him with her eyes, her heart, her very soul, that he was all that she would ever want or need.

"Oh, Claire," he whispered, his voice at once soft and harsh, gentle and violent.

He wanted her desperately, and yet a different kind of despair warned him to leave her alone. But Cole was not heeding warnings on this moonlit night. With wonder, with reverence, he wove his long fingers into the fragrant silk of her cinnamon hair and framed with his tender, reverent hands the loveliness of her face.

Then he kissed her. *He had to.* He felt her lips tremble, joyous and yielding, and tasted first the sweetness of cider . . . and then the magnificent sweetness of her.

This, kissing Claire, loving her, was so very right, and so terribly wrong. Yes, perhaps, *yes*, she was the only way his heart could survive. But at what cost to her?

With the question came anger. Its fury raged within him, roughening his kiss, lacing it with violence, punishing him—and warning her. Run, Claire, his fury commanded. Run *now*, while you still have the chance.

But Claire did not flee. She welcomed him, matching his desperate passion, his ferocious hunger, with her own. She was fearless, and lovely, and delicate, and bold. Didn't she realize that he could crush her with his desire? Couldn't she feel the violence that churned in his veins?

Of course she couldn't . . . because she was Claire. And now something truly astonishing was happening. Her hopefulness was flowing into him, flooding him, warming him, and proclaiming with unabashed joy that this dream, this magic, could last forever. It wasn't forbidden, or dangerous, or impossible. It was merely glorious.

The magnificent illusion shattered swiftly, its dazzling glory splintered by the truth. His love would destroy her. Even the intimacy of his kiss might forever taint her goodness with his evil.

She gasped, so fiercely did he end their kiss.

"You don't know me, Claire." He saw the protest on her startled face and repeated harshly, "There are things about me that you do not know."

"But I *do* know, Cole. I mean, I think I do. It's your father, isn't it? He's hurt you, hasn't he? Hit you. I remember your bruises, and the days when you didn't come to school."

Cole shrugged dismissively. "He hasn't come near me for a very long time."

In fact, it had been years since Jed Taylor had touched his son, years since Cole had become strong enough to defend himself and sent the solemn promise that he *would* defend himself—and gladly.

And before the time when Cole could defend himself? There had been two people, the only two *ever*, who had cared enough to even try—the freckle-faced elf and her elegant great-aunt. Claire's defense of Cole had been unwitting. She had simply cloaked him in her own joy, an invisible coat of armor that enabled him to survive even the most punishing blows.

And as for Aunt Augusta . . . she had guessed the brutality of his life and had wanted to help. She offered to confront his father, to expose his cruelty to the entire town if need be, and she told Cole that he would be more than welcome to live in her home. Her generosity was stunning, overwhelming. And how did Cole respond? By telling her that she was wrong, that there was no abuse, no violence of any kind. Everything was fine at home, he lied. But it might *not* be fine, he added truthfully, if she went to his father with her accusations. Then, there might be brutality after all.

Cole hadn't understood, at age eleven, why he so adamantly refused Aunt Augusta's help. But now he did. He deserved his father's punishment. *He had earned it.* And when Jed Taylor could no longer safely assault his only son? That son took matters into his own hands, by living recklessly, dangerously, and, the most harsh punishment of all, by depriving his heart of hope, of dreams—of Claire.

"My father's very violent. His rage is there all the time, waiting to erupt, and when he drinks, he gets crazy. I'm his son, Claire. I've inherited his genes."

"But *you're* not violent! And when you drink . . ."

"When I drink?" he echoed, wondering what she had observed. "When I drink, Claire?"

"You become quiet. Sad. Not crazy."

She was right about the quietness, of course. When he drank, he became still, silent, not raving. He withdrew into alcohol, a brief death, a time when he stopped thinking, stopped feeling, stopped being. But Cole was surprised that during those times of near-death Claire thought that he looked sad. He had always imagined that he must look happy then, relieved to be so close to death, at peace at last.

"You're not your father, Cole. You would never hurt anyone. *Never.* You're gentle, loving, kind."

"Have I been kind to you, Claire? All these years? When I've ignored you? When I've flaunted my relationships with other girls? Was that loving? Gentle? You need to *see* me, Claire. You need to see who I really am—not who you want me to be."

"But I *do* see, Cole. I'm not blind to what you've done. You *have* hurt me. You *have* been cruel. I . . ."

"You what?"

"I . . . hated you sometimes. But we were different ages. I was a girl, and you were growing up, and it was hard for you, too, wasn't it? Didn't you hate yourself for being so cruel to me?"

"Yes." *I hated myself then, now, always.* "Yes."

"It was difficult for both of us. Me growing up so slowly, you waiting."

"I wasn't waiting for you, Claire. I was trying to keep you away, to drive you away."

"But why, Cole? Because of your father? Because you were so afraid that you might be like him?"

"Partly because of that." Partly. Was he really going to tell

her the rest? Was he going to inflict on himself this final punishment—the loss of her faith in him? Because that would be
the consequence. Her belief in him, her valiant conviction
that he was somehow worthy, despite all evidence to the contrary, would be irrevocably shattered. Was that what he
wanted? No. *Yes.* For her. Because when she heard what he
had done, she would surely run away. He was going to tell
her, and already he felt the loss, the emptiness, the fathomless
sea of blackness in which, once before, he had nearly
drowned. He was drowning now, again, and this time it
would be forever. *But Claire would be saved.* "But mostly,
Claire, because of me, because of something *I* did before you
and I ever met."

The fury of his passion had not scared her, nor had the
harshness of his voice. But now, quite suddenly, Claire felt fear.
What past history could an eleven-year-old have? What could
Cole have done by that age that would have irrevocably tainted
his entire life?

Claire knew so little about his past. He had mentioned his
mother only once, in reply to a query from Claire. *She left.*
That was all he said. But his voice, bitter and cold, spoke volumes about his feelings for the mother who had abandoned
him to endure alone the brutality of his father.

Now she was about to learn something else about his past,
something far worse than a mother's betrayal. She saw that
truth in his eyes, in the anguished stone that had never been
more bleak, more gray.

Cole had killed someone. The boy who believed he had inherited his father's violence had horrible, tangible proof of that
lethal legacy.

Loving him, loving him, Claire asked, "What happened?"

"I had a younger brother. . . ."

Claire expected to hear about that younger brother's tragic
death. An accident, surely. Two boys playing with their father's
gun, not realizing it was loaded.

But the confession Claire heard was not about a tragic accident, but about a courageous decision of love. To save his little
brother, Cole had given him away.

And now Claire knew the truth. Cole Taylor *had* killed someone on that moonlit night in Texas.

He had killed himself.

"I love you, Cole," she whispered. "I love you."

"*I gave my brother away.*"

"Because you loved him!"

"I gave him to a complete stranger, Claire, a man who might have been worse than our father."

"But he *wasn't*! You saw his gentleness, how upset he was when he saw the bruise on your brother's face. There are good people in the world, Cole. Millions of them. That's who your little brother is with. Good, loving people—like you." She reached for him then, her delicate fingers touching the face that had become as hard as his eyes. "It was terrible for you, Cole. But it was best for him. He's safe and happy and loved. I know he is. And you have to believe that, too. *You have to.*"

"Oh, Claire." It was a hoarse whisper of hope.

He had confessed to her his greatest sin, his most shameful secret, his most heinous crime. She was supposed to have run away in disgust, understanding at last.

But Claire was still here, in this moonlit gazebo. And she had forgiven him.

And now her blue eyes were shining even more brightly than before and her slender fingers were weaving into the dark blackness of his hair and she was tiptoeing to kiss his lips.

It was a whispered kiss. "Make love to me, Cole."

His answering reply came from deep within his powerful throat, a sound primal and raw, half laugh, half groan.

"Cole?"

"I want to make love to you, Claire. Believe me, I do."

"Then . . ."

"No," he said softly. "Not now. Not here—and not in my car."

And not until the last vestiges of rage have been washed from my veins. He was just born, awakened from a long slumber of anguish by the gentleness of her love. New, powerful, dazzling emotions pulsed within. But there was violence, too, still. The fury that had seethed within him for so long was not ready to admit defeat, to relinquish its sovereignty over his heart. It would wage a fierce, final battle.

Cole would not make love with Claire until the violence was vanquished.

"We *will* make love, Claire. An infinity of times." His eyes were silver now, glittering with love. "But I want our first time together, every time, to be perfect. All right?"

"Yes."

"Yes," he echoed, sealing the promise with a kiss that was deliberately careful—almost chaste—but which threatened to undermine his vow nonetheless.

It was Claire who pulled away from the kiss, her lovely face set in the determined expression he knew so well. Because she didn't want him to break his vow? No, Cole decided. It was something else. Something far more important.

"We're going to find him, Cole. We're going to find your brother."

Cole started to shake his head, then stopped. This was a night of magic, and she was the weaver of bold dreams, and even though what she was suggesting seemed impossible . . . "How, Claire? How would we do that? He doesn't know his first name, much less his last. Or that I was his brother, not his neighbor. And it's likely, don't you think, that he has never even been told about that night?"

The same winter moon that had guided Cole's footsteps to the truck stop on that long-ago December night was shining down upon them now, smiling at them, enveloping them in a heavenly mist of pure gold.

"No. He will have been told. I'm sure of it. And he will have been wondering about you, wanting to find you. Whether he believes that you were his neighbor or his brother, he'll remember the love, *your* love. And when he hears that you're searching for him . . ." Claire smiled, a radiance that far surpassed the moon's. "And he *will* hear, Cole. You'll tell him yourself. You'll tell the world."

It had been so long since Cole had permitted himself to remember the dreams spun by the elf-songstress of the bayou that it was several moments before he understood her words. But now he did. He would make the appeal to his long-lost brother from the worldwide stage that would be his, *theirs*, the stage from which they would sing their duets of love.

If they truly achieved the fame that Claire had so boldly forecast for them, it might indeed be possible to find a missing brother. But on this night when Cole had already ignored the most ominous of warnings, had *dared* to envision a life of love with her, it was too much, too dangerous and too greedy, to imagine more.

Standing before him, haloed by the golden mist of the winter moon, was everything Cole Taylor would ever want . . . and far more than he ever deserved.

"Do you know what I want, Claire?"

"No. Tell me."

Nineteen-year-old men were supposed to dream of conquering the world, of vast fame and vaster fortune. But the dreams of this nineteen-year-old man were quiet, gentle, simple dreams.

"*You*, Claire. You, us . . . and our babies. I'd like to teach music, and live in a small house like Aunt Augusta's, near a bayou where it sometimes snows for Christmas."

"I want that, too."

"You do?"

"Oh yes. Most of all." She had never cared about fame, only about singing with him—except that now, for him, for his heart, there was a reason to be famous. "But your brother, Cole. We need to find him."

There were times when Claire could not read the messages of Cole's gray eyes. But now the intense fire that blazed deep within him had vanquished all shadows, and the molten silver glittered brilliant—and clear—with love. The silver brightness didn't fade, not really, nor did the dazzling clarity blur in a way that could be detected by anyone but her. But because she loved him so much, or perhaps because it was she who had sparked the small flame of hope from its smoldering ember, just before he answered, Claire saw that tiny flame flicker one final time— and then die.

"No, Claire," Cole said quietly. "I have to let him go."

I cannot dare to dream any more dreams.

Chapter Six

ON THAT DECEMBER NIGHT, BEFORE THEY
left the secluded gazebo at Belle Rêve, Cole Taylor and
Claire Chamberlain made joyous plans for their love. Cole
would graduate in June and attend college nearby; and in two
years, when she graduated, they would marry; and both would
become music teachers; and even though wishes for his happiness would always dwell in their hearts, they would abandon
all thoughts of finding Cole's younger brother.

Their singing would bring private joy, not worldwide ac-
claim, duets of love sung with each other and to their children.
It was a dream more grand than all the shimmering dreams of
fame, a perfect diamond alight, aglow, with its own inner fire.

But the next day Cole became famous . . . and their glorious
dream was shattered, like a flawless diamond struck just so, its
once glittering shards as bleak, as colorless and as cold, as his
winter-gray eyes.

The dream-shattering event began with a knock on the front
door of the small house on Joshua Street where Cole lived with
his father. Cole was in the living room, playing the guitar that
Claire had given him and composing a song of love. In just
three hours he would see her again, for dinner at Aunt Augusta's, and later, before he bid his love good night, he would

sing her this song. It would be ready to be sung by then because, although he had started working on it just late last night, its lyrics had been engraved in his heart for years.

The midafternoon visitor to the Taylor home was Annabelle Prentice.

"Merry Christmas Eve *eve*," she greeted gaily as she brushed past Cole and into the house. "Where is he?"

"I have no idea."

Annabelle frowned at the diamond-encrusted Chopard watch that encircled her wrist. It was three-fifteen. Jed was supposed to be here, waiting for her, and today of all days every minute counted. Christmas might mean absolutely nothing to the two men who dwelled in this impossibly tiny house. But for the rest of Harlanville, and especially the Harlans and Prentices, this was a time of parties, of celebration, of family. Annabelle and her parents were expected at Belle Rêve at five-thirty, which gave her at most an hour to spend enjoying an entirely different kind of celebration with her lover.

Jed Taylor and Annabelle Prentice could accomplish quite a bit in an hour, sixty minutes of dangerously delicious, breathtakingly decadent, and *almost* violent passion—and the heiress who was unaccustomed to self-denial of any kind wanted every one of those minutes.

"Damn him!" Annabelle's annoyance abated dramatically as she looked up from the gold-and-diamond face of her watch to the stone-and-shadow face of her lover's son. "What are *you* doing now, Cole?"

"Leaving."

"That's not what it looks like to me." She glanced meaningfully at the guitar. "Play something for me, Cole. Serenade me."

Cole answered by propping the guitar against the threadbare couch. "Gotta go."

"What's this?"

Cole was already walking away from her, halfway to the door, but her question compelled him to stop. He *knew* what had piqued her interest. He had thought about taking it with him, or at least putting it in his bedroom, but either action would have drawn her attention to it . . . and it had seemed safe where it was, nestled in a far corner of the couch. The moment he left, Annabelle would go to the kitchen to pour herself a drink, and as soon as Jed appeared they would withdraw to Jed's bedroom.

But somehow she had discovered it, and as he turned, Cole's heart stilled. The snow globe, purchased this morning in Lafayette, was held aloft by her perfectly manicured hands, like an offering to the gods . . . one that Annabelle would quite happily drop in sacrifice.

The snowy Yuletide scene encased in glass was a present for Claire; a surrogate until snow came again to the bayou. And since leaving Lafayette, the snow globe had acquired a special significance for Cole as well, a pristine symbol of remembrance—and atonement.

Cole could certainly have found handcrafted snow globes in any of several towns between Harlanville and Lafayette. But he had driven all the way to the place that had once been his home, beckoned there by misty—and mystical—memories of quaint shops adorned for Christmas, and of two boys, two brothers, standing hand in hand as they beheld the splendor of tiny snowflakes falling on miniature glass-encased towns.

Cole had not set foot in Lafayette since his family's late-night flight from their home near Breaux Bridge. He had doubted that he ever would. But as he began his predawn journey in quest of a gift of snow for Claire, it seemed important that he return to his boyhood home, to make peace at last with the ghosts that dwelled there still.

The ghosts were *everywhere*, invisible and taunting, and yet they were nowhere. There was no place, either in Lafayette or Breaux Bridge, where he could confront them.

Their house was gone, as was the trash heap where the brothers had found their treasured tattered quilt, as was the home of the neighbor who had given them the rusty wagon. Even the bayou had changed. Its indigo waters were darker now, hostile and brooding; and the birds sang piercingly sad ballads of loss; and the foliage was so dense, so overgrown, that Cole could not find the places that had been their secret sanctuaries.

And what of the quaint shops in Lafayette where snow

globes were sold? Such charming shops abounded still. But none was the place of Cole's misted memory. His past was gone, lost somewhere in the passage of time and the tangled vines of the primeval forest. Or maybe that past, that time of loving brothers, had never really existed at all. Perhaps, like the ghosts, it was a phantom of his imagination.

Cole bought the snow globe, then drove away from Lafayette, away from his illusory past toward his certain future. Toward Claire.

But the ghosts were with him still. Displaced from their ancient haunts in Lafayette and Breaux Bridge, they had spent the intervening years pacing—restless, angry, and desperate for something familiar to which to cling.

At last Cole had returned, and the ghosts had found him, and they were not going to let him go. Claire might have forgiven him. But the ghosts of the Taylor boys had not. They wanted their pain to be heard. They wanted Cole to be punished—forever—for giving away the brother he loved.

You should have found another way! they screamed. You should have been able to keep him with you—*and to protect him.* How could you have given him away when you loved him so much?

They were angry ghosts, and anguished ones, caught in a netherworld of love and pain. Pacing, restless, they pleaded for peace.

I will give you peace. It was such a bold thought—and so confident—glorious proof that Claire's hopefulness now dwelled within him, too.

Cole Taylor's offering to his tormented ghosts was precisely the kind of gift Claire would have given them: freedom from their restless anguish, their haunting pain. And how would Cole accomplish such a remarkable feat? By transforming the haunted phantoms into tiny snowflakes, perfect crystals of happiness that were enclosed—along with his entire past—within the smooth surface of the small glass globe.

His ghosts would live there forever. They would dance sometimes, floating, spinning, twirling in a delicate ballet of remembered joy. And at other times they would be at rest, sleeping in heavenly peace.

Cole would tell Claire what he had done with his anguished ghosts, and she would welcome them, and they would find their greatest comfort of all cradled in the gentle warmth of her graceful hands.

But now it was Annabelle Prentice who held the snow globe, and her expression of pure petulance sent the warning that at any moment she might smash it on the floor . . . and the ghosts that had traveled with him from Lafayette, at peace within their glass cocoon, would be peaceful no more.

"It's a Christmas present," Cole answered finally. "For Aunt Augusta. It's a gift from everyone who sang in the pageant."

"Oh." Aunt Augusta was sacrosanct—even to the petulant heiress. Annabelle held the globe more firmly as she studied the idyllic scene inside, the ice skaters gliding across the frozen azure pond, the bemittened children putting the finishing touches on the plump snowman, the young lovers dashing through the snow in a one-horse open sleigh, the carolers serenading the merrymakers with joyous songs of the season. "It's very beautiful. I'm sure she'll like it."

Cole nodded, unable for a moment to speak. His heart, which had stopped, was beating again, ravenous now for every molecule of oxygen it could commandeer. And when, with special care, Annabelle set the globe down on the coffee table, it began to race. Claire's white Christmas was safe, and his own ghosts were at peace. . . .

"Please don't go, Cole."

"I'm sorry, Annabelle. But I'm taking the globe to Aunt Augusta tonight, which means it needs to be wrapped. I have the paper and ribbon, but we're out of Scotch tape." Except for the fact that the globe was really a gift for Claire, Cole's words were entirely true. He had been planning to make the short walk to Harlanville's general store as soon as he was happy with the final lyric of his song of love. But now those plans had changed. "I hate to abandon you, Annabelle, but I'm sure he'll be here any minute."

"He'd *better* be. We'd better be in his bedroom, *in his bed,* by the time you get back." Annabelle arched a perfectly tapered eyebrow. "You don't listen to us, do you, Cole?"

In the years that followed, Cole would remember with excruciating clarity what he had been thinking as he walked back to his house after buying the Scotch tape: that he should have taken the snow globe, his guitar, and the gift wrap with him. But he had wanted to get away from Annabelle as quickly as possible, before her demands became even more explicit, before her hands started exploring him as if he belonged to her.

Even as he was walking toward the house, making the turn off Bayou Boulevard onto Joshua Street, Cole was planning his escape. Annabelle and his father would be in bed. After retrieving the globe, the guitar, and the wrapping paper, he would drive to the bayou and sing until it was time to go to Aunt Augusta's.

Cole modified his plan slightly as he neared the house. Jed Taylor *was* home. But his car was in the driveway, slanted crosswise, blocking Cole's.

Cole's car was his sanctuary. On another day the revelation that his private refuge was now denied to him, by a careless, or perhaps purposeful, act of his father, would have pumped angry energy to every cell in his body, a powerful rush of rage that would have given eloquent testimony to what he feared most—that he was his father's son in the most terrifying way, that fury smoldered in his blood, heating his veins, threatening to explode without warning.

But on this day, when the ghosts of his past were at peace, transformed to the purity of snowflakes, and when the violence within seemed already to have been vanquished by a magical love, Cole felt only hope, only happiness.

He would walk to the bayou, and later to Aunt Augusta's, and—

It was then that Cole heard the screams.

The day that marked a joyous beginning for the son signaled an end for the father. The other officers of Harlanville's small police force had been wary of Jed Taylor for quite some time. Everyone in town knew that he became wild when he drank. But not once in eight years had there been anything to suggest that he imbibed while on duty. And yet there were times when Jed's behavior was decidedly bizarre, when he was fully in control but oddly manic.

Was it cocaine? his colleagues wondered. Had one of their own introduced to sleepy little Harlanville the harsh reality of urban life? Was the man who had sworn to uphold the law making a private fortune selling drugs to their children? Was that why, sometimes, their own teenagers behaved with such arrogant defiance?

The other officers finally decided to watch him, each dedicating part of his off-duty time to that pursuit. The effort had finally paid off. Late last night, many hours after most of Harlanville had fallen asleep to the memory of the duet sung by Claire Chamberlain and his son, Jed Taylor was observed exchanging what looked like small packages—of drugs? of money?—with two strangers.

The officer who witnessed the shadowy transaction took no action at the time. But his report, first thing this morning, had prompted a flurry of activity. Harlanville's chief of police immediately placed a call to the force in St. Martin Parish, where Jed once worked, and from which, it was discovered, Jed had resigned, abruptly, when his fellow officers became suspicious that he was keeping for himself a substantial portion of drugs confiscated during arrests.

In retrospect, such a call should have been made eight years ago, when Jed applied for the job. But Harlanville had needed him, and no one could be more convincing than Jed Taylor, and his claim that he had served with honor—in fact, distinction—in St. Martin Parish had been accepted without question.

When Harlanville's chief of police confronted Jed with his concerns, Jed was convincing still. The "strangers" he had met in the shadows last night were old friends, buddies from his football-playing days in Lafayette, and the officer had simply been mistaken about the exchange of any packages. And as for what had caused his precipitous flight from Breaux Bridge? It had been jealousy, pure and simple. He had an impressive record of arrests—with subsequent convictions—and another officer, also in line for promotion, devised a way to discredit him.

There had been no proof. Not then. And not now. The only common denominator, in fact, was a fellow officer acting out of self-interest.

The police chief conceded that they had no proof. But while they "pursued the matter," he wanted Jed's gun and badge. It would be a paid suspension, he assured him, and they would do their best to keep it quiet.

Jed complied with an easy shrug, even as his entire being throbbed with rage. He knew what the chief really wanted—for him to leave, for the problem to simply go away. Well, he *would* leave Harlanville, but not so quietly this time, not without making certain that the hicks in this town would never forget him.

For several years cocaine had been Jed's drug of choice. It made his thoughts clear, his vision precise, his power without equal. Within moments of his suspension, energized by its potent magic, he charted an invincible plan. The first order of business was to punish the officer who had followed him last night. Jed considered swinging by the house to get a hunting rifle. But on reflection he decided that his bare hands would be quite lethal, and there would be a certain pleasure in disposing of the traitor with such intimacy.

And after that? He would, indeed, leave Harlanville. But not alone. Harlanville's very own spoiled princess—the town's most shameless slut—would be going with him.

Annabelle was furious by the time Jed finally arrived. But her anger changed to fear when she saw the gleam of madness in his eyes. She had seen Jed on cocaine. More than once she had shared that empowering danger with him.

But this was something different, something more, something truly terrifying. *And there was blood on his hands, and his knuckles were torn.*

She should have fled. Her mind knew that. But during those precious moments when she might have escaped, Annabelle was stunned into paralysis, mesmerized by the fearsome yet purposeful power with which Jed strode through his house.

Only after he had gathered his rifles, ammunition, and hunting knife did Jed speak.

"Let's go." It was a command. Harsh and brutal—thrilling in his bedroom, but terrifying now.

"No, Jed, I—"

He laughed, and before she could move, she was imprisoned in his arms, the cold steel of the jagged-edged knife angled menacingly against her throat.

As Jed felt her terror, his mind formed a new and suddenly far more appealing plan. He wouldn't take the whore-princess with him after all. There could be no greater pleasure than slashing her delicate flesh and feeling the hot spill of her blood on his hands. Only thirty minutes earlier he had killed the traitorous officer, a carnal death that had merely whetted his appetite. He was ready to kill again, to appease anew his savage hunger.

The knife pressed deeper—and Annabelle screamed.

Cole responded instantly, instinctively, to her cry of terror. He ran toward the house, toward her, unaware of the more distant screams, the wail of police sirens that signaled the fierce pursuit of the man who had murdered one of their own.

When his son burst into the house, Jed Taylor's mouth widened into a delighted grin. He had been planning to kill Cole for a very long time. More than once he had left him for dead, beginning with that day in Texas when Cole confessed that he had just watched his little brother drown.

But beginning that day, Cole had revealed his true identity. He was a phoenix. Again and again he rose from the ashes of death to be punished anew. And after that day, the same day when Cole's mother left forever, Cole's punishment became, for Jed, a game of pure pleasure, a most welcome challenge, a precarious balancing act that demanded supreme finesse. The injuries to his son had to be carefully inflicted, just enough, not too much. Jed learned with each successive—and successful—session precisely how much Cole could endure without dying.

Eventually the brutal game had been abandoned. Cole grew from a defenseless boy to a powerful and angry young man. But the game had never *really* ended. The ultimate victor had yet to be crowned.

Well. That would all change today. Even his phoenix-son could not survive a knife plunged deep into his heart.

"Let her go," Cole commanded.

Jed laughed, and even though he was now far more interested in the liquid heat of his son's spilt blood than of his lover's, he imprisoned Annabelle still.

"Come get me, Cole. You've wanted to for a long time. Now's your chance. You can be a hero. Save the damsel in distress. Come on, sonny boy. Come closer and I'll let her go. Or would you rather watch me slash her pretty throat?"

Jed Taylor was not bluffing. Of that, Cole had no doubt. It would take so little to end Annabelle's life, a trivial effort for his father's heavily muscled arm. And Jed *would* do it, was going to, unless Cole stopped him.

Cole began to walk toward his father, a slow journey of immense resolve. Haste was not necessary. As long as he was obeying Jed's wishes, Annabelle would be safe.

Cole was half panther, a powerful creature stalking his prey. And he was half prisoner, weighted already by the heaviest of chains. Cole did not know that Jed had already killed once today, that he had absolutely nothing to lose by committing another murder. But he saw the ominous truth on his father's face: Jed Taylor was intent on a fight to the death with his son.

Jed had nothing to lose, and Cole had everything to lose.

I cannot be my father's son. I have to contain my violence, to stop him without killing him. *I have to.*

When Cole was within arm's reach, Jed shoved Annabelle away, discarding her in favor of the more appealing victim. The hunting knife flashed brightly in Jed's already bloodstained hand and his eyes flashed brightly, too, gleaming with murderous lust as he envisioned what lay ahead.

Cole would try to dodge his vicious slashes, all the while trying to claim the knife. Not every slash would find a home in his son's muscled flesh. But some would, spilling blood, draining

Cole's strength with each splattered drop. Eventually Cole would begin to stagger, his face white from blood loss—and finally from terror.

Jed frowned. It seemed too easy. *Was* too easy. As he found a remedy, his frown became a smile.

"You need a weapon, don't you, sonny boy?" Jed's grin widened as he reached for the guitar that Cole had left propped against the couch. "How's this? It's about time you put this thing to good use."

With a single powerful blow, Jed smashed the guitar on the floor. The gift from Claire made its final sound, a discordant wail, as its strings vibrated one last time. Or perhaps the agonal wail came from the quivering strings of Cole's heart as he bore witness to the destruction of the beloved instrument and began to sense how much more was about to be destroyed.

The guitar's wooden body splintered on impact. But its neck, although cleanly broken, was connected to its body still, tethered by the slack, mute strings. The guitar dangled in Jed's hand, limp, broken—and useless as either an instrument of love . . . or a weapon of death.

Jed's attempt to create a sharp, piercing weapon had failed. Or had it?

By destroying the only possession Cole had ever treasured, hadn't he, in fact, transformed his reluctant son into a lethal weapon?

Yes, Jed decided with a satisfied smile. *Yes.* Cole's eyes were blazing now, alight with fires of rage.

"Come on," Jed goaded, tossing the guitar away. "Fight me."

Cole had believed—such a foolish belief—that all vestiges of violence had been washed from his veins. But he was so wrong. Familiar fury churned within him, more powerful than ever before, a rushing river compelling him forward. Could he dam this gushing flood of violence? Could he prevent the lethal destruction to which it flowed? *No,* the answer screamed, a hiss of triumph from the strong, swift currents that surged within.

The raging river—the river of his own rage—would carry him wherever it pleased. And when it was through, it would hold him under its angry waters until he drowned. This was the imaginary death that Cole had given his little brother, the fiction created to enable that precious loved one to escape.

But there would be no escape for Cole. This was his destiny.

Death, not dreams.

Violence, not love.

Murder, not magic.

And yet, by some miracle, Cole did not move. The river rushed past him, around him, carrying its violence with it.

It's not too late, an inner voice promised. All is not lost. There can still be dreams and love and—

Jed lunged then, impatient and eager, a sudden movement that caught Cole off guard. Unable to dodge the slash entirely, Cole deflected it with his left forearm. The razor-sharp steel carved deep into his flesh, a memory kept alive and vivid by the brisk spill of hot crimson.

"Touché?" Jed mocked as the sight of his son's blood fueled further his lust. "It's only the beginning, sonny boy."

In fact, the next slashes were poor imitations of the first. Most sliced only air. But because Cole needed to stay close, ever vigilant for the moment when he could grab the knife, some grazed his arms, his torso, his neck. Those cuts drew blood, a scant amount, tiny drops compared with the free flow from his injured forearm.

Cole needed to grab the knife—and soon, he realized, as a sudden twist left him a little dizzy. He needed to curl both of his hands around his father's wrist, to wrest the knife away, and then to hold his father, imprisoning the violence, until the police arrived.

They *were* coming, weren't they? Weren't those sirens he heard above the thunder of his heart?

Cole saw his chance, and took it. He seized Jed's wrist, cuffing it with a hand made of pure steel, and in another moment the knife would fall away. . . .

It was a ferocious battle, the son's power fueled by the promise of magic, the father's by the mandates of madness. The son was gravely wounded, the father was not. And Jed Taylor had a secret weapon, the cocaine that made him invincible.

Still, Cole believed that he would win. His will was stronger, the hope of love the most powerful weapon of all. Even after Jed managed to twist away, Cole believed still. He reached again for his father's wrist, but this time he caught the knife itself, a direct slice deep into the palm of his right hand.

I'll never play the guitar again. Somehow, in the midst of the fight, that truth came to him. It doesn't matter. I can still sing to her. *I can still sing.*

Cole curled his fingers around the blade, intending to clutch it tightly and then pull it away. His fingers would curl—but they would not clutch. Their strength was gone, the tendons all but severed. The hand that had once strummed songs of love, and which seconds before had the power to kill, was as useless, as broken, as his shattered guitar.

When Jed realized what had happened to his son, he laughed aloud, a cackle of pure madness. Then he pressed the knife blade even deeper, scraping bone.

Cole's right hand had been his dominant one, the strongest and most agile; but now, with the left, he grabbed his father's neck, spinning them both, hurling them together onto the floor.

They wrestled, rolling, rolling, the knife wedged between them . . . until Jed rolled onto the discarded guitar. He arched with surprise as a splinter, sharp and piercing after all, pricked his back. It wasn't a lethal stab, not from that shattered instrument of love—but it caused one. As Jed arched, and then twisted away, the blood-slick blade found its final home in his heart.

The fatal plunge was entirely accidental, a fickle whim of fate. But Cole felt his father's final heartbeats as if they were his own. They pounded fiercely, desperately, trying to deny their impending death—to defy it—and yet with that forceful protest speeding along their own demise, as each beat caused the irrevocable loss of yet another heartful of blood.

And where did Jed Taylor's hot, dying lifeblood go? To his son, pumped along the sharp blade of steel, soaking Cole's chest, staining him, claiming him, *branding* him.

The carnage in the house on Joshua had several witnesses. Annabelle saw it all, her own flight blocked by the duel of death. And just at the end, just as the knife made its lethal journey into Jed Taylor's heart, the police arrived.

That the homicide was justifiable, an act of self-defense, was abundantly clear. And beyond that, it was *heroic*. Cole Taylor had saved Annabelle Prentice's life.

And when at last Cole stood—when, at last, he disengaged himself from his father's dead body—Annabelle rushed to him. Her manicured fingers reached for his tormented face, finding the rare places that were safe to touch, the tiny islands of ashen flesh amid the vast sea of splattered blood.

"You saved my life," she purred. Then, suddenly quite aware not only of the police but of the ever-increasing crowd of curious citizens, the princess of Harlanville took her caressing fingertips from the bloodied face of the town's bad boy and breathlessly explained, "Jed Taylor *kidnapped* me! I was out for a walk, before getting ready for dinner with Andrew, and he forced me into his car, and brought me here, and when I told him that I refused to be taken hostage, he put the knife to my throat. But Cole saved me. Cole's a hero. *My* hero."

Annabelle's hero said nothing, nor did his eyes even journey to her. The dark gray gaze was focused elsewhere, on the small glass globe that sat on the coffee table.

Claire's Christmas gift was miraculously intact. But it was no longer pristine. Splattered now by thick droplets of blood, the snowy scene within was all but obscured.

Annabelle was immensely annoyed that Cole was ignoring her adoration. She might have pressed against him, provoking his attention with her sensual body. But Cole was wet with blood, drenched in it, and there was an all-too-curious crowd.

She had to do *something*, though, some small yet memorable punishment for Cole's inexcusable neglect. She reached anew for his face, and when she withdrew, a sharp fingernail left its mark on his skin, a private message of anger.

Cole didn't flinch, didn't move. Finally, with imperial splendor, Annabelle made her way through the wall of police officers, over the body of her dead lover, and outside. There, to the mesmerized crowd, she related her story, sharing the drama in rich, bloody detail. Her words were heard—and repeated and embellished—as news of the incident spread swiftly throughout the town.

Claire had spent the afternoon at her home on Magnolia Avenue, preparing the dinner that she and Aunt Augusta and Cole would share. Augusta would have been there, too, enjoying the festive domesticity with her great-niece, but a dear friend was sick, and sad, and in need of a Christmastime visitor. Claire sent Aunt Augusta on her way with a hug, and set about basting, blending, slicing, and mincing by herself, humming as she did, her heart counting the seconds until she saw Cole again.

When she heard the sirens, she stopped humming, and frowned. A single siren was rare enough in Harlanville, and from the sound of the wails it seemed as if every emergency vehicle in town was speeding its way to some tragedy. Claire's heart faltered, stumbled. Where were her loved ones?

Safe, she assured herself. Both were absolutely safe. Aunt Augusta was at the hospital thirty miles away, the modern medical facility that served Harlanville and several other townships, and Cole, who had been away all morning, was at home. He had called on his return, and Claire had invited him to come help her with dinner, but on learning that Aunt Augusta was away, he had declined.

Nothing would happen, of course. But in Harlanville, and perhaps in all homes where parents cared about the lovely innocence of their daughters, a sixteen-year-old girl did not spend the afternoon alone in an empty house with a nineteen-year-old man—especially not one with a reputation as sultry, as dangerous, as Cole's.

"I don't *care* what people think or say!" Claire had protested.

"But I do," Cole had countered. "I care about you, and Aunt Augusta."

As Claire listened to the wailing sirens, her frown deepened. *Her* loved ones were safe. But she felt guilty at her own sense of relief that the tragedy was not hers. After a thoughtful moment, however, she smiled. There was no tragedy, not for anyone, not on this day when she had enough joy for the entire world. The shrill, speeding motorcade was probably a processional of happiness, an escort for Millicent Theriot, Harlanville's youngest schoolteacher, who was expecting her first child.

But when the phone rang thirty minutes later, the caller was Millicent herself. She had missed the pageant, on strict bed rest in the final days before her delivery, and knew neither of the duet that had been sung nor of the moonlit magic in the gazebo at Belle Rêve.

Millicent knew only that Cole Taylor was in trouble, and if there was anyone in town who might reach him, it would be Aunt Augusta.

As Claire ran to him, through faintly misting rain and the graying winter twilight, the echoes of Millicent's words enveloped her in ever-deepening fear.

The moment his father's body had been removed, Cole had told them all to leave, a command so fierce that even the chief of police had complied. Cole was badly wounded, Millicent said. Before being banished from the house, however, one of the firemen managed to wrap in sterile gauze the two most serious wounds, to Cole's left forearm and right palm. That wrapping had, apparently, stemmed the flow of blood, the continual splashing of huge drops of liquid crimson onto the already reddened floor.

But Cole was in urgent need of proper medical attention—blood transfusions probably and expert suturing definitely. As it was, even if Cole found his way to the best hand specialist in New Orleans, the fireman predicted that the function of his right hand would be permanently impaired.

Claire worried about the wounds to Cole's flesh. But her greatest fear lay with the wounds that no one could see.

No one—except her ... and oh, how she saw those deep, deep wounds.

Cole stood absolutely still, a stark white statue cloaked in blood. His eyes were black, depthless, sightless pools of pain, and the stone-hard lines of his face were granite symbols of pure rage. There was some motion, a whisper of life in the red and white marble. Amid the strong muscles of his neck, that powerful throat which only last night had moaned with desire for her, Claire saw a pulse, proof that his gravely wounded heart beat still—forcefully, *but so slowly.*

Cole's heart should have been racing, spurred to a pounding frenzy by adrenaline and the loss of blood. But its pace was ominously slow, resigned, as if not fighting death but welcoming it.

And when Claire wrapped her arms around him, she felt the icy coldness of his skin and the core of steel that lay beneath.

"I love you," she whispered. *"I love you."*

How could steel become more taut or ice become more cold? Claire had no answer, only that it happened. Then he moved, encircling each of her wrists with his icy fingers. His intent was clear, to disengage himself from her loving embrace, but the act was stalled by the truth. Claire's strength was no match for his left hand, but his right, so strong once, and so talented, was powerless now, unable even to move her delicate hand from his bloodied chest.

For a moment Cole looked bewildered, aware of the injury yet strangely disembodied from it. Then, as he remembered everything, all that had been lost, the fierce bleakness returned to his face.

"I want you to leave, Claire."

It was the voice of a ghost. It belonged to a man who had died when he was still quite young, whose life was over before he could even begin to live his dreams. And that ghostly voice accomplished what his ruined hand could not. Claire stepped back, away, touching him no longer.

"Leave, Cole?"

"I don't want you here."

"You're not your father!"

He smiled then, a faint smile edged with bitter wisdom. "Oh but I am. We both killed today. We're both murderers."

"You didn't murder him. I know you didn't. The police are

calling it self-defense, but I know the truth. It was an *accident*. You were struggling for the knife, trying to get it away from him, so that no one would die."

There wasn't the slightest question in her voice, her confidence in him absolute, and for a moment Cole's heart betrayed him, beating faster, alive with hope. Claire saw the pulse in his throat, and began to move toward him.

"I killed him in cold blood, Claire. I could have gotten the knife away and held him until the police arrived. But I didn't." Cole's heart slowed with the necessary lie, he *made* it slow—more sluggish now, nearer death, even than before. "I killed him."

"I don't believe you! And even if it were true, which it's not, I wouldn't care! I love—"

"*Don't.*"

"And you love me."

"No I don't."

I can't. Cole knew that now. Claire gave him . . . everything. And what did he give her in return? Only hurt, only sadness, only pain. There was violence within him, death within him. It was his birthright, an inheritance so profound, and so tenacious, that even on this day when his entire future had depended on his ability to avert tragedy, he had failed. He had not been able to protect his heart, his dreams—just as, years ago, he had been unable to protect his brother.

But now he had to protect Claire, from himself, from his love. He needed to hurt her until she hated him so much that she would feel only relief when he was gone.

Hurt her, hurt her. The words seemed to come from Jed, goading words. Come on, sonny boy. Hurting Claire is what you do best. *Do it.*

"I don't love you, Claire." Cole saw her pain—and felt it in his own dying heart—a pain so sharp, so piercing, that for a moment he could not speak. But you must speak, sonny boy. Cruel words . . . until she runs away. "What I said to you last night wasn't true. I'd been drinking."

"Sparkling cider, Cole. That's all."

"I'd been drinking all day," he lied, an easy, necessary lie.

For her. On any other day, of course, Cole Taylor would have been drinking. But yesterday, as if he had somehow known about the magic that lay ahead, he had gone to the banks of the bayou, to their cathedral of lacy moss and cypress shade. He had spent the day remembering, and on sheer impulse had gone to the pageant, and Aunt Augusta had asked him to sing the finale with Claire.

Cole had had nothing to drink last night. But he *had* been drunk, intoxicated by a different kind of moonshine—moonlit blue eyes aglow with love.

Those lovely eyes were glowing no longer, shadowed now by winter twilight and stricken by the wintry chill of his own cruel words. But Claire had not yet given up. His angel was as determined as ever, believing still in the wondrous truth that lay beneath his lies.

When Cole would not give her that truth, would not relinquish even a trace of his own resolve, Claire looked away from him—as if she truly believed that somewhere in this blood-splattered room she would find proof of his love.

Her gaze fell first on the guitar she had given him. It lay limp and broken on the floor. Destroyed by Jed, *surely*. By Jed, not by Cole. A little shaken, but still undaunted, her valiant search continued, coming to rest at last on the glass globe.

Cole could not see through the thick rain of blood that coated its crystal surface. But Claire could.

"You bought that for me, didn't you?" she asked, walking toward the crimson glass as if it were a glowing beacon in the winter darkness. When she cradled it in her hands, she turned back to him. "You were going to give me snow for Christmas, weren't you?"

"It was the least I could do."

He had been planning to shatter the globe, to smash it against the brick fireplace, to free the angry ghosts imprisoned within. But the ghosts were already free. Indeed, the peaceful, heavenly sleep to which he had so boldly consigned them had been pure fantasy. The ghosts had never been contained, not for an instant. They had been with him all the time, an invisible aura of evil, deceptively silent during the journey from Lafayette as they lay in wait, smug in the confident knowledge that revenge—vengeance—soon would be theirs.

"The least you could do?" Claire echoed.

In the seconds before he uttered his cruel reply, Cole saw Claire with brilliant clarity. She stood apart from him now. But despite that separation and the ever-darkening veil of twilight shadows, he saw her anguish; and the defiant courage with which her delicate fingers clutched the blood-cloaked globe; and the sogginess of her cotton blouse, soaked crimson from having pressed against his chest; and the places where her cinnamon hair was painted red.

She was tainted, poisoned by him, covered with the blood he had spilled, the blood he had inherited.

"The least you could do, Cole?"

"It's an apology, for having said things to you last night that I didn't mean."

"But you *did* mean them! We're going to be married, Cole. We're going to teach music, and live in a house with a white picket fence and gardens of roses, and we're going to sing to each other and to our *children*."

"Get out of here, Claire. I mean it."

"I love you, and you love—"

"I don't love you, Claire."

Her heart was fully exposed now, and he was stabbing it with a jagged-edged knife. But even with that vicious assault, her love would not die.

"Are you just going to forget about me, Cole? About *us*? The way you've forgotten about your brother?"

Yes. *Yes.* That's my specialty, saying good-bye to the ones I love. Good-bye, Claire. *Adieu*, my precious love.

Cole felt his heart, frantic and desperate now, just as his father's heart had been at the last. But Cole denied his dying heart its final fight, slowing it with a chilling mantra. Hate me. Hate me. *Hate me, Claire.*

And when it was safe, when his heart was frozen, he finally answered her.

"I already have forgotten."

She stayed a little longer, staring at him until he was merely a shadow in the twilight, his silhouette more black than the winter night and more still than death. Then she turned away, ran away, stumbling in the darkness, clutching the snow globe still as she journeyed into a night that wept cold, bitter tears.

An hour later, when Claire returned with Aunt Augusta to the Taylor home on Joshua Street, the house was filled, still, with glistening red vestiges of carnage and of death. But it was quite empty of human life. Cole's car was there, in the driveway blocked by Jed's, where it would remain for the next several weeks.

But Cole was gone.

There were those in Harlanville who believed they saw him that night, a dark figure walking slowly in the rain. But they disputed his destination. The interstate, some maintained, from there to hitchhike wherever the road would lead. But others preferred a different version.

The wounded panther had gone to the bayou . . . to die.

Claire searched for him, in their enchanted forest. Day after day she searched, journeying ever deeper into the lush leafy green, calling to him, singing to him, screaming her anguish. Hating him as he wanted her to hate him. Yet loving him still, *always*, even when at last, after six years, she agreed to marry Andrew.

Claire believed that she would never see Cole again. And she was right. But eight months after her own world had become shrouded in darkness, she heard his voice.

The panther wasn't dead after all. And he was a phoenix still. Risen from the ashes of death, he had soared to the stars as a singer of love songs—seducing the women of the world as once he had so masterfully seduced her.

*C*hapter Seven

Hotel Paradis
Harlanville
Friday, December Twenty-third

NIGHT HAD COME TO HARLANVILLE, AN EN-
veloping cloak of black velvet, its darkness illuminated
by the shimmer of lights. Some of the lights were brightly colored, and twinkling, a celebration of the festive season. Others
merely shone with the golden incandescence that was the year-
round sign of nightfall over the bayou.

Cole stood at the window of his hotel room gazing at the
lighted world outside but so very aware of the darkened one
that lay within. Earlier, when the winter twilight had first begun to cast its shadows into the room, he had reached for a
lamp. And then stopped.

Day or night, her world was black. All the lamplight on
earth, every watt of luminescence, would not brighten it.

Did Claire turn on lights anyway? To illuminate the darkness for others? The porch light at Aunt Augusta's modest
home on Magnolia Avenue had always burned all night long, a
golden symbol of warmth and welcome. Did it glow still?

Yes, Cole decided. Claire would extend that warm, golden
welcome.

And what of the lights inside the house? The living room
ones might shine, cheery signals to potential visitors that she
was at home and would happily receive them. But beyond that

beacon of welcome to those whose eyes could see, there would be darkness. She wouldn't illuminate the light in the back hallway, or the fluorescent one above the stove, or the reading lamp beside her bed.

Claire Chamberlain dreamed, but she did not pretend.

She would have accepted her blindness, adjusted to it, courageously meeting the obstacles—and conquering them. Cole's mind reeled as he thought about the obstacles. Some were large, survival itself, and others, like being certain that the sweater she chose to wear wouldn't clash with the skirt, were, by contrast relatively small. But every one was an obstacle, monumental in its own way.

How did she buy groceries, cook meals, tell the time of day? And how did Harlanville's blind music teacher get to work? Aunt Augusta's house was only four blocks from the school. Four blocks, four intersections. Did Claire walk the short distance still, as always? Yes, perhaps she walked still—but not as always. Her movements along the cracked pavement would be uncertain now, slow and cautious, *or would they?*

A memory came to Cole then: a fallen log, a freckled face, a wide grin, and copper-lashed blue eyes tightly shut. Claire had danced along that log, sightless yet surefooted, and when her daring ballet was through, she had challenged him to do the same.

Even now Cole remembered his reaction, the chill of fear that had iced his veins. Of all the senses, sight had always been the most important to Cole, the most essential to his survival. He needed to see his father's face, to read its ominous messages, the forecast of violence that was to come. Sometimes Cole saw that his punishment wasn't inevitable, that Jed was too drunk—or too drugged—to chase after him if he fled. Mostly, however, there was no chance for escape . . . and it was then that Cole truly needed his eyes, to see his father's fists.

"No," Cole had told the freckle-faced ballerina who wanted him to close his eyes, just for a few moments, just for a game.

Cole heard the fear in his own voice—and so did the eight-year-old elf. Her expression became solemn, thoughtful. She did not understand his fear, or the meaning of the shadows in his dark gray eyes, but she cared, and worried, and wanted to help.

Claire's sightless dance across the fallen log had seemed incredibly bold to Cole—but it was nothing compared to the courageous journey into darkness that she embarked upon next. She reached for him, the golden warmth of her soul reaching out to the icy blackness of his, and when her small hands clasped his larger ones, she tugged.

"I'll lead you, Cole. Please trust me. I promise I won't let you fall."

The challenge that had begun as a game became much more, proof of the trust that was the very essence of their friendship. Cole made himself vulnerable to her, and Claire never let him stumble. He wandered blind through the forest, guided by her, feeling strangely safe, but fearful still.

What if she let go? What if she suddenly disappeared and he was unable to open his eyes? What if he was left alone in the darkness, destined to dwell there forever?

Claire had never abandoned him, of course, never betrayed him, and now it was she who was destined to darkness. Was she alone in that world? No . . . and yes. Until six months ago, Aunt Augusta had been with her. And since Aunt Augusta's death? The citizens of Harlanville had undoubtedly rallied to Claire's side. They were her extended family, people she had known all her life, kind people who were more than willing to help.

But as Cole thought about the girl who danced fearlessly— and sightlessly—along fallen logs, he guessed that as much as possible Claire Chamberlain helped herself.

Cole turned then, from Harlanville's festival of twinkling lights to the night blackness of his room. Before stepping away from the window, he pulled the heavy drapes, shutting out the final vestiges of light.

Then he began his journey toward darkness, toward blackness, wanting to know what she felt, to *feel* it, too.

And what Cole Taylor felt was pure terror. But surely this fright, this fearsome sense of helplessness, was his own private hell, a legacy of horror left over from his childhood. Surely— please—this wasn't a primal fear shared by all living creatures. Please don't let her feel this. Not *this*.

His seeking hands found a lampshade, and with that discovery the promise of a swift end to his torment. But Cole moved on. How many times had *she* reached for the nearest light, praying that when she flipped the switch she would awaken from the nightmare?

At school, surrounded by humanity, Claire probably felt safe. But what about when she was alone in her house? Was she held prisoner by the icy clutches of this bone-chilling terror?

He would know soon enough. His left hand rested now on the telephone beside the bed, his fingers lightly touching the keys as he forced himself to recall the way the numbers were displayed. That was the only demand Cole placed on his memory. Claire's phone number came to him of its own volition.

He misdialed on the first try, a miscue of his fingers, not of his mind. Then the phone was ringing, and he imagined her in the darkness, startled by the sudden sound, as if the phone itself were one of the many monsters she could not see. But she would quickly remember that the ringing telephone was friend, not foe—a link with another human being, a respite from her lonely terror—and she would rush toward it, fearful that the caller would disappear before she answered.

"Hello?"

Her voice was a little breathless, but absolutely fearless. So fearless, in fact, that it seemed to cast a golden light into the night-black room in which he stood.

"It's Cole."

"Cole."

It was then that Cole heard what he had expected to hear—her fear. *Then*, as she quietly echoed the single syllable of his name.

Because she knows the truly fearsome darkness, he thought, the only darkness that can ever really hurt her. *And she knows it's me.*

"Did you decide not to sing at the pageant after all?"

"No," he answered softly. "I want to sing, Claire—with you. I was just wondering if I could escort you?"

Even as he asked the question, Cole wondered if it was any more dangerous—or terrifying—for Claire to walk the four blocks to school at night than in the brightness of day. For her, the darkness was the same . . . and Harlanville's only truly dangerous citizen was long gone, long dead, killed by a hunting knife during a struggle with his son. But now that son was back—and perhaps, once again, the streets of Harlanville were no longer safe.

I won't hurt you, Claire. I just need to know what I came to learn—that the nightmare is mine alone, that you're all right, not terrified, not frantic, not desperate. Then I'll go. Then I'll say good-bye.

"Claire?"

"Thank you, but some of the students are coming by for me. Any minute, in fact. I could . . ."

"Yes?"

"Well, I could use a ride *after* the pageant, if you're planning to go to the reception, that is. It will be at Belle Rêve, as always."

Her voice made it sound as if nothing had changed, as if it was of no consequence to her heart that the bridegroom who had preferred a dead wife to a blind one now lived at Belle Rêve with the new Mrs. Harlan. Or perhaps Claire's heart was remembering something else, something that compelled her to return to the mansion despite what had happened with Andrew. Perhaps she was remembering a moonlit gazebo where two young lovers had shared their magical dreams. . . .

"You really want to go to the reception?"

"Yes. I have to, especially this year, because of Andrew's donation to the music department. Andrew and I have made our peace, Cole. But I guess it wouldn't be very peaceful for you, would it? Everyone would want to talk to you."

"That doesn't matter. We'll go to the reception, Claire, and after, I'll drive you home."

During their childhood, Cole Taylor and Claire Chamberlain had sung countless duets, performing for the snow-white egrets in their cathedral of cypress and moss. They never rehearsed those performances, never needed to. They could not have improved upon their perfect harmony had they tried. And twelve years ago, when Aunt Augusta surprised them both with her last-minute request for a duet of "Silent Night," they hadn't rehearsed either—and many in Harlanville still recalled with reverent wonder that Yuletide gift.

Still, on this night, Cole arrived at the Augusta Chamberlain Theatre an hour before the opening curtain was to rise on Harlanville's traditional Christmas pageant. He was accustomed to rehearsing now, with his band, practicing until each sound was precisely the way he wanted it to be. Cole remembered, of course, that he and Claire had never rehearsed, and he also remembered believing that there had been no need. But surely his memory of that instinctively perfect harmony was a deluded one, blurred by youth and hope and magic. Wasn't it?

He would find out. Tonight. Because it was obvious that he and Claire would not have a chance to discuss their performance, much less practice it. Her attention was wholly focused on her students, a mother hen surrounded by a flock of anxious chicks. On this night, their lovely mother hen wore Christmastime plumage, an ivory blouse and long green-velvet skirt. She smiled, and reassured, and patiently reiterated details that they all already knew by heart.

She wasn't blind, Cole realized. Not to any of her nervous chicks. They made the same demands of her that generations of students had made of Aunt Augusta, needing her confidence to calm their swirling butterflies. Claire's slender white cane was in a far corner of the stage, propped beside the chair where she had tossed her winter coat. The cane was unnecessary here. Her mind had long since memorized every square inch of the varnished stage and its cavernous wings. She could probably dance here, a ballet to rival her pirouettes along the forest's fallen logs.

Do you dance here, Claire? Do you spin and twirl and laugh? Still? As then?

Cole wanted that joy for her, even as an aching sadness constricted his heart. Claire's graceful dances had been *their* joy. She had danced for him, wanting to share with him the exhilarating freedom she felt, trusting him to watch her happiness—and to catch her if she fell.

Had Claire found a man to watch her dance upon this stage? If so, he wasn't here now, nor was he driving her to the reception at Belle Rêve. No, Cole thought. She is alone. If she dances here, it is by herself . . . with no one to catch her if she falls.

The image of the solitary copper-haired ballerina caused such pain that Cole focused firmly on the present. Claire wasn't alone onstage now, and there was a dance of sorts taking place. The nervous performers swirled around her, and although their movements seemed quite random, they were, in one respect, choreographed with exquisite care. Whenever their anxious pacing drew them close to Claire, whether scooting past or pausing to talk, they touched her, every one of them, gentle caresses to let her know where they were. Even the teenaged boys who towered above her, and who undoubtedly harbored at least some adolescent skepticism about adults of all types, made an exception for her. Their large hands touched her as gently as the younger children's did, a gesture that was at once admiring and protective.

"Watch out, Miss Chamberlain!"

Claire's confident stride, on this stage she knew so well, came to an abrupt halt. "What is it, Shelley?"

"My purse," the girl whispered as she swooped to retrieve the holly-red culprit. "I'm *sorry*. That was so dumb of me! I don't know what I was thinking, just dropping it there."

The truth, of course, was that the pretty sixteen-year-old *hadn't* been thinking. Any hope of coherent thought had vanished the moment she saw Cole. She glanced at him now, her young cheeks blushing furiously.

Cole looked at the embarrassed teenager and offered silent reassurance with a gentle smile. But there was nothing gentle about Cole's thoughts. Claire's students knew how special she was, how precious and how rare. But tonight, because of him, that knowledge had gotten jumbled. His presence was causing a distraction, stealing from her—just because of the way he sang songs of love.

As Cole looked from Shelley to Claire, he saw just how much he had stolen. Her confidence, her pride. Had Shelley not suddenly remembered the purse left so carelessly in Claire's path, Claire would have tripped, fallen hard onto the varnished floor. The smoothly polished mahogany would have caused little damage. No telltale splinters would have pierced her snowy palms. But something *would* have been splintered to bits: the illusion that she didn't need help.

The mishap had been averted—everywhere except in Claire's heart. There she had fallen, alone in the darkness, and now her stricken unseeing eyes were telling him even more. He *would not* have caught her if she had begun to fall, nor would she have expected him to. Such trust had perished years ago, severed as irrevocably as Jed Taylor's hunting knife had severed the strength and talent of Cole's right hand.

Claire was alone, in the darkness, and she had been there for a very long time—long before the accident that had taken sight from her brilliant blue eyes. The world of solitary darkness was where Cole himself had left her, twelve years ago, on that blood-drenched twilight before Christmas Eve.

I would have caught you, Claire. You can trust me still. Cole's silent protest was both truth and lie. Had he seen the purse lying so perilously in her path, he would have moved to her, and guided her around it, without ever mentioning to her that it was there.

But Cole hadn't seen Shelley's purse. His gaze had been on Claire's brave, lovely face, not the flowing green velvet that cloaked the confident strides of her ballerina legs.

And if he told her that she could trust him? Her sightless eyes would become earnest and sad, and she would ask, very softly, Trust you to do what, Cole? Hurt me? Break my heart? That's all I could ever really count on you to do.

He was hurting her again, now, *always*. But even as he watched, the desolation vanished, replaced by the determination he knew so well. Claire had picked herself up from her imaginary fall, dusted herself off, and now she was going on. One of the stage crew's teenaged boys needed her—needed to hear again from the woman who dwelled in darkness precisely how he should angle the bright beams of light that would soon fall on the stage.

This time, on this night, Cole Taylor and Claire Chamberlain should have rehearsed their duet. But they didn't. Which meant that they were both completely unprepared for what had happened to their voices during the past twelve years.

They had sung as children, with voices innocent and pure, and as teenagers, old enough to love deeply and forever, yet still quite young. But now . . . he was a man, and she was a woman, and the years of separation and loss had filled their souls with longing, and with a sensuality that stunned them both.

The audience heard only the splendor of the union. But Cole and Claire knew the truth. Their voices were making love, twining together with breathtaking intimacy, and promising that if ever their bodies were permitted such joy, this was the way they would touch, would join, would become one.

And after that glorious union? They would hold each other, unable to speak, yet needing no words. Their tender loving, that magnificent duet of their hearts, would have said it all.

Neither spoke after the pageant ended. Neither could, neither needed to, and as they drove in silence to Belle Rêve, both fought the remembered wonder of their love with stark reminders of the truth.

I love you, Claire. But nothing has changed. I still have nothing to offer you, only my heart, a different kind of darkness.

I love you, Cole. But I wasn't enough for you before, when I could see your face, when—sometimes—I could even read your pain. And now I have nothing to offer you, only my heart, and my world of darkness.

"I wonder," she began when Cole brought the car to a stop on the mansion's white cobblestone drive.

"What do you wonder, Claire?"

His voice was as soft as hers, and for a moment Claire imagined more words from him: *Do you wonder, Claire, if I love you still? I do. I've never stopped loving you. I lied to you the day I left. I lied—*

Don't do this! The command came from deep within her, from a voice that was harsh with wisdom. Don't even *begin* to fantasize. It can't happen. It won't. It's far too late. You know that you could never survive loving him again, not blind, not able to see the stone and shadows of his eyes. *You know that.* You barely survived the last time.

The harsh warning was echoed by the thunder of her pounding heart. The racing heartbeats had begun hours before, the moment she first sensed his presence, and they hadn't slowed, not one single beat, not even when they had been apart.

And they won't slow, the ominous voice cautioned. Not until he's gone. You'd better hope that's soon, too, because this fluttering is very dangerous. No heart can beat this rapidly for long.

"What do you wonder, Claire?"

If I will die tonight, with you—or if death won't come until tomorrow, after you're gone.

Claire drew a breath, reminded herself who she was, *what* she was, and when at last she answered, her tone was matter-of-fact, as it always was when she discussed the limitations of her blindness. "It's awkward for me to use my cane in a setting like this, when the rooms are so crowded and everyone's holding drinks. It's better if I just sit. That's what I usually do. I leave my cane in the car and whoever's driven me to the reception helps me get to the living room, to the sofa closest to the tree. Could you . . . would you get me there?"

"Yes, of course. Unless . . ." Cole frowned.

Claire heard the frown. "Unless?"

"Unless you'd like to mingle together." *Unless you could trust me to guide you, to hold your hand and not let go, to never leave you alone in the darkness.* That had been her pledge to him in their enchanted forest, and she had never betrayed his trust. But he had betrayed hers—and with his cruel betrayal it was he who had been condemned. "Claire?"

"I'd like that very much."

She teetered a little on the cobblestones, but was steadied by his arm, and just before they began their ascent to the front door, Cole said, "Steps."

"Yes, thank you. Twelve of them." She shrugged. "I've become a bit of an expert on things like the numbers of steps at various Harlanville locales."

She needed to concentrate, to recall the height of the steps on this particular staircase, and to silently count each one. But how could she, when Cole cradled her so gently, and when she felt his strength, his heat, even through the thick layers of her winter coat?

She couldn't, and somehow he knew, or perhaps he, too, had begun to count and then lost track. Whatever the reason, when they reached the top, he said, "That's it, all the steps."

"Eight paces then—my size ones, not yours—until we reach the doormat, then one more step up into the house."

"Okay," he said quietly, hating this for her, even though her voice held only a smile. Claire had risen to this challenge as she had risen to every challenge in her life—with optimism and courage. "Lead the way. I'll adjust."

In moments they had traversed the porch, his long strides finding easy harmony with her smaller ones. They were greeted by a butler, who took their coats, a process that necessarily drew them apart. The physical separation was brief, a matter of a few seconds, but for both of them it felt like an eternity—the eternity of darkness, of loneliness, to which at evening's end they were destined to return.

Then Cole found her hand, and carried it with gentle urgency to his left forearm. Claire had been feeling so cold, in just those precious seconds away from his heat, but now she felt fire again—and ice. There was a glacier of it, a hard, massive mound of coldness. It was a scar, she realized, a gravestone of the knife wound that had severed his flesh.

Cole hadn't seen a doctor. She was sure of it. Which meant that the more devastating wound, the one deep in his right palm, had gone untended, too. How long had it wept, raw and open and unhealing? And what had it become, the hand that with such exquisite tenderness had once plucked the strings of a guitar . . . as if they were the delicate strings of her heart?

Claire almost reached for that talented hand then, to feel the destruction, and to make him talk to her about it. She would have, had they been alone, had no one been watching.

But Cole and Claire were not alone, and *everyone* was watching, including the man to whom she had once been married. The exchange with Andrew was mercifully brief and civil. But Claire felt Cole's reaction. His arm turned to pure steel, its powerful muscles ready for violence, eager for it. Even the scar came alive, cold still, but straining to burst open.

Cole was ready to defend her, to hurt the man who he believed had hurt her so much.

Oh, Cole, you have the wrong man.

They spent an hour mingling at Belle Rêve, during which time Cole and Claire exchanged very few words. As she had predicted, there was little peace for Harlanville's superstar. Inquiring minds wanted to know everything about him; and from Cole's replies, Claire learned answers to some of the questions she herself might have asked.

Cole was leaving Harlanville tonight, for New Orleans, then on to London in the morning. London would be his home for the next six months. His upcoming album would be recorded at the Gemstone studio near Hyde Park, and the accompanying music videos would be filmed in England's most grand castles, and, of course, he would appear in concert throughout Europe.

The promise of a new Cole Taylor album piqued the most interest. Would it contain *more* original songs? the townspeople of Harlanville wondered. Or, they asked quietly, knowingly, was "Imagine Moonlight" the only song he would ever write?

Although he had never confirmed it—had, in fact, denied it— every Cole Taylor fan on earth knew *why* he had written

"Imagine Moonlight," and for whom. The breathtaking song of love was an anguished good-bye, a forever farewell to Paulina Bliss, the enchanting actress who had been the love of his life. Paulina was much beloved by moviegoers as well. Even before "Imagine Moonlight," authentic tears of grief had been shed at the news of her death, her brutal slaying on Valentine's Day.

"Imagine Moonlight" had shattered all previous sales records, and was slated to sweep the Grammys, and because Gemstone Records' smash hit had been featured on the sound-track of Gemstone Pictures' *Wind Chime*, it would undoubt-edly garner an Oscar as well.

To the interested citizens of Harlanville, Cole said no, he didn't plan to write any more songs; and yes, if the song was nominated, he would sing live at both the Grammy and Acad-emy Award ceremonies; and it was sometime during his sub-dued answers about "Imagine Moonlight" that Claire learned about the fate of Cole's right hand.

She wasn't sure how it happened, how her hand became en-twined with his. She was lost in his emotion, sharing his silent pain and so saddened that such brutal violence had touched his life yet again. Perhaps she reached for him, without thought and with love. . . .

In fact, Cole reached for her, cradling her small fist within his, then twining their fingers so that her silken palm caressed his ravaged one.

As Claire felt the roughness of his flesh, she had the distinct impression that had he been able to, Cole would have crushed her hand within his own. But he couldn't. His hand, crippled by violence, was now destined to gentleness.

But there was nothing gentle in the voice that abruptly an-nounced that it was time for them to go. It was hoarse and stark, a whisper as harsh as the whisper of twelve years ago, when he had needed to be alone with her, and they had found sanctuary, and magic, in Belle Rêve's secluded gazebo.

Would they go to the gazebo now? Claire wondered as they reclaimed their coats. There, in that once enchanted place, would Cole confess to her his pain, his immense sadness—and rage—at the loss of Paulina Bliss? Would he admit that was the reason he had returned to Harlanville, because he needed to talk to the girl who had been his friend, to share with her the aching emptiness he felt?

If so, if the way in which Cole needed her was to help him survive the death of the only woman he had ever truly loved, then that was precisely what Claire would do.

But Claire was never to know if Cole had planned such confessions in the gazebo . . . because this was not the balmy moonlit December night of twelve years ago. In fact—

"Cole?" she gasped when their journey from the porch had taken them halfway down the twelve steps. "Is it snowing?"

Do you think we'll have a white Christmas? Her voice was as innocent now as when she had posed that eager question as a girl. As innocent, as hopeful, as filled with wonder. Snow had come to their bayou town at last, a Christmas present for those who could see—but six years too late for the woman who had dreamed of witnessing this wintertime delight most of all.

And yet, her sightless eyes were glowing, and she lifted her face to the snowy sky, and she smiled.

"Cole?"

"Yes. It's snowing."

"Tell me what it looks like," she whispered. "Tell me what you see."

I see a flame-haired angel adorned with snowflakes.

"Is it beautiful, Cole?"

"Very beautiful."

"Is everything white and pure?"

So pure, so white, so lovely. "It's becoming that way."

"The trees? Do they look lacy and bright?"

"Yes," Cole answered, marveling that she was seeing more than he, more than he had *ever* seen. Snow was not new to him. Surely the snow-caressed pines at Lake Tahoe looked as lacy as Belle Rêve's white-dressed cypresses. But he hadn't noticed that frilly wonder—until now. And as for brightness? The winter wonderland was aglow, the silhouettes of its trees illuminated by a shimmering silver light. *I see a wedding chapel.*

"That's exactly how they look, Claire. Lacy, and bright, and very delicate."

She turned then, from the snowy heavens to him, her unseeing eyes framed by snow-kissed auburn lashes, her mane of cinnamon hair hidden beneath a pure white veil.

I see a bride.

She was looking to him now, so hopeful, so innocent, silently beseeching him to share with her more descriptions of the pristine wonder she could not see. But Cole had nothing more to tell. Had she not suggested otherwise, the silver-white trees would have been, to him, merely the haunting ghosts of long-dead dreams.

"I can feel the shapes of the snowflakes," Claire said at last. "Each tiny crystal. Each one is different, unique, as rare and distinctive as a fingerprint." She shook her head then, freeing the exquisite flakes from the rosiness of her cheeks and the cinnamon flames of her hair. "I don't want them to melt," she explained. "I don't want their magic to end."

But magic ends. The reminder stayed with Cole throughout the drive to Claire's home. It was a reminder, and a warning, and a truth. Compelled by his own haunting nightmare, he had returned to Harlanville to see her, to make certain that she was fine . . . and then to say good-bye.

Claire wasn't living the dream he had envisioned for her. But she *was* fine. Her life of darkness was a challenge for her, but it was not a lightless world of sheer terror; and she was as beloved by the townspeople of Harlanville as Aunt Augusta had been; and her unseeing eyes saw far more beauty than his sighted ones would ever see; and . . .

"Would you like to come inside, Cole? I could make some coffee, or hot chocolate?"

They were in his rental car, parked in front of her house. The porch light was on, as Cole had imagined it would be, and the living room lights, and there was blinking, too, a twinkling rainbow of color.

She had a Christmas tree.

"How do you do it, Claire?"

"Do what?"

Everything. Smile. Laugh. Survive. "Make coffee, or hot chocolate. Buy groceries. Tell time."

She smiled now. "I get by with a little help from my friends—and with clocks and watches that talk to me." Her face became solemn as the silence told her that he truly wanted to know. "As for groceries, I call in my orders to the Pelican Pantry, and you know those label-making machines, the ones that create letters in relief on strips of plastic? Well, Mr. Gautreau, you remember him, labels each item for me."

"And you read the words with your fingers?"

Claire nodded. It was lucky that, as a girl, she had given her guitar to her friend, the boy she had loved even then, thus avoiding a lifetime of calluses on her delicate fingertips. If that beloved friend still played the guitar, if his hand hadn't been forever crippled by the bone-deep slice of a hunting knife, she might have mentioned that lucky happenstance.

As it was, she merely explained, "They make such label machines in Braille, too, but since I'd spent twenty-two years being familiar with letters, and since the people who do the labeling for me are all sighted, this is easier. Everything's labeled. My food, my clothes, my shoes." *All of your CDs.*

"What about reading?" Cole asked, remembering the girl who had been such an avid reader.

"There are books in Braille, but I'm really not proficient enough to read them. Fortunately, though, there are also lots of books on tape." *And, until she died, Aunt Augusta read aloud to me every article ever written about you.* "And there are so many news shows on television and radio that I'm pretty much up-to-date on current affairs."

"You've adjusted so well."

Claire shrugged. "Why fight something I can't change?"

Her voice held wisdom, and not a trace of bitterness—and most certainly no anger. But her calm acceptance of her fate could not tranquilize the rushes of fury Cole felt. Claire Chamberlain *should* be able to see. It was wrong, desperately unfair.

But she is fine, and in absolutely no peril—unless, that is, you decide to stay. Unless you permit the selfish wishes of your own heart to put her in the greatest danger—the greatest darkness—of all.

"I think I should go now, Claire, to begin the drive to New Orleans before the snow gets even deeper."

"Oh! Yes, of course." *You need to go, and I will never know why you came. Was it to seek my help with your sadness about Paulina? Or could it, perhaps, possibly, have been because of me and the memories of our love?* Memories of a girl who had not been blind?

You need to go, Cole . . . and oh, how I need you to go.

Cole walked her to the front door, a journey so familiar that Claire needed neither her cane nor his touch. Once there he watched as she inserted her key into the lock. Her hands trembled a little, he thought. But the key found its mark cleanly, as if guided by the sharpest of eyesight.

Before disappearing into the house that was dark to her, but where a rainbow of Christmas lights twinkled brightly, Claire turned to him.

"It was nice . . ." *to see you.*

Claire used that phrase still, easily, cheerfully. In truth, she *did* see everyone in Harlanville, in her mind's eye. They were frozen in time, their images as young, or as old, as they had been on her wedding day.

And as for her students, the fresh faces she would never see? The boys were Cole, and the girls were her, and that was undoubtedly why *this* Miss Chamberlain was as beloved as her great-aunt had been—because she smiled at them with such fondness, and with such great hope for them all.

But Claire couldn't merrily say, "It was nice to see you" to Cole. No single image of him was frozen in her mind, but a collage of countless ones, from despair to love; and there were the most important images of all, the ones that she would never know and would wonder about always—the unseeable images from today, tonight, this final moment.

What look had crossed Cole's face when he first realized that she was blind? And when their voices had joined in song, *had made love*? And when her silken palm had kissed his scarred one? And now, when he was leaving, again, forever?

Claire wanted to reach for him, to survey with her never-callused fingertips the hard planes and harsh contours of his face, to read, if she could, the messages in the powerful muscles of his throat and jaw, and in the strong heartbeat in his neck.

But even if Cole would permit such exploration, the most important terrain would be hidden from her still, dark to her always—for even if she felt their coal-black lashes, and the tiny lines etched at their edges, and the smooth heat of their unflickering lids, she would never be able to know what dwelled in the deep shadows of his stone-gray eyes.

Still, Claire felt her hands beginning to move. Bold, renegade, *foolish* hands. Sheer terror enabled her to stop the folly. Terror—memory.

She had reached for him, twelve years ago, loving him so much. And Cole had cast her away. And now, even without touching him, Claire felt his tension, his urgency to leave.

If she let him leave, right now, if she didn't foolishly search for something that she could never find, she could create whatever image she chose for these final moments. She could pretend—forever—that the severe angles of his face had softened with tenderness, and that there had even been a little longing, amid the pity, in his eyes.

Soon, Claire promised her hands, very soon you will be wrapped around something safe, the touchstone you know so well.

The snow globe sat beside her bed. There, encased in glass and crystallized in tiny flakes of snow, were her memories of Cole, of dreams, of love. Tonight, soon, her hands would curl around the globe, like a fortune-teller with her crystal ball.

Claire would not journey to the future, however, but to the past. And tonight, soon, she would encase more memories within the glass. They would be her memories, not his, the ones she would come to believe: that there had been love, still. Not *enough* love, of course. That would never change. But love nonetheless.

"Good-bye, Cole."

It was what he had come to say to her.

But before Cole echoed her words his hands started to move toward her face, the crippled one and its powerful twin, moving in perfect harmony, trembling together . . . until the last moment, when, in unison, they dropped away.

"Good-bye, Claire."

Adieu.

His final stop, before leaving Harlanville, was Joshua Street, to gaze one last time at the small house where he and his father had lived. To a casual observer that place of violence, of torment and of death, was at peace now, cloaked in the purity of freshly fallen snow and glowing brightly from within.

But Cole was far from a casual observer. He saw his home through a crimson veil, a blood-red haze of remembrance and rage.

He closed his eyes, seeking relief. But the redness blazed still. So he lifted his face to the heavens, to the feathery caresses of snow, and he tried to feel what Claire had felt, the unique, perfect shape of each tiny crystal.

But Cole Taylor could not feel the exquisite delicacy of snowflakes. All he could feel was their death. They melted on his cheeks, destroyed by the fiery heat of his rage, and then they turned cold, dampening his face like the most bitter of tears.

Magic ends.

*C*hapter Eight

Drake Hotel
Hyde Park, London
Saturday, December Twenty-fourth

JACK POLITELY DECLINED THE BELLMAN'S OF-
fer to acquaint him with his room at the Drake, tipped him
liberally, and was moving toward the telephone even as the
man was pulling the door closed behind him.

Jack's call was to the police commissioner at Scotland Yard.

"Yes, I'm already here," Jack confirmed. "I took the evening
flight from Dulles. I was hoping it might be possible for all of
us to meet a little earlier than planned."

The muscles in Jack's jaw rippled as he listened to the apologetic reply.

"We had no reason to believe that she might fly the coop,"
the commissioner explained, his voice conveying amazement
that Sarah Pembroke, *Lady* Sarah Pembroke, had orchestrated
such a brazen deception.

"But you must have an idea where she is," Jack countered,
his own voice equally eloquent in his unrelenting resolve.
Christmas Eve or not, he intended to have this meeting with
Sarah Pembroke. The beautiful aristocrat turned elusive journalist would undoubtedly be wearing her blue-blood persona
for the holidays. She would be in the country, ensconced at one
of England's grandest manors, sipping hot buttered rum in

front of a roaring fire. Fine. That's where they would meet. "She must be with family or friends."

"Not family," the commissioner replied. "She has none. Except, that is, for her deceased husband's relatives. But there's no love there. As Simon Beckwith-Jones's widow, she inherited a substantial portion of his family's real-estate empire. The family wanted her holdings, and she obliged, but for a price far above market value. Then she donated every penny of the proceeds to charity."

"Is that why she went to work?" *To war?*

"You mean was she a pauper? Hardly. She had—has—a significant trust fund. She can't touch the principal for years, but the annual interest itself is a small fortune. Rumor has it that she gives most of the interest, along with her salary, to her favorite charities as well."

"What are her favorite charities?" Jack asked, digressing again, wanting to know.

"Haven't the foggiest. No one does. Her donations are always anonymous—as anonymous, I'm afraid, as her friends. She's doubtless involved with someone, but we honestly don't have a clue who he might be."

"Which is the way she wants it."

"Apparently, as evidenced by this disappearing act. In any case, she *does* feel a bit guilty about what she's done. In fact, she's signed a blank check to be made out in your name and for any amount you choose."

"A blank check?"

"To get you back to the States for Christmas with your family. You can charter a private jet, if you like. She's prepared to pay."

And she *will* pay, Jack vowed. But not with a blank check. The fierceness of his thought stunned him. What was he planning to do? *Yell* at her for being such a self-absorbed dilettante? Fume and scold and rage and shout?

That was not the Jack Dalton he knew, the ice-cool master of control. Jack was fully capable of anger—toward the killers he tracked, toward anyone, for that matter, who caused pain to anyone else. But to feel such emotion toward her, this woman he didn't know, herself the intended next victim of a most brutal assassin?

It made no sense. But there it was. Totally without logic, as inexplicable as the urgency he had felt throughout the night flight to London, and astonishingly powerful.

The voice with which Jack finished the conversation with the commissioner of police gave no clue to the emotions that pulsed within. With unwavering calm, he agreed that one o'clock on Monday, the twenty-sixth, would be a fine time to meet with the wayward journalist, and there was even warmth in his voice as he wished the commissioner the happiest of holidays.

Then Jack was alone, pacing restlessly, feeling caged—trapped, held hostage, by *her*, this woman he did not even know.

Because of her—because of the sinister message of the black heart—he was in London, not Maui, his own holiday plans forsaken. It was possible, of course, to journey from London to Maui and back by one o'clock on the twenty-sixth. He could, in fact, share a few hours of Christmas day with his parents, sisters, and brothers-in-law. But a token appearance wasn't what a family holiday was all about.

And besides, there it was again, the feeling that he was *supposed* to be here. Here? Pacing in his room at the Drake? Consumed by inexplicable anger? No . . . not quite.

Jack stopped pacing then, and for a long time he was very still. He was the captor now, imprisoning his own fierce energy, containing it, controlling it, and finally compelling it to find purpose, to focus its random power in a decisive way.

He needed to decide what to do with the next two days, how and where to spend this Christmas. The answers came with surprising confidence—and remarkable calm. He would spend this holiday alone. Somehow that solitude felt right, and not the least bit lonely.

And where would he spend this private time of quiet reflection? In the town of Dickens? Apparently not, because even as the plan was coming into clear focus, he was beginning to transfer two days worth of clothing into his smallest valise. His anger had dissipated, and he was no longer trapped but free, and the only lingering restlessness he felt was eagerness to begin the short journey to Paris.

And what of Lady Sarah Pembroke? She was safe; cloistered, no doubt, with a lover. Indeed, the weeks that lay ahead would be the safest that the intrepid journalist had known in years. Anchoring the nightly news from London was a far cry from dodging sniper bullets in Goražde, and although her own personal assassin, the monster whose calling card was an elegant black heart, would appear sometime before February fourteenth, his lethal hand would not wield its jagged-edged knife until that romantic day.

Lady Sarah Pembroke was fine, enjoying the holidays in her lover's embrace. And as for Jack? He would enjoy his solitary Christmas in Paris, in the embrace of the city to which he had never traveled, but which had always held such a powerful allure.

Jack knew the reason for his fascination with the City of Light: Monique Villeneuve, his high school French teacher, a native Parisian. Madame Villeneuve's love of her city—and its language—had been contagious. Under her enthusiastic tutelage her students pored over maps of the city, describing aloud, in French, how exactly they would get from Montmartre to the Tour Eiffel, and precisely what they would see as they strolled the Champs-Elysées from the Arc de Triomphe to the Place de la Concorde and finally to the Louvre.

Because of Madame, an entire generation of Denver teenagers, none of whom had previous acquaintance with the language, spoke fluent French. Especially Jack. He had a special aptitude, Madame decided. Perhaps, she suggested, it was a gift that extended to all languages.

Which it was. In college, Jack demonstrated the same remarkable fluency both in Russian and Italian. But it was French to which Jack returned, enrolling in the school's most advanced classes. French was the language he preferred, the one that held an irresistible appeal.

Jack hadn't spoken French since college. And he knew from Madame Villeneuve the arch disdain of the French toward any-one—*especially* Americans—who butchered their beautiful language. But Madame had appended a prediction to her warning: Jack Dalton would be able to speak French in Paris. He would be identified as an American, naturally, but the Parisians would be so impressed with his mastery of their language that they would consent to converse with him in French.

It had been less than two hours since his flight had touched the tarmac at Charles de Gaulle, but already Jack had discovered that Madame Villeneuve's prediction was correct. Although halting at first, his words had evoked a receptive reply, beginning—after the requisite test—with the taxi driver at the airport. The test had been a barrage of words, low, rapid, idiom-laced, and when Jack passed with flying colors, with complete comprehension and not a trace of butchery, the driver gave a lavish shrug of his shoulders and obliged Jack with animated conversation all the way into the city.

The concierge at the Ritz had been similarly accommodating, and now, as Jack crossed the rue de Rivoli, en route to the Seine, he made the decision to speak exclusively French. Why not?

Pourquoi pas, he amended silently as he wandered through the Tuileries Gardens, its fountains and statues shadowy phantoms in the misting winter twilight. *Ici, à Paris, je parlerai, et penserai, exclusivement en français.*

Jack could imagine no reason to depart from his plan, even—*spécialement*—when he saw her.

Emotion came before thought, feeling before cognition, slowing his footsteps even as his heart set a new, rapid pace. She, this Frenchwoman standing beside the Seine, was the reason he had come to Paris. She was the reason he had mastered French.

Jack knew all that, his heart did, within seconds, an extraordinary knowledge based merely on a shadowed glimpse. She was staring down at the river, her slender body leaning toward it, as if pulled by a magnet deep beneath the watery depths. Her head was tilted in thoughtful contemplation, a gesture that veiled her face behind a thick curtain of long black hair. That

curtain, that luxuriant flow of lustrous ebony, was an enchantment in itself. But on this misting winter evening, there was
even more: tiny drops of mist adorned the night-black silk like
a glittering galaxy of diamond-bright stars.

I need to see your face. I need to know if these astonishing
feelings can possibly be true . . . and if you feel them, too.

Look at me.

Regardez-moi.

It was then, when the silent command of his heart was issued
in French, that the enchantress obeyed. She turned to him
slowly, a blend of resignation and wonder, as if she couldn't
refuse his command, and yet feared that she should have resisted with all her might.

The mist that had transformed her hair into a sky of diamonds clung to her long black lashes like tiny tears. And the
eyes framed by those glistening lashes? They were dark green,
shaded emeralds, concealing an infinity of secrets in their shadows—yet revealing the most important truth of all. She knew.
She felt it, too.

They were meant to be here, at this precise silvery moment
of twilight on the misted banks of the River Seine. This was
why he spoke flawless French, and why his meeting with Lady
Sarah Pembroke had been canceled, and why he had felt such
restlessness until he made the decision to journey to Paris, and
why now he felt such peace.

She was why. It was she for whom he had been searching all
his life. She was the missing piece, the one that would fill,
would heal, the gaping hole in his heart.

Jack knew all those things about her at once, that powerful
truth, that wondrous joy. But it was only as he moved toward
her, to whisper the unnecessary greeting—because their hearts
were already singing their joyous hellos—that he realized who
she was.

His destiny. *Yes.*

And more.

She was Lady Sarah Pembroke.

Had the master puzzle solver *known* that he would find the
elusive journalist in Paris? Had there been a clue in the articles

he had read about her, something subtle but decipherable by the gifts of his logical mind? If so, the perception had been so deep, so instinctive, that it had dwelled far beneath the surface of conscious thought.

But something urgent and restless had compelled him to London, to her, as quickly as possible, and then had urged him to journey even farther, to Paris, when he had learned that she wasn't there.

And now? Now the mysterious restlessness was calm, *satisfied*. Lady Sarah Pembroke had been found.

And here, on the misting banks of the River Seine, she was a Sarah Pembroke the world had never seen. The warrior unarmed. The woman revealed.

Jack had seen many photographic images of the renowned war correspondent. But now, and for the first time, he felt that he was truly seeing her in color. The realization was startling, and surely wrong. Her reports from lands ravaged by war were always filmed in color, weren't they? Yes, of course they were. And yet they felt oddly black and white—at least *she* did. Then, from the battlefields of misery and death, everything about her was solemn and subdued, a somberness to match the stark grimness of the stories she told.

But on this overcast Parisian day, Lady Sarah Pembroke was a shimmering rainbow against the muted gray sky. Her jeans were blue, her turtleneck yellow, her parka the color of pines. And at her throat, like a Christmas ribbon, shone a ruby red silk scarf.

The brilliance of her clothes paled, however, in comparison to the pinkness of her cheeks and the jewel-bright glitter of her dark green eyes. And her hair? Even without its sparkle of diamonds, there was a deep fire, embers aglow within the coal, and it was styled to complement the lustrous richness, unrestrained and flowing, a cascade of curling silk that bore little resemblance to the single subdued braid she wore into battle.

Sarah Pembroke was not a warrior now.

She was *never* a warrior, Jack realized. Not really. Her warrior persona, the austere veneer that sent the clear message that she needed no one, was merely a disguise, a necessary armor to shield the lovely vulnerability that lay within.

What made her so fragile? Jack wondered. What compelled her to don the stark masquerade?

And why did Lady Sarah Pembroke believe that she needed to be her own warrior, a fortress unto herself? Was there no one willing to protect her against the assaults of the world?

Well. *There was now.*

"Hello," he greeted, in English.

Sarah had begun trembling even before she turned toward him. She had known he was there, a sudden awareness that had come with brightness and clarity and warmth—as if there burned behind her a fiery sun, hidden until now by the darkest of clouds. She had turned expecting to see nothing, *hoping* for that. Anything more, she knew, would be a mirage, a phantom of her mind, terrifying proof of her greatest fear.

But he was no phantom. Just something far more disturbing—a tall, dark-haired stranger whose cobalt blue eyes gazed at her as no man's eyes ever had.

Sarah knew well the gazes of men, the menacing blend of desire and disdain. They wanted to possess her, and they were always slightly angered by the power of their need for her, as if it were her fault, as if she willfully seduced from them their ability to resist. They wanted to punish her brazen seduction, to conquer, and to hurt.

It had been a very long time since Sarah had looked directly into the eyes of any man. It was far too dangerous, a duel of monumental proportions, his desire, her contempt. She would never accede to the man's wishes. But the battle itself would drain her strength, and move her ever closer to the precarious ledge on which she teetered, just one small step away from madness.

Sarah dared not voice her contempt in person. But when she looked into a camera, that faceless eye that could not taunt in reply, she was looking at all men. And the message she sent as she shared with the world the folly, the atrocity, of war? That men were despicable creatures, brutal savages wedded only to violence and to terror.

But here was this man, this stranger, and Sarah could not compel her eyes to leave his. She saw his strength, his power, his *fierceness*—and yet it was such a gentle fierceness, such an intense tenderness . . . as if he were promising to protect, not to harm; to give, not to take. To cherish, even to love—

Fantasy! Hallucination. *Fearsome proof of your perilous dance with madness.*

She needed to flee, to run far and fast. But her legs remained still, and she sensed that if she impelled them to move, they would carry her toward him, not away.

Jack saw the confusion on her mist-caressed face. She seemed conflicted; unable, it seemed, even to speak. If Jack didn't know the truth, that Lady Sarah Pembroke was one of England's titled aristocracy, he might have assumed that she, his captivating Frenchwoman, was struggling to recall what limited English she knew.

At a loss, but determined not to lose her, Jack offered impulsively, *"Bonsoir."*

"Bonsoir," she echoed, reflexively. And flawlessly. It was yet another facet of her madness, this need to escape to Paris, to *vanish* here. Sarah Pembroke, the highest-paid war correspondent on the planet, was known to most households in France. But the woman Sarah became in Paris bore no resemblance to that familiar television image. Here, in Paris, that woman was free, *almost* free.

In all the days and nights that she had spent in Paris, Sarah had never been recognized. Nor was she recognized now.

This man, this stranger, was speaking French to her. To the woman who was almost free.

"Je m'appelle Jacques. Et vous?"

Sarah had no name for the woman who escaped to Paris. In the small hotels where she found lodging, on the Left Bank or L'Ile de la Cité, she always paid for her room in advance, in cash. And when she was asked to sign a guest register? She supplied a first initial and a French surname, never using the same one twice.

It was important that she never name the woman she became

in Paris, that she not be permitted an identity separate from Sarah. Such division of self would have been far too dangerous, too detached from reality, too close to the abyss of madness.

Sarah had read extensively about dissociative disorders, the multiple personalities that evolved as a result of childhood trauma. Such segmentation was a survival mechanism, a primal instinct for self-preservation. Sometimes the only way a young child could deal with the horror of its life was to shatter its single personality into many, each shard coping as best it could, all shards together managing to survive.

Sarah could lay legitimate claim to trauma, to horror, and at the time it had felt as if her young heart would disintegrate into nothing. *Perhaps it had.* But Sarah herself—her *self*—had not shattered. She'd been too old, her personality too fully formed, when the greatest trauma occurred.

She was Sarah, only Sarah. And the woman she became in Paris? She was part of Sarah, a wispy shadow who appeared when the world was bright and vanished when it filled anew with darkness.

The world was bright now despite the mistiness of this winter day. And now the man who had caused such shimmering brightness wanted to know the shadow's name.

The name came to her without conscious thought, and in the moments before she spoke it, Sarah hoped its owner wouldn't mind. She *wouldn't*, Sarah decided. Not that lovely, generous, joyful girl.

"*Claire,*" she whispered. "*Je m'appelle Claire.*"

The wind gusted then, a bitter cold hiss that felt to Sarah like an ominous warning. How *dare* you pretend to be someone you are not? Especially her, especially Claire. It's sheer madness, in any case, as you well know. *A rose by any other name.* Just because you've borrowed her name doesn't mean you can lay claim to her hopefulness and her joy.

Sarah felt the wind as a chilling reminder of her madness. But Jack felt it only for what it was: a reminder that night was falling—a night that, according to the Ritz's concierge, would know a drenching winter storm.

"Come with me, Claire. We'll find someplace warm, a café. Claire? *Voulez-vous dîner avec moi?*"

He was inviting her to join him for Christmas Eve dinner. But to Sarah it sounded like so much more—an invitation to life, to love . . . to a lifetime of love.

Say *no*. Before it's too late. Before he discovers that you are really Sarah, not Claire. Sarah, Sarah, say—

"*Oui,*" she whispered, a defiant whisper embellished by an uncertain nod.

The gesture was slight, little more than a tilt of her diamond-adorned hair. But it caused a spill of mist onto her face. The droplets should have been as bitter cold as the wind, as icy as the hissed warnings she did not heed.

But they weren't.

They felt oddly warm. Like tears of joy.

Chapter Nine

THEY FOUND A CAFÉ ON RUE DE LA PAIX and spent Christmas Eve falling in love—and telling lies. He was Jacques, a businessman from Quebec, in Europe to oversee the opening of offices in London and Paris. And she was Claire, a native of Cannes, now living in Paris where she edited children's books for a major French publishing house.

The falsehoods scarcely mattered. They were quite trivial, virtually inconsequential, compared to the truth they shared. They spoke that wondrous truth with their eyes, and with smiles that forgave every lie uttered by their lips. *Je t'aime. Je t'aime.*

The restlessness Jack had felt, the urgent sense of discovery, of destiny, was now explained. She was found. He felt extraordinary peace—and restlessness still, eagerness to end the charade, to reveal to her precisely who he was.

My name is Jack, he would tell her in English. And I know that you are really Sarah. I've come to protect you from an unspeakable evil, and I will do that. But I want so much more, Sarah. I want you, I want *us.*

Jack would speak those words. But not now. Not yet. The masquerade seemed terribly important to her, a desperate, necessary deception. She clung to each candlelit moment of happiness as if it were a mirage, a golden but essentially false brilliance that was doomed to fade.

It's no mirage, Sarah. Our destiny is brilliance. His dark blue eyes eloquently spoke those words, and for a very long time that was the only way the lovers caressed. Finally, with exquisite gentleness, Jack touched her, a reverent kiss of his loving hand on the ivory satin of her cheek.

But his caress might have been the piercing stab of the sharpest of knives. She pulled away, instantly fearful.

Instinctively fearful, Jack amended silently, as restlessness, itself a razor-sharp knife, ripped through him anew, slicing through the peace, shredding it to ribbons.

The caressing hand that had caused such terror returned to the table, near hers but not touching.

"Tell me what's wrong."

During this Christmas Eve of falling in love, Jack had seen the splendor of a smile of pure joy on the face of the world's most famous journalist. Now, as she willed away her fear, he saw a new smile, brave, trembling—and as false as the answer she gave.

"Rien," she whispered, her gaze unwavering as she spoke the lie. "Nothing is wrong."

It was then that Lady Sarah Pembroke began to drink. She'd had nothing to drink all evening, neither of them had. Their love was intoxication enough. Neither wished to blur its dazzling clarity.

But now she wanted champagne.

Needed it, Jack decided as he watched her drink.

The sips she took were impeccably ladylike, delicate and small. But they were frequent. And after each demure swallow, she seemed expectant, almost hopeful, as if anticipating a familiar effect, the floating euphoria that would make her brave.

Finally it came, her counterfeit courage, and with it her slender white fingers found his hand. Jack welcomed her touch, encircling her fingers with his, wishing that he could capture her other hand as well. But that other hand was committed to another kind of embrace altogether. Curled tightly around the champagne flute, it clung to the false magic of the golden liquid.

We're the only magic you need. Jack wanted to shout the words. Jack who didn't shout.

Sarah had done this to him earlier, before they had even met, evoking new emotions, foreign ones, restless and powerful and wild. The emotions had dwelled within him, hidden and deep, and now, because of her, they had been freed.

Lady Sarah Pembroke might have freed Jack's most primal emotions; but she had given Jack himself no freedom at all. He *would not* shout at her. Could not. He would hold her hand, and pray that she would feel the love in his caress despite the blur of champagne, and that she would come to trust his touch, not fear it.

And he would keep imprisoned every emotion but his love.

Sarah was becoming increasingly bold. Trying, Jack realized, to seduce him. The attempt was both courageous and shy, and so terribly awkward, so achingly innocent, that had he not known that she was the widow of Simon Beckwith-Jones, he might have questioned her experience.

Jack drew to his lips the hand he was permitted to hold. His eyes held hers as he kissed her open palm, and he did not permit his gaze to falter—even when he discovered the secret of her wrist.

She always wore long-sleeved blouses, even in the desert heat, and now, as his lips grazed the unmistakable scar beneath the ribbed sleeve of her yellow turtleneck, Jack knew why.

She had tried to kill herself. Sometime. Long ago. The scar was substantial, the gravestone of an indisputably serious attempt at death, and it was fully healed. But what about the wounds of her soul, the deep gashes that had driven her to such a desperate act?

They were open still, gaping, weeping, crying with pain.

I will kiss your wounds, lovely Sarah. If only you will let me. *I will love them all.*

Jack would have sealed his silent promise with a kiss to the carefully hidden scar. But Jack saw her fear as his exploring lips neared her wrist—and her immense relief as they traveled back to her palm. She believed that her secret was safe, that he had not made the grim discovery.

Your secrets are safe with me, Sarah. And one day, my love, you will feel safe enough to share them.

For the moment Sarah's safety seemed precarious, floating aloft on tiny bubbles of champagne. After taking a final—and generous—swallow, she asked, "Can we go?"

"Where?"

"To your hotel?"

It was, Jack realized, her only possible reply. The lie that she lived in Paris would be exposed if she confessed that her Parisian home was in fact a hotel. But Jack's lie was still quite intact. The successful Canadian businessman would logically be staying at the Ritz.

The promised winter storm had arrived with a vengeance, with punishing wind and pelting rain. The Ritz wasn't far from the café, just across the Place Vendôme; but still Jack asked if she wanted to wait for a cab.

"*Non,*" Sarah replied. And why not? To the woman who had spent last Christmas Eve in the bone-chilling cold of Sarajevo, this Parisian downpour was of absolutely no consequence. "*Courons-nous.*"

And run, they did. It was she who set the pace, a fast, graceful romp that spoke volumes about her fitness. Her muscles were sleekly conditioned, finely toned, just as his were. For Jack, however, such conditioning was a choice, a luxury, the consequence of deciding to run many miles every day in the lush, green hills of Virginia. And for Sarah? Such conditioning was more necessity than choice, the essential fleet-footedness of a warrior.

They arrived at the Ritz scarcely winded, but totally drenched, and by the time they reached his room, the transient warmth of exertion had given way to the chill of rain-wet skin.

Jack might have immediately gathered a stack of plush towels from the marble bath. But his attention was drawn to her—and hers was wholly focused elsewhere, on the four-poster bed. It was quite ready for occupants, having been carefully prepared by the nightly maid service. Its satin coverlet was turned down, and an offering of fine chocolates, in a nest of orchids, adorned the feather pillows.

It should have been an alluring scene of romance. But Sarah's eyes were wary, as if they were beholding a funeral pyre, not a place of love. Wary . . . and determined. Resolved, it seemed, to join him in that bed.

Eventually her gaze left the bed, searching until it found the lavishly stocked bar, then brightening with relief.

Lady Sarah Pembroke would make love with Jack Dalton.

But she needed a little more fortification, a little more courage, a little more alcohol.

Jack knew exactly how much champagne Sarah had consumed at the café. If he hadn't witnessed that consumption, however, he would never have guessed that she had drunk even a drop. She appeared absolutely normal. Her eyes were brilliantly green, brilliantly clear; and the elegant precision of her voice was indistinguishable from the voice that spoke to the world without a slur. And her gait? The graceful gazelle who had dashed across the rain-drenched Place Vendôme could not have been more surefooted.

So there it was, the aching truth: Lady Sarah Pembroke drank to become normal, to be like any other woman in love, to be able to receive the caresses of her lover.

Alcohol was a medication for her, taken to cure—or at least keep at bay—some terrible sickness deep within. And would Jack pour more of that drug for her? So that he could make love to this woman he desired far more than he had ever desired another?

Not in a million years.

But now Sarah was moving to pour the drug for herself, her delicate hands curling around the unopened bottle of Courvoisier as if it were a life buoy in a storm-ravaged sea.

"It's a myth, you know."

She was torn—between the bottle to which she clung and the voice behind her that seemed to promise even greater salvation.

She turned toward him, holding the bottle still, and echoed, *"Un mythe?"*

"Drinking brandy when you're chilled. Yes, it makes you feel warm. But it's a dangerous warmth. You end up dissipating heat, not conserving it." Jack dispelled that myth—one that the warrior already knew full well—with words. And as for the other fiction? Jack dispelled it with the intimate messages of his dark blue eyes. It's a myth, Sarah, pure fantasy, that you need to drink to be touched by me, *to be loved by me.*

"It's late," she whispered with sudden urgency. "Maybe I should—"

"Why don't we each take a hot shower? And then, why don't we just go to sleep?"

"Just sleep? You don't . . . ?"

"Want you? Oh, yes, I want you. But the first time we make love, I want it to last all night." And I want to make love to Sarah, not Claire—to a Sarah who doesn't need alcohol to endure my touch. "And tonight, well, I'm feeling the effects of jet lag and champagne."

It was the greatest lie in an evening of lies. True, Jack hadn't slept last night. He had spent the night flight to London studying the police files on the Valentine's Day murders and wondering—worrying—about the intriguing journalist chosen by the killer as his next victim.

But was Jack truly too tired to spend the entire night making love to Sarah? *Hardly.*

Another woman would have been offended that her allure could not vanquish his fatigue. But not Sarah. She seemed relieved, almost hopeful, until her eyes skittered toward the bed.

"Perhaps I should go to my place," she murmured. "You'll sleep better without me."

"No I won't," Jack countered. "Please stay. We'll sleep late, and spend Christmas together, and tomorrow night we'll make love."

Another woman, experienced with the demands and pleasures of passion, would have known that the moment he awakened he would want to make love. Indeed, such a woman would have insisted that they plan, right now, to spend all of Christmas in bed.

But Jack's words had been spoken as a solemn promise, and Sarah seemed to greet his vow as if it were a stay of execution. As if it were he, not the black-hearted killer, who planned to plunge a jagged-edged knife deep into her heart.

He was promising her a night without intimacy—or was he? No, Jack realized. He was promising her a night of *chaste* intimacy, but of intimacy nonetheless.

In fact, Jack mused, sleeping together, just sleeping, was intensely intimate, a personal privacy he had never before chosen to share. Always before, once the passions had been spent, the desires lavishly satisfied—for both of them—Jack left the beds of his lovers. He was compelled to leave, he realized now, remembering the restlessness he felt, the inexplicable sense of wrongness despite the pleasure.

Oh, Sarah. I've been searching for you for a very long time.

And now, with her, he wanted to share an intimacy that was perhaps far greater than the intimacies of the flesh. Allowing oneself to succumb to sleep in the presence of another required immense trust, the willingness to permit that time of absolute vulnerability, to expose those unguarded hours of nightmares—and of dreams.

"Spend the night with me. Sleep with me." *Share my bed . . . and my dreams.* "I can't offer you a pajama top. I wear only the bottoms when I sleep, and all the never-used tops are at home. But I do have a freshly laundered shirt. And it's all yours."

Jack watched as Sarah absorbed the information he gave her, the description of what he intended to wear to bed and the assurance that her own modesty would be amply preserved. His shirt would be big for her, long and unrevealing, its cuffed sleeves providing complete sanctuary for her scars.

Jack saw fear, and hope. Courage, and—

Sarah looked away then, to the bottle of brandy still clutched in her hand. It was to that glass vial of amber-hued medication that she spoke.

"If I take a glass of brandy with me while I shower, while I'm getting warm from that heat, it would be safe, wouldn't it?"

She looked up then, from the brandy to him, and her green eyes, shimmering with courage and with hope, confessed, If I fortify myself a little more, Jacques, just one more glass, then I can sleep with you, stay with you, *and I want to stay.*

Sarah wanted to stay with him. But, Jack thought, if I deny her request for more brandy, she will leave, will *have* to.

You don't need to drink, Sarah. Not with me. The wild emotions deep within wanted to scream their fury.

But Jack silenced them, imprisoned them. "Why don't you pour yourself a glass while I go find a shirt?"

Jack took his shower after hers, after she had emerged flushed and shy and brave, and wearing the shirt he had given her. Light blue, its expensive threads tightly woven, it afforded the modesty of a young girl's nightgown. Only her legs, the slender white limbs that roamed blood-soaked earth—and ran through the rain like a joyful gazelle—were revealed, and only below the knees.

Jack wanted to tuck her into bed, to kiss her temples, her cheeks, her damp, fragrant hair. But instead he merely smiled, whispered *"Bonne nuit,"* and left her alone.

To pour herself another drink? he wondered. Or to vanish into the night?

Jack didn't know about the drink until the next morning. Yes, she had had more brandy. All he knew that night, when he finished his own shower, was that she was in his bed, a motionless silhouette at a far edge . . . but there.

Was she asleep? Or was she merely feigning slumber?

It was only later, when Jack heard the subtle change in her breathing, that he realized she had been awake.

But now she slept, and he was wakeful still, keeping vigil, worrying, marveling, promising himself that the Christmas Day that lay ahead would be a day of truth, not of lies.

Eventually Jack, too, succumbed to sleep. It was a willful decision, a glorious choice, a wish to share the intimacy he had never shared. He allowed her breathing to become a lullaby, luring his fatigued body to sleep beside hers, welcoming the vulnerability—and the dreams.

All Jack's dreams were of her, and all were wondrous. But the only one he remembered was the last, the one that so boldly seduced him from sleep. Her face was close to his, haloed by a cloud of lustrous ebony, and she was singing, a French song known to children around the world.

On this Christmas morning, in Paris, when Jack was sleeping too late, the song seemed written just for him. Indeed, she had modified the words slightly, making them more personal, more intimate.

"*Mon cher Jacques, mon cher Jacques, dormez-vous, dormez-vous?*"

Jack awakened with a start, his own heart singing in reply, expecting to see her, expecting love.

But she was gone.

It wasn't yet dawn. Despite champagne and Courvoisier, Lady Sarah Pembroke had not lasted the night.

As Jack's eyes adjusted to the shadowy darkness, he saw the note Sarah had left. Propped against a hand-painted porcelain lamp, it was a stark white ghost.

The ghost of a dream . . . because Sarah's letter began with the same term of endearment that Jack had dreamed she was singing to him.

Mon cher Jacques,
   Je suis mariée. My husband and I have been having difficulties with our marriage. I realize I must return to him now, to try to work things out. I know that you sensed my uncertainty when you touched me. I wanted your touch—please believe that—but I felt so guilty. That explains the champagne. I wanted to block the guilt. But I couldn't, not enough.
   Please forgive me, Jacques. I needed to be with you. But I

know now that it can never be. I will treasure the memory of
last evening—always.

Claire

Lies! The pronouncement came swiftly, a fierce wildness
caged too long. The fury raged for a while, a river of molten silver in his veins, until finally the mind famous for its cool logic
imposed its familiar icy control.

Was there any truth to what Sarah had written? that disciplined mind queried. Was it possible, in fact, that she was married to the memory of the husband who had died?

From the articles Jack had read about Sarah, he knew selected details about her marriage. She and Simon Beckwith-
Jones had wed when Sarah was only seventeen. Simon was
forty-two at the time, a close friend of her parents, and three
years later Simon had perished, in a plane crash in Scotland,
with those friends.

Eight years had passed since the dense Scottish fog had
claimed the lives of Sarah's husband and parents. Eight years
might not be long enough for a young bride—and daughter—to
recover fully from such a devastating loss. *Except*, Jack
thought, compelling evidence argued against that young
widow's unrelenting grief.

No love was lost between Sarah and her deceased husband's
family. Scotland Yard's commissioner of police had made that
quite clear. Indeed, it had cost the Beckwith Joneses a substantial fortune to buy back Sarah's inheritance—a fortune that
Sarah promptly donated to charity.

And Mrs. Simon Beckwith-Jones had become Lady Sarah
Pembroke again, reverting to her maiden name, not keeping,
not cherishing, his.

It didn't take a master puzzle solver to deduce that those
weren't the actions of a bereaved widow.

So that part of the ghost-white note, the allusion to her husband, was totally false. And what about the rest? The *uncertainty* she had felt at his touch? Another lie. It wasn't
uncertainty, Jack knew. Nor was it guilt.

It was fear.

I needed to be with you. I will treasure the memory of last evening—always.

A lie? Or the only truth?

Jack would find out tomorrow, when they met again, when Lady Sarah Pembroke was formally introduced to the man who was going to save her heart from a jagged-edged knife.

Jack would save her; of that, there was no doubt.

But as he thought about the woman who could not bear his touch, who had fled under night's dark cover to avoid it, it felt to Jack as if it were his own heart that had been brutally stabbed.

Chapter Ten

Hyacinth House
Cornwall, England
Christmas Day

THE OUTSIDE WORLD WAS STILL VEILED IN darkness as Emma rose from her bed. The world inside the house was dark as well, but warm, the furnace having long since been started by Lucas.

Emma was greeted by warm air, and by a feeling of pure exhilaration. This year, for the first time in the eleven years since the birth of their daughter, Hyacinth House was closed for Christmas. No strangers slept in the spacious guest wing, no one who would awaken early, eager for Christmas Day to begin, to enjoy the gracious hospitality for which the charming Cornish bed-and-breakfast had become so famous.

Today would be a family day, and the eagerness was Emma's. She didn't need to rise before dawn, not today. Jessie would sleep for another hour at least, and Lucas was already at work in his studio, and this family Christmas would not truly begin until ten, when her parents arrived from St. Ives.

Emma could languish in the coziness of her bed, drifting back to sleep, to dreams. But she wanted neither sleep nor dreams. She wanted to live this day, to savor each and every moment.

You know why, don't you? Because you know it won't last. Because every second, every heartbeat of joy, is moving you closer to the time when all this happiness is going to end.

The thought froze her limbs, transforming her into a shadowy statue in the darkness, chilling her as deeply as if Lucas had forgotten to turn on the heat on this cold winter morning. Emma might have forced her limbs to move, walking so swiftly to the warm shower that the chilling thought was left behind. But she did not. It was time to face the thought. *The truth.*

For almost twelve years it had been there, the certain knowledge that her life with Lucas would end. Emma even knew when that end would come: when they had kept all the solemn vows they had made for their daughter, their beloved Jessie.

Emma had known, since before her wedding day, that her marriage to Lucas was not forever. But until now that certainty had been buried very deep, hidden far away. Now, however, it could no longer be denied—because, during the past year, so much had changed.

Jessica was growing up, beginning the dramatic and inevitable transformation from little girl to young woman. Oh yes, Jessie was young still, only eleven, lovely and innocent. But a new grace touched her limbs, and the childish plumpness of her face had given way to sleeker contours, and more than ever before she was aware of the world beyond her home, a world filled with magnificent possibilities.

Every mother since the dawn of time had watched the blossoming of her precious child with a bittersweet blend of pride and loss. Emma knew that. But for her there was more—the promise of greater loss.

Now, in this dark room that had become so cold, Emma forced herself to envision that loss, to face it, to accept it, and then to banish it from her thoughts. She imagined the scene with brilliant clarity. Eighteen-year-old Jessie would be away at college, in her first year at Cambridge perhaps, or maybe even Stanford; and Emma would be in the kitchen, putting the finishing touches on a wedding cake; and Lucas would appear in the doorway.

For a moment everything would seem quite normal—Lucas taking a break from his work, choosing to spend that time with her. But then she would see the solemnity of his face, and even though she wouldn't want to—because suddenly she would *know*—she would meet eyes the color of a forest . . . eyes that had never lied to her . . . and that deep, dark green would be honest now, as always, and so very gentle, as the man she loved told her good-bye.

"We did it, Em," Lucas would say. "Our daughter's life has been safe, happy, filled with love. Just as we promised each other it would be. We've kept that promise, Emma, and now it's time for us to get on with our lives."

Already, during this monumental year, Lucas *had* gotten on with his life, the one he would live without her, the one he had always planned to live but had abandoned without a backward glance when Emma's pregnancy had compelled them to wed.

Since the day he had learned of that pregnancy, the talented hands of Lucas Cain had unselfishly given themselves to other pursuits. Before Jessica's birth, when Emma was so sick, the hands that could turn stone to flesh, *were meant to*, had instead set about converting her parents' run-down bed-and-breakfast into a place that could support them all—and eventually Hyacinth House had become the toast of Cornwall.

And after Jessie was born, those strong and gentle hands found new purpose, wondrous purpose, the love of a father for his child. As an infant, Jessie knew the cradling tenderness of those hands; and when she was learning to walk, when her small, sturdy legs needed to make their all-important journeys, Lucas enabled the exploration, but never let her fall; and when their bright little girl added language to her repertoire, he always had time for her words. He would kneel before her, his gifted hands resting lightly on her shoulders, and he would listen with absolute attention, and never a trace of impatience, to every eager, earnest word she had to say.

The greatest wonder of Lucas Cain's hands, their greatest glory, was in the nurturing of his daughter. But that was a private joy—precious, and fleeting. Jessie was growing up. She didn't need him as she once had, not every minute of every day, and his hands, feeling the emptiness, had returned at last to the art, the passion, that had once meant everything to him. Already, during the past year, Lucas's success permitted them to close their home to guests whenever they chose. By this time

next year it would be possible to close Hyacinth House permanently, if that's what they wanted.

Emma knew that it was not what she would want. She
needed Hyacinth House, and in truth the bed-and-breakfast had
become more hers than his, something she could do on her own.
Would she run Hyacinth House still, after Lucas was gone?
Would she achieve her own minor fame, the Cornish innkeeper
who played hostess to England's most romantic weddings?

After Lucas was gone. This past year had given Emma a terrifying taste of that future loneliness. Lucas had traveled,
overnight jaunts to London and one five-night trip to the
States. She had missed him so much when he was away, had
slept anxiously, fitfully, alone in their bed. And, she noticed, he
had dark circles, too, when he returned—as if, without her, Lucas slept fitfully as well.

But at least when Lucas was away, Emma had Jessica. Until
two weeks ago, that is. Then, with virtually no warning, Lucas
had taken Jessie with him to London. The trip was scheduled
for December eleventh, a date when Emma *had* to be in Cornwall, and with surprising sternness Lucas had told her that his
meeting in London could no more be postponed than her party
in Cornwall could.

Indeed, Emma's "party" had been scheduled for months.
The twenty people who would crowd into Emma's spacious
country kitchen to watch as she crafted her gingerbread house
could not be forsaken. Nor would they be. As always, Emma
would open her kitchen, and generously reveal every trick she
knew, from the secret ingredients of her royal icing to the special way she made her glazed caramel windows glow with a
deep amber light.

The traditional gingerbread extravaganza at Hyacinth House
was an event at which Emma's most able and enthusiastic assistant had always been her daughter. But not this year.

Jessie was in London with her father, and she returned to
Cornwall with happy anecdotes about their adventure. But her
voice quavered as she admired the gingerbread house that had
been made during her absence. At Emma's suggestion, they

made another house, an exact replica of their own lovely home—and this year Lucas helped, too.

The talented hands that had transformed Hyacinth House from rustic quaintness to elegant grandeur carefully re-created miniature gingerbread versions of its roofs and walls. Lucas built, and Jessie and Emma decorated; and as if nothing had changed, would *ever* change, they crafted the final authentic touch, orderly lines of hedgerows fashioned from plump green gumdrops.

Emma shivered now as she remembered the aching loneliness she had felt while Jessie and Lucas were away. Her reaction had seemed extreme at the time, and terribly selfish. But, she realized, her subconscious mind had been at work, envisioning the future, when both her husband and daughter would be gone.

Where would Lucas begin his new life? Emma wondered. Would her American husband return to his California roots? Or would the gifted sculptor seek out places that had always been more important to him, where he felt bonded to the masters of marble who had lived long ago? Would he go to Italy? To Florence, perhaps, the city of splendor where he and Emma had met?

Or Venice, where they had . . . fallen in love? No, Emma knew. She and Lucas hadn't fallen in love in the City of Canals. *He* hadn't. And in truth, long before that weekend of romance, she was already hopelessly in love with him.

For her, the nineteen-year-old innocent, it had been love at first sight. He was twenty-two, sensual, worldly, experienced, and she was bedazzled, an infatuation that was both instant and unexpected. She would, quite happily, have devoted herself to distant adoration, watching him, admiring him, giddy at even his slightest smile. Indeed, she never imagined more, never even *fantasized* about it. She was just plain Emma, after all, and he was Lucas, a black-haired, green-eyed god. It seemed beyond imagination that she would ever feel the touch of his hands, or that there could come a time when the full attention of his appraising gaze would be focused solely on her, as if *she* were a work of art, as intriguing as the statues he regarded with such wonder.

But on that weekend in Venice, Lucas *had* looked at her, and he had touched her. And, that weekend, they had created the most wondrous work of art, the precious treasure for whom they had decided to marry.

And what had Emma known, then, about the man she was to marry? Very little—and everything. Somehow the innocent country girl had sensed the truth about the man with whom she had fallen in love. Somehow she had seen the nobility that dwelled beneath the dangerously sensual facade.

Lucas Cain had planned to devote his life to his only true passion, his only true love. His art. There would be women in that life, of course, many of them, intense liaisons of breathless pleasure. The artist was a lover, and a loner. A poet, and a rogue.

But there were other truths about Lucas, ones hidden even from him: the kind of father he would be, his sense of honor, his abiding integrity. Before they wed, he made solemn commitments to Emma and their unborn child. And Lucas Cain had kept every one.

And he will keep them. There it was. Emma trusted him absolutely. Their pact, the solemn vow they had made, had been to raise their daughter together. They had never discussed what would happen when Jessie was grown. That time had seemed so far away. But it was implicit.

Lucas would leave.

Emma and Lucas had been young when they wed. And they would be young, still, when they parted. Just thirty-seven and forty. Many people *began* their families then.

Emma's mind traveled to the future: Lucas at forty. He would be handsome still, *always*. In fact, he would be more handsome than ever. His coal-black hair would be slightly silvered, and the eighteen years spent as a loving father would be etched on his face. Already there was a solemn wisdom, a quiet joy.

At forty, Lucas Cain would possess the serenity that came from knowing he had gifts to give, and that he had given them to his child. So many gifts, such a deep well of love. At forty, he could even—

Emma intercepted the thought. It was too painful. But her heart was already reeling. The damage was already done. So she allowed the anguished thought its freedom. *He could even have more children.* She couldn't, but he could, and perhaps when he left—

Are you so certain that he will leave you? The question caught Emma by surprise. In the predawn shadows of this Christmas day she had permitted her darkest thoughts to surface. The winter night's darkness was dissipating now, pierced by the first gray light of day, and with that silver light came this astonishingly hopeful thought—and it wanted to be heard as well. Are you so very certain that Lucas doesn't love you?

I *know* he loves me. I'm the mother of the daughter he treasures above all else, and he and I are good friends, best friends. We respect each other, trust each other, rely on each other.

But you're also his wife, *and his lover.* Have you forgotten what happens in bed?

No. Never. For the past twelve years the talented hands that could turn stone to flesh had turned Emma's flesh into trembling desire. The effect of his touch hadn't diminished with time, not at all, and during this past year when so much had changed, Lucas's passion for her—oh yes, it *was* passion—was more intense than ever, at once fierce and tender. It was as if he, too, sensed the future—the inevitability of their parting—and was tormented by it as well . . . and yet powerless to stop it.

And what of the expression you sometimes see, when he's looking at you, *staring* at you, so entranced that he's forgotten you can see him, too? It's pure emotion, you know it is. Some ferocious passion that you do not understand.

Emma couldn't explain that expression. She knew only that it terrified her. It spoke of secrets—*and she and Lucas had no secrets.* Sometimes her desperation to have the terrifying expression end almost evoked a frantic scream, a cry so startling that it would break the mesmerizing spell. Instead, however, and very softly, she would speak his name; and Lucas would hear the call of her heart, and his dark green eyes would focus, vibrant and intent, a caress of love that made her want to weep with joy.

He loves you, the silvery thought proclaimed. Perhaps he's struggling with that, this artist who believes that to achieve his greatest work he will need to be alone. But during the next seven years, as together you guide your beloved daughter toward adulthood, he will realize the truth.

Seven more years.

Seven more Christmases.

I am not going to spend the next seven years counting Christmases, Emma vowed to the bedroom that was now shimmering with light. I'm going to live each day, each second of each day, loving him, loving Jessie. And not thinking about the future.

With that, Emma pushed the dark thoughts away. She wrapped them tightly, and with great care, as if they were Christmas presents, not Christmas fears. She adorned those blackest of thoughts with a bright silver wrapping of hope. But, she vowed, I won't be fooled. I won't expect more than the magnificent gift I've already been given.

She smiled then, and as she crossed the bedroom toward the shower, the feelings that had awakened her on this day returned and she felt warm again, enveloped in her own joyful anticipation of the family Christmas that lay ahead.

"Oh Mummy, you're already awake. We were going to *surprise* you!"

"I am surprised," Emma said as she greeted her daughter.

Emma was in her robe, still toweling her shower-damp hair, and Jessie—and Lucas—were fully dressed. And looking so much alike, Emma mused as she beheld father and daughter. Jessie had inherited from Lucas his lustrous black hair and his stunning good looks. Somehow the features that were so masculine in him, so hard and strong, softened to delicate prettiness in her.

But Jessica's eyes are *yours*, Emma. That's what everyone

said, in the next breath after remarking on the striking resemblance between Lucas and Jessie. As if it might actually have bothered Emma that her daughter had inherited so much from him. It was, of course, what Emma would have wished for Jessie, that she be blessed with her father's elegant bones and dramatic coloring rather than the distinct ordinariness of her own.

In truth, their daughter's eye color came from both of them, a rare blend of Emma's bright blue and Lucas's dark, dark green. But the shape—and the sparkle—were all Emma's.

The blue-green eyes were sparkling now as Jessie approached. "Happy Christmas, Mummy!"

"Happy Christmas, darling," Emma echoed as she accepted the large box that Jessie offered.

It was a present, for her, and Emma's heart stumbled as she looked at the wrapping: pure silver, as hopeful as the first light of this Christmas day, the same shining color in which she had just so carefully wrapped her darkest thoughts *forever*.

"What's this, Jessie?"

"A present! Daddy and I got it for you in London. It's the *real* reason we went to London, Mummy."

To get a present for me? Emma's heart tripped again. *That's why you went to London? It wasn't to prepare me for the time when I would lose you both, when you would choose to spend your college holidays in Italy with your father?*

"You have to open the card first," Jessie said. "Then the present will make sense."

"All right," Emma murmured, setting the glittering box on the bed as she withdrew the envelope from beneath the mauve satin bow.

The paper was parchment, elegant and expensive, an invitation engraved in gold. *Lillith and Timothy Asquith request the pleasure of your company at a New Year's Eve of celebration and romance. . . .*

The romance would be provided by Cole Taylor, in concert at the Royal Albert Hall, and the celebration to follow would be a champagne-drenched dinner buffet at the Imperial Ballroom in Hyde Park's Drake Hotel.

Emma knew of Cole Taylor's upcoming New Year's Eve concert. She had read about it in the Sunday *Times*. There had been no mention, however, of the black-tie gala to be hosted by Gemstone Records' billionaire owner and his aristocratic wife. That would be a private affair, and an extravagant one, a grand party to which would be invited London's glamorous elite . . . and, as well, the Cains of Cornwall. For many years Lillith and Timothy had been loyal patrons of Hyacinth House—a patronage that now extended to Lucas and his art.

As Emma frowned slightly at the invitation, Lucas spoke for the first time. "Lillith remembered a conversation the two of you had last June, about how much you like the way Cole Taylor sings. You do, don't you?"

Of course Emma liked the way the superstar sang. The emotions, the longing and the love, reminded her of her feelings for Lucas. She could listen forever to Cole Taylor's songs of love— save one, the most famous of all, "Imagine Moonlight." The song was indisputably sensational. Lyrical. Poignant. Compelling. But it tore Emma apart. Because "Imagine Moonlight" was about *them*, Lucas and Emma, an impassioned farewell to a love that did not want to die. And yet did.

Cole had written "Imagine Moonlight" in memory of Paulina Bliss, the actress who had been brutally slain last Valentine's Day. At least, that was what Emma had heard. But, to her, it wasn't a farewell to a woman who had died, but to one who was alive—and yet inaccessible to him—a woman for whom his love could never be.

"Emma? You do like Cole Taylor, don't you?"

"Oh yes."

"But you're frowning," Lucas offered softly.

"Don't you want to go, Mummy? We thought you'd love to. You and Daddy are going to spend two nights in London, at the Drake Hotel, and I'm going to stay with Nana and Granddad, and we even bought you a sequiny evening gown, and Daddy's going to wear a tuxedo—"

"Of course I want to go," Emma interjected, smiling brightly even though her daughter's enthusiastic words triggered a new round of worry. "I'm just overwhelmed. I can't believe it."

"*Believe* it, Mummy," Jessie urged. "Open the dress now. We bought it at a boutique called Pearl Moon, and it's going to look *so* beautiful on you."

Emma's bright smile held as she reached for the gift-wrapped box. But, as if she were suddenly inside her own Christmas package, the one that cloaked the darkest of thoughts, she felt herself faltering. "How would you like a fashion show, Jessie? Let me finish drying my hair, then I'll come downstairs and model the gown. I don't even want to *open* it until my hair's completely dry."

"That sounds like a good plan," Lucas concurred.

"I'd better do some hugging now, though, Miss Jessica Cain," Emma said as she embraced her daughter. "Thank you, my love. What a wonderful, wonderful Christmas present."

"You're welcome, Mummy." Then, with the scrupulous honesty she had learned from both parents, Jessie confessed, "It was Daddy's idea."

Emma couldn't quite look at him, having vowed to dwell neither on bleak thoughts nor soaring hope. She focused elsewhere while Lucas suggested to Jessie that she scamper downstairs, to prepare for the fashion show. He would be down soon, he promised. But he needed to talk to Mummy first.

Then they were alone, and Lucas was standing in front of her, and Emma's gaze was downcast still.

"What is it, Em?"

"Nothing. I'm just . . . I really am overwhelmed."

"I think there's something else," Lucas countered quietly. "Would you rather not do this? We don't have to."

"No, I *want* to." Emma looked up at last, to Lucas, his night-black hair silvered by the early morning light. *Lucas at forty.* "Do you?"

"Of course I do. It was my idea, remember?"

"Why?" she asked, steeling herself, preparing her heart to hear the truth: that it was mostly business, a chance to mingle over champagne with the wealthiest men and women in the British Isles, art collectors all, potential clients whom Timothy Asquith wanted Lucas to meet. "Why, Luc?"

"Why?" he echoed, touching her then, tracing the hollow of her cheek with a single talented finger. The touch was a mere whisper, but it heated her cheeks, her blood, her heart. "Well, we've never gone away, just the two of us, not since we've been married. We've never had a honeymoon. And the timing seemed right."

"The timing?"

"You always seem a little sad after Christmas."

"I do?" *Have I been counting Christmases all these years, mourning the loss of each one, not even knowing it—and yet somehow revealing that sadness to this man who knows me so well?*

"Don't you?"

"Yes, I suppose I do."

"Then let's do this, Em. Let's greet the new year with happiness and celebration. This should be a good year for us. A wonderful year." He smiled. "Okay?"

"Yes. Okay."

Her heart was dancing now, twirling, leaping—and then stumbling, as she thought about being alone with him for an entire weekend. What would she say to him during their honeymoon in London?

Here, at Hyacinth House, talking was possible—effortless and easy—from the idiosyncrasies of their guests to the trimming of the hedgerows to the menu for Sunday brunch. And there were far more important conversations, too, the ones that truly mattered, about their daughter, their love for her, their hopes, their dreams.

Someday, perhaps in the year that lay ahead, she and Lucas would discuss how they were going to broach the revelations—and admonitions—that every girl becoming a woman needed to know. Love. Sex. The powerful urges of young men and the romantic notions of teenaged girls.

Emma and Lucas were experts on such reckless passion.

And somehow, when she and Lucas discussed the parental counsel they would give, Emma would be so adult, so terribly objective, that her heart would not ache as they considered ways to help their daughter avoid the same passionate, romantic mistake that they had made.

That conversation would happen soon, and Emma would be a grownup when it did—so surely that grown-up woman, that wife, that mother, could think of something to say to her husband during their weekend of love songs in London. . . .

Except that now, in this brightly shining room, Emma was nineteen again, wanting only to be near him, to breathe the very air he breathed, to feel the cool shade of his long shadow. And so bedazzled that speech was impossible.

The bedazzlement silenced them both. Lucas gazed at her, marveling at her loveliness. Her shower-damp hair was beginning to curl, to frame her face in unruly tendrils. Emma rarely talked about herself, especially her appearance; but when pushed—when, for example, he told her how much he liked her hair—Emma's reply was authentically surprised. A hopelessly tangled mop, she would murmur with a self-deprecating frown. You know that, Luc. No matter its length or how rigorously I try to subdue it.

A tangled mop of spun gold, he would counter, startling her anew. And silently he would add, A luxuriant symbol of you, my lovely Emma. Natural, unaffected—and shimmering.

Oh, Em, how I love you. I wonder if you have any idea how much.

No, Lucas thought as they stood, mute and bedazzled, on this Christmas morning. Of course she doesn't know, *can't* know , , , because I can never confess to her the shattering proof of my love.

Lucas wanted to take her to bed, right now, to make love to her until they were so close that there was no room for secrets between them.

But there would always be a secret between them—his secret—the betrayal that could destroy forever the trusting radiance of her shining blue eyes; and their daughter was downstairs, waiting for her mother to model the gown of lilac-and-lavender sequins; and now, as the silence lingered, Lucas saw shadows of worry cross Emma's lovely face, as if she somehow sensed the perilous darkness of the secret he must always keep.

So Lucas smiled, and whispered, "Happy Christmas, Em."

It was a private Yuletide tradition, begun twelve years ago, between the wide-eyed romantic English girl and her sexy, reckless American man.

Now that English girl smiled, wide-eyed still, romantic still, and she whispered, as if *she* were the Yankee, "Merry Christmas, Luc."

Chapter Eleven

"IT'S COLE, CLAIRE. MERRY CHRISTMAS."

"Cole," she whispered, clutching the telephone, wondering if this was real or merely her imagination come to life. Ever since he had disappeared into the snowy night she had been wishing, hoping, dreaming. Aching, grieving, dying. "Merry Christmas. You're in London?"

"Yes."

"The connection is so clear." *If you listen carefully, Cole, you'll hear the beating of my heart. It's that frantic, fluttering, soaring sound.* "Did you have a nice Christmas?"

"Sure. I had dinner with the band. How about you?"

"I was with Millicent Theriot—you probably remember her from school—and her family." *Why are you calling me, Cole? Tell me quickly, please, so that my heart can slow again. Already it's aching, gasping, pleading to be permitted to resume its solemn tempo of grief.*

But Cole's words did not slow Claire's racing heart. Instead, they sent a challenge. *How much faster can you go? How much longer can you maintain this death-defying pace, teetering on this brink of exhaustion, this very edge of hope?*

"Come to London, Claire. Come sing with me. We'll sing

duets, just like we always planned." *Just as you always dreamed*. It was *your* dream, Claire, so generously shared with me, and now it's the only dream I can give you in return.

"I . . . Cole, you can't . . ."

"Can't what, Claire? *Mean* it? I do. I've given this a lot of thought. Now it's your turn."

"No."

"No?"

"No, I don't need to think about it." I *can't* think about it. "And yes, I'll come to London to sing with you."

"Beginning New Year's Eve? At the Royal Albert Hall?"

The Royal Albert Hall? In concert with Cole? In just six days? Claire answered with breathless giddiness. "Why not?"

The flock of tiny birds that had been fluttering in her chest— and creating thunder in her ears—became still then, just for a moment, just long enough for her to hear with glorious clarity the happiness in his voice.

"I'm so glad," he said softly.

"I . . . me, too. London."

"You've been here, haven't you? When you visited Sarah."

Cole didn't need to be specific about the date of Claire's visit to England. Both knew when the much-anticipated face-to-face meeting of the pen pals was to have occurred—that summer, twelve years ago, six months after he left Harlanville.

"I didn't go to London that summer after all. Sarah and I lost touch." *I lost Sarah, just like I lost you, and on that same December day. I expected too much of her, demanded too much of our friendship, and that summer, instead of going to Europe, Aunt Augusta and I stayed at home—in case you returned.*

"But you know about Sarah, don't you? That she's a journalist, a war correspondent?"

"Yes, I know."

"And do you also know that beginning in January she'll be anchoring the news from London?"

"Yes." A smile touched Claire's voice. "That announcement gets made about every thirty minutes on Global News Network."

"You'll want to get together with her, won't you, while you're here?"

Want to? *Yes.* But . . . "No. I don't think so."

"What happened, Claire? The two of you were so close."

I was so close to you, too, Cole. I loved you. Claire trembled, a shiver of pure ice that came with a chilling warning. *You can't go back to that love. It's over. Too much has happened. Too much has changed. You have changed. He's asking you to sing with him, that's all. Don't you dare imagine more.*

"Claire?"

"We just grew up, that's all. We just grew apart."

Both fell silent, remembering two other best friends, a renegade boy and an innocent girl who had grown up . . . and apart . . . and then, for one glorious moonlit evening, had come together once again.

"So." Cole's voice broke the silence with exquisite gentleness. "When should I come get you?"

"Oh! You don't need to do that."

"I'd like to."

"It's really not necessary."

How calm she sounded, as if she were an experienced traveler, as if, even since the accident, she had logged thousands upon thousands of sightless miles. In truth, Claire had never flown, not before her accident or since.

So where did that calm voice come from? From a place of wisdom deep within, a place that knew *why* she needed to fly to London on her own—so that she would be able to return to Harlanville *on her own*, when she could endure no more, when being with Cole, unable to see the shadowed messages of his stone-gray eyes, was finally more painful than the specter of living the rest of her life without him.

Claire would leave London then, making the monumental journey home to Louisiana the same way she made even the tiniest of trips—by retracing the carefully counted steps that had gotten her there. And could she make those indelible, retraceable memories of her journey to London with Cole at her side?

No, the wise voice counseled. You could not. If Cole were with you, your heart, that wildly fluttering thing, would be unable to supply your brain with enough oxygen to record any memories at all.

"I can make it over on my own, Cole. Thank you."

"I'd like to meet your flight, though. Would that be all right?"

Would it? Claire wondered. Or would his presence even at the end of the voyage ruin her eventual escape, erasing even the memories that had come before, as if they were as perishable as Hansel and Gretel's trail of crumbs? Surely not. And once in London, if need be, she could practice the final leg of the journey, the taxi ride between Heathrow Airport and Hyde Park's Drake Hotel.

Cole *would* meet her flight, they agreed. She would plan to arrive on the thirtieth, and would let him know the flight number and arrival time as soon as the reservations had been made. Their Christmas night conversation ended then, quite abruptly, an impulsive, necessary good-bye that came from Claire.

Her entire being had begun fluttering, the same dangerous pace set by her trembling heart, and she was shivering now, pricked by ice-cold stabs of doubt.

You can't do this. You *can't*. Being blind in Harlanville is one thing. You knew the town with your eyes closed even before the darkness fell. But London? Europe? Are you crazy?

And what about Cole? The boy you loved—yes, all right, the man you love still—is a superstar now, *and a businessman.* The gifted musician within him hears, as you do, the magnificent harmony of your voices. But what if his legions of female fans don't *like* the duets, don't *want* to share the seductive intimacy with any other woman? Then what? How much time will pass between the moment when Cole, the businessman, wants you to leave and you finally sense that truth? And even if the duets are well received, won't you wonder, every second of every day, what emotions lie in the dark gray shadows you can never see? Won't you wonder, always, if his eyes are smoldering with pity—or icing over with disgust?

The questions bombarded her, guided missiles that found their mark in her heart. What possible defense did she have against such a vicious—and logical—assault?

Only one, the delicate weapon crafted of glass—and memories of love—that sat on the nightstand beside her bed.

Claire had made the journey to her bedroom countless times, surefooted—always—in the darkness. But now she staggered, stumbled, tripping on furniture that hadn't moved in six years, her sense of direction suddenly as confused as she. Some invisible magnet was wreaking havoc on her internal compass.

Some magnet? No, just one. His name was Cole, and he had spun her entire world out of control.

When Claire reached her bedroom at last, she curled her trembling fingers over the smooth contours of the globe of snow. She found peace in its glassy calm, and warmth—and strength—in the memories of love that dwelled within. Memories of Cole were there, dancing amid the tiny snowflakes she could not see, and the glass encased other memories as well, of the great-aunt she had loved so much.

During the years between Cole's disappearance and Aunt Augusta's death, the relationship between the Chamberlain women had changed, grown, deepened, matured. No longer were they great-aunt and niece, but just two women, similar in so many ways, especially in the men they had loved. Augusta told Claire about her beloved Cajun boy, how glad she was to have given herself to him before he died, how she would regret always that their forbidden passion had not left her with his child.

"Oh, Aunt Augusta," Claire whispered in the darkness. "Can I really do this?"

Yes. The answer came not as sound but as warmth—warmth, and strength, from the dome of glass cupped so tightly in her hands. You *can* do it, Claire. And you must. Go to him. Be with the man you love—and love him in whatever way you can for as long as you can bear.

"I will," Claire vowed. "I *will.*"

There seemed an even greater warmth then, beneath her hands and shimmering in the air, and Claire felt herself floating, floating . . . until she was beside the deep blue waters of the bayou once again, enveloped by a fragrant, steamy heat.

It was that long-ago day in June, when she and Cole first met, and magically, mysteriously, Claire felt exactly as she had felt then, a creature of boundless wonder and untarnished joy, an eight-year-old girl who knew no fear.

I *am* going to London. The confident pronouncement came from that brave young girl, and with it Claire actually felt the defiant jut of her once-freckled chin. I'm going to sing with him, and love him, and I'm going to give him the only gift I can give. That tormenting sadness lives in his heart still, I know it does. And now I have the chance to heal that weeping wound, *and I will do it.*

Claire smiled then, the radiant smile of the girl who had believed in all dreams.

And maybe, just maybe, when I'm in London, I'll even find the courage to give Sarah a call.

Sarah, Sarah, Sarah. Where are you, bitch, on this Christmas night? The killer's eyes gleamed at the blade of the jagged-edged knife, and the shining weapon seemed to gleam back in brilliant reply, a bright silver promise of carved flesh, of spilled crimson, of triumph, of terror. *Enjoy this Christmas, Lady Bitch. It will be your last.*

*C*hapter Twelve

Scotland Yard
Monday, December Twenty-sixth

PERHAPS THE FBI CONSULTANT WOULD AD-
vise her to leave London, to flee to a place ravaged by
war where the killer would not or could not follow.

It wasn't the first time the thought had danced in Sarah's
mind. And now, as her limousine neared Scotland Yard, delivering her precisely on time for her one-o'clock meeting, the
dancing thought took on even greater hope. Maybe the consultant would *insist* that she leave.

Sarah wasn't afraid of the killer, but of London. Her decision to return to the city, to actually *live* amid all its ghosts and
demons, had seemed quite bold. But, in fact, it had been a final,
desperate, necessary act.

She would permit herself only one weekend a month in Paris,
she had decided, only one weekend of pure escape; and she
would greet the new year with the firm resolve to stop drinking
altogether; and in time she would be harder, stronger, tougher.
Better?

No, not better. But hopefully, *please*, at least in some sem-
blance of control. For a long time, too long, she had been flirting with the very edges of madness, succumbing to every
opportunity to hide, to escape, *to not be Sarah*.

And what did that mean, that lack of control, that systematic denial—destruction—of self? It meant that *they* had won. They. Her husband, her parents, the three brutal strangers. All six were dead. But their ghosts ravaged her still, punishing her, compelling her to punish herself.

Sarah had to reclaim some of what they had taken from her. *Had to*, before all that remained for her was madness. Already the places on earth where Sarah Pembroke could survive had been dramatically curtailed.

There was war, of course, the place where Sarah felt safest of all. The battlefield was her asylum, where her own sanity was never questioned because everything was insane—and where, she believed, she had a chance of making a contribution to the world. And when she wasn't safely cloistered in the lunacy of war? She escaped to Paris, a nameless Frenchwoman who roamed the streets, her black hair flowing and her clothes rainbow-bright.

During her sojourns in the City of Light, as in the faraway lands drenched with blood, Sarah Pembroke never drank, not a drop. She didn't need to drink in Paris, *hadn't* needed to . . . until him . . . until Jacques.

Paris was no longer a safe haven. *He* was there, and even after he left the Ritz, he could still be found. She merely needed to ask the concierge to forward a letter to the man who had paid for the room from which she had fled in the darkest hours of night.

And then what? Would she go to him and confess all? Every lie and every truth? Would she tell him that no man had ever made her feel the way he did? So safe. And so afraid. Would she admit that she had feared his touch, had reason to, but that she had wanted it, too—and that when it had come, a caress of such tenderness, the trembling power of her own wanting filled her with an entirely new terror?

Such confessions were impossible. Sarah knew that. But her shadow, the Frenchwoman who was almost free, did not fully share that belief. She could not be trusted. She might try to find the man named Jacques. Which meant that Paris was no longer safe, not even for one weekend a month.

Sarah would have to remain in London, every night and

every day, confronting without hope of escape the ghosts that caused such harm. You're going to confront them *without* alcohol? an inner voice taunted. With nothing to numb the old memories of pain—and the new, more painful ones of Jacques?

You can't do it. You're far too damaged, too brittle. Such courage will backfire, and it won't be long until you find yourself making a mad dash—a *mad* dash, Sarah—toward that abyss you fear so much. And you will be running so hard, so fast, that your momentum will hurl you right over the edge.

Choose your madness, Lady Sarah Pembroke. The depthless abyss itself—or the blood-soaked sanctuary of war.

Maybe the FBI consultant will suggest that I return to war, Sarah thought again as she emerged from the limousine. If not, *I* will.

Sarah greeted Scotland Yard's commissioner of police with gracious apology.

"Please forgive me again for vanishing. I hope your Christmas was a happy one?"

"Yes, indeed."

"Good. Is the FBI consultant still in the States?"

"No, he's here. He didn't return home. Which reminds me . . ." The commissioner handed her a cream-colored envelope. "Here's your check."

"Thank you," Sarah murmured. "Where is he? I thought we'd be meeting together."

"He's in an office down the hall. We decided that I'd meet with you first, to explain his role in the investigation, then leave the two of you to discuss the specifics. So let me get right to it. He's interested in this case and has generously offered to remain in England until it's solved. Because of his expertise, we'll be following his lead, taking his advice, working cooperatively with him."

Sarah gave a faint, wry smile. "All of us?"

"Your participation is essential."

Sarah's smile held even as her hope faded. No one was planning to send her back to war. She was going to have to stay in London, to face the trivial threat of a cold-blooded killer and the far greater threat of her own cold-blooded ghosts.

"From this moment on, I shall try my best to be part of the team," she promised.

The commissioner smiled at last. "Well then, shall I introduce you to Mr. Dalton?"

"*You lied to me*. You followed me to Paris, didn't you? You knew precisely who I was but pretended not to know."

"I wasn't the only pretender, *chérie*. I wasn't the only one who lied."

"The reason I go to Paris is to get away. If someone doesn't recognize me, as you pretended not to, I don't reveal my name."

"I'm not talking about that lie." I'm talking about the *other* lies, Sarah. The important ones. Like pretending to fall in love, and promising to trust me with the vulnerability of your nightmares and your dreams. And then there was the note, Sarah, those lies inscribed on stark white paper. "You're not married, are you?"

"No."

"Not even to the loving memory of your husband?"

"No."

She stood before him, her magnificent green eyes ablaze with fury. And something else, a dark shadow of despair that had been there from the moment she whispered *You lied to me*. Jack saw that shadow clearly now, amid the flames of her anger, a shadowy darkness that held pain—not rage—at his betrayal.

"I didn't know you were in Paris, Sarah." A truth? Or yet another lie?

A truth. He had not known, not consciously. Perhaps his incisive mind *had* seen a clue. Or perhaps his restlessness had been compelled by something else entirely—something inexplicable, fanciful—and wondrous. Either way, whether their Parisian rendezvous had been the consequence of his gift, or the mandates of something far more mystical, it had happened because of who he was . . . who she was . . . who they were.

And now the man who was so famous for his cool logic embellished softly, "It was destiny."

It is not my destiny to love, or to be loved. It was a harsh thought, a bitter truth, and when she spoke again her voice should have been edgy and sharp. But at the last moment the Frenchwoman who dwelled within her smothered all traces of harshness, and Sarah heard only her own astonished hope.

"Destiny?"

"Mais oui."

His voice was a tender caress, spoken to that woman she had dared to be, that Parisian impostor, the shadow woman for whom haute couture was shimmering rainbows and flowing black hair. Sarah felt that woman now, wanting to stage a defiant coup, to split away from Sarah Pembroke entirely and leap boldly—but with such joy—into the abyss of madness that was her only true destiny. It would be a swift descent, but a glorious one. For those few glittering moments, she would surrender completely to fantasy. *I can love again without being destroyed. And I can* be *loved, for the first time ever.*

Oui, Jacques, oui—

No, Sarah commanded. *No.* When she spoke again, the wonder was gone, the lacy phantom of a rainbowed shadow. "Shall we get to it, Agent Dalton?"

Jack wanted to hold her, this strong and fragile warrior who stood before him. Her slender body was taut, alert and wary, ready to fend off the gentleness that seemed to threaten her very life.

His warrior was even dressed for battle. Admittedly, her attire wasn't what she wore in the field, but it was solemn nonetheless. Faultlessly elegant—and timelessly tasteful—her suit was as black as night, its austerity scarcely softened by the ivory silk blouse she wore beneath; and her hair was imprisoned, not the single braid worn in war but a sleek knot captured tightly at her nape. Sarah's anchorwoman armor did have a few embellishments: pearls at her ears and neck, and the most subtle of makeup, impeccably applied.

She might have been Lady Sarah Pembroke, patroness of worthy causes, having heard that Scotland Yard wished to sponsor a safe home for runaway children and wanting to offer her help. She would play hostess to a lavish charity ball. A Valentine's gala, perhaps.

But Sarah had not been invited to Scotland Yard to discuss her role in a black-tie affair to be held on the most romantic day of the year. She was here to discuss a killing that was scheduled for that day, a murder at which she would be both hostess and honored guest.

And now she wanted to get to it, to discuss with him the battle that lay ahead, and she was fully armed, cloaked in an invisible armor that warned him to stay very far away.

"It's not Agent Dalton. I'm merely a consultant to the FBI, a private citizen, not a government employee. My name is Jack, Lady Pembroke . . . Sarah."

She had never heard her name spoken with such tenderness, not as a daughter, not as a woman, not as a wife. It was the same way in which the man named Jacques had spoken *Claire*, as if he believed both Claire and Sarah to be the same, equally worthy, neither phantom nor shadow.

He is so dangerous, a voice warned. Far more dangerous than the haunting ghosts of London or the live missiles of war. You must fight with relentless ferocity the powerful temptation to offer him your heart, your trust, your love. You know all too well the consequences of such foolishness. You are so badly damaged, so bitterly disappointing, that any gift of yourself would be promptly returned. How would you survive after that?

And you *must* survive, remember? It was an abiding truth of Sarah's life—or perhaps the ultimate proof of her madness. But there it was: the belief that she must stay alive, that it was not yet time to yield to the enticing wish to slumber in eternal peace beside the tiny grave in Norfolk.

Jack saw her torment and wanted desperately to rescue her. But Sarah didn't want his help, his love, not yet. Indeed, she seemed quite terrified of it.

So, Jack commanded his own fierce restlessness, for now simply concentrate on saving her life.

"Please have a seat," he said quietly.

They sat in Jack's office, separated only by the narrow expanse of his wooden desk. The distance between them was little more than it had been on Christmas Eve, at their candlelit table in the Parisian café.

But there were no candles now. And they weren't Claire and Jacques, falling in love, but Sarah and Jack, discussing death.

Jack began with a request that surprised her. "Tell me why you forwarded the letter to Scotland Yard."

"Because it seemed so evil."

"A heart is a symbol of romance, of love, and even though this heart is imprinted in black ink, it's still stylish—elegant and appealing. At least that's what I was told when I showed it to several women at Quantico. They thought it was quite beautiful, and didn't instantly link it to violence. But you did. Why?"

Because for me love and violence have always been linked. "It just felt sinister to me, menacing. Perhaps because of my work, I'm more alert to danger."

Now it was Jack's turn to register surprise. "More alert than Paulina Bliss or Ashley Alexander?"

Sarah frowned. "Paulina Bliss and Ashley Alexander?"

"Do you recognize their names?"

"Yes. Of course." Sarah knew that both were famous actresses, although she had never seen their work. Sarah Pembroke escaped with alcohol—or by traveling to Paris or to war—not with the celluloid fantasies offered by Hollywood. She hadn't known that either actress had died, much less been murdered. Last February fourteenth, and for several months beyond, the renowned journalist had been far away, immersed in a different kind of brutality from the one that had tarnished Tinseltown on that romantic day. "I hadn't realized . . ."

"Both women were very savvy, amply aware of the dangers associated with their celebrity and not the least bit shy about calling the police when something—or someone—caused concern. Both received the same letter you did. But neither notified the police, or even the private security firms they employed."

Sarah shrugged. "Maybe I'm psychic. Like you."

"Psychic?"

"According to the commissioner, you're an expert in murder. He said that you're able to discern the identity of killers when no one else can. I assumed that meant you had some psychic connection with them."

"No. I use logic, problem solving, not psychology."

"You believe there's method to everything, even the madness of murder?"

"That's exactly what I believe," Jack affirmed. "It's a conviction that requires rigorous attention to detail, Sarah, even seemingly irrelevant ones. Which is why I'm pushing you now, wanting to know why you sensed the danger. Did the symbol trigger something? A distant memory of a black heart?"

"No. Nothing specific." *Just a lifetime of trying to love black-hearted people.*

"Okay," Jack relented easily, because that was what she wanted, and uneasily, because he knew she was hiding something, this woman with such secrets who told such lies. "Let's go on, then. I want—well, need—to tell you a few facts about the other murders. Both actresses received three letters. Neither kept the envelopes, but there's an obvious order of receipt. First, the imprint of the black heart alone, identical to what you received. Then the addition of typewritten words—*Be mine* on what's presumed to be the second, and *Valentine* on the third."

"I can't believe that didn't seem ominous to them."

"It's likely that each woman believed she knew who was sending the letters and therefore didn't feel threatened. In fact, each *did* know the killer. She permitted him into her home on the evening of February fourteenth and shared a bottle of champagne with him shortly before she died." Jack was trying to keep their discussion analytical and professional. But now an intensely personal—and intensely painful—image came to him: Sarah drinking champagne, so that she could bear his touch . . . as if *he* were a killer, as if *he* were planning the brutal murder of her lovely heart. "The killer seems patient, calculating, organized. The most probable scenario is that he plans to strike again on Valentine's Day. He'll be someone you know, Sarah, someone you feel comfortable entertaining in your home."

Then he doesn't exist. There was no one, man or woman, whom Sarah Pembroke felt comfortable permitting into the sterile place she called home. "You keep referring to the killer as *he*. Did he, were they . . . ?"

She didn't shiver, not visibly, but Jack sensed the deep quiver of fear. It hadn't been there before, when Lady Sarah Pembroke uttered words of death—*murder, killer, victim*. She had spoken them effortlessly, and without apprehension of any kind. Impersonal. Analytical. The warrior-journalist at work.

But now there was fear, in the word she did not speak. Was it, for her, a word that conjured an invasion more intimate, more brutal, than death?

"Raped?" Jack finished softly. "No. They weren't raped. That the killer is a man is merely a guess—an educated one, but a guess nonetheless."

"You mean there's no physical evidence, no trace of him at all?"

"Not a fingerprint, not a lip print, no blood, no skin—nothing. The victim's champagne glass was empty. But the killer's was full, and wiped clean of all prints. The police guess that they drank together, but that he washed and refilled his glass before leaving."

"The police," Sarah echoed. "But not you."

"Refilling the glass seems a strange—and calculated—thing to do. As if he wanted to create the impression that he hadn't had anything to drink."

"And thus leave a clue? When he'd obviously been so careful to leave none?"

Jack smiled. "There's method even in the madness of murder. I just have to figure out what it is."

"But there must be other clues. The paper? The typewriter? Surely the symbol itself."

"The paper's high-quality parchment, sold in fine stationery stores everywhere, and counting the typed address on the envelope he sent you, three different typewriters have been used. The symbol, however, is a major clue—or could be, if we could find out where it was made, and by whom. It's hand-carved, in stone, as distinctive as a fingerprint. LAPD can't find any stone carvers in L.A. who admit to making it, so either the killer carved it himself, or had it made elsewhere—perhaps even ex-U.S."

"Like Hong Kong."

"Yes." *Exactly like Hong Kong.* "What makes you say that?"

"My . . . husband. He lived in Hong Kong before we were married and became accustomed to using his hand-carved chop in place of his signature. It was an affectation he maintained even after he returned to England." Sarah's mind's eye saw an image, the symbol that was Simon Beckwith-Jones's name—in Chinese—imprinted in gold ink and glittering brightly on their marriage certificate. *Too* brightly. Even now its remembered glare caused blinding pain. "Is the killer wealthy, do you think? A world traveler?"

"A world traveler? Maybe. Wealthy? I think so. Neither actress seemed to have any qualms about permitting him into her home. The champagne they drank was Cristale, presumably purchased by him, and he apparently arrived with long-stemmed red roses as well. The usual Valentine's Day props, but in both instances pricey ones."

"And ones that worked," Sarah murmured. They wouldn't work for her, of course. A seduction of champagne and roses? *Never.* Quite obviously the killer didn't know her—not yet. "This should be easy, shouldn't it? The killer's presumably a man, from L.A., someone I will come to know between now and Valentine's Day. He'll be somewhat of a celebrity, I suppose, an actor, a journalist, someone who'll be able to contrive a plausible reason to meet me. And because last time neither victim went to the police, he'll feel completely safe. He won't imagine that we're on to him."

"That's the ideal scenario. And maybe it will be just that straightforward. But his home may not be L.A. Both actresses traveled extensively, could have met him anywhere. We know, with certainty, only that he was in Los Angeles last February fourteenth. Even the letter you received, postmarked from Beverly Hills, could have been mailed for him by someone else. He could already be in London, Sarah. Someone you already know and trust."

Jack expected Sarah to consider his words for a moment, to search her London acquaintances for a man who might have a connection with the other victims and who had *her* trust. But without a heartbeat's hesitation, Sarah shook her head.

"I'm going to need names, Sarah," Jack persisted. "Lovers, admirers . . . especially rejected ones."

Her midnight-black head was still now, and remained that way. But her green eyes answered with brilliant clarity. There was no such list. No admirers. No lovers. Rejected or otherwise.

Except me. "Please think about it, Sarah. I'm sure you'll be able to come up with someone."

Jack saw that he was losing her. For a while they had been a team, working together to solve this puzzle of death, intently focused, harmonious in their resolve. But when the discussion became truly personal—more personal, apparently, than her impending murder—Sarah began to retreat behind her invisible armor.

Jack needed to engage her again, to once more compel her bright mind to focus on the problem at hand. And that would be easy, he realized. Far easier than asking the woman to name her rejected suitors. He merely needed to address the warrior, not the woman, to involve her in a discussion of strategy for the battlefield of her death.

"Why don't we discuss the specific plans?"

"Plans?"

"For your safety."

"But I'm already perfectly safe. I'll notify Scotland Yard the moment I receive the next letter, or if I sense that someone—an old acquaintance or a new one—is trying to get close to me. And if he can't be arrested beforehand, if he needs to be caught in flagrante delicto, officers can be waiting for him at my home on Valentine's Day."

Jack felt a rush of fury at her dismissive nonchalance. But his voice was as calm as ice.

"Here are the plans, Lady Pembroke. You will be guarded, *protected*, twenty-four hours a day. At work, at home, and at all times in between. It's my understanding that the security at Global is extremely tight, but I'm going to put an officer inside with you anyway. She'll be a woman, working undercover as your assistant. At all other times, you'll be guarded by men." Jack waved away her instant indignation at what seemed to be overt and incontrovertible sexism. "This man murders women, Lady Pembroke. He *loves* to murder them. We already have one woman in jeopardy—you—and we're not going to expose another to undue risk. It would help immensely if you didn't play games with the officers assigned to keep you safe. But this time they'll be prepared. They won't lose you."

They won't lose you. You can't get away. They were words from her past, from that terrifying time when she was under constant watch. For her own protection, she was told, to prevent her from coming to harm. From harming herself. But even then Sarah had known that her imprisonment had another purpose, that there were others—more important than she— to protect. Her parents. Her husband. By hiding her away, they were protected from the awkward embarrassment of her madness.

"No," Sarah whispered. "Please."

It was a soft entreaty, and a desperate one. And, Jack realized, it wasn't even spoken to him. Sarah's eyes were unfocused, and very far away. "Sarah?"

It took a moment for his gentle voice to reach the place where she had gone, and a moment more for her to journey back to him.

"Please don't have me guarded, Jack. I'm not the criminal, am I?"

"Of course not."

"And he's not going to suddenly attack me in the street. He's going to send me two more letters before Valentine's Day, at which point he'll appear on my doorstep bearing roses and champagne."

"He's *probably* not going to suddenly attack you," Jack amended. "But what if he gets impatient, Sarah? Or angry? He's a madman, and therefore unpredictable. He may not have the control he had a year ago."

"I'll be careful."

"*Careful?* What does that mean?"

"That I can take care of myself."

"Do you carry a gun?"

"This isn't America. We're not routinely armed over here. We have no need to be."

Lady Sarah Pembroke was telling him that she lived in a civilized country, unlike his; that the colonies born of revolution had, apparently, never abandoned that heritage of violence. Jack was not about to argue that the American way was better.

But he had a question for the warrior. "How will you protect yourself?"

"I've taken classes in self-defense. And I'm strong, Jack. Very strong." She sat before him, determined and proud, an army unto herself, reliant on no one else. "I'll carry a can of pepper spray if it would make you feel better."

"And you'll do what, Sarah? Squirt a little spray with one hand while you're twisting the knife away with the other?"

"The knife?"

"The hunting knife."

Jack had assumed that she knew, had imagined that when the commissioner informed her that she was the murderer's next target, she might have been a little curious about the way the monster chose to kill. But quite obviously she hadn't been. Was she truly so casual about her own death—or merely so confident in Scotland Yard's ability to protect her?

Her beautiful green gaze had been unwavering, defiant. But now it fell away, downcast, intently focused on the hands folded demurely in her lap. Was she envisioning the scars hidden beneath the cuffs of her ivory silk blouse? The places where her delicate flesh had once before felt the sharpness of a blade? Would that memory, in concert with the revelation that the madman's weapon of choice was a jagged-edged knife, make her more reasonable about being protected?

Jack hoped so. But the eyes that finally met his again were defiant still—and oddly triumphant.

"Actually," Sarah said, "a knife should be relatively easy to defend against. Far easier than a gun."

"It wasn't easy for either Paulina Bliss or Ashley Alexander, both of whom had guns in their homes."

"They weren't prepared, weren't expecting—"

"It wouldn't have mattered. Would you care to see why?"

Jack Dalton had not planned to show Sarah Pembroke the crime-scene photographs. Indeed, he had not even considered it. But now it seemed necessary.

She had been to war, had borne witness to all manner of horror. But Jack was nonetheless quite confident that these photographs would have an impact on her.

And they did. Immense sadness shadowed her lovely face. Sadness, and outrage. But not a trace of shock.

And when at last she spoke there was only quiet analysis.

"He slashed their throats first, didn't he? Before doing . . . the rest."

The rest. Vicious stabs, scores of them. Then, during the horrifying calm that followed what had so clearly been a storm of rage, his hands, steady now, had left the perfect imprint of the stone-carved heart. The ink wasn't black this time, but red, the victim's own blood. And the symbol wasn't placed on expensive parchment but on the ivory flesh of the dead woman's left breast.

"Monster," Sarah whispered.

"Yes, Sarah. He's a monster. Which is why you need protection, twenty-four hours a day."

Sarah placed the color photographs on the wooden desk between them, returned her hands to their ladylike clasp in her lap, and met his eyes. "No, Jack. I absolutely refuse that sort of intrusion on my privacy."

"A trivial intrusion compared to murder, wouldn't you say?"

"But my choice, wouldn't you say?"

At that moment Jack Dalton was quite relieved that he was not an official representative of the United States government. As such, he would have been obliged to know the fine print of English law, its various guaranteed freedoms, and he would have been obligated to abide by the law of the land. Here, as in the States, there were undoubtedly prohibitions against such invasions as phone taps and electronic surveillance, and quite probably against personal surveillance as well.

But Jack Dalton, private citizen, had only one concern—the safety, twenty-four hours a day, of Lady Sarah Pembroke.

And she would be safe.

"Your choice," he conceded. "But I want this monster, Sarah."

"I want him, too, Jack."

"Good. Then in exchange for your privacy, I need some promises from you. You must be very careful, very wary. You must let no one—*no one*—into your home without notifying Scotland Yard first. And I want to hear right away about letters, phone calls, anything that's the least bit unusual, no matter how trivial it seems. Agreed?"

"Yes. Agreed."

She looked so hopeful, so grateful. *I'm lying to you, Sarah. I'm betraying your fragile trust, your delicate hope. I have to.*

"It's still necessary for me to see your workplace and your home. If that feels too intrusive, I'm sorry. But if you suddenly need help, the police have to know how to get to you without delay. Okay?"

"Yes."

"So where shall we begin?"

"I'm not scheduled to return to the bureau until tomorrow morning. Could we do this then?"

"We'll do your office tomorrow. But let's do your home today."

Chapter Thirteen

HER HOME. SARAH DIDN'T WANT JACK TO
see it, not ever. But Sarah Pembroke knew all too well
the sometimes impulsive mandates of madness. Despite the
killer's intent to slay again on Valentine's Day, he might pay a
surprise visit before then.

The police needed to be able to get to her, through the doors
electronically secured at the building's front entrance as well as
the two dead-bolt locks that sealed the door to her condominium itself.

"Who else has copies of the keys?" Jack asked when they
stood in the foyer on the building's top floor. Three doorways
intruded into the smooth granite walls. One, at the far end,
opened to a stairway, for use in the event of fire, and one permitted entrance into Sarah's penthouse, and the third, directly
across from Sarah's, belonged to another unit, the mirror-
image twin of her own. "Your neighbor?"

"What? Oh. No. No one lives there. It's empty."

"Until the killer moves in." *Or until I do. Until I betray your
trust, defy your wishes, yet again.*

"He won't. He can't."

"Because?"

"Because I own it."

"Okay," Jack said evenly. "Then back to the issue of keys. The building manager must have a set."

"No."

"The locksmith, then. I'll need his name."

"All right. But . . . I actually hired two locksmiths, one for each lock." Her expression said the rest: trust no one.

But Sarah would have to trust Jack. She would have to give him the set of keys she had given no one else. As she turned to open the door, she seemed weighted by an invisible heaviness, as if some colossal hand from the heavens were pushing down, trying with all its might to crush her.

Jack saw the fragile shoulders that refused to bend beneath the enormous weight and chastised himself for his own heavy-handedness. This tour of her home *could* have been scheduled for tomorrow, before they had seen her office, or after. Sarah would have been quite safe overnight. He would have seen to that.

But Jack had wanted to be with her, this warrior-woman who owned his heart. Such a selfish wish, he realized now. Quite obviously Sarah did not want him here.

"I've seen messy apartments before," he assured her. "And I do need to see the inside of yours. But if you'd rather post-pone this until tomorrow, I'll just wait out here while you get me the extra set of keys. I do respect your privacy, Sarah. I'm trying to."

Sarah hesitated before responding to his offer. Her condominium wasn't messy at all, of course. Just the opposite. Like her, it was impeccable, fastidious, not a hair out of place. And sterile, and dead, a place where she lived, barely survived, whenever she was in England.

Could she transform it overnight? Yes, absolutely. Money could do anything. By tomorrow morning it could be filled with brightly colored furniture, and a collection of cheerful paintings could adorn the ice-white walls, and there could be all manner of knickknacks, each looking as if it had personal meaning, a treasured memento.

The truth of her existence could be camouflaged beneath a brilliant facade. But such bright plumage would be yet another lie, another disguise—and it might intrigue him anew, as he had been intrigued in Paris by the shadow woman dressed in the bold, vivid hues of a rainbow.

You don't want him to be intrigued. *You don't dare.*

"No," she answered finally. "Now is fine. Please come in."

Jack had expected clutter, and his mind had even set the scene. Sarah didn't officially begin her new role as Global's anchorwoman until January second, so she was on a hiatus of sorts. But Jack imagined that there would be newspapers strewn everywhere, this morning's editions from around the world; and there would be notes, in her own hand, scribbled on lined pads of yellow paper; and although he could not quite imagine unwashed breakfast dishes piled in her kitchen sink, he envisioned this morning's coffee mug teetering precariously on the bulky arm of an overstuffed sofa.

In short, Jack assumed that he would see proof of who she was, the dedicated journalist, hard at work even when she didn't need to be.

But Jack was not greeted by clutter, only by starkness. Elegant starkness, like the cold, stark elegance of a heart carved from stone. A black lacquer coffee table was in evidence, but there was no sign of this morning's mug. And as for an overstuffed sofa? There was no such bulky coziness here. The furniture was sleek and trim, in austere shades of ebony and bone, and even the incandescent light came from a somber source, a lamp of black porcelain etched in gold.

There was no clutter in Lady Sarah Pembroke's living room, and no color. Unbidden—and unwanted—Jack's mind conjured an image of brilliant hues. It was a logical image, because this place where Sarah lived looked like a place where someone could die. Indeed, death would become this austere room, adding color and even more elegance: crystal champagne flutes shimmering with honey-gold Cristale, a lush bouquet of blood-red roses, a snow-white body with midnight black hair . . . and that final adornment, that most vivid splash.

Sarah had worn such a splash in Paris, a silken scarf the color of rubies. But here, in that scene of death, the jewel-bright tint would come from within, a glistening liquid spill from her severed silken throat; and in lieu of the mist of tiny diamonds that had caressed her hair as she stood by the Seine, the droplets here would be gemstone red—rubied tears that wept from wounds carved deep into her flesh.

I have to get you out of here, Jack thought. Because even though I plan to stop the killer long before he ever sets foot in this place, you—your heart and your soul—will surely die here.

Jack didn't trust himself to look at her, not then, not yet. Sarah would see too clearly the raw urgency of his thoughts. He scanned the room instead, a searching gaze in hope of finding something that would calm the restlessness he felt, the impatience to hold her, to protect her, to love her.

Jack believed his search would be a futile one—until he saw the statues displayed on the black marble mantelpiece. The sight did little to calm the pace of his heart; but it subdued the restlessness. *We are meant to be together. We will be.* Someday the specter of death will be behind us, and there will be no more lies. There will be only the truths of love shared by Claire and Jacques . . . and confessed, in English, by Sarah and Jack.

The mantelpiece was massive. But in this penthouse of so many stark and empty spaces, it seemed odd that the statues, thirteen in all, would be congregated in a single place. Yet there they were, crowded together—as if the choice had been theirs, as if the eclectic community of spaceship and swan, and ballerina and butterfly, and hummingbird and harlequin, and panther and peacock, and Dalmatian and dagger, and clown and cowboy had come to life and demanded to be placed beside their compatriots. Or perhaps they had been led to the mantelpiece by the prancing hoofbeats of their winged leader, the mythological Pegasus.

Jack knew everything there was to know about the society of statues that was huddled—as if in search of warmth—in this place of ice. All had begun their lives as tiny shards, three-dimensional clues that, when assembled correctly, yielded the stylishly elegant shapes.

Pegasus Enterprises released one new puzzle a year, on December first, in time for the Christmas rush. The most popular and least expensive format was teak. But as Pegasus puzzles became more prized, there was an ever-increasing demand for more exotic options—silver, crystal, obsidian, and gold. And once, in a limited edition for the most avid of collectors, the original puzzle, the winged horse, had been offered in white marble.

Jack turned to her at last, to the woman who was, apparently, such an ardent collector. "Do you have the new one? The sailboat?"

Of course she did. She had placed an order for the puzzle, in crystal, in July. And on her return from Moscow, even before going to her office—where the letter from a killer was waiting—she had gone to the shop on Bond Street to claim it. She had wanted, needed, to hold in her hands the box of crystal shards. But she had postponed the pleasure—the escape—of assembling it. In January, she told herself, half command, half promise. She would need it then, during the long, sober nights in London.

But Sarah had needed to assemble the crystal sailboat yesterday, on Christmas, when it had been so important to keep her mind focused, fully engaged . . . and when she had needed something else, something the Pegasus puzzles had given her from the very start—the bold promise that something wonderful could be crafted from even a myriad of shattered shards.

Assembling the crystal sailboat had been the perfect way—perhaps the only way—to endure the day and night after leaving the man named Jacques.

She had completed the puzzle just before dawn, an accomplishment accompanied by despair, not triumph. How would she spend tonight? she had wondered. Tomorrow night? The night after that? Sarah hadn't had an answer, not then. But now she did. She would spend the long nights that lay ahead forbidding herself to drink, and thinking about a man named Jack . . . and reminding herself how dangerous he was to her heart.

"I have the sailboat. In fact, it's already assembled."

"Already?"

His voice was soft, and Sarah saw such tenderness, and an expression that looked like pride—in her. *Oh, Jack, you would be so disappointed if you knew the truth about me.* The bitterness of that truth armed her with defiance. "It took me sixteen hours, a little less time than the others, all of which have taken me less than a day. Does that shock you, Jack?"

"Not at all."

It didn't shock him. Nothing about her would. But Jack was intimately acquainted with the demographics of the millions of people who eagerly awaited Pegasus Enterprises' annual pre-Christmas release. The overwhelming majority were men. Was the ability to solve such puzzles genetic, some innate gender-based aptitude? Or was it merely acquired, a predictable consequence of gender-oriented socialization? Such questions were the stuff of endless speculation and debate. But the simple fact remained: Little boys spent untold hours assembling model boats, planes, and cars; little girls did not.

Pegasus puzzles provided a grown-up outlet for that childhood fascination—and an extreme test of the skill involved. As *the* Christmas gift for the man who had everything, the statues stood in executive offices around the world, ornamental trophies that offered eloquent testimony to their owner's possession—and mastery—of whatever mysterious facility it was that conferred the skill, wits, and patience to assemble them.

Lady Sarah Pembroke had an office. But *her* puzzles were on display here, in the stark austerity of her home. Why? Jack wondered. Was it a reluctance to draw attention to herself? The same reserve that prompted her generous donations to charity to be anonymous ones?

Or was it something else? Did Sarah worry, perhaps, that the mysterious aptitude she so clearly possessed might make her seem too much the warrior?

And who was it who gave her the puzzles? One of the admirers she claimed did not exist? Or did she give them to herself, a challenge to the incisive mind he had seen at work in his office at Scotland Yard?

"I'm not at all shocked," Jack repeated. "In fact, as one of the owners of Pegasus, I'm delighted that you've been sufficiently happy with the puzzles that you have every one."

"One of the owners?" *You're responsible for these puzzles*

that mean so much to me? That help me escape, and give me hope?

"Pegasus is a family affair—my parents, my sisters, and me. The others do the lion's share of the work. I'm just the guinea pig, the in-house test market. My father creates the puzzles, then sends them to me to assemble, to decide on a piece-by-piece basis if changes need to be made. We want each puzzle to be a little more difficult than the last, but not so frustrating that we lose customers. It's a business, after all."

"And you're a businessman in your spare time?"

"No, although there was a time when that was my plan. I entered college with the intention of getting a degree in business."

A smile touched her lovely face. "But you got sidetracked into your life of crime."

Jack smiled in reply. "Yes. I took a course in criminology and was hooked. It's a different kind of puzzle solving, but the principle's the same—you begin with a seemingly random assortment of pieces, otherwise known as clues, and you fit them all together."

"But . . ."

"But?"

"Well, when you're dealing with a crime, no one gives you the pieces, the clues, do they? You have to find them on your own, decide which ones will ultimately fit and which can safely be discarded."

"That's exactly right. You have to be very careful not to throw something out just because it doesn't *seem* to fit, and when you've made a firm commitment to a clue, when you're convinced that it's an essential part of the puzzle, you must find a place for it, no matter how difficult that may be."

"Like the Pegasus puzzles. There are always a few pieces that, on the face of it, can't possibly fit, that seem to have been included as one would introduce red herrings in a murder mystery."

"We get letters all the time from customers who've decided that we've done just that. Have you ever been tempted to write?"

"No. You . . . your company . . . wouldn't do that."

"You trust us."

Sarah greeted his words with a thoughtful frown, and then a tentative smile. "Yes. I guess you could say that."

Then trust *me*, Jack implored silently to the woman for whom the admission of trust seemed a betrayal of self. Trust me to find all the pieces in this puzzle of death. Help me find them, Sarah. Share with me the bright insights of your mind. And when we've solved the mystery of the black-hearted killer, trust me still, with the most intriguing puzzle of all. *You.*

Sarah seemed to read his silent command, and for a fleeting instant Jack saw an answering flicker of hope. Then she frowned anew, distracted, searching for a memory.

"What, Sarah?"

"I remember hearing—or perhaps reading?—that the company was founded by a sixteen-year-old. That was you, wasn't it, Jack? Pegasus is actually yours."

"That was me, yes. But from its inception thirteen years ago, the company has belonged to my family, to each of us equally. All I did was recognize the commercial potential of the puzzle my father had made. Rubik's Cube was already a sensation, and as far as I was concerned, my father's winged horse was much more interesting. Not to mention the fact that, once assembled, you had something to show for the challenge." Jack shrugged. "I simply solved the puzzle of how to form a company, get a patent, and put a product into distribution—all pretty trivial compared to creating the statue itself."

Trivial, perhaps, Sarah mused. But something that had been parlayed into an immense fortune—which Jack had shared with his family.

"Your father didn't make the Pegasus to be sold?"

"No. He just made it for me."

"For you? Why?"

"Out of sentiment. When I was young, he made puzzles for me all the time. I was almost four years old before I could—or would—speak more than my name. But my motor skills were advanced for my age. Instead of obsessing about my inability to speak, my parents focused on what I could do with my hands, and, I suppose, with my brain. We didn't have a great deal of money, in fact very little, so my father, a carpenter by trade, made things for me. An elaborate set of building blocks at first, then the jigsaw puzzles. The puzzles were far more complicated than those available for children, and more interesting, too— and more personal."

"Personal?"

"He created scenes from our life, portraits of our family. Our house, our dog, my sisters, all of us. You can custom order such personalized jigsaw puzzles now, by sending in photographs. But they're cardboard, chipboard at best, and the ones my father made were wooden, sanded smooth so that I wouldn't get splinters and then hand-painted by my mother."

"Do you still have those puzzles?"

"They're at my parents' home in Denver, waiting for their grandchildren, the first two of whom will be arriving in March."

"One of your sisters is having twins?"

"No, my twin sisters, Marcy and Krystal, are each having a baby sometime that month—which makes this the first truly *twin* thing that Krys and Marcy have ever done. Twins are supposed to be completely wrapped up in their own world, especially as children. But my little sisters—they're eleven months younger than me—spent those years turning the full force of their twin energy on me. I had my own personal stereo system, in the form of my sisters, supervising me, encouraging me to speak—generally bossing me around."

Sarah heard the fondness in his voice and saw the light in his indigo eyes. Jack had *allowed* his little sisters to supervise him. The older brother had seemingly given them control; but the entire time, even when he was nearly mute, he had been in charge.

"You're very close to them still, aren't you?"

"We're all still very close, all five of us."

Earlier, when Jack had first seen the starkness of Sarah's home, his mind had conjured a crimson image of carnage and death. Now it was Sarah who envisioned a faraway scene: a young boy, brilliant yet inexplicably silent, sitting on a clean but well-worn carpet as he stared with eager anticipation at the array of brightly colored puzzle pieces that lay before him. His parents were there, the talented carpenter who so carefully sanded the wood and the loving mother who painted the vivid colors; and his twin sisters were there as well, chattering words of encouragement to their older brother who was so terribly smart but who could not speak.

Jack had wanted desperately to take Sarah away from the image he had seen. But Sarah felt no comparable wish about the vision that danced in her mind. It was a joyous portrait of love, of family, something she had never known—but knew to cherish.

Sarah had no wish to steal Jack from that wonderful image of love.

But I already have.

"You were planning to spend Christmas with your family, weren't you? If it hadn't been for the black heart . . . for me. I'm sorry, Jack. I'm sorry that I prevented you from being with them."

"You're not responsible for the black heart," Jack reminded her. Then softly, meaningfully, he issued another reminder. "But you are responsible for the way I spent Christmas Eve. And I'm not unhappy about that, Sarah, not at all. Except for the way it ended."

"That was—" a fantasy, an illusion, a *del*usion of a madwoman's bold shadow "—a mistake."

"Which part, Sarah? Christmas Eve? Or leaving my bed before dawn on Christmas Day?"

"Christmas Eve."

Jack gazed at the woman-warrior who was so very accomplished at telling lies. Was she lying now? Jack couldn't tell. She was fully shielded by her armor.

"Well, I don't agree. I think the only mistake was that you left." And the mistake I can make now, Jack realized, is to push you. I see your fear, Sarah. I hate it, but I see it. "So, Lady Pembroke, why don't you give me the rest of the tour?"

The remainder of the place Sarah called home was as spacious—and as spartan—as the living room. She had an office, state-of-the-art and sterile. And then there was her bedroom. It was the most heartbreakingly solitary room of all, its only adornments the just-assembled crystal sailboat *and his blue shirt.*

Jack had discovered that the shirt was missing late Christmas Day, as he packed for his return to London, and he had toyed with both hopeful and cynical reasons for its absence. Sarah wanted his shirt as a treasured memento of their evening *versus* she was in such a hurry to leave, to escape before he awakened, that she simply grabbed her clothes and fled. In that cynical scenario, his shirt was crumpled in a trash can somewhere along the Champs-Elysées, or drowned deep in the murky waters of the Seine.

In fact, his shirt, her modest nightgown, was neither crumpled nor drowned. Smoothed with great care, it lay at the head of her impeccably made snow-white bed, as if she had worn it last night and planned to wear it on this night as well.

"I was going to have it laundered," Sarah explained in a rush. "I was going to send it to the Ritz to have them forward it to you."

"Keep it, Sarah."

"But I—"

"Keep it, Sarah," Jack repeated. "Wear it."

I see your fear, Sarah. I hate it, but I see it. Your fear . . . and your hope.

A battle was being waged deep within the warrior, fear against hope. And fear, Jack realized, was about to win. In another moment Sarah would shove the shirt into his hands, crumpling it after all—and drowning all hope.

Jack moved away from her, to the wall of windows on the far side of the bed. The vista confirmed what he had already assumed—that this room was as safe from outside intrusion as all the others.

The starkness of Sarah's home might pose great jeopardy for the survival of her heart. But any assault launched by a killer would necessarily be made through the double-locked front door.

Lady Sarah Pembroke's penthouse was a fortress. But could Jack truly trust the gatekeeper herself?

No. He would merely pretend that he could.

"You're positive that you wouldn't like around-the-clock protection?"

"Positive."

"Okay. You'll let no one in, not a soul, without notifying Scotland Yard first."

"I've already made that promise."

"Just checking. I do want you to carry the pepper spray, as well as a personal alarm. And in addition to writing them down, and carrying them with you always, I want you to commit to what I'm assuming is your photographic memory a few important phone numbers—mine—my office at Scotland Yard, my hotel room at the Drake, the pager I'm going to wear. Agreed?"

"Yes. Agreed. Thank you, Jack."

Jack looked at her, this impeccably bred lady who was offering her gratitude, her formal words of thanks—but who seemed truly amazed that he was concerned for her welfare.

They were separated still, by the stark expanse of her pure white bed, the place where Sarah dreamed—or was haunted by nightmares—all alone.

But wearing my shirt, Jack thought.

Her hands were touching his shirt still, resting on that single spot of color in the vast whiteness of the room.

Not the only color, Jack amended as he met green eyes that glittered brightly, bravely, with hope. And now, in response to her polite, amazed words of gratitude, he smiled, and answered, very gently, "You're most welcome, Lady Pembroke."

Chapter Fourteen

Gemstone Recording Studio
Waverton Street, London
Tuesday, December Twenty-seventh

C OLE CHOSE TO WAIT UNTIL THE END OF the night's rehearsal to inform the band of his decision to have Claire sing with him. The decision was Cole's alone to make. It was his name, his voice, that made them all so very rich.

But since Cole knew that the response of the band would be surprise, perhaps even anger, he elected to defer the announcement until the end of one of the few remaining rehearsals before New Year's Eve. The upcoming concert mattered, Cole's music mattered, above all else. It had been that way from the very beginning, from that day, six years before, when he presented himself to Hollywood's premier talent agency.

Cole Taylor's path to superstardom was a legend within the music industry, well known to the elite inner circle, but not highly publicized beyond. He was the exception that shattered every rule, a true overnight sensation. If any of Tinseltown's talent agencies or recording companies believed that it was even remotely possible that another Cole Taylor—another gold mine—would just stroll in off the street, they would have kept their doors open twenty-four hours a day.

But it *wasn't* remotely possible. And to advertise what he

had done would merely cause a flood of Cole Taylor wanna-bes. So they kept the legendary story to themselves. . . .

"I'm a singer. I'd like a recording contract."

Those were Cole's first words, spoken as soon as he and Elayne Seymour were alone in the inner sanctum of her opulent office. He had appeared at Meteor Talent Agency without an appointment. Such drop-in visitors were normally triaged in one of two ways. If the prospective client looked at all promising, a determination reserved for a rare few, he or she would be told what was necessary to even be *considered* for an appointment—a professional portfolio, résumé, and photographs. More likely, the aspiring star would be sent back outside, to the sunbaked pavement of Wilshire Boulevard, never to shadow Meteor's doorway again.

But Elayne herself had been breezing through the agency's reception area, caught a glimpse of the black-haired, granite-eyed man whose sensuality literally steamed up the room, and ushered him into her office.

During the short journey she had already begun marketing him, imagining the lucrative assignments that could be his. Print ads, she decided. He would go right to the top. He was stunning in what he wore now, faded jeans and denim work shirt, and there was absolutely no doubt that he would be equally devastating in both more and less. It wouldn't matter. As long as he wore that face, that body, he could sell anything. And if the product happened to be named "Passion's Inferno" or "Midnight Desire," its sales would go sky-high.

Could he act? Elayne wondered. Again, it scarcely mattered. He could just be himself, a portrait of sex, of danger, of arrogance and anger. A rogue, she thought. A rebel. But as she saw the stone-hard expression that accompanied his pronouncement that he wanted to sing, Elayne was compelled to amend her assessment slightly. This was not your usual petulant, purposeless—and immensely profitable—Hollywood rebel. He was something else, something quite rare: a rebel *with* a cause.

"A singer?" she echoed. This was the new era of music, the

epoch of MTV. Performance videos were part of the business. He would be spectacular in that forum, of course; any visual of the astonishingly sensual creature who stood before her would definitely help sales. But superstardom in music was the trickiest career path of all. "Someday, perhaps, but why don't we start you out as a model? Maybe even get you some acting lessons?"

"No."

"*No?* Modeling can be extremely lucrative, even for a man. It's competitive. Cutthroat. But I'm telling you right now that I can get you assignments—good ones—as early as today."

"No modeling. No acting. Just singing."

Elayne drew a steadying breath, and smiled. "Okay. Tell me where you've performed."

Beside the blue waters of the bayou . . . at the Harlanville Christmas pageant. "Nowhere."

Cole hadn't sung a note in six years, not since the afternoon spent perfecting the never-sung song of love for Claire. So what *had* Cole Taylor done since that December night when he had vanished into the storm, when he had allowed the pelting rain to wash the thick coat of blood from his shivering skin? The years were mostly blurred—by drugs, by alcohol, by loss. But there had been bursts of purpose, the memories of which remained vividly clear despite the misty haze.

Cole's first task had been to heal his crippled right hand. He treated the injury himself, as an animal would tend its wounds, acting on instinct, heedless of pain. He kept it clean by dousing it with disinfectants—alcohol and iodine. Such care ignited liquid fire in the open wounds, searing, burning—but, miraculously, preventing serious infection.

Cole knew that his hand would never be the same, its strength irrevocably impaired, but there appeared to be two options for the way in which it could ultimately heal. If he immobilized his hand while the scar tissue matured, an approach that would be accompanied by almost no pain, the result would be a claw, frozen forever into a slight clench and totally useless.

Cole chose the more painful route, enduring a course of self-imposed physical therapy that was far more rigorous than any doctor would have prescribed, reopening the wound without mercy, breaking the scar tissue before it hardened, compelling it to loosen and stretch. The result was a hand that was weak but mobile . . . a hand that could no longer write, or play a guitar, or even hold a full bottle of whiskey . . . but could caress still, could touch, could feel, could love.

At the same time that Cole worked to salvage what could be salvaged of his right hand, he undertook the training of his left. For nineteen years, it had been strong but not terribly agile, a helpmate to the right. The process of retraining was surprisingly difficult, enragingly frustrating—but eventually successful.

Cole's right arm retained its power above the wrist, and his left became powerful and agile throughout, and Cole put both limbs to work, assigning them physical labor that was more harsh, more severe, than any he might have encountered had he killed his father on purpose and been condemned to a chain gang by a jury of his peers. For six years, he toiled, going from job to job, from state to state, farther and ever farther away from Louisiana.

Until the day he returned to Harlanville, unable—or perhaps simply unwilling—to resist. The day. *That* day. Her wedding day.

Cole spent less than twenty minutes in the bayou town that had once been his home, and as he turned his back on Harlanville the vision of his stone-gray eyes seemed hopelessly blurred. But Cole knew where he was going, and precisely what he was going to do. He would sing, just as Claire had always predicted *they* would sing, dazzling audiences around the world, selling albums in record numbers, winning Grammys and Oscars, and . . . *why?*

To spite her? No. *No.* To celebrate her, perhaps, to keep her memory close by living her dream. Claire was living the more important dream, the only one that mattered, of family and of love. But this less important dream was left for Cole.

It was half a dream without her. Not even half. But a fraction of a dream was all the dream he would ever have.

Elayne Seymour looked at the purposeful rebel who stood before her. "I don't even know your name."

"Cole Taylor."

"Well, Cole Taylor, you want to be a singer? Why the hell not? By the way, can you sing?"

"Yes. I can sing."

Cole sang, a cappella, for three of Gemstone Records' top producers. The audition was held as a favor to Elayne, who handled some of their most successful artists, and all three producers had already mentally scripted their apologies to her.

Her client needed experience, they would say. A few years crooning in smoky dives. He needed to pay his dues—*just like everyone else.*

But even before Cole Taylor started to sing for them, the three producers shared a similar thought. The solemn twenty-five-year-old might not have logged any hours in smoky dives. But he most definitely had paid his dues—far more, already, than most men twice his age.

Still, they didn't give him a break. They asked him to perform "I Will Always Love You," the song that had set new standards of success throughout the industry, and that no one else dared to sing. But as they listened to Cole's stunningly emotional rendition, once again the producers shared a common thought: What if Cole Taylor had recorded that song?

Cole was offered a contract with Gemstone on the spot, a substantial offer to which he responded with absolute calm, as if he had expected as much, as if he were on a mission that could not be denied. He had requirements of them, these people who were going to make him a star.

He wanted privacy; and the right to sing only songs he chose; and he wanted it written into his contract that he would always sing alone. No duets. Not ever.

"But your voice and Barbra's would be *magic.* And what about Dolly? Or Whitney—"

"No duets. I sing alone."

"But you'll sing with backup singers, right? You'll be willing to perform with a band? That's really necessary, Cole, both for concerts and albums. You can have anyone you want, a group of your friends, *whoever.*"

Cole had no friends. But he acceded to Gemstone's wish that he have a band. They were willing to facilitate the process, to parade musical groups—or even individual musicians—before him, to be interviewed by him, to be found personally acceptable, compatible, or not.

Personal compatibility did not matter to Cole, nor did age, sex, race, or physical appearance. Musical compatibility was the only criterion. As a result, he selected his backup band simply by listening to performance tapes.

The band was Amethyst, a group already in the Gemstone stable. Amethyst's success had been less than expected. Despite the talent of its three members, and the indisputable attractiveness of two of the three, the listening public had not been bewitched. They were missing that magic ingredient, a lead singer whose voice was absolutely *necessary* to the hearts of millions.

Cole provided that voice, that magic, and now, six years and six albums later, the once little-known members of Amethyst had all been catapulted to stratospheric fame. Because of the celebrity of Sydney Quinn, Mick Maitland—and even, remarkably, David Slater—Cole was able to enjoy his own all-important privacy. He was grateful for the popularity of Amethyst, and generously enhanced it. Thanks to Cole, David was recognized as a premier lead guitarist, a talent to rival Eric Clapton; and the past three albums had featured songs written and performed by Sydney and Mick. And, naturally, all three band members had become fabulously wealthy.

Unless Cole was in the company of the band, he was virtually anonymous, a chameleon who so artfully blended with his surroundings that he was scarcely noticed. Onstage, he always wore black. But in public, he wore generic jeans, or restrained ensembles of jackets and slacks. His coal-black hair was only slightly long, not a flowing mane, and although his vision was quite perfect, he frequently donned horn-rimmed glasses, a gift from Ashley Alexander, the actress with whom he shared the closest thing to friendship since Claire.

"Glasses like these are all that separated Clark Kent from Superman, after all," Ashley teased. "They'll *work*, Cole. You'll see. You'll be absolutely incognito—especially if you wear your Ivy League clothes."

People, *women*, looked at him, of course. Even the most conservative attire and scholarly glasses could not mask his allure. But he was rarely recognized as the man whose voice seduced their hearts and touched their souls.

Cole's relationship with his band, as with his public, was cordial but remote—and definitely distinct. They were Cole Taylor *and* Amethyst, singer and backup band, not a musical group with four equal parts. They were not, nor would they ever be, Obsidian—a name change suggested in celebration of him, a perfect name, it seemed, for a man with coal-black hair and stone-hard eyes . . . and who smoldered with volcanic passions.

Quietly but emphatically Cole had resisted the name, had resisted becoming one of them. He remained separate, distinct. Cole Taylor would survive—flourish—without Amethyst. Despite the individual fame of the members of the band, the reverse was not necessarily true. Which meant that Cole called the shots. He accepted their input, adapted whenever he could. But ultimately the decisions were his.

And now, at 6:00 A.M., as their all-night rehearsal drew to a close, Cole informed the members of Amethyst of the most recent unilateral decision he had made.

"Beginning with the concert on New Year's Eve, someone else will be singing with me."

As expected, the announcement was greeted with surprise. Sydney, Mick, and David all knew of Cole's firm resolve never to sing duets. In fact, less than a month ago, they had witnessed firsthand his refusal of a seductive, and then frankly aggressive, invitation to sing *just one love song* with one of the world's top-selling female vocalists.

"You caved in after all?" Sydney arched an eyebrow. It was an exquisitely beautiful eyebrow, as was everything about Sydney Quinn. Her eyes, for which the band had been

named, were truly a brilliant purple, and her hair, untouched
by dyes of any sort, was really platinum blond. She was a
natural beauty, so natural, so fresh, that—for fun—she had
done a guest spot on *Baywatch*, playing a lifeguard visiting
from Honolulu, tan, sleek, sunny, fit. But it was the cover of
Cosmopolitan, and her own cover-girl looks, that resulted in
the nickname—*Elle Syd*—by which she had become known
around the world. Now Amethyst's drummer, keyboardist,
and sometimes actress and cover girl, was affecting a teasing
pout. "How could you *do* this to us, Cole? You know her
reputation, her *ego*—"

"It's not her."

"Meaning you've finally seen the light and are going to sing
duets with our very own Syd?"

The question was unassuming, as all queries from David Slater
invariably were. David looked like death, painfully thin, worri-
somely sallow. In the music world, grim diagnoses came immediately to mind: a diet more rich in amphetamines—specifically
crystal meth—than in calories; the ravages of AIDS; cachexia re-
sulting from a lifestyle that was nocturnal, dissolute, antithetical
to every normal biorhythm. In fact, David was extremely healthy,
a rigorous vegetarian and marathon-caliber runner. His devotion
to purity of body—and of soul—compelled him to forsake chem-
ical intrusions of any kind.

Of the three members of Amethyst, Cole felt closest to
David. Not that they had ever shared anything even remotely
personal. But of all of them, Cole had decided that he and
David were most alike—dedicated musicians who kept their
own counsel and in whom the still waters of their public de-
meanor ran private and deep.

There was, however, one unconcealable truth about David.
His adoration of Sydney. Cole guessed that at some time David
and Sydney had been lovers, as had she and Mick, and that
David still carried a torch for her. It was always in the context
of Sydney that David broke his usual silence, as he was doing
now by asking if the woman with whom Cole had decided to
sing duets was Elle Syd herself.

The campaign for a Cole-and-Sydney duet, quietly spearheaded by David and forcefully endorsed by Mick, was not new. But because it was so important for Amethyst not to anger their superstar, the crusade had been one of subtle prodding, not overt exasperation. No one had demanded, for example, why a musician as gifted as Cole couldn't tell that his voice and Syd's, both so smoky and sultry, would be stunning together.

"Apparently not," Sydney offered finally, and with a smile, as she read the apology on Cole's face. "So who's the lucky lady, Cole? You *are* planning to sing duets with a woman, aren't you?"

"Her name is Claire Chamberlain."

"*Never* heard of her."

Mick Maitland made no attempt to hide his skepticism. Of the Amethyst trio, Mick was by far the least politic, the least careful about annoying their superstar. Cole knew the reason for Mick's disdain. As the band's lead singer before Cole, it was *he* who should have propelled Amethyst to at least minor fame. But Mick had failed—inexplicably, because there was absolutely nothing wrong with Mick Maitland's singing voice, or with the way he played the guitar. And his striking good looks, at once classic and sensual, could not be denied.

The antithesis of David, Mick was the portrait of health. His shoulder-length brown hair glittered with kisses from the California sun, and every muscle in his body was sculpted with elaborate care. Indeed, in an unlikely meeting of the minds, the editors of *Rolling Stone*, *Vanity Fair*, and *Gentleman's Quarterly* had described his appearance as "flawless, utterly male." In its debut year, Mick's calendar had actually outsold the Fabio offering in most markets, and there were constant calls from movie executives. But Mick had no intention of abandoning his music career—or Amethyst. Was Mick waiting, Cole wondered, for the day when fans would demand that Mick, not Cole, become the principal singer of love songs? The day when Cole Taylor would fall, would *fail*?

"No, Mick," Cole conceded. "You wouldn't have heard of Claire. She teaches music in a small town in Louisiana."

"*Excuse* me? Was there some queen-for-a-day sing-with-the-superstar contest that we didn't hear about?"

"Claire and I have known each other since we were kids. We sang together then." Cole anticipated the next question and answered it. "And we sang together again two days before Christmas." Then, addressing other issues that he knew would arise, in their minds if not aloud, he said, "This won't have any impact on your income. I'm going to pay Claire directly from my share."

"What songs are the two of you going to sing?"

"I'm not sure yet, I'll need to check with her, but I'm thinking about 'Somewhere Over the Rainbow' and 'When You Wish Upon a Star.' "

"I beg your pardon?" Mick's hostility was unconcealed, a lack of control, and of discretion, that wasn't helped by his addiction to drugs. Mick Maitland, portrait of health, was a true connoisseur of foreign substances. As a matter of routine, he imbibed, smoked, snorted, and even shot the latest designer concoctions. Once an expert himself, and once, too, a connoisseur, Cole knew well the danger of drugs, the insidiousness of the damage they caused. But Mick was not interested in sage advice from the singer who had achieved all that he could not.

"Those aren't exactly love songs, Cole," Sydney offered.

"No, they're not."

They're two of the songs that she and I sang in our forest beside the bayou. Two of her favorites.

Claire had loved all types of music, but was particularly fond of musicals. She seemed to know them all, and Cole—who had long since banished music from his life—knew none. But that was of no consequence to Claire. She was an enthusiastic teacher, and he was a quick study, and whenever they sang her musicals, she insisted that they sing the entire soundtrack, in order, never skipping a song.

Which meant that then, and quite by accident, Cole and Claire sang songs of love. "Some Enchanted Evening" from *South Pacific.* "Till There Was You" from *Music Man.* "Somewhere" from *West Side Story.* But then, as children, all that mattered was the purity of their young voices. The lyrics had little meaning.

Cole and Claire were adults now, and even their duet of "Silent Night" had shimmered with intimacy. And if they sang songs of love, longing, of need? Claire would know that every love song he had ever sung had been sung to her, impassioned confessions of his love still. Always. His *impossible* love.

I have nothing to offer her. The reminder was punishingly harsh. Nothing—except for this unimportant dream that I'm living, and the night-black violence of my heart.

"I decided that 'Somewhere Over the Rainbow' and 'When You Wish Upon a Star' would be good songs for New Year's Eve."

"They're terrific, Cole," Mick scoffed. "Truly inspirational. But we're not in the show-tune business, remember? And New Year's Eve? Are you *kidding*? We're going to perfect two new songs in just four days?"

"No, Mick, I don't expect that. Claire and I won't need musical accompaniment for the duets."

"You mean on New Year's Eve? Or ever? Are you trying to tell us something, Cole? Is the marriage of Cole Taylor and Amethyst heading for an ugly divorce?"

"No. Claire and I will just sing the two songs on New Year's Eve. The remainder of the concert will be exactly what we've planned—except that I'm pulling 'Imagine Moonlight.' "

"Pulling 'Imagine Moonlight'?" Sydney echoed, shocked. "You *can't*. It's still at the top of all the charts. Everyone will be expecting to hear you sing it."

"Everyone can hear me sing it all day every day on the radio." *And I can't sing "Imagine Moonlight," not with Claire anywhere nearby. If I do, she'll realize that I wrote it for her, a final farewell to our love.*

"Does Timothy Asquith know you're planning to omit Gemstone's all-time number-one recording?"

"Timothy doesn't decide what songs I sing. No one does." Cole's voice held an unmistakable note of warning. "I expect you all to welcome Claire."

Sydney smiled. "*Of course* we'll welcome her, Cole."

"And I want you all to help her."

"Help her?"

How he hated this, saying these words aloud. Cole wanted gentler words, a gentler truth for Claire, ones that offered even the faintest glimmer of light. *She doesn't see very well. Her world is a little gray, a bit shadowy.*

But that wasn't truth. *She doesn't see at all. Her world is black.*

"She will need your help," he said softly, hating his own voice . . . that voice that had made them all so famous and so rich. "Claire is blind."

Chapter Fifteen

Eight forty-five, they had agreed before Jack left yesterday afternoon. That was when he would arrive in Mayfair to accompany her to work. Jack knew the building's security code, but at precisely 8:45 he punched in a different combination of numbers, ones that rang the telephone in her penthouse.

"Hi. It's Jack. Shall I wait here or come up?"

"You can come up if you like, but it will be a minute before I can buzz you in. I have to call Scotland Yard first, to notify them that I have a visitor."

Jack answered the tease in her voice with a smile. "Very nice, Sarah. Very cooperative."

"I told you I would be. Is the limousine already there?"

"Yes."

"Then I'll just come down."

The Rolls-Royce limousine was provided by the network, a luxurious precaution that predated the threat posed by the black heart. Sarah was a celebrity, and therefore a target. Timothy Asquith was determined to keep his star reporter as safe—and as happy—as possible.

Jack had planned to tell Sarah during the drive from Grosvenor Square to Belvedere Road who he was going to be, the pretense he would use to explain his frequent presence in her office—and in her life. The plan already bore the imprimatur of both the commissioner of Scotland Yard and Glo-bal News Network's billionaire CEO. And Jack hoped, based on the light tease that had greeted him, that Sarah would accept his plan without protest—and perhaps even with a smile.

But the tease was merely a bewitching memory. The Sarah Pembroke who sat beside him in the limousine was a silent creature, intensely serious and apprehensive, with an anxiety that seemed to crescendo as they crossed the Thames via Waterloo Bridge and the shining silver glass of Asquith Towers came into view. The shimmering edifice was where Sarah worked, where she was the *star*. Was it actually possible that she dreaded the day that lay ahead?

When they stood on the pavement of Belvedere Road, before the building that housed the most influential news organization in the world, Jack finally broke the silence. He asked the question for which he already had the answer, but he posed it anyway—conspiratorially—a reminder to Sarah that, together, they were going to solve the mystery of the black-hearted killer.

"Who shall I be, Sarah?" *An acquaintance from America? A lover from Paris?* When his question merely caused confusion, Jack clarified, "The killer may be someone you work with. You can't really introduce me as the FBI consultant who's here to help Scotland Yard with the case."

"No. But it won't come up."

With that, Sarah looked away from him and toward the graceful arch of the building's main entrance. Her expression was quite extraordinary. It was, Jack supposed, the way that someone—with great courage and pride—might face a firing squad. Courage, pride, and dread.

It made no sense. Asquith Towers should have been a symbol of all that Sarah Pembroke had achieved. It should have been her home. Jack had assumed, had hoped, that it would be.

Haunted by the desolate memories of her penthouse, he had convinced himself that where Sarah truly lived, where she smiled and flourished and thrived, was at her office.

But that was clearly not the case. And within moments of walking into the shining granite lobby, Jack knew why. The reason was mirrored on the faces of everyone they encountered: Lady Sarah Pembroke was not liked. Not at all. Not even a little bit. When some greeting was inevitable, when it was impossible *not* to say something, the words of her co-workers were curt and cool.

Was Sarah a known tyrant? Jack wondered. An impeccably bred lady subject to venomous fits of pique? Was she imperious—and merciless—with subordinates, firing them for even the slightest mistake?

Jack had no doubt that Sarah was a perfectionist. But he guessed that her demands for perfection were first and foremost placed on herself.

And, Jack realized, there was no fear on the faces of her co-workers, no latent terror that Lady Sarah Pembroke might suddenly issue a command that could cost them their jobs. Indeed, if there was fear at all, it belonged to Sarah. She was the stranger in this alien world, the pariah, the outcast. *She* was the one who did not fit in.

There should have been friends for Sarah here, colleagues who embraced her with admiration and respect, and with whom she could even share the personal aspects of her life. But the star journalist had no friends here. No friends anywhere.

It was something Jack should have known. The woman who had been alone at Christmas was alone—always.

Not anymore, Sarah. I'm here. I care. I want to be your friend . . . if you'll let me.

Jack's smile of reassurance went unseen. Sarah was too distracted to notice it, too wary. The warrior was making her way through a minefield. And if in that field of mines there lurked an assassin with a knife? She would not notice that lethal peril until it was far too late.

But Sarah Pembroke was not going to be attacked within

these glittering silver walls. Even if the killer was here, and had decided on a seduction in her office, not her home, it couldn't happen. The security in Asquith Towers was simply too good.

Yes, one could get in with a bottle of Cristale and blood-red roses. But a hunting knife, even a penknife, could not elude the ultrasensitive metal detectors, manned by armed guards, through which all who entered the building were required to pass.

Sarah could not be murdered here. She could only be deeply wounded by the people who so clearly did not want to be her friends.

By the time they reached the twenty-eighth floor, Jack knew that Sarah had already run a gauntlet of sorts. Her pace quickened as they neared her office, as if she had almost made it. Soon, very soon, she could retreat behind a tightly closed door.

Did she even remember that he was beside her? She *would* remember, Jack vowed. As soon as they were secluded, alone, in the inner sanctum of her office. He would wait until she focused on him, truly saw him, then he would tell her the truth.

I'm your friend, Sarah. Her eyes would flash, surprised, disbelieving, and with the faintest glimmer of hope. And to that hope, Jack would repeat the words, very slowly this time, the most solemn of promises. *I am your friend.*

Jack's plan was preempted twelve feet from the doorway of Sarah's sanctuary.

"Adrian wants to see you," her secretary announced. That was the only greeting, and it held an unmistakable note of anticipation—as if her boss was in trouble, and *she* was secretly pleased. "He's in your office."

Jack had decided that, wholly distracted by her own private war, Sarah had forgotten his presence. But he was wrong. She turned to him and offered a quiet apology. "I guess I'll have to ask you to wait out here for a few moments."

"That's fine." Jack smiled the tender smile that had been born, in Paris, just for her. "I'm entirely at your disposal."

After choosing the *London Times* from the selection of newspapers in the reception area, Jack settled on a nearby couch. He had been quite aware of the curious stare that had been following his every move, and before he read a single word, Sarah's secretary spoke.

"Would you like some coffee, Mr.—or is it Officer. . . ?"

"It's Mr. My name is Jack Dalton. And no, thank you, to coffee."

Jack made a quick assessment of the woman who, at the very least, resented her role as Sarah's secretary. Young. Pretty. And smart, Jack decided. And curious. He put aside the *Times*, far more interested in the kind of news she might impart than in the world events of the day.

"There *was* a police officer here," she insisted. "Before the holidays."

"Yes. I know. It was a false alarm."

"Oh. So who are you then, Mr. Dalton?" she pressed, confirming Jack's impression that she undoubtedly aspired to Sarah's job and couldn't resist the chance to practice her investigative skills. "Someone she's interviewing for a story?"

"No. And please call me Jack."

"All right. And I'm Frances." With a questioning tilt of her head, she asked, "Sarah's *not* interviewing you?"

"No, in fact, it's just the opposite. I'll be doing the interviewing. I'm writing a book about Sarah."

"But . . ."

"But?"

"I mean, she *knows*? Mr. Asquith knows?"

"Yes." It was a half-truth. Sarah didn't know about the pretense, the false identity that Jack Dalton would assume. But Global's owner did. "Why does that surprise you?"

"Well, it's just that I thought Sarah absolutely refused to have a book done about her. Ever. The last time the idea was broached, by Mr. Asquith himself, she flatly said no." Frances arched a provocative eyebrow. "I'd always believed that Timothy Asquith was the world's most persuasive man. But I guess maybe you are."

"Who I am, Frances, is Sarah's friend."

Jack had planned the words for Sarah, and had anticipated surprise and disbelief. But now he spoke them to Frances—who was stunned. Sarah's *friend*? Impossible! The ice queen doesn't have friends, *especially* not a man like you.

Quite suddenly the would-be reporter's perplexed expression transformed to one of glowing triumph. "*You're* the sender of red roses, aren't you? *You're* Sarah's mystery man. I never really quite believed—" Frances stopped with a gasp. "I mean, well, you have wonderful taste. In roses."

"Thank you," Jack replied with deceptive calm. "You think Sarah likes them?"

"I *know* she does. But why don't you ever sign your name?"

"Don't you think Sarah knows who they're from?"

"Yes, of course she does."

"But?"

"Well, why all the mystery? Why send instructions, and cash, but no name, to the florist? I suppose I can answer that myself, can't I? Sarah wanted your relationship to remain private. She must have told you that extravagant bouquets of roses might trigger a little curiosity around here. That someone might check to see who sent them."

"Someone—like you."

"*Please* don't tell her, Mr. Dalton. Jack? Please?"

"I won't," he promised, managing a reassuring smile despite his own private anger. No rejected suitors, Sarah had told him. No mysterious admirers. Just expensive bouquets of blood-red roses anonymously sent.

At that moment, the door to Sarah's office was flung open. The door, that inanimate object made of wood, seemed to have taken on life, emotion, a private anger that rivaled Jack's. Even before the red-faced visage of Adrian Gilbey appeared, the message of rage was loud and clear.

"*Bitch,*" Adrian hissed, a word that would have been his parting shot had Jack not blocked his path. "Who the hell are you?"

"This is Jack Dalton," Frances offered. "Jack, meet Adrian Gilbey." She looked meaningfully at Adrian as she embellished, "Jack's writing a book about Sarah. He and Sarah are friends."

Frances gave *friends* an explicitly sexy meaning: *lovers.* Adrian greeted the revelation with unconcealed surprise—and disgust.

"God help you."

With that, Adrian brushed past him. Jack didn't watch the seething retreat. His attention was on the open doorway, on Sarah.

Her face was ashen, her green eyes stricken, shadowed with such pain that they were almost black. Jack saw her anguish and comprehended it with exquisite clarity. Sarah knew *exactly* what they all felt about her; and although it hurt her deeply, terribly, to be so disliked, she accepted it, as if she were truly made of ice, not human at all, and wholly deserving of such disdain.

There was another message in Sarah's eyes, one just for Jack: What hurt most of all, at this moment, was that he was bearing witness to this most shameful truth.

Jack's anger that Sarah had lied to him about the existence of admirers—*secret* no less—dissipated swiftly. With a gentle smile, and an even gentler hand on her rigid arm, he guided her into the privacy of her office.

When they were alone, the wooden door closed securely behind them, Jack repeated the words Sarah had overheard.

"I'm your friend, Sarah." Frances had cloaked *friend* in the provocative intimacy of sex. But Jack cloaked it in something even more intimate. *Love.*

His pronouncement caused the familiar war within her, the fierce battle between the forces that commanded her to shake her head in harsh denial and the ones that clung, disbelieving, to hope. Sarah's shining black head remained absolutely still. But harshness proclaimed its victory in her voice. "You told Frances you're writing a book about me?"

"It's my cover story, a plausible explanation for why I'll be around, talking to your colleagues and meeting with you."

Why does this bother you? Jack wondered. You're the mistress of falsehoods. And yet this lie, so inconsequential compared to the others, is obviously upsetting to you. "It's a necessary lie, Sarah. If you like, if it would make you feel better about the pretense, I'd be happy to actually begin writing about you."

"*No.* No. It's just, I wonder, could we amend what you're doing to a book about all twentieth-century war correspondents, something like that?"

"Sure," Jack agreed easily.

But he was amazed by her request. It didn't matter. *There would never be a book.* It was all a ruse. And yet even the idea of someone writing about her was so troubling that she wanted the lie to be altered. *Why?* Was Sarah fearful of what a biography might reveal? Or was she just convinced that there was so little of interest to say about her? A chapter at best, but not—never—an entire book.

Jack could write volumes about Lady Sarah Pembroke, beginning this moment, before he received even one scrap of the information requested from Scotland Yard: a dossier on the Valentine's Day killer's next victim, everything that could be uncovered about Sarah's past. Was it a necessary request? An essential piece of the professional puzzle? Or was it merely personal, the search for clues to the mystery of the woman-warrior?

Would Jack Dalton, murder maven, have made a similar request if the next victim had been someone else, someone he didn't love? *Yes.* Because that was the way he found killers, by overlooking nothing, by pursuing every conceivable link. The FBI consultant with a gift for finding murderers needed to know everything he could about Lady Sarah Pembroke.

But she would hate me if she knew. It would feel to her like a betrayal of trust, a shattering of promises. Just like all the other promises I'm shattering. I have to, Sarah. *I have to.*

"The part about the book may be false, Sarah, but what I told Frances about being your friend is the absolute truth."

His words, or perhaps the rawness in his voice, caused the battle within her to rage anew. Hope—battered but not quite dead—valiantly reentered the fray. The struggle was furious for a while. But finally, *finally*, there was a little calm, a shaky truce, and her cheeks, which had been the stark white of surrender, bloomed a pale, delicate pink.

"Thank you," she whispered, as she had whispered in her bedroom, a blend of gratitude and disbelief.

And now as then, gently, and with a smile, he answered, "You're very welcome. So my first question as your biographer—and as your friend—is who the hell is Adrian and what's his problem?"

Sarah answered Jack's vehemence with a trembling smile. "He's the producer of the *International News Hour,* and his problem is me. Adrian and I have artistic differences about what constitutes appropriate—newsworthy—visual imagery."

"Let me guess. Adrian believes that colorful footage of dead bodies, the more graphic the better, enhances the story." It was more than a guess. Sarah Pembroke's reports from war were conspicuous for their lack of gratuitous violence. "And you believe that such photographs are an unacceptable invasion of privacy."

"Yes, and . . ."

"And?"

"Well, the dead aren't truly the story, are they? The survivors are. They suffer still, hurt still. But the dead are lucky. They're at peace."

Lucky? Jack was stunned by the word—and by the absolute seriousness with which Sarah spoke it. True, the dead no longer suffered, no longer felt pain.

But to believe that those whose lives were over were luckier than those who lived was a grim pronouncement for a twenty-eight-year-old woman to make. Quite obviously, however, it was what Sarah believed. And not only, Jack decided, in the context of war. Her words were intensely personal.

The ex–Mrs. Simon Beckwith-Jones was not, Jack knew, tormented by the death of her husband. So who was it she had lost, and for whom she suffered still, and who she needed so desperately to believe was lucky—and at peace? Her parents? Or someone else she had loved?

"It sounds like you know."

"I've been there, Jack. I've been to war."

And she was going there now, becoming the warrior again, shielding herself, shutting him out. So Jack resumed their discussion of the apparently safely impersonal battle with her producer.

"How will the artistic differences with Adrian be resolved?"

"We'll do it my way. I agreed to become the network's anchor with the proviso that I have editorial control over everything—script and visuals. Apparently the memorandum from Timothy Asquith detailing that agreement went out yesterday afternoon."

"And if Adrian's next stop is Timothy Asquith's office?"

"It probably will be. But it won't matter. When Timothy agrees to something, it's etched in stone."

Jack and Sarah spent the next two hours touring her workplace. With each step, from the vast stretches of deserted granite corridors to the immense tomblike library of documents and film, Jack reminded himself of the building's state-of-the-art security system. Even if the killer worked within these silver walls, he could not strike her—at least not with his preferred weapon of death. Besides, in all likelihood, the knife-wielding madman had not yet made his appearance in Sarah's life. He would be arriving from Los Angeles, a man so famous in his own right that Sarah would be intrigued to meet him.

Still, as they stood on the set of Global's evening newscast, pitch-black now and vacant, a killer's dream locale in which to accost and slay, Jack asked, "Do you have the pepper spray?"

"In my office."

"You should carry it with you at all times."

"He's not going to come after me here."

"Humor me, Sarah. Please."

"Yes . . . all right."

The final stop on their tour of Sarah's workplace was far more ominous than the darkest shadows of the broadcast studio. It was the rooftop, her own secret haven. Just one small step from death forty floors below.

She could be so lost in the glory of the view, or so relaxed far away from disapproving eyes, that she would abandon her wariness, would not hear the stealthy footsteps—

"Promise me that you won't come up here, Sarah, except with me, until this is all over."

"Except with you?"

"Except with me," Jack affirmed. "This seems like a good place for us to meet. We can talk privately here, and we will need to talk, Sarah, to share developments, significant or otherwise."

"You mean like my arguments with Adrian?"

"Exactly like that."

"That was hardly significant."

Meaning that such encounters were commonplace, Jack thought, minor—but exhausting—skirmishes in her ongoing battle to do what she believed was right.

"Maybe not," Jack agreed. "Probably not. But let's make that judgment together. I need to hear everything, Sarah. Everything."

And you're not going to tell me, are you? You're too ashamed of what such disputes mean, of how disliked you are. You don't want me to know . . . even if it kills you.

"Tell me who sends you roses."

"Roses?"

"*Dammit*, Sarah. I know that someone has been sending you expensive bouquets of roses. *Blood*-red roses. And I even know that they're sent anonymously. But I have a feeling that you know the identity of the sender. Am I right?"

She couldn't look at him, couldn't meet his dangerously invasive—and dangerously tender—dark blue eyes.

She turned away instead and stared across the Thames toward the majestic silhouette of Westminster Abbey.

"Yes," she admitted, speaking to the spires that pierced the dappled pewter sky. "You're right. I do know. But you'll just have to trust me when I say that the person who's sending me roses is—" *not a killer* "—no one you need to worry about."

Not a killer. Sarah intercepted the words before speaking yet another lie. In fact, the sender of roses *was* a killer, the worst kind, one whose victim had been an innocent unborn life. It hadn't been a calculated murder. She had tried *so hard* to nurture that tiny being, that precious son. But in the end she had failed.

"The sender of the roses is no one you need to worry about, Jack," she repeated, her voice as gray now, as cold and wintry, as the December sky.

Jack heard her anguish, the despair that dwelled in her wounded heart. And he knew the truth. *Oh, but she is*, he thought. *The sender of the roses is the person I worry about, care about, most of all.*

Sarah sent the roses to herself. Of that, Jack had no doubt. But why? There were wonderful reasons, of course. Such a lavish gift to oneself could symbolize glowingly healthy self-esteem—justifiable pride in one's accomplishments and a robust confidence that was hard earned and well deserved.

But Jack did not believe it was buoyant self-confidence that prompted Sarah to send roses to herself. Rather it was despair, and sadness, and loneliness, and pain. She needed to prove something to the people with whom she worked, these women and men who were not her friends. She didn't need to convince them of her intelligence. If so, she would have long since displayed her Pegasus puzzles for all to see. The staff of Global News *knew* that Sarah Pembroke was brilliant, a warrior beyond compare. But what they didn't know, and what Sarah wanted desperately for them to see, was that she was a woman, *worthy* of being loved. Even though it was a lie.

"Okay," Jack said. Then speaking a lie of his own, he added, "I trust you. I won't push. But just so you know, as of this morning Frances—and therefore everyone else?—believes that I'm your secret admirer. And, Sarah, that's something I don't plan to deny."

Sarah trembled at his gentleness. Jack Dalton was so dangerous to her heart, far more lethal than the vicious slashes of a jagged-edged knife. Did he realize that she sent the roses to herself? Yes, she believed he did. The master puzzle solver had deduced her shameful neediness—and yet it didn't seem to matter, didn't make him withdraw in disgust.

Why was he being so kind to her? Because he truly cared?

No! He needs your help, that's all. He's in London to catch a killer, and you just happen to be that madman's bait, the most important clue to this challenging riddle of death. Something about you is beckoning to the killer, some hidden longing, perhaps, some secret desire that you share with the other victims.

And you know, don't you, how Jack is going to discover that all-important link? By learning everything he can about you—and your heart. He'll take it apart as if it were a Pegasus puzzle, piece by quivering piece. And when he finds shards that don't seem to fit, and are of no use to him at all, he'll simply toss them away. You're disposable, *remember*?

Sarah had been staring at the piercing spires of Westminster, not his piercing blue eyes. But now she turned to him—and saw a gentleness that matched his voice. *False* gentleness, she reminded herself. Merely a ploy to convince me to expose my damaged heart, to reveal whatever clues to the puzzle of death might be hiding there.

"You know what would be really clever, Jack?"

The warrior was on attack now, a valiant—and somehow necessary?—assault of pure fury. As if she were a general who had just discovered a spy within her ranks.

"No, Sarah. What?"

"For the killer to be the man assigned to solve the case, the expert who seems above reproach, who has keys to the victim's home, and asks whatever questions he wishes, and himself is never challenged."

"You want to challenge me?"

"Yes." *No. I want to believe you, the part that's telling me this is far more than a puzzle to you, far more than a game . . . the part that seems to be saying that even when this is all over you will be here still.*

"Go ahead, Lady Pembroke. Challenge me."

He won't be here. You know he won't. "All right. Tell me where you were last Valentine's Day."

Jack sighed. "What are you doing, Sarah?"

"What? No alibi, Jack?"

"I was in Virginia, with a woman, an attorney who works in Washington."

"So you spent the night making love in front of a roaring fire?"

"No." His voice was fierce with frustration. "That was only how I had hoped to spend the night. In fact, we argued. She'd decided it was time to make more permanent plans for our relationship—and I wasn't interested."

"Your interest was limited to getting her into bed? Is that your specialty, Jack?"

"Why are you doing this, Sarah? What's the point?"

Sarah frowned, and then smiled. "There's no point. Just conversation. Just getting to know you better. But I do have work to do. I really should get back to the office."

She moved away from the edge of the building then, from the place that was just one push, one stumble—or one desperate, lonely leap—away from eternity, and brushed past the strong male body that had become taut with its own rigidly contained fury.

Jack might have glowered at the pewter sky, his vision veiled as much with smoke from within as from the grayness of the winter day. But instead he watched her hasty retreat—and saw what happened, the almost imperceptible fall of her proud shoulders, the slight tilt of her midnight-black head . . . and finally, the gazelle gait that slowed, faltered, and then stopped.

He walked to her, until he stood behind her, close enough to touch. But not touching. His hands were suspended in midair, above her shoulders. And yet she must have felt the heat of those hands, the power, or perhaps she was a marionette, connected to him by invisible strings, because after a moment she began to straighten, and then she turned, a ballerina's twirl of pure grace.

"I'm sorry, Jack."

"No, Sarah, I'm sorry. I shouldn't have gotten angry with you."

"Yes."

"No." Jack smiled. "I told you the cardinal rule of crime-solving, Sarah. You can't overlook anything, not even the most minute—or implausible—detail. Such as me."

She smiled at last, and for a moment they were in Paris, falling in love by the Seine on that misting day of diamonds and rainbows when the lies scarcely mattered and the menace of murder seemed very far away.

But this was London, not Paris, Jack reminded himself. And there were such important lies here, such monumental betrayals of her trust. There had to be, to keep her safe. And if she knew?

Jack felt a deep quiver of ice, followed by a hot rush of restlessness. *Show yourself,* he commanded in restive silence to the black-hearted killer. Let me put an end to your menace before my betrayal of Sarah puts an end to all hope of our love.

Jack had no expectation that his impassioned command would be obeyed. But while he and Sarah were standing on the rooftop going to war—and then falling in love again—a call had been made to her office by a man from Los Angeles, a superstar she could not refuse to meet.

Chapter Sixteen

"*T*HERE YOU ARE!" BEFORE TODAY FRANCES'S greeting might have been scolding, accusatory. But now it merely held excitement, and her expression radiated respect. Frances had learned extraordinary things about Sarah today. First, the existence of Jack, Sarah's gorgeous lover. And now this. "Cole Taylor called. *The* Cole Taylor. He wants to see you. He suggested dinner tonight, at the Drake, but if that's not convenient for you, he says he'll adjust to whatever you prefer. *Cole Taylor*, Sarah! Do you know him well?"

"What? No. Actually . . . no, I don't. I suppose Timothy's behind this," she murmured, frowning even as she spoke the words. Timothy *might* want to orchestrate a rendezvous between Gemstone Records' crown prince and Global's very own princess. But the very proper Timothy Asquith would not have done it like this. The invitation would have come from him, not from Cole.

Frances clearly concurred. "I don't think this is Mr. Asquith's idea," she said. "It sounded far more personal than that. In fact, Cole Taylor gave the reason he wanted to see you. He wants to talk to you about someone named Claire."

* * *

"How well *do* you know Cole Taylor?"

The question was Jack's, at once soft and piercing, and posed to her the moment they were alone.

"I . . . We've never met."

"Has Claire met him?"

Sarah knew what Jack was asking, and that he might understandably, *justifiably*, have raged the question at her. "Is Claire the name you use with all your men, Sarah? With Cole Taylor, and me, and countless others?" But his voice was quiet, needing to know.

"Sarah?"

"Claire is Claire Chamberlain. She and I were penmates— pen *pals*, I guess you say—when we were girls. Claire lived in Louisiana, in a small town named Harlanville, and Cole lived there, too. In Paris, when you asked me my name, hers was the one that came to mind. I've never used it before."

"Okay." Jack's easy smile rescued them all. Sarah and Jack, and Jacques and Claire. "Why would Cole want to talk to you about Claire?"

"I honestly don't know. Claire and I stopped writing twelve years ago."

"Because?"

"Because—" *my life shattered, splintered into madness* "—we grew apart."

"What about Claire and Cole?"

"I don't know anything about them now. I've read a few articles about Cole, but her name has never been mentioned."

"But was there a time, in Harlanville, when Cole and Claire were close?"

Sarah frowned thoughtfully. "The letters Claire and I exchanged were like diaries."

"Meaning you feel you might be betraying a confidence by telling me?"

Sarah's expression foreshadowed the apology in her voice. "I suppose so, especially since it doesn't—" She stopped abruptly. "Oh, but maybe it *does* matter."

"Maybe," Jack concurred quietly. "Maybe Cole Taylor's a

piece of the puzzle, and maybe he's not. But at this point it would be careless not to view him as a person of interest. Especially given his relationship with Paulina Bliss and Ashley Alexander."

"He knew them?"

"Yes. Both of them. Very well. At the time of her murder, Paulina Bliss was Cole Taylor's lover. His name is all over the police reports."

"As a suspect?"

"As someone who was questioned extensively. Cole apparently expected Paulina to come to his Malibu home late that night, and when she didn't show, and didn't answer her phone, he drove to her house in Bel Air. He couldn't get in, claims not to have had a key, and called the police from his car phone."

"But he was never charged?"

"No. Much to the chagrin of many people in the prosecutor's office. But they couldn't charge him. There simply wasn't sufficient—in fact, any—physical evidence to link him to the crime. The case would have been entirely circumstantial, a prosecutorial nightmare in any capital murder case, but especially one involving a celebrity defendant." The virtuoso puzzle solver's cobalt eyes focused the full force of their keen incisiveness on her. "You didn't know about Cole's relationship to either of the actresses, and yet I get the distinct impression that you think he could be the killer. Tell me why."

Sarah shrugged. "He's from Los Angeles, the celebrity we've been waiting for."

There was more. Jack was sure of it. Something else Sarah wasn't telling him, a confidence, perhaps, once shared with Claire.

"I take it Claire and Cole *were* close once, in Harlanville?"

"She cared about him. Very much." *And he hurt her terribly.* "But that was a long time ago. When they were teenagers."

"And now Cole is here, wanting to talk to you about her."

"Yes. And I *am* going to talk to him, Jack. I'm going to have dinner with him tonight, just as he's suggested."

"And will you be careful?"

Her unflickering eyes answered first, and in the brilliant green depths Jack saw a truth that even Sarah could not hide.

There *was* more, a troubling—and possibly lethal?—secret that she knew but would not reveal.

"Yes," she promised. "I will be careful."

From birth Sarah Pembroke was a disappointment to her parents. They wanted only one child, one distraction from the more important pleasures of their life, and they had very much hoped that their legal issue would be a son. But their baby was a girl, and she was so frail, so fragile, that it was difficult to believe that she was theirs. What had become of the genes that made them excel in all pursuits of the flesh, from the hunting of foxes to the ecstasies of sex?

Lady Sarah didn't *look* the way their daughter should, either. Her skin was sickly white, not aglow with health, and her hair was raven-black, not glittering gold, and even though from infancy her striking, aristocratic beauty was abundantly clear, it wasn't enough, *she* wasn't enough. Not for them.

Robert and Geneva Pembroke could not be bothered to waste very much of their time on their disappointing daughter. Sarah knew that. But still she tried. *Oh, how she tried.*

She would rehearse words to say when she saw them next, during those fleeting moments when they would breeze into her life. Her words were desperate, frantic; and they were often accompanied by desperate, frantic acts.

"Look at me, Mummy! I've learned to ride my bicycle all by myself. Watch me, *please*. I'm athletic, really I am, just like you and Daddy!"

But the woman who would one day run with the gracefulness of a gazelle possessed no such sleek elegance as a child. And during those rare all-important seconds when she had her parents' undivided attention, what fragile coordination she had would fail her. She would teeter and fall, disappointing them all the more, a ballerina who could not dance a single step, a tennis player who could not hit a single ball, a horseback rider who was terrified of the powerful steed she was meant to control.

It didn't matter that Lady Sarah Pembroke was terribly bright. *That* was expected. Her parents were bright as well.

What mattered was awkwardness where there should have been grace, failure where there should have been success, despair where there should have been only smug and certain calm.

This is who I am, Sarah's young heart pleaded. *Love me for who I am. Please?*

On Sarah's eighth birthday, as a gift to themselves, Earl and Lady Pembroke announced their decision to send Sarah to boarding school, to the prestigious L'Académie des Jeunes Filles in Val-d'Isère in southern France. It was for the best, they said, and Sarah agreed. Maybe in France, in a place where no one knew anything about her, she could start over, make friends. . . .

But the desperation that had become as much a part of Sarah as her dark black hair and snow-white skin was immediately apparent to her new classmates. The urgency with which she wanted to be liked drove everyone away. Sarah had no friends in Val-d'Isère, just a school full of girls who sensed that if given a chance, Sarah would want far more from them than they were prepared to give.

Sarah's third year at L'Académie marked the arrival of a teacher from Harlanville. It might be fun, the new arrival decided, not to mention educational, for her pupils to have pen pals in the United States. She wrote to Augusta Chamberlain, her own favorite teacher, and together they hatched a plan. Since fluency in French was as useful for the students in Harlanville—on the fringes of French Louisiana—as it was for the girls in Val-d'Isère, at least some portion of every letter would be written in French.

It was Sarah Pembroke's great fortune, great joy, that her name was withdrawn from Aunt Augusta's straw hat by Claire Chamberlain's freckled hand. Their letters became intimate chronicles of their lives, diaries in which they shared secrets and dreams—bold confessions of the heart made only and always in French.

Sarah confessed to Claire her loneliness, and the generous girl from across the sea replied by embracing Sarah with encouragement and hope. Claire shared Aunt Augusta with

Sarah, painting an image so vivid that Sarah could almost feel Augusta's welcoming warmth. And Claire also told her far-away friend about the other person she loved, the boy she met in the forest beside the bayou . . . the boy who, during the years when the girls were pen pals, grew away from Claire, becoming a young man who treated with mocking cruelty the lovely girl who had once been his friend.

Claire's portrait of Cole was cloaked in love, no matter what he did to her. Sarah lived each of Cole's betrayals with Claire, *felt* each one deep within her own heart. There was a difference, however. Claire was absolutely blind to the cruelty of Cole Taylor. Sarah was not. Her own teenage years, her own blossoming into a rare if austere beauty, had taught Sarah new, painful lessons about love, how selfish it was, how self-centered.

The young aristocrats with whom her parents insisted that she mingle wanted her, desired her, *desperately*. But their affection was as conditional as her parents' had always been. They wanted her only if she made *them* look better, only if she gave *them* pleasure. Sarah greeted the never-ending advances with icy disdain, a mask of contempt that concealed her true loneliness and her ever-increasing despair. These boys didn't want to befriend her, to know *her*, any more than her female classmates did.

Lady Sarah Pembroke had one friend, her pen pal in Louisiana; and when it came to Cole, Sarah felt torn. Should she reveal to Claire *her* thoughts about Cole, a jaded view based on her own experiences with "love"? Or should she continue to believe, as she always had, that everything would be different for Claire, *should* be different—that the girl whose heart shone with pure sunshine would find perfect happiness? Perhaps Claire was right about Cole, that he deserved her love, and that—despite persuasive evidence to the contrary—he was loving and kind.

Sarah didn't share with Claire her concerns about Cole. They were difficult to express, in writing, even in French. Besides, she decided, if ever her concerns were to be expressed, it should be in person, face-to-face.

Which it could be—because the pen pals were going to meet, a rendezvous that would also include Aunt Augusta.

Claire and Augusta were coming to London in June, and Sarah was going to show them *everything*, and they would talk non-stop, and—

Six months before the much-anticipated visit, tragedy struck. It claimed both girls, separate incidents of shattering brutality an ocean apart, distinct and entirely different acts of violence—and yet they shared a remarkable coincidence: the separate tragedies occurred on the same December day, at precisely the same hour.

For Claire, the day that would end with the death of Cole's father was gloriously joyous until its devastating end. The same was not true, however, for sixteen-year-old Sarah. That twenty-third day of December began ominously and only got worse.

Just before the winter dawn, Sarah and her parents were kidnapped. The three heavily armed men broke into their Norfolk estate, forced them back to sleep with chloroform, and transported them in a windowless van to the musty cellar where they were to be held pending payment of the ransom.

Money, lots of it, was the only motive for the crime. All three kidnappers were British. None had a political ax to grind—save the age-old one, the perennial struggle between the wealthy and the oppressed.

"We're modern-day Robin Hoods," the men proclaimed, their contemptuous sneers evident even through their stocking masks.

The theme was reprised hours later, as they waited to make the final phone call to Simon Beckwith-Jones. As both a close family friend and the Pembrokes' personal solicitor, Simon was given the task of assembling the ransom *without* notifying Scotland Yard.

"You're really quite a looker, aren't you, Maid Marion?" The kidnapper was speaking to Sarah, his eyes gleaming through nylon slits, smiling, mocking, terrifying. Then, consulting his comrades in crime, he queried, "What do you think, mates? We deserve a reward, don't you agree? Our own personal ransom? Who better than this lovely maiden? You *are* a maiden, aren't you, Lady Sarah?"

Sarah could not speak. But she was waiting, her heart was, to hear two other voices.

Touch my daughter over my dead body, her father would warn with such conviction that the kidnappers would abandon their plans in shame.

Take me, her mother would implore, an unnecessary plea in the wake of her father's command—but an urgent and heartfelt one nonetheless. *Take me, not my innocent girl.*

In her heart, Sarah actually heard those voices. But they were hallucinations, she realized, merely taunting phantoms of her own foolish hope.

There was only silence, and when she looked to her parents, their expressions were familiar, and so clear, even in the shadows.

What was about to transpire was disturbing to Earl and Lady Pembroke. Of that, there was no doubt. Disturbing. Distasteful. And disappointing. Their daughter's body lacked the grace to run, to dance, to ride. But now, in lieu of those *approved* endeavors, that graceless—yet womanly—body was about to engage in something truly unsavory . . . and with the most vile of criminals.

The savage intimacy was performed on the concrete floor at the feet of her parents. In standard measurements of time, the rape of Sarah Pembroke could be counted in minutes. But by the invisible timepiece of the heart, and the spirit and the soul, those minutes of pain—and betrayal—were an eternity.

Sarah wished for death, prayed for it. Surely she was losing so much blood that it would happen soon. If only she could lose consciousness in the meantime.

But Sarah did not lose consciousness. *Could not.* Her mind was eerily alert, incredibly aware—already ominously cognizant of what this betrayal would mean. The madness that was to come.

It was possible that Sarah might have died, or that her rapists might have become bored with her near lifeless body and turned their violent lust to her mother. Sarah might have seen her father's courage then, a ferocious fight to the death to prevent them from touching his wife. But before her attackers grew weary of her, while they still found pleasure in the ripping of her tender flesh, the Pembroke family was rescued.

The kidnappers had been taking turns with Sarah, watching when it wasn't their turn—as well as guarding Sarah's parents. The latter task was a casual process. It was abundantly clear that neither parent was going to make any attempt to save their daughter, and they would have had to clamber *over* the sexual carnage in order to flee.

The men were scarcely attentive to their captives. But they were quite alert to other, more remote sounds. They heard the opening of the distant door, followed by the hushed thuds of rapidly approaching feet, and by the time the police arrived, the kidnappers were ready for them. Indeed, they met them halfway, and with open fire.

The gun battle that ensued was protracted and thunderous, a tumultuous storm during which the Pembrokes were all alone. From their vantage point in the darkened room, it wasn't clear who would emerge victorious, the criminals or the police. Assuming it was the latter, however, the sight of Lady Sarah Pembroke lying ravaged and bleeding *would not do.*

Pillars of society and mavens of etiquette, Sarah's parents moved swiftly to erase all scandal—all truth—from the scene. Using torn remnants from her daughter's nightgown and robe, Geneva Pembroke wiped away the most incriminating spills of blood, stuffing the bloodied remains into the pockets of her own silken robe when she was through. Then both mother and father lifted their naked daughter to her feet, finishing their parental—societal—ministrations by swaddling Sarah in the earl's massive silk robe . . . just as the first policeman rounded the corner.

Did Robert and Geneva Pembroke feel remorse? Did they realize that in those moments in the dank and shadowy cellar they had crossed the line from imperfect parents—neglectful and self-absorbed—to truly deplorable ones? Did they vow to atone?

Perhaps. Perhaps not. Any traces of such parental contrition vanished swiftly as Sarah passed the Christmas holidays in virtual silence. Their disappointing daughter was behaving badly again, *still*. She needed to *forget* about the unfortunate incident. It was *over*. But Sarah didn't rebound as Robert and Geneva wanted her to, and as time passed, the failure, the blame, became hers, not theirs.

Sarah overheard her parents sharing the ordeal—an edited version—with their friends, a breathless accounting steeped in drama and always closing with the pronouncement that as uncharitable as it might sound, they were very glad that all three kidnappers had died on the scene.

Unfortunately, they would add in hushed whispers, the sight of the dead men, their bodies riddled with bullets, their lifeless faces unmasked, had been too much for Sarah. She simply wasn't bouncing back from the trauma the way she should have.

By the time Sarah should have returned to West Heath, the exclusive boarding school in Kent to which she had transferred at age thirteen, Sarah had become, in her mother's words, "positively unbearable."

"She doesn't eat, doesn't speak," Geneva complained to Simon Beckwith-Jones. "In fact, she doesn't even *move* unless prodded. She just stares into space."

Some vague corner of Sarah's mind wished that she could stare at her parents, could communicate to them with mute yet eloquent clarity that *they* were the true criminals, thieves and murderers who had stolen every shred of hope from their child and then killed that hope forever. And, Sarah thought, her parents were kidnappers as well. They had held her heart hostage all those years, taunting her with a fool's ransom, the promise that she could be loved, could *earn* their love if she really tried.

Earl and Lady Pembroke were guilty of heinous crimes of the heart. But they were not guilty of lesser crimes, smaller lies. Indeed, for Sarah's entire life, they had been telling her that she was unworthy of being protected, of being loved. The sacrifice of their virginal daughter on the cold concrete floor was merely the ultimate proof of that truth.

Sarah was not precious, merely disposable.

And now she was becoming a nuisance, an embarrassment. She wasn't a huge problem in London, in the house in Regent's Park where the Pembroke family lived during the week. There she was little more than a potted plant. The housekeeper could water her occasionally and move her away from the window whenever there was a draft.

But at their country home in Norfolk, where one of their great pleasures was hosting parties for the weekend, Sarah was definitely in the way, an awkwardness that was becoming too cumbersome to explain.

The Pembrokes needed to dispose of their disappointing daughter—again.

"Help us, Simon," Geneva implored. "You're to blame, after all. If you hadn't gone against the kidnappers' wishes and called Scotland Yard—"

"You wouldn't have been rescued."

"Quite right. We'd be dead as doornails, and better off for it!" The tease left Geneva's voice, replaced by a foreboding hiss. "I think she's quite mad, not a raving lunatic, not yet, just a mute one. Isn't there *somewhere* she can go?"

There were special requirements for the place where Lady Sarah Pembroke would be sent. Discretion was essential, from the psychiatrists to the cook. The official story would be that Sarah was in Switzerland, attending a finishing school near Lucerne. It had been her decision to leave England, they would say. Sarah yearned for the tranquillity of the Alps, far away from the unpleasant memories of the Christmastime kidnapping.

In fact, Sarah was in England, at Avalon, an expensive and exclusive asylum in Cornwall. There *were* alps nearby, near St. Austell, mammoth white mountains formed from powdery waste as clay became china.

And as for tranquillity? Could that be found within the stone walls of Avalon, the fortress nestled in the heather-cloaked granite of Bodmin Moor? Such serenity might have been possible here, for those whose hearts and minds were at peace. This was the land of King Arthur, after all, and of the magic of Merlin, and the purity of Galahad. To the north was Tintagel Castle, where the legendary king was born, and just south of the asylum lay Dozmary Pool, where Excalibur was returned to the Lady of the Lake. Even the name, Avalon, recalled the legend. It was to that island that Arthur journeyed after his final battle, his wounds to be tended, to be healed, by the fairy enchantress Morgan Le Fay.

Was this modern-day Avalon a place where mortal wounds could be healed? Not for Sarah. For her, it was more prison than sanctuary. But like the Avalon of old, the asylum was an island, in a sea of heathlands, from which there was no escape.

Not that Sarah ever contemplated escape. Why would she? She had no place to go. But she wished for privacy, for even a moment away from the shadowy figures who watched her every move, reporting everything they saw, the progression of her madness, her ever more tangled mane of hair, her endless pacing in the gardens—and who listened intently for the words that would spill from her lips when at last she broke her silence.

Less than a month after the event that had condemned her to madness, Sarah felt a presence beyond the shadowy shepherds. It was a wondrous presence, and it seemed to come from deep within—a tiny flame of hope that lighted her way and promised that she would never be alone again . . . if only she would cherish it.

And cherish, she did. She began to eat again, and to rest, and to sleep, for her daughter. Her *daughter*. Sarah believed without question that her baby was a little girl, a miracle of Christmas, pristine and pure, not a symbol of the violence that had shattered her life just two days before.

Sarah talked to her daughter, silently at first and then in whispers. *I'll protect you,* she vowed. No one will ever hurt you. You'll be safe and happy and loved, and we'll have such fun, won't we? We'll laugh, and talk, and play. And there will never be a time when I'm too busy for you. Never. You will always be the most important part of my life.

Always.

Chapter Seventeen

"SHE *LOOKS* BETTER," ONE OF SARAH'S CARE-takers reported. "She's brushed her hair at last, gotten rid of the unruly mass of snarls. She wears it smooth as silk now, and shining clean, and she even captures it in a colorful ribbon at her nape." The caretaker sighed. "I'm afraid, however, that in all other ways she's worse. Oh, she's talking, all right. But she's invented some imaginary friend to whom she talks constantly and with great passion. From the bits and pieces I've overheard it sounds as if she's making plans."

"For escape?"

The question came from Sarah's psychiatrist. But it was answered first, and with imperious warning, by Geneva Pembroke. "She had better not escape."

"The plans sound extremely vague," Sarah's watchguard assured. "Scattered. Delusional. She's obviously hallucinating."

Sarah managed to delude them all. The rosy flush to her cheeks was ascribed to the long walks she took, as well as her exuberance for the fantasy world in which she lived. And her pregnancy itself was easily concealed beneath the loose-fitting clothes that were de rigueur for all asylum inmates.

214 / KATHERINE STONE

Sarah permitted her shadows to overhear small parts of what they believed to be her imaginary conversations. But the most important plans were uttered so softly that no one but her daughter could hear.

We'll have to live with my parents for a while, until I'm eighteen. I'll have money after that, a trust fund, and we can be on our own. We *will* be on our own, though, even when we're living with them. I won't let them near you.

But they'll have to take us in, to welcome us with open arms. In fact, they'll have to do *everything* I say. You know why? Because I'm stronger now, with you inside me. Already I feel the way a parent *should* feel—willing to do anything to protect her precious baby . . . ready to lay down her own life to save her child.

My parents are despicable. I know that now. And the *world* will know if they don't do whatever I say. It's blackmail, but I don't care! It's a small crime compared to theirs. There's this man, called Timothy Asquith. He used to come to their parties, although he hasn't in several years. Perhaps he's just too busy. But maybe he knows the truth about them.

One time, you see, when I was nine, they wanted me to ride in front of all their friends. It was intended to embarrass me, I suppose, to shame me into overcoming my fear. But I was too terrified even to get on the horse, much less to try to ride. I started to cry, I couldn't help it, and even though they were secretly furious with me, they laughed at my tears, mocking me.

Timothy Asquith was there, and he whispered something to my parents, and within seconds everything changed. They began putting on a show of their own, hugging me as if they truly cared, reassuring me that horseback riding couldn't matter less. I don't know what Timothy Asquith said to them, whether he came to my defense or merely announced that he considered watching a nine-year-old girl ride a horse an unspeakable bore. Whatever it was, though, it saved me, *he* saved me. And my parents seemed flustered, actually afraid, as if they knew it was terribly unwise to anger Timothy Asquith.

So what I've decided is this: If my parents refuse to take us in, I'll threaten to tell Mr. Asquith what *really* happened during the kidnapping. I wouldn't undo that day now, not for anything, because of you. But my parents won't know that. They'll only know that, if they don't take us in, I'll ask Timothy Asquith to tell the world what they did. He *can* tell the world, you see, because he owns an entire television network.

Such brave plans, and infinitely possible when she was empowered by the tiny new life growing inside her. Everything was possible then. Happiness. Love. Joy.

But such a happy life was not to be.

By Sarah's calculations, her daughter would be born sometime in September. But when she went into labor on August tenth, an event that stunned the asylum personnel, Sarah wasn't alarmed in the least, felt no foreboding whatsoever. In fact, just the opposite. Her daughter was obviously ready to be born, as eager as Sarah to begin their life of love; and her baby girl was healthy enough, robust enough from Sarah's nurturing, that she could arrive a little early.

But in the end, despite all Sarah's promises, all her brave and joyous plans, her baby must have known that life with Sarah would not have been worth living.

Her baby—her hope, her light, her love—was born dead.

It had been a fantasy, a delusion after all. Eloquent, devastating proof of her madness. Oh yes, she had been pregnant. That, alone, was not an illusion. But her baby was a little boy, not the daughter she had imagined, and even at the moment of her baby's birth she was hallucinating.

She was groggy, in the twilight sleep of anesthesia, but she believed she heard her baby's cry. It was music, clear and pure, a melodic hello, the first note of a lifetime of song . . . not the anguished strain of a requiem.

But there had been no music, neither overture nor dirge. The cry was merely hallucination. Merely illusion, merely fantasy, merely madness, merely death.

The news that her infant son had died before leaving her womb came from Geneva Pembroke. Her mother's expression held a sorrow that Sarah had never seen before, as if she might have been a loving grandmother after all. Sarah's father was there, too, at her bedside in the hospital in Penzance. The earl seemed to be mourning as well, grieving—as did Simon Beckwith-Jones.

"No," Sarah cried. "He's *not* dead. He can't be. I don't believe it! I want to see him."

They let her see him, and hold him. Her beautiful dead son. As her trembling lips placed tender kisses on his small, cold, alabaster face, strands of her long black hair entwined with his, a perfect, lustrous match.

"I love you," she whispered. "I love you always."

Sarah didn't return to the asylum. She was not, after all, as crazy as they had supposed. She hadn't been speaking to a phantom friend but merely, and quite coherently, to her unborn child.

Even as Avalon's psychiatrists were pronouncing their patient to be sane, if a little strange, Sarah was realizing the depth of her madness. Her parents realized it, too. The asylum's physicians, however, refused to readmit Lady Sarah Pembroke to their cloistered sanctuary on the moors. In their professional judgment she no longer needed their expertise; and they were more than a little offended by Earl Pembroke's verbal assault when he discovered that Sarah's pregnancy had been overlooked.

While her parents pursued other avenues, a faraway place where Sarah could languish forever, they hired round-the-clock supervision for their bizarre daughter.

Bizarre? *Ghoulish,* Geneva proclaimed. Sarah was obsessed with death—at least with her dead baby. He was buried in a churchyard near their Norfolk estate, a place where, if Sarah had her way, she would spend every day—and night—talking to him still.

Their daughter had become a ghoul—and worse. Her obsession empowered her. Before, she had been silent and docile, a potted plant; but now she ranted and raved, tormenting them until they made firm commitments for yet another graveyard visit.

Every Saturday afternoon, her parents promised. We'll spend weekdays in town, and weekends in the country, and you can see him—his *grave*, Sarah—every weekend, every Saturday, without fail.

Saturday *and* Sunday, Sarah countered defiantly, a demand that was met in the interest of peace.

It was during the week, when she dwelled entirely within the walls of their London home, that Sarah discovered alcohol. *It helped so much,* numbing the pain, muting the cries of her heart, stilling her thoughts. Those who were paid to watch her made no attempt to prevent her from drinking. Their job became so easy, effortless really, when their crazy charge drank. Sarah would spend hours in one place, as silent as an alabaster statue and as still—except for the graceful rhythmic motion of her right arm, as crystal glasses of bourbon rose and fell from her lips.

Sarah had a vague but inconsequential notion of how destructive her drinking was. It simply didn't matter. Alcohol was the only way she could survive the endless days in London, and on the weekends, when she sat for hours by the tiny grave, she never drank a drop.

Besides, she realized finally—*and with such peace*—she wasn't going to have a lifelong relationship with alcohol . . . with anything.

"**I** want to marry her."

"That's in very poor taste, Simon. Not the least bit funny."

"I'm dead serious."

"You want to marry our lunatic daughter? That's lunacy in itself." Geneva's eyes narrowed shrewdly. "You haven't squandered your fortune, have you?"

"I still have more money than the two of you combined. But what I don't have, and what I've wanted for a long time, is Sarah."

"She *won't* marry you, Simon. The old Sarah might have, but this new Sarah isn't nearly as compliant. Unless, that is, you propose to her in London, when she's so drunk that she could be convinced of anything."

"I can convince her, and I plan to do so here, this weekend, while she's stone-cold sober. I don't need your blessing, not really. But as a courtesy—"

"You *have* our blessing, Simon. And if you can pull this off, you'll also have our eternal gratitude. As a matter of interest, though, how precisely do you intend to convince her?"

"By promising her what she wants most." Simon smiled. "A baby."

"But Simon, you've had—"

Robert Pembroke's protestation of surprise was preempted by the sudden appearance of Sarah's nurse. She was from the nearby village, a clinic nurse who was delighted to supplement her income by spending her weekends watching the Pembrokes' daft daughter.

On this night, however, the nurse's face held worry, not delight.

"Have you seen Sarah?"

"That's your job."

"Yes, I know. But she wanted a bath, and it seemed safe to give her privacy, to wait outside the door, and as I fancy good long soaks myself, it was a while before I started to worry. When I finally called to her, and got no answer, I barged right in. I understand now why you've taken the locks off all her doors. I was afraid of what I might find. But she wasn't there, and the window was flung wide open."

Robert swore, tame epithets compared to those offered by his wife.

Finally, with a heavy sigh, Geneva confessed, "I suppose it's only a tragedy if she's found running naked through the village. Which, fortunately, she won't be. We know where she'll be, don't we? In the graveyard, talking to her moldering son." Geneva arched an aristocratic eyebrow at Simon. "You don't really want to take this on, do you?"

"Yes. I do. Sarah needs someone who truly cares about her."
"*Cares*, Simon?" Geneva mocked. "*Truly* cares?"

It was December twenty-third, the one-year anniversary of the day her beloved son had been conceived. Sarah had chosen this date for their reunion, had *waited*—with such desperate, eager, impatient joy—for this night to come.

But she shouldn't have waited! The ground that enveloped his small coffin was frozen now, *frozen*. He must be so very cold.

"Just a moment more, my little love," she whispered as she hurriedly sliced the flesh of her wrists to the bone. "You'll be warm soon, and you'll never be alone again."

Sarah watched the blood gush from her severed wrists, spilling onto the icy earth, melting the tiny crystals of frost with a river of crimson heat—and glistening love—as it began its journey down to him, to warm him.

But the journey of her blood, her love, into the frozen ground was far too slow. *He was still so cold.* Sarah began to dig then, a frantic excavation, a clawing into the ice-hardened dirt with shredded fingertips and bloodless hands.

Eventually, as far more of Sarah Pembroke's blood cloaked the frozen earth than pulsed within, her movements became less frantic, *she* became less frantic. Indeed, when Simon found her, Sarah was smiling a smile of pure joy. She was almost dead, just moments from death, from eternal peace.

Sarah didn't recognize Simon. But she did not resist his touch, or his swift, harsh binding of her bleeding wrists. To her floating mind he was an angel, and it made sense that he would not want her to drip blood on their journey to heaven. The man-angel whispered gentle words to her—"Sarah," "love," "baby"—and Sarah closed her eyes, knowing she was safe at last. Her sadness was finally over, and when she awoke, she would be with her son.

But she awakened in a hospital, the same sad and aching Sarah—and yet different. Nothing had died, not one sliver of her stabbing pain. But something had been born, a deep and abiding sense of purpose. She wasn't meant to die, not yet. That peace was a faraway promise. For now she was to remain on earth, to endure the pain.

Why?

The answer was astonishing, and joyous: to have another baby. It seemed impossible that she would be given this second chance. But there it was. Simon wanted to marry her, and he trusted her to bear his children, to have babies that would survive, flourish, with her love. Simon didn't believe her to be crazy, merely terribly sad, and he vowed to make her happy.

But all the happiness—all the pleasure—belonged to Simon.

Mr. and Mrs. Simon Beckwith-Jones lived in London, in a mansion in Belgravia. There was a nursery in their elegant home, a bright, cheerful place decorated by Sarah and located just a few steps from the master bedroom . . . where she and Simon tried—and failed—to create a new little life.

Simon's sexual tastes, at least with her, were quite straightforward. Not brutal, not violent, not bizarre. But still, for Sarah, because of her memories, every time felt like rape. She hid that truth, that terror, from her husband. She was a willing—desperate—participant; and because of the baby she wanted so much, the promise of that unborn joy, she didn't drink, *wouldn't*, no matter how shrill the silent screams of her heart.

The Beckwith-Joneses had been married, and childless, for three years when Sarah's parents and husband made the fateful journey to Scotland. Sarah chose not to accompany them on the weekend of hunting and parties. She wasn't *encouraged* to join them, of course—nor did she want to.

The weekends when Simon and her parents were away, enjoying sensual pursuits of the flesh, were the times when she traveled to the graveyard in Norfolk. Such visits were carefully rationed, more severely than before; and again, Sarah was a willing participant. She knew how important emotional factors were in conceiving a child. Too much focus on the son who had died might interfere with her ability to become pregnant again.

But on that weekend, when the accident occurred, Sarah was in the churchyard in Norfolk, speaking to her son.

The fog shrouding Balmoral was dense. So dense that Simon Beckwith-Jones should never have tried to land the plane. But he—and Geneva and Robert—knew the pleasures that awaited them. They were greedy for the delights to begin, too greedy to sacrifice even a moment of pleasure in the name of caution.

Betrayal. That was her legacy, her inheritance, from her parents and husband. There was not financial betrayal, however. In that one arena Simon Beckwith-Jones and Earl and Lady Pembroke had been immensely generous—or immensely careless, having neglected their wills because their deaths seemed so remote.

The betrayal was emotional, calculated, unspeakably cruel; and it was revealed to Sarah within hours of their deaths. A doctor arrived to see the bereaved widow, a man who belonged to the same exclusive men's club as Simon and Robert, and who had been Simon's personal physician as well.

"I've brought along some pills, Sarah, tranquilizers to help you sleep."

"Thank you, but no. It would be best not to take anything, wouldn't it, in case I'm pregnant?"

"Pregnant? But that miracle won't happen, Sarah. You know it can't. Oh, dear child, maybe you *don't* know."

Simon Beckwith-Jones could not father children. It was a choice, made long before their marriage, a decision secured by a surgeon's scalpel—the success of which Simon had reconfirmed shortly before he and Sarah had wed.

Simon knew that his wife would not become pregnant. And her parents knew it as well. For three years Simon had, in essence, raped her, and by their silence her parents had given their blessing for her destruction *again*.

Sarah discovered even more betrayal as she sifted through papers at her parents' London home. In the deep recesses of a locked drawer in her mother's antique desk, she found a letter from Claire. Thick, never opened, it had been written four years before, just hours after the lives of both sixteen-year-old girls had been shattered by violence.

Claire's letter began in French, the romantic language in which the pen pals had always revealed the secrets of their hearts. In flowing, elegant, lyrical French, Claire shared the magic of her love for Cole, the duet they had sung at the Christmas pageant and the moonlit splendor that had followed in the gazebo at Belle Rêve. Claire wrote, in French, of Cole's confession about the brother he had loved so much—and given away—and of their own joyous confessions of love.

Then, abruptly, Claire changed to English, flowing no more, but eloquent still, in her pain, as she recounted the events of the following day, the act—and then accident—of violence that signaled the end of all dreams.

Sarah had wondered about her friend, and the letters from Louisiana that had stopped arriving coincident with her own life-shattering Christmastime trauma. Had Claire somehow sensed what had happened to her? Not the rape itself, perhaps, but its meaning—that Sarah had crossed the line from innocence to madness?

It was just as well that Claire stopped writing precisely at that time. Indeed, if Claire hadn't ended their correspondence, Sarah would have.

But Claire hadn't stopped writing after all. She had sent a most intimate letter, an honest outpouring of emotion and grief; and now, four years later, Sarah responded in kind, revealing everything, *everything*, pages and pages in English, a drowning sea of betrayal and despair. There was a small island of joy in that vast sea of pain; and when she wrote about her baby, the tiny flame of happiness that had glowed inside her, Sarah wrote in French.

Sarah never mailed her letter to Claire. Their friendship had long since lapsed. Why resurrect it with a chronicle of sadness—and madness? Why taint Claire's happiness with a saga of bitterness and pain?

Claire *would* be happy now, again. She would have moved far beyond the loss of Cole. Happy again, in love with someone new. *She had to be.* That was the only destiny Sarah would willingly imagine for lovely, generous Claire.

And as for Sarah? Her destiny? It was there still, that voice inside that commanded her to live. Her purpose had not been to bear another child. She had been so very foolish to believe *that.* But there was something she was meant to do, something that would not permit her, not yet, to once again slash her wrists to the bone.

Something elusive—but important.

Perhaps she was meant to tell the world about war, to expose its folly in the hope of helping the entire planet move toward peace. That was a worthy mission, and it evolved in a way that felt like fate, a chance meeting, after so many years, with Timothy Asquith, the man who—perhaps—had come to her defense when she was an awkward, frightened child.

She was Sarah Pembroke again by then, a decision of love not for her parents, of course, but for her son, so that her surname would match the one engraved in marble on the gravestone in Norfolk. Sarah was attending a charity gala to benefit orphaned children, and Timothy was there as well, and emboldened by champagne, she heard herself telling him how appealing a career in journalism would be to her.

Sarah didn't clarify, to Timothy, the reasons for the appeal. But she knew them. News was *real*, concrete and tangible. However horrible or tragic, it kept one tethered to reality—far from the beckoning abyss of madness—and if one was an observer, focused intently on the happenings of the outside world, perhaps in time the screams from deep within would become muffled . . . and maybe, in time, even mute.

Selfish reasons? Yes. But Sarah would do her job well. She would devote herself entirely to it.

Timothy Asquith assigned his new reporter to Global's local—United Kingdom—telecast, specifically to the ever-engaging drama of the royals. What better palace correspondent than the aristocratic Lady Pembroke?

But Sarah balked at the regal assignment, and despite the

fact that the media mogul was quite unused to being counter-manded, Timothy relented. If the articulate, photogenic reporter wanted to tell her fellow citizens about London's most heinous crimes, then so be it. And when that same reporter asked to be sent to Baghdad, on the eve of Desert Storm, Timothy Asquith acceded to Sarah's wishes yet again.

Now the battlegrounds where she felt so safe, so sane, had become too dangerous for her, and she had acceded to Timothy's wish that she return to London. Away from war? Hardly. Sarah Pembroke had her own battles to fight right here. She had to confront her demons, to control them at least and to conquer them if she possibly could, before it was too late. Before they conquered her.

And there was something more, that voice again, and it seemed to be promising that, in London, her life's true purpose would finally be revealed.

What greeted Sarah on her return to London was a communiqué from a murderer. Was *that* her destiny? To catch a killer? To avenge the deaths of two women she did not know?

No, because now there was much more, the link to Claire. Was this, then, the reason Sarah had survived? To unmask Cole Taylor as a killer? To avenge not only the deaths of the two actresses but Claire, her friend, the lovely girl to whom Cole had been so cruel?

Cruel, yes. But a *murderer*?

Sarah didn't know.

But she was going to find out.

Chapter Eighteen

Drake Hotel
Hyde Park
Tuesday, December Twenty-seventh

*H*E LOOKS LIKE A KILLER. SARAH'S ASSESS-
ment was immediate and decisive, made the moment she
caught her first glimpse of him. She was already seated at their
table in the Colonnade Room, and Cole was coming toward
her, his powerful body moving with predatory grace and menacing stealth. He wore black, as Sarah herself so often wore,
the austere and somber color of death.

Sarah subdued her crescendoing apprehension with the
soothing reminder that here, in the hotel's elegant dining room,
she was perfectly safe. She had acquiesced, without the slightest
protest, to Jack's request that she permit an undercover police
officer to dine nearby. And she had promised to resist any suggestion made by Cole to retire to a more private location.

And remember, Jack had said. I'll be just upstairs, in my
room. Call me, Sarah, and I'll be right down to join you. Tell
Cole that you'd like him to meet your biographer, or that as a
celebrity biographer I'd like to meet him myself.

Sarah had agreed to protection, to caution, and as much as one
possibly could, she had prepared herself to dine with a murderer.

Now Cole Taylor was here, and the shadows of his face were
illuminated by candlelight, and the deep breath Sarah might have
instinctively drawn in fear became a shallow gasp of surprise. His

eyes weren't the eyes of a killer. Sarah had seen killers' eyes, in the masked faces of her own rapists and countless times since, at war. She knew the various guises of such eyes, sometimes glistening, shimmering with lust, sometimes flat, unseeing and dead.

But gleaming or clouded, in the most essential way the eyes of killers were all the same. They had no conscience. No soul.

The dark gray eyes that greeted her now belonged to a man with a soul, albeit a tormented one, and even though they glinted with unrelenting intensity, there was gentleness as well.

Gentleness? In a man's eyes? As they looked *at her*? Before Christmas Eve such an impression would have been pure folly, an optical illusion, an hallucination of her own deluded mind. But in Paris a man named Jacques had gazed with exquisite tenderness at a woman named Claire . . . and in London a man named Jack gazed the same way at a woman named Sarah.

"Hello, Sarah."

His voice, too, was gentle. So gentle that it stole from her all images of slashed ivory throats.

"Hello, Cole."

"Thank you for agreeing to see me."

"Of course. I'm delighted to."

Had Cole Taylor been the black-hearted killer she had worried he might be, he would have focused entirely on her, wanting to know *everything* about her, pretending to, as if she were the most fascinating woman on earth. The singer of love songs would have embarked on a journey of seduction that would begin tonight and end in her death on February fourteenth.

But as soon as they had declined cocktails and placed their orders for dinner, Cole said quietly, solemnly, "I wanted to talk to you about Claire. I know it's been years since the two of you stopped writing, and I sense from Claire that that was your choice. Please understand that my intent is not to convince you to reconsider that choice. But Claire is coming to London. She'll be at the concert on New Year's Eve and at the party here as well. I know from Timothy that you've been invited to both, and if you're planning to attend, there's a chance that you and Claire might meet. I wanted you to know because I want to avoid any awkwardness for her."

He's not trying to seduce me, and there isn't the slightest pretense that I'm fascinating at all. He's just here to implore me not to hurt Claire *again.*

"The decision to stop writing to Claire was a choice, Cole. But it was also *not* a choice. It just wasn't possible for our correspondence to continue. It had to do with me, not with Claire. Does she truly believe that I *wanted* it to end?"

"I think so. She didn't give me details, but that was my impression."

Details. Sarah knew them. And now, for the first time, she realized what they had meant to Claire. Her friend had sent a deeply emotional letter, and when Sarah had failed to respond, Claire concluded that Sarah had been repulsed by the tragedy—and brutality—she had so bravely revealed.

I should have written to her, even after four years had passed. I should have known, and reassured her.

"It's a misunderstanding, Cole. One that I'd very much like to clear up. Will she see me?"

Sarah expected him to smile, an acknowledgment of the greatest truth about Claire: her lovely generosity, her willingness to forgive. Quite obviously, Claire had forgiven Cole his cruel rejection of her love on that long-ago December day. Surely Claire would be willing to forgive her penmate as well? At least be willing to hear her out?

But there was no smile on Cole Taylor's face, and his gray eyes darkened to black. He was a killer now, a stone-eyed panther ready to maul, to mangle, to destroy.

But I'm not his prey, Sarah realized. His dark, lethal rage is directed somewhere else.

"Cole?" she asked softly—and without fear. Hadn't she just pronounced him a killer? Yes, and no. Because amid the mortal rage, she saw the tenderness of his soul. "Cole?"

"Claire will want to talk to you, Sarah. I'm sure of it. But she won't be able to see you."

It was almost ten, the hour at which Cole Taylor was supposed to begin his nocturnal rehearsal at Gemstone's recording studio on nearby Waverton Street. At any moment the phone would ring—Sarah, with the report that their dinner was over and Cole was gone, or the undercover police officer with similar reassuring news.

Jack was restless to get that call, had been restless from the moment the dinner rendezvous began twenty-six floors below. But he had put the edgy energy of the past two hours to good use.

"I want everything you can find on Cole Taylor," he told a private investigator in L.A. "Every article ever written, every videotape, whatever you can get, no matter how trivial it seems. I also want information on Paulina Bliss and Ashley Alexander."

And to a colleague at the FBI Jack said, "I need a background search, from the moment Cole Taylor was born. And will you check on his travels ex-U.S.?"

Jack placed the calls to the States on the second of the three phone lines in his room. The first line was sacrosanct, for Sarah only, and the third was dedicated to the fax machine through which the data he requested would arrive.

The first line rang, at last, at 10:05.

"It's Sarah. I'm in the lobby with Cole Taylor. He needs to leave in a few minutes, to practice with his band, but I wanted you to meet him. Would that be possible? Are you free?"

"I'll be right there."

During the elevator ride to the lobby, Jack thought about Sarah's voice. How relaxed it was. How free of fear. It was possible, in fact likely, that Cole had been within earshot when Sarah had made the call. If so, she was an actress even more gifted than Jack had imagined—for what he heard sounded far more like an authentic invitation to meet a friend than the ruse they had devised should Sarah become fearful of a killer.

The impression that sometime in the past two hours Sarah had abandoned her wariness of Cole Taylor was confirmed the moment Jack saw them standing in the lobby. Even though she and Cole were sharing no words, Sarah seemed perfectly at ease, as relaxed as her voice had been . . . *until she saw him.*

She stiffened then, suddenly wary, and the voice that greeted him was taut. "Jack."

"Hi."

"Jack Dalton, meet Cole Taylor."

As Jack offered his hand to the man who had known both victims of last year's slayings—and had been the lover of one of them—he looked directly into Cole's winter-gray eyes . . . and for an immensely powerful moment inscrutable blue met pure steel. Their gazes locked, solemn, appraising, unwavering; gazes that might never have faltered had their hands not touched.

With a wry smile and an expression that implored Jack to follow suit, Cole looked down to his right hand. And when Jack followed that command, Cole turned his hand palm up, to reveal the stellate scar that provided ample explanation for a handshake that was surprisingly weak for a panther.

The revelation was not reassuring to Jack. *Not at all.* Indeed, he now knew the disturbing answer to one of the many questions that needed answering about Cole Taylor.

I hope you're acting, Sarah, he thought. Because it's terribly dangerous, and dangerously premature, to embrace as innocent this seductive singer of love songs.

"Sarah says that you're writing a book—"

"Cole!"

No one needed to turn in the direction of the new voice because in seconds Sydney was there, standing between Cole and Jack, her amethyst eyes sparkling with interest—and with obvious approval—at both Sarah and Jack.

Sydney knew Sarah, of course—knew *of* her, and greatly admired her work. She said as much when they were introduced. Then, turning her full attention to Jack, Sydney asked, "And you are?"

"Jack Dalton. I'm writing a book about Sarah and other war—"

"A biography of Sarah? That sounds so . . ."

"Final?" Sarah offered.

Sydney laughed. "Hardly. So *impressive.* In fact, I think it's about time that someone did a biography of Cole Taylor, superstar. It would sell like hotcakes, until the fans discovered that all the inside pages were blank. Cole's a bit mysterious about his past—his present, for that matter."

"But *not* about his future," Cole countered amiably. "It's a future that will be quite grim, Syd, filled with two not-so-happy guitarists, if you and I don't leave for the studio now."

"You think that Mick and David are already at the studio? On *time* for rehearsal?"

"I know they are. They wandered through while Sarah and I were waiting for Jack."

"Then you're right. We'd better go. Sarah? Jack? Are you coming, too? I'm sure Cole agrees that you'd be welcome."

"More than welcome."

"Thank you," Sarah replied. "Maybe sometime after Claire arrives?"

"You know Claire, Sarah?" Sydney asked.

"Yes." *We were, are, maybe, friends.*

"Well then, why don't the three of us girls do something elegant and ladylike? Dinner at Claridge's, or high tea at the Savoy? *Without the guys.* Would you like to?"

Sarah felt a sudden rush of gratitude, and admiration of her own. Sydney Quinn was more than stunningly beautiful. She was smart. Her flamboyance was an act, a vividness that was undoubtedly a calculated counterpoint to the darkness of Cole—and for that matter to the silence of David and the moodiness of Mick.

The famous Elle Syd was the bright plumage for the band, the charming ambassador, and now she was graciously offering to be the same for Sarah and Claire, a confident, cheerful liaison.

"Yes," Sarah answered finally. "Absolutely, Sydney. That would be very nice."

"Cole is very nice." Sarah's words broke the silence that had fallen as soon as Cole and Sydney left.

"Really?"

"Yes. *Really.*"

"What did you talk about?"

"Claire." Sarah frowned as she remembered the solemn revelations of the evening. "Cole and I just talked about Claire."

"Shall we go somewhere a little more private?"

"Why?"

"So you can tell me what Cole said."

"It's not relevant. He's not . . . he *couldn't* be."

Jack sighed, took her arm, and steered her gently but firmly
to a secluded corner of the hotel lobby. "We knew he would be
clever, Sarah. A master of seduction."

"He wasn't trying to seduce me, Jack!"

"But he *did* seduce you, didn't he? Despite everything, after
one candlelit dinner you believe absolutely in his innocence."

"Everything?"

"He's from L.A.," Jack said patiently. "He knew both victims very well. And, Sarah, Cole Taylor is left-handed."

"The killer is left-handed?"

"Probably. In both instances the lethal slash to the throat
was made from right to left. Which means that at least for that
time the knife was held in the murderer's left hand. The rest of
the wounds are equivocal."

"So you wouldn't rule out a right-handed killer."

"No. But, Sarah, I also wouldn't instantly dismiss a left-
handed killer who appeared on cue." His quiet admonition
caused no surprise—merely disappointment; which prompted
further clarification from him. "I have no idea if Cole Taylor is
the man we're looking for. I'm certainly not saying that he is. It's
simply far too soon to reach any conclusion, in either direction."

Sarah knew that Jack was right. One didn't solve puzzles either by seizing the first clue that came along—or by ignoring it.
Especially not a man like Jack Dalton, paragon of cool, dispassionate logic. He was so very calm now, so reasonable, so infuriatingly rational.

With a purely irrational rush of emotion—for Cole, for
Claire—Sarah repeated, "It's not Cole. It's just *not*. Besides, he
isn't even really . . ."

"Really what, Sarah?"

"Nothing." She shrugged, then sighed. "I'm very tired. I
need to go home."

"Okay. I'll ride with you—in silence."

"No. Thank you. In fact, I think I'll walk. It's not far, and it's completely safe, isn't it? I mean, especially if the prime suspect is in a recording studio until morning?"

It *was* completely safe for Sarah Pembroke to walk the night-darkened streets of London, no matter who or where the black-hearted killer happened to be. Jack knew that, had made certain of it. Still, had Sarah not been so obviously eager to get away, to begin her solitary journey into darkness, Jack might have reminded her of the promise she had made to be careful . . . and he might have reiterated that he had not proclaimed Cole Taylor to be guilty, only worthy of further scrutiny . . . and that if the superstar was innocent, then the knife-wielding madman might be lurking in the shadows just outside the hotel.

But Jack saw the truth. Caution did not matter to Sarah, not tonight. All that mattered was that she could be free to walk by herself into the misting blackness.

What the hell had Cole Taylor said to her?

The roses were pink and white, and they arrived in a silver vase, and the card, this time, was signed.

"Jack!" Frances raved the moment she saw him. "I *love* them!"

Jack smiled. Good. But does she? "Where are they?"

"In Sarah's office, *naturally*. She was truly surprised, even a little worried, I thought. Since you'd always sent red ones before, I suppose she wondered if she had *another* secret admirer."

"I imagine she has many, don't you?"

"Oh! Well, *yes*, of course. I admit I considered the possibility that this batch might have come from Cole Taylor."

"Were you disappointed?" *Was she?*

"Of course not! Mr. Taylor and I are becoming fast friends over the phone."

"He called again today?"

"She's talking to him right now." Frances glanced at the telephone for confirmation. "I stand corrected. It looks like she's finished with the call."

"She is finished," Sarah confirmed quietly from the doorway. "Hello, Jack."

"Hello, Sarah."

Her eyes were bright green, and her alabaster cheeks flushed a glowing pink.

Not just any pink, Jack realized when they were alone in her rose-fragrant office. The delicate pink he remembered—and had chosen to send.

It was to those roses, that carefully selected gift, that Sarah spoke. "They're lovely, Jack. Thank you."

"You're welcome. They seemed like you." *Soft, fragile, and far better than the color of blood you choose to send yourself.*

It would have been so nice to talk forever about roses, about pink blooms the color of her cheeks and white ones that were the pure snow of her silken skin. But more shimmered in the air in Sarah's office than the perfume of roses. The specter of her just-completed telephone conversation with Cole was here as well.

Cole, and lies, and secrets . . . and death.

With a sigh that gave Jack hope, a wistful signal that she, too, would like to linger forever over the roses, Sarah looked from the flowers to him.

"I've decided I need to tell you about Claire, about what happened to her. Then you'll understand."

"Okay," Jack agreed. And when you're through telling me about Claire, I'll tell you what I've learned about Cole—and then *you'll* understand.

They went to Sarah's sanctuary atop Asquith Towers. The pearl-gray winter twilight announced its presence with a wind that was bitter cold and piercingly sharp.

But the icy chill that enveloped them was appropriate for the moment. Because Sarah's news about Claire was bitter cold—and piercingly sharp—as were the truths Jack had learned about Cole.

"She's blind, Jack, and it's tearing him apart. He says that she's an absolute trouper—and I'm certain that she is, because that's Claire—but he hates it for her. A monster wouldn't feel such compassion. A murderer wouldn't *care*. That's why I'm so confident that Cole couldn't possibly—"

"Cole murdered his father, Sarah. With a knife."

That chilling fact had arrived, by fax, early this morning, and as soon as the workday had begun in Harlanville, Jack was on the phone with the town's chief of police, learning all about the bad boy of the bayou. It was a history that began when Cole was eleven, the year that he and Jed Taylor had arrived in Harlanville. And as for Cole's younger years? He had been born in Breaux Bridge, a week before his parents were wed, and another birth certificate, for a second *Baby Boy Taylor*, was recorded several years later.

Shortly after that second son turned two, Jed Taylor was accused of stealing drugs. The family of four fled St. Martin Parish, essentially vanishing until Jed and Cole appeared in Harlanville. Quite obviously, at some point during the intervening years Mrs. Jed Taylor herself had fled, taking her younger son with her and leaving Cole to fend for himself against his brutal father.

The missing years in Cole Taylor's early life were not of great interest. They would merely confirm what Jack already knew: that it had been a blueprint for disaster, a childhood that virtually assured a future of reckless rage and explosive violence.

The violence had come, in a most dramatic form, when Cole was nineteen . . . a lethal chapter which, Jack realized, did not come as any shock to Lady Sarah Pembroke.

"You *knew*, Sarah? You knew that Cole has killed before, and *with a knife*?"

"It was an *accident*, Jack! The police may have called it self-defense, but even that's too strong."

"I can't believe you knew and didn't tell me."

"It's hardly a secret! All of Harlanville—"

"It was a secret to me, Sarah. A secret you kept from me. Last night, when I told you Cole was left-handed, you started to disagree—because you knew, didn't you, that he wasn't left-handed by birth but by violence?"

"He's *not* a killer, Jack."

"I honestly don't give a damn about Cole Taylor's innocence

or guilt. That's not what this is about." *It's about us.* Jack ran a powerful hand through his thick sable hair and gazed beyond Sarah to the ever-darkening winter sky. "I wonder if we're ever going to trust each other?"

The question was more rhetorical than real, and posed to the glowering heavens, not to her. The only reply Jack expected was from that dark, scowling sky—a resounding *no.*

"*Yes.*"

Jack looked from the sky to her. He wanted to see the woman who had so boldly proclaimed that one day there would be trust, and whose impassioned voice seemed to promise even more. But she was already gone, that spokes-woman of Jack's dreams. All he saw now was confusion—as if Sarah was truly bewildered that such astonishing words had flowed from her lips.

Still, and softly, he asked, "Really, Sarah?"

It was the shadow woman who had spoken. That foolish phantom. That gossamer symbol of sheer madness.

"Yes," Sarah murmured, but without conviction. The shadow woman was gone, her courage a mere memory, her fantasies merely a lingering fear. "Really."

"When, I wonder?" This time Jack got no answer, at least not one spoken aloud. But he saw Sarah's apprehension, and the dark shadows of all the secrets she intended to keep. "What else aren't you telling me, Sarah? That Cole's favorite cham-pagne is Cristale? That the two of you shared a bottle last night?"

"No. Neither of us had anything to drink last night."

You didn't need to drink to be with Cole Taylor, to dine with a man who might be a murderer, but you had to drink glass after glass to be with me?

Sarah saw it then, at last, the flash of anger in his eyes, the searing blue fire. She had known the fury was there. *It had to be.* But until this instant Jack had kept it hidden, buried deep beneath a glacier of control.

But now . . . now the blaze of blue fury was gone again, the inferno doused, conquered so swiftly that it seemed merely a fiery mirage.

"I think there's more you're not telling me, Sarah. Another little bombshell about Cole. Like the fact that his birthday is February fourteenth?"

"I knew that," she confessed with a whisper. "But I'd honestly forgotten."

"So something else."

"Well, yes, there *is* something. But it's not a bombshell, Jack, and it has nothing to do with murder." It's because we're alike, Cole and I, bonded by our love for Claire. She was the bright light for both of us—Cole, the angry, alienated boy, and Sarah, the lonely, desperate girl. And now . . . "It's a favor Cole has asked of me. Something I'm *going* to do."

Jack saw her defiance. It had been there from the start, the woman-warrior valiantly holding her ground, defying him, defending Cole.

Sarah was defiant still, unwavering still. But suddenly fearful. As if she was afraid that Jack might try to prevent her from granting this mysterious favor to Cole.

She's afraid of me . . . but not of Cole.

Molten fury filled his veins anew. But this time he chilled the fire before it flamed in his eyes.

His rage was frozen deep within. And now Jack felt new warmth, a most powerful heat. Not rage. Not fury. Just love.

He loved her, this complicated woman who told so many lies, and now his frozen heart was beating again, just for her.

"Tell me, Sarah," he said softly. "Tell me what Cole Taylor wants you to do."

Chapter Nineteen

Moisant Field
New Orleans
Friday, December Thirtieth

C LAIRE CHAMBERLAIN HAD NEVER FLOWN
in an airplane, not when she was sighted, not since
she'd been blind. When she made her reservations to London—with an open return—she mentioned her blindness,
in case it mattered. It did matter, the reservation agent affirmed. She would be assigned a specific seat, in the event of
emergency, and the flight attendants would be advised in
advance.

In truth, Claire had never traveled at all. She had packed for
a trip only once in her life, for her honeymoon with Andrew.
Now, for London with Cole, those same suitcases were filled
anew, and with some of the same never-worn items she had
packed six years before, remnants of the marriage that was
over before it ever began. *Dazzling* remnants, useful at last.
Onstage at the Royal Albert Hall, she would wear an emerald
flow of satin and silk, and for Timothy Asquith's gala to follow there would be more satin, ivory this time, a long-sleeved
floor-length evening gown.

Claire packed other clothes, familiar and worn, and surely
soft enough, bulky enough, that she could have nestled the
snow globe in their downy midst. But Claire left the globe
in her bedroom in Harlanville, something to return home

to . . . glass-encased memories of love that could never be shattered.

Claire had booked her reservation in coach. But when she reached the airport, accompanied by Millicent, she learned that she would be flying first-class, a change that had been made and paid for by a Mr. C. Taylor.

The first-class cabin provided spacious seating, the offer of a champagne brunch, and extremely nice flight attendants. But even that location of luxury, and the cheerfulness of those around her, could not calm Claire's terror.

The jet engines seemed so loud, surely *too* loud; then the plane began racing down the tarmac, a frantic sprint of trembling steel; then its nose lifted off, seeking the heavens, engaged in a battle against gravity that it could not possibly win; then the mammoth man-made creation was airborne, an unwelcome visitor in the skies, punished for that presumptuous intrusion by a raging storm.

Claire felt every lurch and skitter as if it were the last. Any moment the plane would shatter in midair, the splinters of its silvery body falling to earth like shooting stars. Or they would crash into a mountain, a towering mass of granite that was unseen until it was far too late.

The captain spoke to his passengers, a matter-of-fact voice from somewhere overhead. He described the ride as "a little bumpy," and requested that they keep their seat belts fastened. But, as if he truly believed that they would all survive this ordeal, he talked about their anticipated *on time* arrival and the current weather conditions at their destination. The flight attendants were similarly calm, serving the sumptuous brunch—which Claire declined—despite the "bumpiness."

Claire felt as if she alone knew the truth. Her eyes were unsighted, but she heard what others could not, the steel that creaked at its seams, the rivets that threatened to give way, the wings that were about to be severed cleanly from the body.

Claire heard every skirmish in the monumental battle between the fragile plane and the rage of nature, and she waged her own monumental battle against fear.

I am going to be with Cole. Someday, some *other* day, I can perish in a plane crash—on the flight home from London, perhaps, when the dream has come to an end.

But not now.

When Claire felt the beginning of the plane's descent, long before the pilot announced that change in trajectory, she believed that all was lost. The jet was hurtling toward earth, and even though her heart wasn't ready to die, her body prepared for the collision with muscles that became ever more taut and fingernails that plunged ever deeper into her already tender palms.

Then the plane landed, a stunningly graceful hello as rubber kissed asphalt, and for a moment Claire felt sheer, euphoric relief. The moment was fleeting, however, because as the customer service representative guided her down the jetway to the first-class lounge, her nerves quivered with an ominous reminder. They had just landed at JFK. The long transatlantic journey into darkness was still to come.

But Cole will be at the end of that journey of terror.

And then the truly terrifying journey will begin.

"**C**laire?"

The voice was familiar, elegantly accented and British, and heard often, in her years of blindness, as she listened to TV. "*Sarah?*"

"Yes, it's me," Sarah affirmed, marveling—and unprepared, despite what Cole had told her. *She won't seem blind. Her eyes will be clear and bright and focused, and she'll look right at you.* That was happening now, as if Claire's vision was quite perfect. Her years of sightedness guided her gaze not to Sarah's lips, the source of the sound, but higher, to Sarah's eyes. Just as Cole had promised. But there was something more about the sightless blue eyes, something that Cole had not forecast: they were smiling. "I hope you don't mind."

"Mind, Sarah?"

"Cole said that you were adamant about making the trip on your own, but—"

"Cole? He sent you?"

"Well, no. He didn't send me. I *wanted* to come, Claire, to talk to you, to explain why I never answered your last letter. Would that be all right? My assigned seat on the flight to London just happens to be next to yours. Is that okay?"

Claire answered with pure relief. "Oh, Sarah, it's more than okay. It's lovely."

There wasn't just one unanswered letter, Sarah learned, but many.

"I finally wrote to your mother, to make certain that you were all right. She answered promptly, explaining that you were attending a finishing school in Switzerland and that you were so happy there, so involved with a new circle of friends, that past friendships—such as ours—had apparently lapsed."

"I only knew about one letter, Claire, the one you wrote the night Cole's father died. She must have thrown the others away."

"But you read that letter, Sarah?" *The one in which I confessed everything—too much for our friendship to bear?*

"I read it, Claire, but not until four years later. Four years. It felt like a lifetime. So much had happened. Too much. Still, I wrote a reply."

"You did? I never received it."

"Because I never sent it. I *should* have, Claire, to let you know why I'd stopped writing, to be certain that you knew it had nothing to do with you or the letter you sent me. But my letter—and the way I was feeling about life at that time—was so negative, so relentlessly hopeless, it seemed best to keep all that negativity to myself."

"Your letter couldn't have been more negative or more hopeless than the one I sent you."

"But it was," Sarah countered, an assertion based on fact, not on false memory. Sarah had saved both of their letters, the final missives of the penmates who had shared so much. And last night she had reread them both. "Despite everything, your letter held a glimmer of hope. And you were *right* to be hopeful, Claire, to believe that you and Cole would be together again."

"We're *not* together, Sarah. Cole is just being nice. Kind."

"It's more than that, Claire. I've heard his voice when he talks about you. I've seen . . ."

"His eyes?" Claire finished softly. And she wondered: Could Sarah be her eyes? Could Sarah read for her the messages hidden in the darkly shadowed gray? No, because already Sarah had been deceived by Cole. Already she had seen messages, something *more* than kindness, that could not possibly be true. "Cole's very hard to read, Sarah. Besides, we had our chance, and it didn't work."

"But here we are, Claire, on a flight to London. You're going to sing with Cole again. He *wants* you to."

"Yes. But it's nostalgia, sentiment for the boy and girl who were such good friends and who dreamed of singing duets to the world. Cole's giving me that dream now, Sarah, and in return . . . Do you remember my writing to you about Cole's brother? It was in that letter."

"Of course I remember." *I read about that courageous act of love just last night.*

In fact, despite the lateness of the hour, Sarah had almost called Jack, to read the passage aloud to him. *Listen to this, Jack. Listen to what kind of human being Cole Taylor truly is, how loving he is, how heroic.* He's not a murderer, Jack! The boy who gave his brother away, because he loved him so much, could not have grown up to become a killer.

But Sarah had not made that late-night call. For two reasons. No, for three. First, the revelation was a secret, shared by young lovers in a moonlit gazebo. Claire's secret, Cole's secret; and not Sarah's to share. Secondly, and quite logically, Jack might assert that one act of love notwithstanding, Cole Taylor fit—indeed, *defined*—the classic profile of a murderer: raised in violence, brutally mistreated himself, abandoned by his mother to endure alone his father's cruelty and rage.

Then there was the third reason not to place the late-night phone call. Sarah *wanted* to talk to Jack, for any reason, any excuse. Even when she infuriated him, even when he had just cause to be immensely frustrated by her deceit, there was gentleness still, *tenderness*. And how much did she need Jack? Desperately, dangerously, a need more potent—and destructive?—than her need to escape to the numbness of alcohol, or the asylum of war, or the bold fantasies of the shadow woman in Paris.

"Cole hasn't found his brother?"

"I'm sure he hasn't even tried. His search would necessarily have been a public one. I would have known about it."

"There must be reason he hasn't searched. I suppose he's afraid of what he might find. That his brother's new home was no better than the Taylor home, perhaps? And that his brother loathes him for what he did?"

"Yes, but I think there's even more. Even though it was an accident, Cole blames himself for his father's death, for failing to prevent it—as if that proves that Jed's violence lives within him, as if *he* is a murderer, too. I imagine Cole's decided that his brother would be better off not knowing anything about him. But he's wrong, Sarah. I believe that with all my heart. That's why I'm going to orchestrate their reunion."

"By making the appeal yourself?"

"Yes." The golden flecks in Claire's sightless blue eyes glittered with determination. " 'Imagine Moonlight' will undoubtedly be nominated for several Grammys, as well as for an Academy Award. If I'm onstage with Cole at either of those events, I'll make the announcement myself. And if not, if I'm already back in Harlanville, I'll arrange to have someone else make it for me."

"But those award ceremonies are quite soon, aren't they, Claire? In February and March? Surely you won't have returned to Harlanville."

"I don't know, Sarah." *I don't know how long I can bear to be with him, loving him, wondering about his pity, worrying that he wants me to leave.* "If, by then, I've found someone I can trust to make the announcement, my mission will be accomplished and I'll be back in Louisiana teaching music."

Claire shrugged, then smiled. "Anyway, my plan to find Cole's brother *will* work. The audiences for those shows are gigantic, and it's a story the media will definitely pursue, don't you think?"

"Absolutely. But it's also a story for which there may be a legion of impostors. More than one unscrupulous man might decide to claim the fabulously wealthy superstar as his long-lost brother."

"Yes, but you know when a crime's been committed, when there's a murderer on the loose and the police purposefully withhold key information?"

Yes, I know, Sarah thought. *I know, for example, that the LAPD carefully suppressed the symbol of the black heart and the killer's lethal left-handed slash.*

Cole Taylor is *not* that man. *He is not.* "You plan to withhold certain information, Claire?"

Claire nodded. "Just describing the circumstances—the truck stop in West Texas in the middle of a December night twenty-seven years ago—should be enough, don't you think? Other details, like the rusty wagon and the tattered quilt, could remain hidden. And there was a song, a favorite lullaby, that Cole sang that night. I don't know what it was, but his little brother might remember. Well, maybe not. He was only two."

"What if Cole's brother was never told about that night?"

"The man who became his father will remember. Cole described him as fairly young at the time, no older than their own father, so . . ."

"So he's still alive, and you're really going to do this, aren't you?"

"Yes. I am. I have to." *I saw the flame that died in Cole's heart when we abandoned that dream. It was a tiny flame, engulfed by the dazzling splendor of the other dreams we shared. But those other dreams are gone now, burned to ash, and the dream of finding his brother is the only ember that remains.*

The flight was astonishingly smooth. Even the roaring engines muted to a contented purr. It was Sarah's presence, of course, the calm voice that offered instant reassurance whenever the plane made even the slightest dip. And it helped, too, that the storm that ravaged the East Coast had not followed them out to sea.

But there was turbulence still, a private storm. Claire heard it, felt it, as Sarah described her own Christmastime horror, the mercifully short but terrifying hours during which she and her parents had been held hostage. She went a "bit mad" after that, she admitted. In fact, she confessed, she went totally "off the deep end."

And, at the end of *that* year of madness, she did something even more crazy. She married Simon Beckwith-Jones, a man her parents' age whom she did not love and who died, with her parents, three years after they were wed.

"There's more, isn't there, Sarah?" Claire asked when Sarah had finished her brief and unemotional recounting of those four years. "Something horribly painful—even *more* painful than what you've already told me."

"Yes, Claire, there is more." *Rape, betrayal, the loss of a beloved child; then more rape and even more betrayal.* "But it's truly not worth telling. It's ancient history."

"Except that whatever it was caused you to write a letter to me that was too pessimistic to send."

"Yes, well, my letters were always far more negative than yours. That one was just far and away the worst. Anyway, I've moved on."

"I'm glad." *I hope it's true.* "Is there someone in your life, Sarah?"

"No."

The "no" was emphatic and immediate. But Claire smiled. "My hearing has gotten very good during the past six years. That sounded like a yes to me, Sarah, or at least a maybe?"

"Your hearing *is* good," Sarah murmured fondly. "He's . . . it's business."

"Business?"

Yes, you see, I've been targeted for murder, and he's going to solve the mystery before my death. His approach is extremely logical, as it should be. Cool, dispassionate, calm. He's not a man who rushes to judgment. Nor has he done so. But guess whose name he has calmly—and logically—placed on his list of suspects? He's had to, of course. The master puzzle solver truly has no choice.

Just as now I have no choice about speaking the necessary lie.

"He's writing a book about war correspondents in the modern era, including me."

"*Of course* including you, Sarah! And his name is . . . ?"

"Jack Dalton."

"Will I meet him?"

"Yes. He'll be escorting me on New Year's Eve, both to your concert at the Royal Albert Hall and to Timothy's party afterward."

"That sounds more like romance than business."

Oh no, Claire, it's all business. Just a cold-blooded search for a cold-blooded killer. Isn't it?

Chapter Twenty

Heathrow Airport
London
Friday, December Thirtieth

ONE WOMAN WAS A SCHOOLTEACHER. HER blue eyes could not see and she had never before set foot on foreign soil. The other was a famous war correspondent. Her green eyes had seen too much, blood-soaked earth in nations of the world ravaged by war.

But on this day the two women shared an experience that was entirely new for both of them. Both were greeted, at the airport, by men who loved them.

Jack wasn't supposed to be here! Yes, he had offered to come. But Sarah had countered, quite emphatically she thought, that she didn't need to be met. *I'm accustomed to getting myself home from the airport, Jack!* Accustomed to returning from war—alone.

"But I'd like to meet you, Sarah."

"No, really. It's not necessary." *And it feels too dangerous, too much like love.* "Besides, Cole will be there. I'll ride into town with Cole and Claire."

Cole. That was, of course, the real reason Jack had suggested the airport rendezvous. To observe Cole, a watchful, appraising, unemotional search for clues. Business, not romance.

Except that now, as she and Claire approached, Jack wasn't watching Cole. He was looking at her, his expression gentle as he silently posed questions that had nothing to do with murder. Did it go well, Sarah? This all-important reunion with your friend?

Claire's hand was curled around Sarah's arm. But, Sarah thought, *I'm* the one who's clinging, who's gathering strength and courage from Claire.

Sarah's smile gave Jack her reply. *Yes, it went well . . . thank you.*

"We made it."

"Yes, you did. Good flight?"

"Very good. Perfectly smooth. Oh! Claire Chamberlain, this is Jack Dalton. Jack, Claire."

"Hello, Jack." Claire extended her hand to him, exactly where it should be to meet his, and her auburn head tilted upward, at just the right angle, as they exchanged warm hellos.

"Did you sleep?" Cole asked, his first words, soft and concerned.

"Not a wink," Claire replied to the place where the softness—and his heat—hummed in the air. "We didn't even try. There was too much catching up to do. It was good, Cole, *wonderful*, that Sarah met me in New York."

"**D**id you notice the way Cole looked at her, Jack? At the airport and all the way into town?"

"I noticed." And I saw your expression, too, as you watched them. Thoughtful. Hopeful. And now, in the starkness of your penthouse, I see the passion of your fight for the happiness of your friend.

"Then you saw, *must* have seen, that Cole is not a killer. *Couldn't* be."

Not a killer. The remarkable and defiant assertion had danced in Jack's own mind while he waited with Cole for the arrival of the flight from New York. That Jack Dalton and Cole Taylor would have anything in common seemed improbable, as did the notion that their silence could feel more companionable than awkward. But as they waited at Heathrow, Jack and Cole were not hunter and prey, not murder maven and possible madman. They were just two men, waiting for the women they loved, and worrying about them, hoping that their reunion had gone well.

And when those women arrived, Jack saw the way Cole greeted Sarah—with gratitude, for what Sarah had done for Claire. Gratitude. Not bloodlust, not cunning, not seduction.

But that meant nothing, Jack knew. If one could diagnose a psychopath simply by looking at him, the world would be a very safe place indeed. The danger of psychopaths, the key to their sinister success, was precisely their ability to appear perfectly normal. *That* was their cunning, their most masterful seduction of all.

"He couldn't be," Sarah repeated.

"Maybe not."

"Maybe not?"

"I admit it feels too easy. Cole Taylor arrives, on cue, from Los Angeles. He knew both victims, and has no trouble whatsoever in approaching you. He's left-handed, his birthday's on Valentine's Day, and, the icing on the cake, he even comes nicely packaged with an enticingly violent past, a death—albeit perhaps accidental—in which the lethal weapon was a hunting knife."

"I agree, Jack. It's too easy."

She was standing near the fireplace, her eyes shimmering with hope. Behind her, on the marble mantelpiece, stood the Pegasus statues, and they seemed to shimmer as well . . . until Jack remembered what they were: *puzzles*, assembled with patience, care, and the rigorous application of logic.

"We're puzzle solvers, Sarah. You and I. We like our puzzles challenging and tough—which is what this puzzle *would* have been had you not so promptly recognized the significance of the black heart. That's the reason this seems so easy. Because we've been waiting for him."

"So you're not dismissing Cole as a suspect?"

"You know I can't."

Even though I want to. It was an amazing realization. Emotional. Irrational. Not typical of Jack. And even more startling was Jack's reason for wishing for Cole's innocence. For Sarah, yes, of course, because of Claire. But mostly the wish was for Cole himself. Jack saw the way Cole looked at Claire, the emotional duet of desire and of torment, of longing and of love.

And Jack wanted what? Cole's *happiness*? Pure joy for the man whose greatest longing, greatest desire, might be to splatter crimson droplets of Sarah Pembroke's blood all over this stark penthouse of ebony and bone? Whose torment would be at peace when the shimmering Pegasus puzzles were cloaked in red?

"You can't dismiss Cole as a suspect, either, Sarah."

"I *can* . . . but I won't."

"Thank you."

"And thank you for meeting me at the airport."

"I wanted to. And I'm looking forward to tomorrow night."

"So am I. I know that when you hear Cole singing love songs with Claire—"

"Listening to Cole sing songs of love is not the reason I'm looking forward to the evening," Jack interjected softly. "I'm talking about after the concert. Timothy's party."

She could barely speak. The tenderness, the intimacy, had stolen her breath. But she had to reclaim what had been stolen, because in another moment Jack might believe that it was a gift, freely and so joyfully given. You can have my breath, Jack, and my heart, and my soul, and my—

This is business for him, remember? The immensely fascinating business of catching a killer. *That's* what fascinates Jack Dalton. That challenging puzzle of death, not the disappointing mysteries of you. "You want to see who approaches me? What murderers might be lurking in the shadows?"

Jack answered with a smile, and from the depths of his indigo eyes Sarah saw the unshadowed desire of the man who could, with no weapons whatsoever, cause the swift and brutal murder of her heart. "No, Sarah. What I'm looking forward to is dancing with you."

Claire's room at the Drake Hotel was a one-bedroom suite on the eighteenth floor. Cole had been shown every available suite in the hotel and had chosen this one.

Its location was good, a short, straight walk to the bank of virtually silent elevators. Twelve of his strides; eighteen, he'd decided, of hers. And the layout of this suite was the best Cole had seen, the most easy to navigate in darkness—more easy now, since he had rearranged the furniture.

"Let me tell you about the room," Cole offered when Claire's luggage had been deposited in the bedroom and the bellman was gone.

"All right."

"Well, everything is to the left of where we're standing. The living room is first and then—" Cole was stopped by an emphatic shake of shining cinnamon. "What?"

"I can learn those details myself. In fact, that's the way I *need* to learn them. But I'd like to know what color the walls are, and the carpet and furniture and drapes, and . . . there are roses nearby, aren't there?"

"Yes. Quite a few roses."

Claire smiled. "Please tell me about them first."

"Okay. Well, they're pink—as, for that matter, are the carpet and drapes."

"What color pink, Cole? Are the roses and carpet and drapes the *same* pink?"

Oh, Claire, you ask too much of me. You ask me to be your eyes, to see the world as you would have seen it. But for me, except for those times when I've been with you, my world has been entirely gray.

Now Claire was asking him to describe colors to her. And, to his surprise, Cole *did* know colors. He was, in fact, an expert on certain shades of blue and pink and copper and gold—the colors of Claire: her eyes, her lips, the glittering fire of her hair.

What color were the roses? Cole knew precisely: the radiant flush of her cheeks on that moonlit night at Belle Rêve when he had framed her beloved face in his hands. But it would be of no use to Claire for him to tell her that. Such a revelation would not color her blackness. He alone had seen that enthralling pink, that ravishing hue of pure joy.

Claire was asking him to guide her now, as she had once

guided him through their verdant forest, when his eyes were closed and he trusted her not to abandon him in the darkness.

But now *he* was abandoning *her*—because, without Claire, Cole knew only darkness. Except that now, as then, Claire was rescuing him, leading him from his world of blackness into her glorious realm of color and light.

"Are they light pink?" she asked. "A happy, joyful pink?"

"Yes." *Exactly that pink—of happiness, of joy . . . of love.* "A happy pink, Claire."

The carpets and drapes were happy as well, they decided, although slightly more subdued than the roses, just the proper tincture of English decorum having been added; and the furniture, seen by Claire through her sensitive fingertips, was upholstered in floral brocade, and—

"I hear rain."

"Yes you do."

In fact, the sudden downpour was torrential; but it was muted to near soundlessness by the double-paned glass. Indeed, had the windows in Claire's suite been small, a minimum surface area on which the raindrops could splash, their sound might have been inaudible even to her acute ears.

But one entire wall of Claire's happy pink suite was glass, a discovery made by her as she moved toward the chorus of raindrops.

"I must have a view," she murmured as she touched the glassy expanse and felt the familiar—and comforting—smoothness beneath her hands.

Her snow globe was at home, but here was this entire wall of glass. And instead of encasing her tiny town of wintertime celebration, this glass promised a whole new world—of plump, singing raindrops, and the vast future she had yet to live . . . and a view.

The view from Claire's suite was the best the Drake Hotel had to offer. Had he wanted this spectacular view for her? *Yes,* Cole realized now. It had been a factor in his choice of this suite, just as he had been influenced by the happy shades of pink. *As if she could see.*

She believes she can see, will be able to see, with my help. *Oh, Claire, I have so little to offer, such meager help. Without you, I, too, am blind.*

"The view's of Hyde Park. There's nothing to see now, with nightfall and the rain—"

"But there must be lights."

Yes, there were lights, the jewel-bright dazzle of London after dark. And on this soggy night, the lights were blurred by raindrops, a liquid flow of color; and after a moment Cole heard a voice. Was it truly his own?

"There are lights, Claire, and it's as if each one is a small sun and each raindrop is a storm unto itself—and when the two meet, there are rainbows. And as for the lights that don't have their own private raindrops, they're twinkling brightly, like stars."

So now she knew something about her wall of glass, the splendor just beyond its smooth surface. No snowflakes danced there. No tiny perfect crystals of remembered love. But there were rainbows here, and stars, symbols of her future not her past . . . for tomorrow night, with Cole, she would sing of places over rainbows and wishes made upon stars.

Chapter Twenty-One

London
Saturday, December Thirty-first

THEY SPENT THE AFTERNOON AT THE BRIT-
ish Museum, wandering amid the riches, marveling at
the splendor they beheld. As they stood in reverent silence before the Elgin marbles, Emma's mind floated back in time, to
other marbled treasures . . . and the beginning of her love for
Lucas.

It was an experiment in education—and goodwill—a social
and academic marriage of students from two of the world's
preeminent universities. For many years Stanford University
had maintained a campus in Italy, the three-story Villa San
Paolo in Florence. But always before the eighty students housed
within the villa's frescoed walls had been American, imported
from the school's parent campus in Palo Alto.

During that experimental year, however, half of the students
were English, undergraduates at Cambridge. Invited to spend
the fall term in Florence, as guests of Stanford, they would return the favor in January, in England, hosting the forty Americans there for the remainder of the academic year.

Emma Louise Lloyd was the last British student to learn
that she would be journeying to *Firenze*. The youngest mem-
ber of the group, she was on the alternate wait list until just
twenty-four hours before the charter flight from San Fran-

cisco was due to touch down at Heathrow to collect the English contingent.

But Emma was at Heathrow the following day, wide-eyed, eager, and accompanied by her slightly shell-shocked parents. The past year, Emma's first at Cambridge, had been wrenching separation enough. Now their beloved—and so innocent—daughter was journeying much farther away, and ever closer to her ultimate and inevitable independence from them.

Did Eleanor and Jonathan Lloyd show their concern? They did not. How could they, when Emma's eyes shone so brightly as she envisioned the grand adventure that lay ahead?

The forty Cambridge students who boarded the plane at Heathrow were subject to intense scrutiny by their American counterparts. The Stanford students had already taken stock of one another, during the long flight from San Francisco, and now they assessed the English half of the group, an appraising search for future friends . . . and future lovers.

Emma was oblivious to the scrutiny, lost in the excitement of the moment, and the idea of viewing strangers with such calculated appraisal was absolutely foreign to her. She imagined that everyone in the group would be friendly, and she would have blushed furiously at the thought of anyone becoming her lover.

One Stanford student did not partake in what eventually became the boisterous welcome of the classmates from Cambridge. He was reading a guidebook of Florence, absorbed in that study—and uninterested, it seemed, in the revelry that surrounded him. Much later Emma would come to understand that he didn't need to study the English girls, to decide even before the jet left Heathrow if there was one he wanted to pursue. She would come to understand, much later, that Lucas Cain could have whomever he wanted, whenever he wanted her.

For the two-hour flight from London to Milan, however, Lucas had no choice about his female companion. Emma's assigned seat was next to his.

As she settled in, Lucas looked up from his book and greeted, *"Buon giorno."*

He stole her breath, literally. Her breath, her speech, her ability even to think. The theft only grew worse as his glittering green gaze intensified in response to her silence.

"It means 'good day' in Italian."

His words caused a wobbly smile amid ever-pinkening cheeks—and, at last, a brief, breathless reply.

"Yes, I know." Of course she knew. Everyone, including the alternates, had taken at least one term of intensive Italian. Emma's comprehension was excellent, and she could write the language flawlessly. But she felt terribly self-conscious about speaking it. *Buon giorno* ranked with *grazie*, *prego*, and *ciao* as one of the most frequently used phrases. Frequently used—and, for Emma, extremely difficult to speak. *Buon* was supposed to be "*bw*one," not "bone," and *giorno* required a rolling of the *r* that required a boldness she did not possess. She had spent the summer wishing a joyous *buon giorno* to the gulls that soared in the sapphire skies above Cornwall, and to the heather and hedgerows and clouds and waves. And there were times when the words sounded *almost* right.

But Cornish seabirds were one thing, and this black-haired, green-eyed American was quite another. His pronunciation wasn't perfect, merely uninhibited and slightly amused, as if nakedness of any sort was of absolutely no consequence to him. And why would it be?

"I know," Emma murmured again. "Hi."

Lucas smiled. "I Ii."

Emma couldn't speak to Lucas Cain during the flight to Milan, and words did not come, either, in the classes they shared, or when they passed each other in the villa's hallways, or when, arriving in the dining room at the very last moment, he found an empty chair at the table—for eight—where she sat.

Emma couldn't speak in his presence, could barely breathe. But her legs worked very well—and of their own accord. Brave, foolish, renegade legs. She followed him, for heaven's sake, like a puppy dog, thrilled just to be near.

It happened *mostly* by chance, the first time, or so she told herself. The class schedule was conducive to exploration of the world beyond the villa's stucco walls: mornings only, Monday through Thursday. Weekday afternoons were dedicated to discovery of the wonders of *Firenze*, and long weekends were designed to encourage journeys to the nearby treasures of Siena, Rome, Vinci, Naples.

It was a Tuesday afternoon in late October, a brisk, clear autumnal day in Tuscany. By then, eight weeks into their Florentine sojourn, many of the students felt they had done ample justice to the city's lavish offerings. They had climbed Giotto's campanile, and knew by heart every Renaissance masterpiece housed within the Duomo. They had admired Ghiberti's *Gate of Paradise*, bronze scene by bronze scene, and had visited the baroque mausoleum where the Medici grand dukes were entombed. Every one of them could point to the precise spot in the Piazza della Signorìa where the fanatic monk Savonarola had ignited his bonfire of the vanities, and all could describe in vivid detail Botticelli's *Birth of Venus*.

There were afternoons now when some students remained at the villa, drinking cappuccino in the cantina, reminiscing about their recent adventures at Oktoberfest, and avidly planning other upcoming excursions. Others left the villa not for the museums and palaces, but for the city's many markets. There they would barter—in Italian—for leather goods, sweaters, and trinkets made of gold, and afterward they would celebrate the shrewdness of their purchases with gelato at Perchè Non. Some strolled across the Ponte Vecchio, watching the Arno rise, predicting with grim certainty that the flood of 1966 was about to recur—and wondering aloud why no one was doing anything about it. And some went to the ancient village of Fiesole, to share carafes of *vino* while enjoying the panoramic view below.

Emma knew that she had not exhausted the treasures Florence had to offer. She never would. Every time she stood before the Fountain of Neptune, or wandered through the Giardino di Boboli, or viewed Da Vinci's *Adoration of the Magi*, she saw something new, ever deeper layers of meaning, of richness.

On this brilliant blue October afternoon she had decided to visit once again the Palazzo Strozzi. But when she saw Lucas walking just a block ahead of her, her plans changed. She followed him, unable not to, a cloak-and-dagger journey all the way to the Galleria dell'Accademia.

Lucas wanted to see Michelangelo's *David* again. And again and again. It was remarkable that he even noticed Emma. When he was here, in this place, he was always focused on the splendor of the art, intently focused—exclusively focused.

But for some reason his gaze left the exquisitely sculpted foot of the giant slayer and fell on the alabaster visage of the timid English girl. She was standing on the other side of the magnificent statue, looking up, her expression enraptured.

Compelled by something he could not name, Lucas joined her, and when Emma looked from the sculpted marble to him, Lucas was greeted by an expression that was enraptured still.

"*Buon*—" He smiled. "Hi, Emma."

"Hi, Lucas."

Emma had believed that she knew quite a bit about the masters of the Renaissance. She had taken art history classes at Cambridge, after all, and had done extensive reading on her own, and there were daily lectures on Renaissance art and artists at the villa.

But on that afternoon with Lucas Cain, Emma realized how little she knew about Michelangelo, or Ghiberti, or Donatello, or Cellini; and how much Lucas did. It was as if he had actually met those gifted artists of the past, as if he were a sorcerer who had traveled through the centuries and become friends with those extraordinary men. He explained, as if he knew firsthand, precisely how those master sculptors made stone-hard marble appear to be the most supple of flesh.

Over the next three weeks, they met—she followed him—eight times. But Emma did *not* follow Lucas to Venice. That encounter was pure happenstance, an authentic whim—or per-haps mandate—of fate.

It was the last weekend in November. Most of the other students had gone south, seeking the sun. Northern Italy had been drenched in rain for two weeks, and it was rumored that the weather in Naples was quite balmy. Capri beckoned, promising golden warmth and bright blue seas. Or one could journey south to Pisa, to confirm that the tower was leaning still, *really* leaning, then travel on to Portofino, the jewel of the Italian Riviera.

Venice was a most unlikely destination in late November. The tourist season had long since ended, with good reason. The glass factories were closed, and San Marco Square was knee-deep in water, and much of the fleet of night-black gondolas were in hibernation for the winter, and even the piazza's famous pigeons had flown to higher ground.

Lucas and Emma had already been to Venice. In September the entire group had spent five days in the City of Canals. But for some reason, on this soggy November weekend, both decided to return.

Lucas made the discovery that he was not alone the moment he stepped off the train. She had obviously been on the same train from Florence, a few cars back, and now she was being Emma, blinking at the floating gray mists of Venice as if she were Dorothy blinking at the dazzling brilliance of Oz. Smiling her shy and lovely smile, she seemed at once overjoyed, and overwhelmed, at the splendor she beheld.

Emma had no idea that she was being observed, no inkling that Lucas was at the train station in Venice, too. He could easily disappear. She would never know.

But Lucas didn't disappear—any more than he tried to escape from her in Florence. He knew full well that she sometimes followed him. He allowed her to, *wanted* her to, adjusting his long strides so that she wouldn't lose him and even backtracking to the villa when he realized he had begun his afternoon journey a little too soon.

That he welcomed Emma's companionship truly stunned

him. But he did. He enjoyed sharing the things that mattered most to him with this lovely English girl.

"Hi, Emma."

"Oh! *Lucas.*"

"Hi," he repeated softly.

Emma kept waiting for him to make his gracious exit. *Ciao, Emma. See you back in Firenze.* But even as she was waiting for those words of farewell, they were sharing a vaporetto along the Grand Canal, then finding a pensione on Riva degli Schiavoni, then making plans for dinner; and over spinach lasagna they talked about what they would see the next day, and the next.

Saint Mark's Basilica, of course. They could easily spend the entire weekend in that exotic place, marveling at its golden mosaics, mysteriously luminous in the haunting gloom. But there was also the Doge's Palace, with its pride of winged lions without and its almost decadent opulence within; and how could they possibly leave Venice without wandering once more through the Accademia di Belle Arti?

And over cappuccino and candlelight, they talked of other things. At his urging, Emma told him about her home in the West Country, and Lucas heard much more: her love for her native Cornwall, that enchanted place of Arthur and Guinevere and Merlin and Camelot; and her love, most of all, for her parents.

Lucas didn't tell Emma about *his* home. There was little to tell, and none of it had anything to do with love. But on this night of mist and magic in *La Serenìssima*, Lucas Cain told Emma Lloyd about his dreams.

"I'd like to be a sculptor."

Emma already knew who he was. A sculptor if he wanted to be, *anything* he wanted to be. But mostly Lucas Cain was a modern-day Merlin, a sorcerer who could conjure all manner of magic, and who could travel through time to befriend the masters of the Renaissance, and who possessed a wisdom that was ancient and worldly, sensual and—"Really?"

"It's not a very modern career choice, Emma, or a very prac-
tical one. What I'd like to do is work in marble."

"Like Michelangelo."

"Well . . ."

"Have you done any sculpting?"

"I've carved wood for years, since I was a kid. And I've done
a little work in stone."

"And you're good, aren't you?"

Lucas laughed. "Who knows? But I hope to find out."

"You will. And you'll be wonderful." *You are wonderful.*

So are you, Lucas thought as he looked at bright blue eyes
aglow with candlelight—but mostly, and so brilliantly, aglow
with confidence in him.

In truth, Lucas did not need Emma's confidence. He already
knew that he had great talent. But talent wasn't enough. Lucas knew that, too. To achieve his ancient yet modern dream
would require everything he had, his heart, his mind, his soul.
He had to be relentless, unwavering, passionately committed.
That was the easy part, of course, because there was absolutely
nothing else that Lucas wanted . . . nothing else that mattered
to him at all.

But there would be no harm in kissing this lovely English girl,
would there? Lucas had kissed many girls, and all had enthusiastically kissed him back. Kissed him, made love with him—
and wanted far more than he was willing to give. But that was
easy, too. So very easy to say good-bye.

Lucas wanted to kiss Emma, more than he remembered ever
wanting that intimacy before. But he did not even touch her.
Not that night. And not any of the thousand times he wanted
to the next day, as they marveled at the glittering gold of San
Marco, or later, when her face was damp with mist and rosy
with happiness as she gazed with appreciative wonder at the
graceful arch of the Bridge of Sighs.

What harm could there be? *So easy to say good-bye.* Wasn't
it? Yes. *Yes.*

Just a good-night kiss, a celebration of the glorious day they had just spent, and a promise that tomorrow would be even better.

But it wasn't *just* a kiss. How could it be, when he wanted her so much; and when she responded with such surprised yet eager joy?

Emma was warm and sweet and soft, and as hungry as he.

"We'd better stop," he whispered, his voice low, and deep, and raw with need. His words should have caused no confusion. But Lucas saw a lovely frown on her passion-flushed face.

"You don't . . . ?"

"Want you?" His laugh was needy. "Oh yes, Emma. I want you. But you've never done this before, have you?"

Her golden head answered, a shake of dancing curls that glittered more brightly than all of San Marco's gold. And her eyes answered, too, bright blue—and fearless.

"I'm not afraid, Lucas. I want to."

"I don't have anything with me, Emma. No birth control."

"But it's *okay*. I mean, it's safe. I just finished my . . . I won't get pregnant."

It's safe, Lucas. How many times he had heard those words before—albeit differently? Always before, they had been spoken in provocative whispers with confident hands that eloquently embellished their intent. *Come on, Lucas. Make love to me.*

But there was nothing—and yet everything—provocative about the young Englishwoman who stood before him. Just honesty. Just brilliant blue candor. Just shy yet bold desire.

Never before had Lucas Cain risked his dream. Never before had he placed the fleeting pleasures of the flesh above his abiding passion for marble.

But now he did, without a second thought.

"Are you sure, Emma? This is what you want?"

Emma had never been more certain of anything in her life. And now he was looking at her as if *she*—plain little Emma—was a work of art, an alabaster statue of extraordinary beauty;

and his eyes, those gleaming green eyes of the sorcerer, were promising to show her magic.

"Yes," she whispered. *"Yes."*

It didn't hurt, not even for that breathtaking instant when they became one. She had told him that she wasn't afraid, but she *was*, and he knew that, and he was so very gentle, so tender and careful, that all her fear melted away.

And the talented hands that were strong enough to carve statues from stone? They caressed her as if she were porcelain, delicate, fragile—and so very precious.

For Emma, in that magical weekend in Venice, the hands of Lucas Cain were filled only with love.

*C*hapter Twenty-Two

"**Y**OU SLEPT WITH HIM, DIDN'T YOU?"
Emma stared at her American roommate. Ashley
Alexander was startlingly beautiful, always. Even now, when
she was so obviously displeased.

"You had sex with Lucas, didn't you, Emma?" Ashley
pressed. Then, exasperated with Emma's silence, she asked,
"Are we having a language problem here? I can be a little more
explicit, more vulgar, if you like. Did you and Lucas—"

"Yes." *No. It wasn't sex. We made love.* "Yes."

Ashley sighed, and a look of sympathy replaced the displea-
sure. "Oh, dear. And it *meant* something to you, didn't it?
Don't answer. I can tell just by looking at you." Ashley sighed
again. "But, Emma, it didn't mean a thing to him."

Yes it did! How could it not?

"Sit," Ashley commanded. "It's time, *past* time, that you
learned the truth about Lucas Cain."

*I know all about Lucas, how wonderful he is, how gentle
and loving—*

"I've known Lucas since our freshman year. We were involved then. Yes, Emma, I've slept with him. *Everyone* has.
He's a terrific lover. You don't have any perspective on that,
though, do you? Lucas was your first, wasn't he?" When

263

Emma's response was a faint nod, Ashley's voice became impassioned. "I blame myself. I should have *warned* you about him. Not that there's anything wrong with him, of course. It's just that he's wrong for someone like you, someone who expects anything more from him than sex. For Lucas, sex is *pleasure*, nothing more. And, as I'm sure you discovered, nothing less. He's a connoisseur—and a classy one at that. Unlike other men I've known, Lucas doesn't talk about his sexual encounters. There are no notches on his bedpost. Sex isn't conquest for him. How could it be, when women always come to him? He's slept with almost every girl in our group, Emma. It's true—although until now, no one knew but Lucas and me."

"He told you?"

"No, I just told you, he is *extremely* discreet. He doesn't talk about sex, he just *does* it. Often. I know about the others because I know Lucas. And I was right about the two of you, wasn't I? Besides, sampling as many women as he can is a major reason Lucas is spending this year abroad."

"No it's not!"

"Oh?"

"He's here because of the art, the artists, the Renaissance sculptors."

Ashley's eyes widened. "My, my. I'm truly impressed. Lucas actually told you about his plan to become a sculptor? He really was pulling out all the stops, wasn't he? Strong, silent, sexy Lucas Cain decided that he needed to talk a little, *confess* a little, to get you into bed. You should be flattered, Emma. He usually doesn't go to such trouble, doesn't need to."

"He's not planning to be a sculptor?"

"Oh yes, he is. I've seen his work. He's gifted, Emma, truly, *truly* gifted." The beautiful young woman who was destined to become an Academy Award–winning actress paused. It was a short pause, but a significant one, a dramatic foreshadowing of the revelation that was about to come. "I don't suppose that while Lucas was seducing you he happened to mention Daphne?"

"Daphne?"

"I didn't think so. She just happens to be his fiancée, as well as my best friend. She loves Lucas, and he loves her—as much as he will *ever* love anything that isn't made of stone. And thanks to Daphne, he'll be able to devote himself to that passion. Daphne's father makes movies, which makes Daphne very rich. Lucas will never need to do anything but sculpt, all day every day—and make love to Daphne, of course, *only* to Daphne. They're planning to get married in June, and he's promised her that he'll be faithful once they're wed. So this European adventure is his last chance, his final fling, and, quite obviously, he's taking full advantage. Daphne knows what he's doing, although not the specifics. In my letters to her I always write that Lucas seems lonely, and I'm sure his letters are filled with his love for her, and for Michelangelo, and no one else. Which is the truth, Emma. That's one thing about Lucas Cain. He may omit the odd detail here and there—like his engagement to Daphne—but he doesn't lie. He didn't tell you that he loved you, did he?"

No . . . but the way he held me and touched me and—

"No," Emma admitted. "He didn't."

"Oh, Emma. I'm *sorry*. But you needed to know this, didn't you? The sooner the better? You had a one-night stand—a one-weekend stand—with Lucas, and you should never regret it. Now that you know just how terrific sex can be, you won't settle for anything less. And now you'll know, too, not to confuse spectacular sex with promises of love."

"Emma?"

It seemed impossible that she could hurt more than she already did. But his voice, and his smile, and those concerned green eyes made the knife that pierced her heart twist ever deeper.

Why was Lucas talking to her here, at the villa, *at all*? He was supposed to be done with her, done *sampling* her, and on to the next.

"Lucas."

"Hi. You've been avoiding me."

"I've been studying for finals."

"Will you come to Assisi with me this weekend? I thought we could stop at Perugia en route, to stock up on chocolate to fortify us for all the walking we'll need to do in Assisi. In addition to the cathedral I thought it might be interesting to climb Mount Subasio. What do you say?"

Yes, her aching heart implored. Say yes. And why not? You have nothing to lose. You couldn't possibly hurt any more than you already do. This is what college is all about, Emma! Experiencing new things, meeting new people, falling in love. Be cheerful! As Ashley said, after Lucas you'll never settle for anything less.

But Emma couldn't say yes. She couldn't agree to just having sex with Lucas . . . couldn't settle for less than love.

"No, thank you. I think I'll stay here this weekend."

"I'll stay with you then. We'll study together."

"No. Thank you." *No, no, no.* Leave me alone! *Please.*

"Tell me what's wrong, Emma." His gaze was as caressing as it had been in Venice, as if he truly cared, as if there was even more magic the sorcerer wanted to show her. "Do you regret last weekend? Did I hurt you? Are you bleed—"

"No. You didn't hurt me." *You just killed me.* "I have to go, Lucas. I'm meeting Ashley for a study break." *You remember Ashley, don't you, Lucas? One of your many lovers—not to mention Daphne's best friend?*

Lucas persevered. But Emma wouldn't talk to him. And the more he pressed, the more frail she seemed—a frailness that was enhanced by whatever virus claimed about half the students during that final week before the Christmas holidays, their final week in Florence.

Lucas wished her "Merry Christmas," and Emma whispered "Happy Christmas" in reply; and he promised himself that they would talk in January, when they saw each other again at Cambridge.

But Emma wasn't at Cambridge. The registrar's office confirmed that she had officially withdrawn for the remainder of the academic year. Lucas didn't have her home address, but he knew where she lived—at her parents' bed-and-breakfast, a place called Hyacinth House, in Cornwall, just south of St. Ives.

Lucas had formed a clear image of Hyacinth House. Based on Emma's loving description of her seaside home, he expected charm and grandeur, a stately structure that endured with regal dignity the harsh winds and raging seas that battered the rugged Cornish coast.

Hyacinth House *was* potentially grand. But in its present incarnation it was somewhat bedraggled, tired and worn; yet welcoming nonetheless.

Lucas's impression of welcome would have been instantly dashed had he climbed the steps to the dilapidated verandah and rung the doorbell. In that event, he would have been met by Eleanor and Jonathan Lloyd—a greeting that would have been decidedly cold.

As it was, however, before reaching the house, Lucas caught sight of Emma. Despite the blustery January day, she was standing on a cliff above the sea, her hair pure gold in the pale light of the winter sun.

She didn't hear him approach. His footfalls were lost in the thunder of crashing waves and the loud howl of the chilling wind. By the time he spoke he was very near.

"Emma?"

She spun, too quickly. The dizziness that had been a constant companion for almost six weeks sent a whirling protest.

She wobbled—and he caught her, holding her to him as he searched her wary blue eyes. "You're pregnant, aren't you?"

Emma stepped back, out of his embrace. "It has nothing to do with you."

"It does if it's my child you're carrying. And it is my child, isn't it?"

The punishing wind caused strands of golden silk to lash her eyes. But she did not blink. "Yes, but it's my responsibility, not yours. I'm the one who said it was safe to . . ." *make love.* "I *did* believe it was safe, Lucas. I really *had* just finished my period. I want you to know that."

Lucas believed he had prepared himself for this truth, this explanation for her illness in Florence and her absence from Cambridge. He had even told himself what he would do, must do, if what he imagined was true. But it had been abstract, not real, never real—until now.

And now, as Lucas inhaled, needing a breath, he found only ice-cold air. Everything became frozen then. He felt it happen, felt his dream become encased in ice, a glacier so mammoth that it would never melt.

His dream was frozen, and in another moment the blood in his veins would still to motionlessness and even his heart would cease to beat. But as Lucas gazed at her lovely, anguished face he felt warmth amid the chill, and then he heard words, *his* words, spoken so gently he scarcely recognized the voice as his own.

"I know that's what you believed, Emma. But *I* know, have known for years, that a woman can become pregnant at virtually any time in her cycle. I knew that, Emma, although maybe you didn't. I made the choice to take that risk. I'm responsible, perhaps even more than you are, and I accept that responsibility."

"I'm *going* to have the baby!" With the defiant pronouncement, Emma stepped farther away and her hands drifted to her lower abdomen, as if to protect that unborn life—from him. "I'm going to have him, and keep him, and *love* him."

"I'm not asking you to terminate the pregnancy, Emma. I never would. Him?"

Emma shrugged, a gesture of shoulders only. Her protective hands remained where they were. "It's silly, I suppose. But I feel—so strongly—that he's a boy." *That he's your son.*

Lucas looked away from her then, from her wind-lashed face to the wind-lashed sea. Emma could see his profile, a portrait of harshness silhouetted against the pale winter sky. He glared into the fierce assault of the winter wind, his jaw set strong and firm. Against an assault from within? she wondered. Were the powerful muscles fighting to keep inside the angry words he wanted to hurl at her?

"Lucas," she whispered. "You don't have to—"

"But I do, Emma. I do." His voice was hoarse, raw, ravaged by the winter wind. And by wintry remembrances of his own. "My father took the same risk once, the night I was conceived. But he didn't feel responsible for the choice he had made. He disappeared before I was born, leaving my mother with a child she didn't want—especially since that child reminded her so much of him."

"I'm sorry, Lucas. That must have been terribly difficult for you."

He was facing the sea, confronting the full force of the howling wind. But Emma saw the sexy half smile touch his lips. "It wasn't all that bad. I didn't mind being alone. In fact, I liked it. According to my mother, that was something else I inherited from him." *He was a loner, Lucas. Selfish, arrogant, completely incapable of love. And you're just like him.*

Emma watched as the sexy smile faded, and the lips that had caressed her with such tenderness became grim. "But I learned something from my childhood, Emma. A son needs his father." Lucas turned from the sea to her, and he was like that sea. Ravaged, wintry, and intense. "At least, my son needs his."

But he's *my* son, too! How can I possibly live without him? Emma's heart offered a swift, confident reply. *Because you love Lucas most of all.*

"Then take him," she said, so softly that her words were torn apart by the wind.

"What did you say?"

"Take him. You and Daphne will be married by the time he's born—"

"Who the hell is Daphne?"

"I know all about her, Lucas. She's your fiancée."

"I don't know a Daphne, Emma. But I *do* know that there is no fiancée. Let me guess," he said with chilling calm. "Ash is behind this, isn't she? She's the one who told you about the fictional Daphne."

"Yes."

"*She's* Daphne, Emma, or wants to be. We dated a few years ago. It didn't work, at least not for me. Ashley wanted more than I wanted to give. But we remained friends—or so I thought. What else did she tell you?"

Emma answered with a shrug. But it wasn't good enough. The sorcerer wanted all the truth. "What else, Emma?"

"Well, she said that your only love, your only real passion— is for your art, for the statues you plan to carve."

"That's true." His quiet confession held a note of apology. "That's who I am." *A man who will never fall in love.* "But I'm someone else, too. Now. I'm a father. And I want to be a good one, Emma. I want to give my son a home where he feels safe, wanted and loved, by his parents." His gaze fell to the pale white hands still splayed protectively across her lower abdomen, then returned to her face. "You do want him, don't you?"

She nodded, a slow dance of brilliant gold in the fading rays of the winter sun.

"Then marry me. Help me love him. I'm going to need your help."

But you're a connoisseur of sex, a wizard of pleasure, a sorcerer of magic, and I'm just Emma.

"What, Emma? Tell me what you're thinking."

"That you'll want other women, and that that will be very difficult for me."

"Other women? Oh, I see. This is more helpful information from Ash, isn't it? I've had lovers, Emma, I won't deny it. It happened, I enjoyed it. And there was never a compelling reason to resist."

"You . . . slept with . . . almost every girl in the group."

Lucas swore, and at last his fury truly flared, a fearsome green fire. But even as Emma watched, mesmerized by the passion of that raging inferno, it was vanquished by his lazy, sexy, wicked smile. "I may just have to kill Ms. Ashley Alexander."

"But, Lucas, she obviously cares—so much—about you!"

"No, Emma. Ashley cares about Ashley. She makes a habit of getting exactly what she wants, no matter what, or who, stands in her way."

Just like Lucas Cain, he mused. Just like the man who was never going to let anything—and certainly not *anyone*—stand in the way of his dream. He had been so careful, always. Until

Venice. And now? Now his dream had been destroyed, shattered, by his own desire.

Lucas turned away from her, toward the horizon far beyond the rippling waves, where the sun, that brilliant sphere of pure gold, was falling, falling, into the cold, dark sea. The fiery star would drown there, buried in a watery grave, like his own golden dream . . . and all the magnificent words that had once defined his life.

Marble. Chisel. Sculpture. Stone. How Lucas loved those words, the very sound of them, the way they felt on his lips and in his heart. But they were vanishing now, falling into the winter sea, to gasp, to suffocate, to drown; and as the sun bid its final adieu, its golden splendor spent, new words began to fill the colorless twilight.

Responsibility. Commitment. Father. Son. Those words had nothing to do with Lucas Cain, with his passion, with his soul. They were hated words, and terrifying ones, and now they froze his blood anew. How could he do this? How could he spend the rest of his life without the only thing that had ever mattered?

He couldn't. But he had to.

Responsibility. Commitment. Father.

Son. Sun. The golden star was a memory now. His dream was a memory. And the infinite promises of the horizon were no longer his. There was only the stark gray twilight, and the bitter winter wind, and her.

Her. The woman who was carrying his child, *and who wanted her baby so much,* but who would have given that precious son away, to Lucas, *for* Lucas.

He turned then, from the lost horizon to her, and in the twilight shadows Lucas saw her fear. She was terrified, too. Her life, too, was irrevocably changed.

We're in this together, she and I. As father, as mother, as husband, as wife.

The ice that filled his veins began to melt again, as if *she* were a glowing sun, warming him, and imploring him to follow her light to an entirely new—and glorious?—horizon.

"I haven't made love with anyone except you, Emma, not since last summer, since before Florence. I came to Europe to see the works of the masters. It was a solitary pursuit, one I couldn't imagine wanting to share. But I did want to share it—with you—and the sharing made it even better. And as for what happened in Venice, I wanted that, too, Emma. I wanted to make love to you. I think you know how much."

"Lucas . . ."

"If you agree to marry me, I will always be faithful to you. I promise. It's an easy promise to make, Emma, and to keep." So very easy, he thought as he gazed at her. It was an astonishing thought, an astonishing awareness. "We have to be honest with each other. Always. I want to marry you, to raise our son together. That's the truth. But I need to know what you want. The truth."

The truth. She wanted to marry him, this man she loved . . . this man who would never love anyone as much as he loved the feel of stone in his powerful, gifted hands. "But what about your art, Lucas? All the magnificent statues you're going to carve?"

"The baby comes first, Emma. Our son comes first. I'll find a job, a steady income." His smile was wry, his voice gently teasing. "Don't look so worried. I'm almost a college graduate. There ought to be something I can do."

"I wasn't worrying about that." Then, smiling, too, but without the trace of a tease, she said, "Once the baby's old enough, I'll go to work, and that way you can sculpt—"

"That's not going to happen, Emma. Not that scenario. We'll take it one day at a time, okay? Right now, the most important question is, will you marry me?"

Lucas didn't love her. That, Emma knew. But he enjoyed being with her, sharing with her, *making love* to her. He would be honest, and faithful. And she had more than enough love for them both.

"Yes," she whispered. "I will marry you."

Eleanor and Jonathan Lloyd did not receive the news of their daughter's impending marriage with happiness. Even before meeting Lucas Cain, they disliked with a passion the man who had so callously misused their innocent girl. And when Lucas stood before them in Hyacinth House's musty parlor, Eleanor and Jonathan felt sheer alarm.

He was *all wrong* for their precious daughter. To her parents, Emma was a delicate flower of exquisite, yet understated, beauty. She wasn't glamorous, or dazzling. Just lovely. And far too quaint, too serene, for this menacingly handsome, and menacingly sexy, American man.

Lucas was wrong for Emma, for *any* woman who hoped for a loving father for her child or a faithful husband for herself.

It would never work.

Eleanor and Jonathan wanted happiness for their beloved daughter. And since it was abundantly clear that such happiness could never come from Lucas Cain, they vowed that when the marriage fell apart, the blow would be softened by the billowy cloak of their love. To that end, they suggested that the newlyweds live with them at Hyacinth House—a suggestion that they secretly hoped would cause Lucas to bolt straightaway. He was as wrong for the pastoral tranquillity of Cornwall as he was for Emma. He belonged elsewhere, in some fast-paced world of sophistication, sensuality, *sex*.

But the idea of living at Hyacinth House appealed to their future son-in-law, even after the revelations that not only would he and Emma and the baby have to live in the gardener's cottage but that the revenue from the dilapidated bed-and-breakfast was so meager that it would be stretched to the limit to support them all.

Lucas did not bolt. He merely surprised them by a suggestion of his own. Would they permit him to renovate their home? he wondered. He had experience, several summers spent working for a remodeler in California, and with a few more bedrooms, and a new coat of paint, and a little shoring up here and there, they could attract more business, couldn't they?

The suggestion was made with quiet solemnity, not the brash arrogance the Lloyds would have anticipated from him. Indeed, Eleanor and Jonathan could not figure Lucas out. They had imagined a charmer, a con artist, a master seducer who made extravagant promises he would never keep.

But that wasn't the young man who stood before them. Or was it? Was this unembellished seriousness the greatest con, the most masterful seduction, of all?

Eleanor and Jonathan didn't know. But they would find out, by insisting that Lucas complete the academic year at Cambridge. By June he would have his degree, an important credential should he and Emma ever decide to move from the ancient charm of Cornwall to the modern sophistication of London, or even of the States.

Eleanor and Jonathan assumed that Lucas would vanish sometime that spring, even after he and Emma had wed. But he arranged his class schedule to fulfill his commitments in Cornwall, spending at least three days a week at Hyacinth House, hammering, plastering, converting its musty, cavernous spaces into luxurious bedroom suites. And the moment he graduated, he helped them run their newly popular—and now truly grand—bed-and-breakfast by the sea.

Did they trust him? Not really. He would be gone before the baby was born.

But that prediction was based upon incomplete information, upon a truth that Eleanor and Jonathan Lloyd did not know, that no one knew, not even Lucas, until it was almost too late . . . until the night Emma gave birth to his child . . . the night that she herself almost died.

The truth. Lucas Cain, who was never going to fall in love, had fallen in love with his pregnant young wife. That it would happen *ever* seemed improbable, especially during those months when Emma was so terribly ill. Confined to bed by her worried physicians, she was groggy most of the time, blurred by drugs designed to lower her blood pressure to a safer range; and her body, once so delicate, was puffy and bloated.

Emma was embarrassed by the way she looked. But to Lucas she was breathtaking, her radiance more brilliant than ever, shining brightly from the beauty of her soul, from that place of love that offered every ounce of her self for his baby.

Lucas was an artist. He knew true beauty.

And as a man, Lucas learned about true love, on that August night when she awakened with sheer terror as their bed became a pool of blood. . . .

"Happy Anniversary, Em."

"Anniversary, Luc?"

"Don't you know?"

Of course she knew. One year ago, in the soggy but enchanted City of Canals, she and Lucas had first made love. "Yes. I know."

"I've been thinking that today, rather than February fourteenth, should be our anniversary. For Jessie's sake."

"I think so, too."

"Good. Then I'll engrave our rings with that date."

"Our rings?"

"It's time, don't you think? Your fingers aren't swollen anymore, and given the success of last summer, we can definitely afford wedding bands. Your parents agree."

Her parents. How dramatically Eleanor and Jonathan Lloyd had changed their minds about Lucas. Emma had known of their skepticism, of course. As subtle as they thought they had been, as clever and discreet, their concern had been abundantly obvious. But even before they saw Lucas hold their granddaughter, a cherishing caress that brought tears to their eyes, Eleanor and Jonathan had revised their wariness about their son-in-law.

And as for Emma herself? She loved Lucas more than ever—and was more wary. Her pregnancy had been difficult, and terrifying. She feared losing both the baby and him. She and Lucas couldn't make love. The doctors advised against it. Not that Lucas would have wanted to anyway.

He *did* touch her, though, during those endless months when she was a groggy, edematous blob. His lips placed gentle kisses on her cheeks, chaste caresses that wished her hello, good-bye, good morning, good night. And his hands, those talented hands, touched with exquisite tenderness her distended abdomen, and his dark green eyes gleamed with wonder whenever he felt a fluttering kick, an exuberant sign of life from the son who turned out to be their daughter.

Emma had no memory of Jessie's birth. She remembered the terror before—the hot, gushing flow of her own blood; and the floating realization that she was going to die; and the fear Lucas tried so hard to conceal. Emma remembered, too, the joy that came after, when both she and her newborn daughter were cradled in Lucas's arms and he whispered softly, hoarsely, *"I love you."*

Emma didn't doubt his words. She was the mother of his most precious treasure. Lucas would always love her for that.

Now it was November, four months since Jessie's birth, four months of loving their baby girl. They took turns holding her, comforting her, kissing the soft silk of her shining black hair and the smooth satin of her plump, rosy cheeks. And when it was time for Jessica Cain to fill her small stomach with her mother's nourishing milk? Lucas did as much as a father could, arising from bed in the middle of the night, bringing her to Emma's waiting breast, watching that marvel of nature, and then carrying Jessie back to her crib when the nurturing splendor was through.

Emma and Lucas had married for their child, because of her. And as for the other facets of marriage, the intimate moments between husband and wife? Those moments didn't exist. They had not made love since Venice. Not for a year.

Lucas had promised to be faithful. But had he really meant celibate?

No, because now, on this first anniversary of the night when they became one, his dark green eyes were glittering with desire. "How shall we celebrate, Emma?"

Emma saw his desire, and was emboldened by it. "By making love."

"Are you sure, Em? Is it all right? Are you healed?"

"Yes."

Yes. She hadn't been healed, not truly healed, before they made love. But Lucas healed her . . . with the tenderness of his passion and the gentleness of his love.

"Earth to Emma."

His voice was smiling—and whispering, as if they were in a library rather than the Duveen Gallery at the British Museum. Emma turned from the fragment of marble at which she had been staring, unseeing, for quite some time, and looked up at him.

"*Buon giorno,*" Lucas greeted, as if he knew where she had been. Then, as he had always done with the nineteen-year-old innocent who had been too shy to roll her *r*, he amended, "Hi, Emma. What were you thinking?"

"A thousand thoughts."

"Happy ones. I didn't want to interrupt. But if we're going to make Cole Taylor's concert—and be dressed for it—we'd better go."

"Okay."

"Would you care to share just one of those thousand happy thoughts before we go?"

A thousand thoughts. But really only one: how much she loved him. Then. Now. Always. More every day.

"I was just thinking about . . . everything."

Lucas smiled, pulled her into his arms, and as his lips brushed against the golden silk of her hair, he whispered, "Then I'm glad that everything is so happy."

Chapter Twenty-Three

Royal Albert Hall
New Year's Eve

"THERE YOU GO, CLAIRE. PERFECT." SYD-ney's voice smiled. "It's too much makeup for the real world, of course, but just right for the stage, for your concert debut."

"Thank you, Sydney. I really appreciate your doing this for me."

"My pleasure." Sydney paused a beat. "What about after the concert, Claire? You'll want to wash all of this off, but would you like me to do your makeup for the party? You don't need much, your natural coloring is terrific, but a little mascara, a touch of lipstick, maybe a *soupçon* of blush?"

"Oh, that would be . . ." Claire frowned. "I was planning to go back to my hotel room to shower and change. Cole said that he would be changing into a tuxedo, and I have an evening gown." Claire's frown deepened.

"Don't *worry*, Claire! I'm planning to change out of my concert clothes as well. I might wear skintight leather pants and a sleeveless velvet vest to another black-tie gala—in fact, I would—but not to one that's hosted by my boss. Propriety is paramount to Timothy Asquith. He's terribly upper crust, don't you know?" Sydney affected an impeccably upper-crust accent. Then, pure California again, she said, "Anyway, I'll be wearing an incredibly subdued and proper evening gown, and I'd be delighted to pop by your room after I've changed. We could make the grand entrance together."

"The grand entrance?" Sydney's words were echoed by Cole.

He stood in the open doorway of the brightly lighted dressing room, an imposing shadow staring at the reflection he saw in the mirror, *glowering* at it. Cole had never seen Claire with makeup, and even though it had been artfully applied, and was exactly right for the stage, he didn't like it. It was wrong to add more paint to a picture that was already perfect.

"To Timothy's party," Sydney clarified. "I'm going to help Claire with her makeup and we'll arrive together. I fully expect breath-held wonder when we do."

A grateful smile touched Claire's made-up face. She had, uncharitably, decided that the famous Elle Syd would not be an ally. It was a conclusion based on articles read to her by Aunt Augusta, as well as vignettes reported on *Entertainment Tonight* and by MTV.

Sydney was a free spirit, dazzling, bold, wild; a whirling dervish who could leave a blind woman in her dust and whose own astonishing amethyst eyes might flash with impatience—and discomfort—in response to the limitations of Claire's.

But Sydney had been welcoming, and not the least bit awkward, helpful but not hovering.

"You don't need makeup, Claire."

It was the second time during this last day of the year that Claire had heard those words. Hours before they had been spoken by Sarah. She would be happy to help Claire with makeup for Timothy's party, she said. But, she added, your coloring is so rich, Claire, so vivid, that you really don't need makeup at all.

Now the pronouncement came from Cole, and it was harsh, an assertion not of Claire's innate radiance but of the insurmountable darkness in which she dwelled.

What's the point? the harshness seemed to ask. Why embellish eyes that cannot see? Why draw attention to that sightlessness? And what was the *future* of such folly? It was impossible, wasn't it, for Claire to ever become adept at applying makeup herself? Wouldn't such an endeavor be a constant source of embarrassment, splattered dots of mascara here, a smear of lip-stick there?

The dressing room fell silent, a charged atmosphere in which Claire correctly assessed the soundless exchange between Sydney and Cole. Amethyst's dazzling drummer was glaring at the singer of love songs, furious at the insensitivity of his remark and demanding that he apologize to Claire.

Would Sydney prevail? Did she have that kind of influence over Cole?

Apparently not, because the next words that were spoken—with forced gaiety—were Syd's. "Well, I think I'll leave you two kids alone. I have equipment to check, and you have duets to rehearse." The fingers that had artfully applied Claire's makeup squeezed Claire's shoulders. "I can't wait to hear you sing, Claire. I know you're going to be great."

All I ever do is hurt you. He had hurt her now, crushed her confidence, muted her radiant glow.

"I'm sorry," he said, moving to her. "You misunderstood what I meant. You look wonderful without makeup. You don't need any. But if you want to wear it, that's fine, too. Whatever you want, Claire."

Oh, but Cole, I can't have what I want.

Claire took a breath. Her fluttering heart was in desperate need of oxygen, and she needed time to find a voice that would sound cheery and calm.

But there was no oxygen in this dressing room at the Royal Albert Hall. With each frantic breath she became more breathless. Her already racing heart galloped even faster, and her head began to spin, and there was an odd—and ominous—feeling deep inside. *A sense of doom.* There was no other way to describe it . . . and with the description came awareness.

She was having a panic attack. Claire had never had one before, but she recognized the symptoms, having heard about panic attacks from television talk shows. Most talk show topics did not apply to Claire. But she was interested nonetheless, experiencing vicariously a range of life's adventures, and perils, that she would never know.

Two years ago, Oprah—and therefore Aunt Augusta and Claire—had spent an hour with an author who believed passionately that women were at their most confident, their most daring and bold and free, when they were girls. They had no fear then, and their dreams knew no limits. But as those free-spirited girls became young women, their daring confidence and soaring dreams were pruned and shaped by the constraints and expectations of society.

Claire's own bold dreams had been severely pruned. Not by society, however, but by fate. *By Cole.* Still, in one regard, the author was entirely correct. There had indeed been a time when Claire's confidence was limitless and her dreams knew no bounds. It had been when she was a girl, during those days of splendor and sunshine and song—with Cole—beside the bayou.

That episode of *Oprah* had definitely applied to Claire, and there were others: shows devoted to relationships, to unreciprocated love and the dangers of loving too much; and ones that exposed the profound impact of one's childhood on adult behavior. Sons of physically abusive fathers were many times more likely to be physically abusive of their "loved ones" than those raised in nonviolent homes. *Many times* more likely to be brutal, violent—

But not Cole, Claire protested as she listened to the staggeringly grim statistics. *Not Cole. Never Cole. No matter what he believes.*

Claire had listened with sympathy, but not true understanding, to the stories of people tormented by various forms of panic. There were testimonials from actors and actresses who experienced pure terror every time they had to perform. And there were everyday folks who confessed to paralyzing fear of the darkness of night, or the brightness of day, or of addressing the PTA, or going to the grocery store, or, in the case of agoraphobia, even of leaving their homes.

Claire knew about the "sense of doom," the frantic breaths

that gasped for air—and inhaled only fear—but she never imagined such terror would be hers. Even her blindness hadn't imprisoned her. Until now.

"Claire?"

He was close to her, so very close, kneeling, it seemed, on the floor in front of her. Claire felt his smoldering heat and sensed his searching gray eyes rake over her theatrically made-up face.

Then he was touching her, cradling her trembling hands in his, and she felt those hands, one so very strong, the other gentle, crippled by violence.

"*Claire.* What's wrong? Talk to me."

"*I can't sing.*" Claire frowned as she heard her own words. She should have shrugged, tried to smile, and confessed, *I . . . can't . . . breathe. Silly . . . isn't it? It's not a panic attack . . . not really . . . just a touch of panic.*

But instead, in a single airless breath, she told him that she could not sing. And it was true. She could not. Not tonight. Perhaps not ever.

But that's why I'm here! To sing duets with Cole.

No it's not—not really. You're here to find Cole's brother, remember? This is about Cole, not about *you*, and now you have to pull yourself together. For him.

"It's okay," Cole said. "Claire, it's okay. You don't have to sing tonight."

"I feel . . . silly." Silly. But suddenly more calm. *For Cole.* She even managed a wobbly smile. "Stage fright, I guess."

How Cole wished that were true, that she was just understandably apprehensive about performing in the Royal Albert Hall. But Cole knew that Claire's fright went far beyond the specter of the stage. He saw her terror, her *terror*, and knew it was because of him.

What have I done to you, Claire? I've taken you from a world of darkness that didn't frighten you at all and brought you here, to be with me, and now you're terrified. And so worried that I will see that truth.

"Stage fright," he agreed gently. "It's not surprising, Claire. Not at all."

"Well." She shrugged. "Thank you. I wonder if I should go

back to the hotel. I'm feeling a little tired. Jet lag, I suppose. I'd like to recover a bit before the party." *I'm breathing now, barely, and I'm afraid that the doom will descend again, with a vengeance, when I hear you sing "Imagine Moonlight."*

Where she really needed to go was home, to Harlanville, to that safe place where she could curl her hands around her snow globe and dream and remember and pretend.

No, a voice commanded. It was a defiant voice, and it sounded very much like an eight-year-old girl with boundless courage. You're going back to your room at the Drake, *and no farther,* and you're going to stand in the shower until you're certain that you've scrubbed every speck of makeup off your face, and you're going to concentrate on remembering only one thing. This isn't about you. It's about Cole. His brother. *That* dream. "Would that be all right with you, Cole?"

"Of course. I'll take you there."

"No. If you could just have someone call a cab, I can easily get myself from the lobby to my room."

The glaring spotlight beat down upon him like the hot Louisiana sun unsheltered by the gossamer veil of moss and leaves. Searing. Scorching. Punishing. Blinding.

Cole could not see beyond the brightness into the darkened theater that was filled to overflowing with those who had come to hear his songs of love. In the brightness, in that blinding light, Cole saw only an image of fright, of fear, *of terror*—a breathless angel with sightless, bewildered blue eyes.

Claire could not sing. Not tonight. Not with him.

And neither could he sing. Not tonight. Not without her.

Oh yes, his lips were moving, and some sound was coming from his powerful throat. But it would be a mediocre performance at best. The thought came vaguely, and without a care.

His music didn't matter. Nothing mattered. Except Claire.

And the dread he felt, that eerie, ominous sense of doom? *That* was for him, what he deserved. It was a stage fright of sorts, a private terror, the aching realization that he was destined to sing alone, forever . . . and that he would force himself to do so, a punishment more searing than the most blazing of suns, a reminder that even when he tried to give his angel her dream, he only caused her great pain.

This was his destiny, his punishment. The anguished loneliness of the stage and the excruciating emptiness of his solitary voice.

Cole Taylor did not sing "Imagine Moonlight" on that New Year's Eve at the Royal Albert Hall. But the omission did not matter. No one noticed. No one missed it. The audience got its money's worth, even without that famous song. Indeed, they bore witness to the most stunning solo performance Cole had ever given.

What no one in the audience knew, a truth hidden even from Cole himself, was that it hadn't been a solo performance at all. In his heart, and in the voice that entranced and enthralled, every song of passion—of longing and of love—had been a duet sung with Claire.

Chapter Twenty-Four

"I FEEL LIKE THE SECOND MRS. DE WINTER. You know, Sarah, in *Rebecca*?"

"I know the book. But in what way do you feel like her, Claire?"

"Well, remember the costume ball where she wore the same gown that Rebecca had worn? And how angry Max was when he saw her?"

"Yes, I remember. But Cole wasn't angry that you didn't sing with him tonight, Claire."

"I know. I guess the comparison I'm making is how foolish she felt, and how I feel. I *panicked*, Sarah. I couldn't speak, couldn't breathe, couldn't have remembered a single lyric if I'd tried."

"Who wouldn't feel panicky about performing with the world's top-selling male vocalist to a packed house at the Royal Albert Hall? And don't forget what the second Mrs. de Winter did, Claire. She simply put on a new frock and went to the ball."

Sarah's voice remained positive despite the grimness of her thoughts. One didn't want to delve too deeply into potential similarities between Claire and Mrs. de Winter. The night of that fictional ball at Manderley had ended in tragedy, with the discovery of Rebecca's murdered body.

No, Sarah told herself. There was absolutely no point in making comparisons, not between the two heroines, and most definitely not between the two men. Maxim de Winter might have murdered his faithless wife, but Cole Taylor most definitely had *not* slain his actress-lover Paulina Bliss.

He had not.

Sarah banished thoughts of murder and recalled instead her most recent image of Cole, backstage after the concert. He had been swarmed with well-wishers, surrounded by members of the entertainment press. But the instant she appeared, as if he had been watching for her, waiting for her, he broke free of the admiring throng, his face a portrait of concern and relief.

Would she be willing to stop by Claire's hotel room en route to Timothy's party? he wondered. She might be sleeping, he said. And she needed sleep. But it was obvious that Cole needed something, too: to be certain that Claire was all right.

Claire hadn't been asleep when Sarah arrived. Freshly scrubbed and wearing a bulky bathrobe, she was at a crossroads. Should she go to bed, for much-needed sleep? Or should she go instead to the New Year's Eve gala?

The issue was far more complex than the simple choice between wakefulness and sleep. Sleep promised safety, the coziness of satin sheets and feather pillows, the enveloping comfort of dreams, whereas the black-tie gala promised more heart-racing moments of breathlessness with the darkest shadow of them all.

But encouraged by Sarah, and by that defiant eight-year-old girl within, Claire dressed for the party.

"You certainly don't *look* foolish, Claire Chamberlain," Sarah asserted with a smile. "You look quite lovely." Indeed, Sarah mused, in the flowing gown of ivory satin her friend looked like a copper-haired angel. "Shall we go? Cole and Jack are waiting for us."

Claire drew a deep breath, inhaled oxygen not panic, and answered, "Yes."

She had to go to the party. Because how in the world

was she going to find Cole's brother if she couldn't even be with *him*?

Claire's instant impression of Timothy Asquith was *almost* accurate. She imagined impeccable elegance, the graceful carriage of an aristocrat combined with the aura of calm that came with immense power and success. Had Claire been able to see Timothy, however, she would have wondered about the calm. The aura was there. But her perceptive blue eyes, if sighted, would have seen what lay beneath the tranquil facade, the deep hunger, the depthless torment, the haunted worry.

As it was, Claire knew only Timothy Asquith's gracious charm—a charm that compelled him to instantly include *her* when he announced to Cole that the princess, among others, was eager to meet him.

"Thank you, Timothy," Claire replied. "But I think I'll just wait here."

Claire liked the place where she and Cole had been standing. Away from the crush of the crowd, it was caressed by a breeze that wafted through windows opened to the night air—a cool caress filled with a bountiful supply of oxygen.

The windows were about twelve feet high, Cole had told her, and the handles looked to him like pure gold, and the heavy velvet drapes were some kind of pink.

"Some kind of pink?" she had pressed bravely, encouraged by the smile in his voice.

"Dark pink," he clarified. Then, after a moment's hesitation, he asked, "Do you remember the sunsets in late summer? The pink just before the sky became dark purple? The drapes are that pink, Claire, exactly that pink."

"Mauve," she whispered.

"Mauve," he echoed softly.

Now Claire stood in the Drake Hotel's Imperial Ballroom, near windows framed by the velvet mauve of a bayou sunset, waiting while Cole met a princess. Claire was here . . . and she was in their shaded woods beside the bayou, transported to that magical place by the soft wonder in Cole's voice. And she felt? *Calm.* Hopeful. Eight years old and infinitely brave.

This is who I must be, she told herself. That girl whose grand vision of life was not yet pruned; who feared nothing; who didn't know the meaning of panic.

I must be that girl. I will be.

I am.

The night air became balmy then, and Claire heard the wind rustling through cypress trees, and the splashing of canoe paddles in azure waters, and the melodic song of a seabird overhead.

Then quite suddenly Claire heard a sound that was distinctly out of place in *her* bayou. Raucous and menacing. The sound returned her to London, where the night air wasn't truly balmy, her cheeks were merely flushed; and where the rustling wind was just the *swish* of silken evening gowns; and where the splashes came from dancing fountains of champagne; and where the seabird's joyous song was an orchestral violin.

And as for the menacing noise that had no bayou equivalent? It was a human laugh, and it belonged to Adrian Gilbey.

It wasn't actually menacing, Claire supposed, merely strident. Still, her memory of the man who would be producing Global's *International News Hour with Sarah Pembroke* was distinctly unpleasant. Because of Sarah, she realized. Because there seemed to be contempt in Adrian's voice when he uttered Sarah's name.

As Adrian's raucous laughter faded, Claire banished the uneasy memory and listened anew to the sounds of the ballroom—the ballroom, not the bayou—and when she did, she heard an entirely different kind of music. Silk and champagne sang together, a duet of sophistication and glamour, a serenade to the cosmopolitan world in which, for a while, the bayou girl was going to dwell.

And how was she doing, that bayou girl? Fine. Calm still, and enjoying this stylish symphony of sound.

Then came a familiar sound, beloved and awesome, a breathtaking harmony of power and grace. It was a sound that had made her heart pound then, years ago. As it pounded now.

But I'm fearless now, she reminded herself. Just as I was fearless then.

Claire turned from the caresses of the night air to the familiar footfalls of her panther. "That didn't take very long."

"It's Jack, Claire."

"Oh! Jack." She frowned. Apparently, in this new world, even remembered sounds of the bayou would be distorted. "I thought you were Cole."

"He and Timothy are still making the rounds, and Timothy has just commandeered Sarah as well."

"The price of fame."

"Yes."

"Not a price either of them likes very much, is it?"

"No," Jack agreed. She sees so much, he thought, this woman who cannot see. But can her remarkable sightless eyes see a monster? They were seeing something now, something troubling. "What is it, Claire?"

"Did they ask you to come be with me?"

"Absolutely not. I'm here because I want to be. Unless you'd rather I left?"

"No, of course not." Claire shook her head. "What a night. First stage fright, and now paranoia."

"The stage fright was entirely understandable. And as for paranoia, well, *what* paranoia?"

Claire smiled. "Thanks, Jack." No panic, no paranoia, not for the bayou girl.

"This is all a pretty big change for you, Claire."

"Yes. And it's pretty clear that I need to get my bearings, to become intimately acquainted with my new city as soon as possible."

"Sarah will help."

"She already is. We're spending tomorrow together. And the following day, when she officially begins as network anchor, I'll begin exploring on my own. I'm sure there are lots of excellent sight-seeing—sight-*hear*ing—tours of London. Don't you think?"

"I'm sure there are."

"I know I'll learn a great deal that way," Claire elaborated. "All sorts of interesting tidbits."

"All sorts," Jack agreed. Far more, he decided, than a sighted tourist, because Claire would listen attentively to every word. You are remarkable, Claire Chamberlain. You and Sarah. Remarkable penmates.

They talked about the *sights* Claire planned to *hear*, from the changing of the guard at Buckingham Palace to the chiming of Big Ben. It was an animated discussion, punctuated with laughter, but it ended abruptly when Jack announced that Cole was about to join them.

Claire stiffened in response to the news. Then, as if giving herself a mental shake, she relaxed, and her bright blue eyes glowed even brighter.

"I like Jack," Claire offered when she and Cole were alone, when Jack had left to find Sarah. "Don't you?"

Like? Cole didn't think of most people in such terms, with that degree of intimacy. And yet his reaction to Jack Dalton was quite distinct from the austere detachment he usually felt. There was something about Jack, something centered and confident and *whole*, and as Claire's question compelled him to try to define what *it* was, the answer came to him with remarkable clarity: Jack Dalton was a man fully in control of his passions—and of his dreams. Under no circumstances would Jack Dalton have permitted Jed Taylor to die, not even by accident, not when such a death would have meant as well the death of all dreams.

"Cole? Does something bother you about Jack?"

"No. Not at all. What were you two talking about?"

"Me, and my plans to explore London. Since the band rehearses at night, my days will be free, won't they?"

"I'd been planning to change the rehearsals to daytime."

"Because of me. That's *not* necessary, Cole. And maybe even disastrous? Sydney says she's always been a night owl, and that Mick is positively surly before ten P.M." *Day and night make no difference to me, Cole. And here, in this place where duets are sung between silken gowns and splashing fountains of champagne, I'm not a schoolteacher anymore.* "Please don't change the rehearsal schedule on my account. I can easily adjust. And I really do look forward to having the days free to explore the city."

"You're sure?"

"Positive."

"All right."

An uneasy silence fell then; and even the glamorous sounds seemed to vanish; and all Claire heard was the hiss of the chilly winter wind.

Then Cole spoke—"I thought we might explore London together"—and the world changed anew. The night air warmed, and hummed with joy, and they were beside their bayou again, the lonely boy and the joyful girl.

Close your eyes, Cole, and I'll show you our enchanted forest in an entirely new way. Don't be afraid! Just take my hand. I won't let go. I promise. Trust me.

Chapter Twenty-Five

I WANT TO DANCE WITH YOU.
You want to see who approaches me? To see if any black-hearted killers are among the invited guests at Timothy's black-tie gala?

No, Sarah. I want to dance with you.

She and Jack hadn't danced yet. But it would happen. His cobalt eyes had been sending that dangerous warning since the evening began.

So now she was going to drink. Had to.

Jack stopped a short distance away, before she sensed his presence, and simply gazed at her. Sarah wore black, an elegant gown of midnight satin—long-sleeved, of course, a sheer weave of silk that both veiled and revealed the snowy whiteness of her slender arms. But at her wrists there was black satin again, solid and concealing, permitting no glimpse of the scars that lay beneath. Her hair was piled atop her head, a lustrous ebony crown, and at her neck and ears Lady Sarah Pembroke wore diamonds.

The evening gown had been retrieved from mothballs, she explained, and the diamonds from a vault at her bank. It had been years since she'd attended a black-tie gala such as this. But she was here tonight because of Claire, the lovely woman whose name Sarah borrowed on that Parisian evening of mist and love.

At that moment, as Jack was remembering Christmas Eve in the City of Light, Sarah turned, a pirouette of pure grace, a slow twirl from the silver fountain of golden champagne to him—to Jacques.

He *was* Jacques again, and she was Claire. She wore black now, and by the banks of the Seine she had been a rainbow. But Jack saw rainbows still, rainbows at midnight as prisms of light from the crystal chandeliers caressed the black satin of her gown and the shining silk of her hair. The Parisian mist had glittered like diamonds, and there were real diamonds now, and now as then the eyes that answered the silent call of his heart shone bright with wonder.

"*Bonsoir,* Sarah."

"*Bonsoir* . . . Jack."

Sarah and Jack were not supposed to speak French. That magical language of love belonged to Jacques and Claire, those illusory shadows who did not exist.

But they *do* exist, Jack thought. *We* exist, no matter where we are or what language we speak.

Softly, in French, he queried, "What are you doing here, Sarah, beside this river of champagne?"

Her gaze fell to the crystal glass she held by its delicate stem. The champagne flute was full, honey tinted and sparkling.

"Practicing . . . for Valentine's Day."

In English, her words would have been as piercingly sharp as a murderer's knife, an edgy reminder from the warrior who believed that she would be meeting her killer alone—and that she could trust no one but herself to save her. But spoken in French, Sarah's words were surprisingly mild.

And, Jack realized with dismay, they were entirely false.

"There's another reason that you're drinking, isn't there?" he asked, a tender, yet urgent, demand for the truth.

"Yes," Sarah confessed to the sparkling golden bubbles, and then to him. "I'm preparing myself to dance with you."

"Is that so terrifying?"

"*Oui. Et non.*"

"Can you tell me why?"

"*Non.* I can't, Jack. Not yet."

"But someday?"

"*Peut-être.*" Her "maybe" was far from a provocative tease, a bewitching invitation to him to seduce from her the enticing secrets she had not yet shared. Rather, it was the hopeful wish of a shadow woman. *Maybe* I can tell you, Jacques, on some faraway day. And maybe, *s'il vous plaît,* when you learn the truth about me you will not run away in disgust. "*Peut-être.*"

"*Bon,*" Jack replied as he claimed from her the crystal champagne flute. "You don't need to practice drinking champagne for Valentine's Day, Sarah. He's never going to get that close to you. I won't let him." *I will protect you from that monster.* "And you don't need to drink champagne to dance with me."

"I . . ."

"You don't, Sarah." *I will protect you from myself, from the immense power of my love, until you are ready.* "Come on. I'll show you."

Lucas Cain danced the way he roamed the planet. Sensually. Gracefully. Powerfully. Emma was so very aware of his body, and of its sudden change, a different kind of strength, steel-taut, a warrior armed, a lover no more.

She looked up at him with alarm. But Lucas was quite oblivious to her worry, to *her.* His face wore the expression she had seen on those rare, unguarded moments, that intensely passionate, and truly terrifying, duet of longing and of rage.

Was he glowering, as always, at a phantom that only he could see?

No, Emma realized as she followed his glare. It seemed, but surely this was wrong, that he was staring at a woman, not a gossamer ghost; a stunning creature whose alabaster flesh was draped in flowing black satin and adorned with diamonds that sparkled like stars.

Lady Sarah Pembroke was *not* supposed to be here. Indeed, it was something Emma and Lucas had specifically discussed. Would Timothy's very own princess be attending his gala? she had wondered, hoping so. She would have liked to meet the famous war correspondent, and Emma Cain would even have found the courage to say a few words to Sarah Pembroke. Heartfelt words of respect, admiration, and gratitude.

You've become the voice for all mothers on earth, Emma would have said. We, all mothers, wish for peace for our children above all else, and by waging your war against those who choose violence over peace, death over love, you're articulating our most fervent wish.

But Lucas had told her, as if he had actually checked with Timothy, that Sarah would be absent from the New Year's Eve festivities at the Drake. Yes, she would be in London, about to assume her duties as network anchor. But apparently Lady Sarah Pembroke was *not* a partygoer.

Except that now she was here, dancing nearby, and quite oblivious to Lucas's stare, despite its chilling fury. Sarah was lost in her own dance of love—as wondrously lost as Emma had been, until she felt her husband's powerful muscles turn to steel and his sensual grace stiffen to near motionlessness.

"She's very beautiful, isn't she?"

Emma's quiet words might have been drowned by the splashes of champagne and the music of the orchestra. In fact, they *would* have been, had she managed to sound as casual as she had intended. But despite her best efforts, Emma's voice held a note of despair; and it was that desperation that Lucas heard.

He looked at her, startled, gentle, and questioning.

"Who, Emma?"

"Lady Sarah Pembroke. I thought you were looking at her."

"No."

He's lying. The truth pierced her heart. Lucas was lying. Lucas. The man who never lied. The man who would one day say to her with heart-stopping honesty, We did it, Em. We've done everything we promised we would do for our precious daughter. And now, Emma, it's time for me to go.

"It seemed . . . Do you know her, Lucas?" Why was she doing this? Why was she *confronting* him with the lie?

"No. I don't know her."

Emma had to look away, had to. Lucas was lying. Could he
really do this? Could he caress her with such tenderness *as he
lied*? Had he lied to her before? Emma didn't know. How could
she know, *how could she know*, when his gaze, even now, was
so sincere?

Now one of his talented hands found her chin and lifted.
"You're the one who's beautiful, Em."

"Lucas . . ."

"You haven't met Cole Taylor yet. Do you care?"

Of course she didn't care. She had her own black-haired
singer of love songs. Didn't she? Yes, *please*.

*For as long as we're together, I have to trust him, to believe
in him, as I always have.*

"No. I don't care about meeting Cole."

"Then let's go. I want to be alone with you, Emma. I want to
make love to you."

It was love, and lust.

She was wife, and mistress.

Bride . . . and courtesan.

And he was knight, and sorcerer. Husband . . . and
conqueror.

Their loving had never been like this. It *could* have been.
This daring passion and unashamed lust was virtually soundless, a hushed symphony of whispers and sighs. They could
have made love like this in the privacy of their bedroom at Hyacinth House. But they never had.

And as she lay in his embrace in the aftermath of their loving, and his hands touched her, claimed her, wherever they
chose, Emma felt exhilarating rushes of joy, a euphoric sense of
wholeness.

She was complete, fully a woman, *his* woman; quite capable
of satisfying every need, every desire, every passionate whim of
this most magnificent male. And what of *her* needs? Her de-

sires? Oh, they had been attended to with exquisite care. Stunning care. Breathtaking care.

But it was what she was for him, so important, so *essential* somehow, that mattered most.

This is not very modern thinking, Emma mused as he placed kisses on her nape and his gifted hands caressed her with such intimacy. Possession. Surrender. Sheer elation at the words *I am his*, as if that were the most significant accomplishment of her life.

Never mind that in her short career at Cambridge she had achieved the highest marks; or that of Mr. and Mrs. Lucas Cain, she was the one who had mastered computers; or that she was known among all parents in Cornwall, mothers and fathers alike, as an undisputed wizard at math. And never mind that her hands, like Luc's, possessed special talents, that her wedding cakes, adorned with sugary bouquets of roses and lilacs, were truly works of art.

I am his.

"Emma? Are you okay?"

"Okay?" she echoed in a voice she had never heard before, a voice that smiled with new confidence and ancient wisdom. He is a sorcerer, and I am his fairy enchantress, and I have gifts to give him, gifts he *needs*, from *me*. "Yes. I'm okay. And you?"

"I'm just fine, Em."

She turned then, in his arms, and found his mouth with hers. "Are you?"

His answering laugh was deep, surprised—and needy. "More, Em? Already?"

"More," the fairy enchantress whispered between kisses. "Already."

And it began anew, their extraordinary passion, and this time, as they loved, Emma's thoughts became as complete, as whole, as she.

I am his . . . and he is mine.

"*Que pensez-vous*, Sarah?"

What was she thinking? Brave *and so dangerous* thoughts. If only I could dance with him, like this, forever. If only the single truth that mattered was the truth of this moment. No past. No future. Just now.

Tell him that, an impulse urged. It's not a terribly risky confession, after all. What's the worst that can happen? It would be nice to dance like this forever, Sarah—he might say—but, unfortunately, we have a murder to solve. Or . . . but, unfortunately, Sarah, this chaste intimacy is of only limited appeal to me. I'm going to want much more, *chérie*, and if you're not willing—

"Sarah?" Jack repeated as he saw the expression of hope, which had prompted his gentle query about her thoughts, yield to one of pure despair.

"That glass of champagne you took from me was my last glass. Ever." Her words, the truth, were spoken in English; a harsh reminder, a punishment in fact, to the shadow woman and her bold and foolish fantasies. I have to stop drinking, you see, Jack. I've become far too dependent on alcohol. It's my liquid asylum when I can't escape to Paris, or to war, and when the next Pegasus puzzle is still a Christmas away.

Her thoughts, punishing and harsh, were silent. But it was as if Jack Dalton *did* see, and worried, and cared.

"Will that be difficult for you, Sarah? To stop drinking?" He knew the answer, of course. For her, alcohol was medication, not pleasure. Without it the wounds that needed to be numbed, to be balmed, would be open wide, raw and exposed. Abstinence would be difficult. And solitary. His brave, lovely warrior would fight this battle on her own.

Tell him it will be *easy*, that relentless shadow woman urged. Tell him that alcohol never meant much to you at all. Lie to him, Sarah! It's your only hope of dancing—not forever, that's sheer folly, but at least a little longer, at least into the new year.

"Yes," she said. "It will be difficult for me. But necessary."

Idiot! Do you realize what you just admitted to him? The dance is over, Sarah. First you flee his bed in Paris because you fear, and want, his touch; then you show him your home, that stark place devoid of life; then he deduces the shameful truth that you send roses to yourself; and now this.

Adieu, Jacques. *Adieu, mon cher.*

"And terrifying?" he asked softly, dancing still, worrying still, *caring* still.

"Yes."

Jack smiled then, a most gentle caress, an eloquent promise that he would be there, helping her, if she would permit him to be. "As terrifying as dancing with me?"

A smile touched Sarah's lips in reply, a defiant and eloquent promise from the Parisian phantom herself, a brave vow not to disappear, not yet.

"No," she said. *Nothing is as terrifying, or as wondrous, as that.*

*H*ow *clever you are, Lady Bitch.* Oh yes, I saw you tonight, witch, *pretending* not to care. I *did* like your gown, however. Black becomes you, Sarah Pembroke. *Just as death will.*

What color is your blood, I wonder? It could very well be pitch—witch—black. I wouldn't be at all surprised.

Well. We'll find out, *won't we?*

Chapter Twenty-Six

Scotland Yard
Thursday, January Fifth

"I'VE JUST RECEIVED A LETTER. I HAVEN'T opened it yet, because of the fingerprints that may be inside. I think it's from him, Jack. Like the other envelope, this one is typewritten, with no return address, and it's marked *Personal and Confidential.*"

"And the postmark?"

"London. Yesterday."

"Why don't we open it together, Sarah?" *Why don't we see each other again, at last?*

Five days had passed since he had wished her good night, and Happy New Year, at her penthouse door; five days during which they had spoken daily, by telephone, about death, murder, and all the possible murderers Sarah might know, the many men who would happily slit her throat.

Sarah had no list of admirers to give him. But she gave Jack other names, so many names, so many men who had been provoked to rage by the warrior-woman, her toughness, her iciness, and the fame that gave her the power to insist that things were done *her* way.

There was Adrian, of course. Perhaps his fury about her editorial control was significant after all. And there were at least six cameramen with whom she had significantly clashed, and a producer with whom she had worked in Mogadishu, until she'd had him replaced; and the list went on and on.

Jack knew what Sarah was doing: exonerating Cole, trying to, for Claire, and at her own expense. And was Sarah wasting Jack's time by conjuring bogus clues, false pieces of the puzzle of death?

Not at all. Jack was not wedded to the idea of Cole Taylor as cold-blooded murderer; *au contraire*. And as Sarah herself observed whenever she called, these many men who despised her were *logical* suspects—especially given the potential links to Ashley Alexander and Paulina Bliss. True, the world in which Sarah worked was brutally real, and the murdered actresses had achieved their fame in a realm of pure fiction. But the *format* was essentially the same. All three women appeared on camera, a process that required a small army behind-the-scenes. Maybe a cameraman with whom Sarah had clashed in Bosnia had practiced his photographic skills in Hollywood first. Or maybe there was a gaffer, a key grip, a director.

Jack could not dispute Sarah's logic and diligently pursued every name. And because she was right, because any of these men might be the killer, he could not stop her daily recitation of the enemies she had made. But he hated her confessions, heard her pain despite the elegant calm of her voice—her pain, her shame, as day after day she reminded him that she was so terribly disliked.

Finally, yesterday, Jack told her that these men who didn't like her were aberrations. Then made a confession of his own: that he happened to know one man who would happily dance with her forever. Jack's confession was greeted with silence, and then, in a rush, with the announcement that she was late for a meeting with Timothy.

Jack hadn't heard from Sarah since, and had been wondering when he would. But now she was calling, *had* to call, because the black-hearted killer had apparently just sent his second warning.

"Sarah? Shall we open the letter together?"

"Yes. All right. I could come there. I have time before the newscast, and it would be best, wouldn't it, to open the letter in private and then send it directly to the lab?"

"I think so. Okay. I'll see you soon."

And in the meantime I'll put away two of these files. There weren't just two files that Sarah didn't know about. Merely two that Jack was quite confident that Sarah would be unhappy to discover. She would most certainly not be pleased to learn of the manila folder on *her*, the scant facts that could be uncovered about her personal life. Nor, Jack imagined, would she be happy about the folder that bore the name of a man she knew well, and should have logically mentioned because of his obvious links to the slain actresses.

But Sarah had not mentioned that man's name. Which meant that her analytical mind had a blind spot where he was concerned—exactly the kind of blind spot that had, perhaps, been lethal for Ashley Alexander and Paulina Bliss.

Dear Lady Pembroke,

My name is Enid Duckworth-Parker. For nearly fifty years my husband, Albert, had an obstetrics practice on Bishop's Avenue in Hampstead. He shared an office with your mother's internist, Jeremy Sloan, which explains why it was Albert who was contacted eleven years ago, on August tenth, and asked to deliver your baby. Naturally, he promptly agreed, and within an hour was on a private jet en route to Penzance.

Six years ago, shortly after you began your career as a television journalist, my husband and I spent a weekend in Cornwall, at a charming bed-and-breakfast called Hyacinth House just south of St. Ives. Since that visit, we've returned at least once a year, although until three months ago, I had no idea why. Not that I ever objected, mind you. Hyacinth House is delightful, as are its proprietors, Lucas and Emma Cain, and their daughter, Jessica.

Jessie is *your* daughter, Lady Pembroke. My husband had known there would be an adoption, of course. The circumstances had been explained to him—the ski vacation in Gstaad, the three young men, aristocrats all, who found you so attractive, and your understandable attraction to them as well, and your own inexperience with alcohol, as well as with the opposite sex. He was sympathetic to the circumstance, *you were so young*, and was told that everyone, yourself included, agreed that all things considered, adoption was for the best.

Albert never talked to you about the adoption. You didn't *want* to talk about it anymore, he was told, your decision was made. And since the delivery commenced just moments after he arrived—after which he immediately returned to London—he didn't really have a chance to speak to you at all. Which is why, I suppose, when he saw you on the telly, saw *how much* you cared about children, he began to wonder, and worry. He contacted obstetricians in Penzance, found the one who arranged the adoption, and convinced the man to reveal the adoptive parents' names.

That's why we made our trips to Cornwall, you see. Albert wanted to be very certain that Jessica was fine. And she *is* fine, Lady Pembroke. She's a happy, joyful, lovely child. She resembles you, she definitely does. But her resemblance to her adoptive father is so striking that her relationship to you would not have occurred to me had I not been told.

My beloved Albert died last week. His final wish was that I write this letter to you. This has been torment for him, seeing your compassion for children and yet knowing how happy little Jessie is with the Cains.

Perhaps you already know about Jessica. I hope so. After all, it was your own husband, Simon Beckwith-Jones, who handled the adoption. You probably *do* know, have known all along. But Albert had a feeling—perhaps the folly of old age—that you didn't. And he believed, as I do, that you should.

Please forgive my Albert, Lady Pembroke. He was a good and honorable man.

Jack had opened the letter carefully, with tweezers, and neither he nor Sarah had touched it as they read.

But Sarah was touching it now, needing to touch it, as if somehow her trembling fingers could reach the daughter who had been given away.

It hadn't been madness. Her baby had been a little girl, and the music she had heard in the delivery room had been that daughter's joyful greeting. And the inner voice that had promised purpose to her life? And had prohibited her from draining her blood, *all* of it this time, into the tiny grave in Norfolk? Not fantasy either.

This was the reason for that voice.

Her daughter was the reason.

But now there was new madness, screaming deep inside, and the ghosts that had already caused such great harm seemed to be cackling at this, their most magnificent betrayal of all. *How we laughed when you mourned for that little dead boy, Sarah! And when you decided to open your veins, to warm the frozen ground—and him—with your own blood. That was truly foolish, Sarah. Truly mad, truly marvelous!*

Sarah heard the cackling ghosts. Her mother. Her father. Simon Beckwith-Jones. They had won. And they knew it. She would never survive this betrayal. She would simply scream until she died.

Then there was a new sound, strong and gentle and raw with love.

"Sarah?" *Dance with me, my love. Let me hold your pain, your sadness, close to me.* "Talk to me."

She followed his tender command, not to dance, not yet, but at least to speak.

"They told me she was dead . . . and that she was a boy . . . and they even gave me a precious little baby boy to hold, to kiss, to love. *I have to see her, Jack!*"

"I know."

"*I have to!*" Sarah repeated, not hearing his quiet words, because the cackling ghosts drowned out all else. *I have to see him!* she had cried, all those years ago, to those ghosts. *I have to go to his grave and talk to him.*

"I know you do, Sarah."

She looked up then, beyond the gossamer blur of ghosts to him. And it was then that the dance began, the gentle waltz of hearts.

"You know?" *You understand?*

"Of course I know." *I love you.*

"When should I see her?" she asked, not desperately now, not the way she had pleaded to the ghosts—*When can I go to his grave?*—but with hope, and with trust. "When, Jack?"

"This weekend. It's still two days away, but that will give you a little time to adjust."

This weekend. And every weekend? As the ghosts had permitted her to do, until that December night when she tried to kill herself and Simon had made promises he knew that he would never keep.

"We'll leave first thing Saturday morning," Jack said.

"We?"

"I'll drive you." *You can't go alone. I won't let you. We're dancing, Sarah, you and I—forever.*

But the waltz began to falter then, as Sarah stumbled on her own fears, her memories of ancient madness and her terror of the new insanity that was yet to be.

You can't come with me, Jack. I don't know what I'll do when I see her. What if I start to scream and cannot stop? What if I have to finish what I began on that long-ago December night? What if I'm supposed to see her just one time, and then die?

But I'm not going to die. I can't. Not yet. I have a friend who is blind, and deeply in love, and I must help that friend. That friend.

"Claire and Sydney and I were planning to have dinner together this Saturday. I'm sure Sydney wouldn't mind rescheduling, and then Claire—"

Claire. The name meant so much to her. Her penmate. Her lovely, generous friend. The shadow woman loved by Jacques. But, quite suddenly, *Claire* sounded sharp and piercing, and the ghosts began to cackle anew.

Talk about *betrayal*! How's this: A mother, let's call her Sarah, takes her good friend Claire to see Sarah's long-lost daughter. And who else will know of that sentimental journey to Cornwall? *Cole.* What if you're wrong about his innocence? *Dead* wrong?

Geneva Pembroke's crimes would seem quite trivial by contrast, wouldn't they? A mother who allows her daughter to be raped is one thing. But that transgression pales completely, merely a minor maternal lapse, when compared to a mother who leads a knife-wielding murderer to her daughter's ivory throat.

Jack watched in silence as understanding dawned on Sarah's face. Understanding, and anguish.

"Let me drive you to Cornwall, Sarah."

You won't scream. You *won't*. Somehow you'll keep that madness deep inside. And you *need* Jack with you. You need his strength and his calm. "Thank you, Jack."

He smiled. "You're most welcome, Lady Pembroke. So, I'll place a call to Cornwall, to reserve two rooms for us at Hyacinth House this Saturday night."

"No."

"No?"

"It might be too difficult for me to stay there. I won't know until I get there . . . until I see her."

Chapter Twenty-Seven

❧

Drake Hotel
Thursday, January Fifth

*P*LUM. CLARET. PEACOCK. JADE.
Burnt sienna.

"Burnt sienna, Claire?" Cole had echoed when she made the smiling—and triumphant—proclamation.

On that rainy afternoon they had been strolling in the Asian Garden at the Drake. A celebration of the flowers of the Orient, the vast indoor garden was in fragrant bountiful blossom even in the dead of winter.

"I think so," Claire had replied. "I mean, if the color's really the same reddish-brown as the pigment at the center of Aunt Augusta's tiger lilies, then it's definitely burnt sienna."

This was how, together, Cole and Claire *saw* London. Cole had believed that the only colors he knew were the colors of Claire. But on New Year's Eve, when he described to her the mauve velvet drapes—by recalling for her the summertime sunset over the bayou—he realized that, in Harlanville, with Claire, his entire world had been vividly bright.

For the past five days they had seen the colors of London through shared memories of shades and hues they had known as children—the myriad greens of their forest, the reds and purples that signaled the fall of the sun from the sky, and the serene pastels that heralded its return. The lettering on the street signs of Harlanville was taupe, they decided, and all those years ago the Hotel Paradis had been painted teal and cream.

Only once did Claire respond with a frown to an image Cole described.

"Remember that skirt you wore, Claire? It was really a kilt, I guess, dark green with red and yellow stripes."

Of course she remembered the skirt, and only too late did Cole recall when Claire had worn it; and this time it was he who had crossed the invisible line that kept them apart. Claire had been thirteen when she bought that skirt, and Cole had been sixteen, and they had been strangers then, were *supposed* to have been. They were not supposed to have been looking at each other, noticing each other—indeed, it was during that same year when Claire bravely challenged him to stop drinking, and he so cruelly drove her away.

But now, in London, as Cole described a plaid skirt he should never have noticed, a colorful relic of that forbidden time, his voice held such fondness, such longing—and oh, in her darkness, and in the air that shimmered between them, the softness of his voice even sounded like *love*.

Claire saw the colors of London through Cole's gray eyes. But it was she, the joyous elf-angel, who had created the palette of brilliant memories that enabled his charcoal eyes to see. And it was Claire, in London, who made Cole discover his other senses in ways that he had never known.

Fish and chips, Cole. Don't they smell wonderfully British? And the taste, Cole. *Taste the sea.*

Listen! she urged during the changing of the guard at Buckingham Palace. Listen to the hoofbeats, how crisp and rhythmic they are. And do you hear the creaking of leather? And that jingling sound, like sleigh bells?

Listen, Cole. Close your eyes and really *listen*.

Years ago, with her, Cole Taylor *had* closed his eyes. He had taken her hand, and trusted her to guide him through the darkness. Cole and Claire touched now, as they explored London, his hand at her elbow, her hand atop the glacial scar on his arm. But Cole did not close his eyes, did not dare—for then they would both be blind.

It was Cole who guided Claire through the darkness now; but now as then it was he who felt the greatest light, because it was her radiant joy that illuminated the blackest places of his heart.

Claire was the bayou girl still, that cinnamon-haired angel of sunlight and dreams. But here, in London, Cole's intrepid bayou girl could no longer sing.

Tonight, she would proclaim with the bravery he knew so well. I'll sing at the rehearsal, *tonight*.

But even as she was making the bold pronouncement, it would begin to falter. She would become breathless, just as she had at the Royal Albert Hall. Breathless, bewildered—and betrayed.

Singing was part of her, a symbol of her happy soul, and now that happiness had been stolen from her as surely as sight had been stolen from her sky-blue eyes.

Cole knew who had stolen Claire's ability to sing. Cole Taylor, crooner of love songs and thief of dreams.

I will give her music back to her, he vowed. By sending her home to Harlanville? That would work, of course, would restore to Claire the stolen piece of her soul.

But Cole believed that Claire wanted more, as he did; not just her voice but theirs, joined together . . . making love.

"**W**ere you able to nap?"

Cole's question, posed the moment she opened her door to him, was expected. The old Claire—that young, brave, sighted girl—would *never* have napped. Her energy then had been as boundless as her dreams. But in this foreign place, where every single step taken in the darkness was entirely new, and potentially treacherous, she readily fatigued.

This foreign place, with him. Claire knew full well that there was much more to her fatigue than the challenges of London, the heightened awareness—and concentration—required of her in this wholly unfamiliar place. What needed rest, far more than her mind, was her heart, the hummingbird inside her that fluttered frantically whenever Cole was near.

So Claire napped, her hummingbird heart did, awakening refreshed, eager, and now, as she greeted him, fluttering anew.

"I had a wonderful nap." She smiled, and because it was expected, too, she asked, "How about you?"

Did Cole *ever* sleep? she wondered. The band didn't rehearse every night, but when they did, Claire would return to the hotel by midnight, escorted by Cole. She would sleep until dawn, and he would rehearse until then, but still he met her for breakfast at eight o'clock, after which they would wander the streets of London, where she would assign exotic, enchanted names to the colors they had known as children.

Panthers never slept. How could they? Nonetheless Claire's panther usually responded to her query with a vague yet pleasant "Sure. Enough."

Usually. But not now.

Now Cole was silent, his gaze compelled to leave her naturally radiant face by another glow, a brilliant yet artificial luminescence, and a worrisome one. Claire usually illuminated two lamps—for him—to light his way in the winter darkness.

But tonight Claire's hotel room was ablaze with lamp glow *except* for the usual two lights.

"Cole? Is something wrong?"

"Did you turn on lights for me tonight?"

"Yes. Didn't I?"

Yes, Cole thought. But because they were already illuminated, along with every other light in the room, when you thought you were turning them on you were actually turning them off. "All the lights are on, Claire. Except for those two."

"Oh." Her expression became thoughtful, then decisive. "Remember how dark you said the sky was this afternoon? How early the twilight? When the women from housekeeping came to clean they must have turned on all the lights and then simply forgot to turn them off."

"But you're frowning, Claire."

"Am I?"

"Yes, you are. Is something out of place? Did you sense that someone had been in the room?"

"No." Her reply was empatic, truthful, and embellished by a lovely smile. Was something out of place? *No.* Just her own relationship with reality. Had she sensed someone in the room? No, not someone, just some*thing*—a golden glow.

Get a grip, Claire. You *did not see* a golden glow. Nor did you see sparkles of silver when you gazed at the heavens on that snowy night in Harlanville. And yesterday, when you believed you saw a flash of scarlet at Buckingham, the bright red coat of a palace guard, that was an illusion as well. You are *blind*, Claire. Forever. It's just that eight-year-old girl inside you believing in the impossible. She can't sing anymore, that bayou girl . . . but she still can dream.

Stop dreaming.

"No, Cole, there's nothing—except my ringing telephone. Probably Syd," she added as she moved with surefooted grace toward the phone.

The caller was Sydney, returning Claire's call.

"The operator didn't call you, did she, Syd? I asked her to hold the message until you called to check, in case you were asleep. . . . Oh, good. Well, here's the reason I called—Sarah can't have dinner with us on Saturday after all. . . . What? No, I'm sure it's something else, something to do with her job. She wouldn't do that. . . . No, not even for him. Anyway, I wondered if we should reschedule? Sarah really wants to come with us. She says any night next week is fine, after her newscast of course, so I thought Wednesday, since the band won't be rehearsing that night? Unless you have other plans . . . Oh, good. Let's plan on it then. Wednesday at nine. Great . . . Tonight? Well, Cole and I were going to try that place on Waverton, you know, the one right next door to the studio? Would you like to come with us? You'd be more than welcome . . . Yes. *Absolutely.* It's settled. We'll meet you in the lobby in twenty minutes."

Claire replaced the receiver and turned toward the place

where Cole had been standing. Was he there still? Or had the panther moved, a motion of such stealth that even her sensitive ears had not heard his graceful prowl?

No, Claire decided. He's just where he was. *I see him.* A dark shadow silhouetted against the golden glow.

There is no shadow.

There is no golden glow.

Stop dreaming, and smile!

"Syd's going to join us for dinner." She shrugged. "I guess you heard."

"I heard everything. I couldn't help it."

His voice came from precisely where her imagination envisioned his mouth to be. His mouth, that sensual place that described with such care, such fondness—and such love?—the colors of their childhood; and that once confessed so much to her, trusting her; and with which he had shown her how much he wanted her, *hungered* for her. *Stop!* "That's fine, Cole. There wasn't anything you shouldn't hear."

"What was Sydney asking about Sarah? Something you said Sarah wouldn't do?"

"Oh. She was speculating that the real reason Sarah was canceling our plans for dinner this Saturday was because she had a date with Jack." *A hot date with that gorgeous Jack* were Sydney's exact words. "I'm sure that's not the reason."

The shadow was silent in the golden glow. Silent and still.

"Why don't you come with me to Monte Carlo?"

"Monte Carlo?"

"Timothy wants me to fly there tomorrow, to meet with the promoter for our concert at the Sporting Club in April. The meeting will be brief. In fact, I'd planned to make the round trip in one day. But since we don't rehearse again until Monday night, we could stay for the weekend."

"I'd like that," Claire heard herself say, *barely* heard above the frantic fluttering of her heart.

It was sheer folly, of course. She was just beginning to feel comfortable with the foreignness of London, and now Cole was inviting her to travel to another foreign place, with him, for the entire weekend.

But she had to go with him *now* to Monte Carlo. Because? Because she would not be with him, in April, when he returned. By then the world would know about Cole's missing brother, and perhaps that beloved sibling would even have been found, and Claire Chamberlain would be teaching music in Harlanville, if she still *could* teach music, and her hummingbird heart would be calm . . . forever.

"**W**hy don't you take a nap while I meet with the promoter?"

Claire nodded, too tired to speak. Her heart had fluttered all night, preventing sleep, and although the short flight from London to Nice had been faultlessly smooth, it had been exhausting nonetheless.

Could she nap in Monte Carlo? Would her racing heart comply? *Yes*, because the sea breeze was balmy, *bayou* balmy, even on this January day. And the seabirds sang a hushed lullaby.

Claire awakened to the quiet knock on her hotel room door. Her hair was tousled from sleep, and she wore only her modest cotton nightgown. But in another moment he would be gone, consigning her to additional sleep she did not need.

"Cole?" she called as she scrambled from her bed. "I'm awake. Just a moment."

The room Cole had reserved for her at Loew's was quite small—at her request. So much easier to learn about, for just a weekend, than a spacious suite. But Claire didn't yet know the details of her room, and the short journey was a groping one.

"Cole?" she asked again when she reached the door.

"Yes, Claire. It's me." Claire opened the door, a vision of tousled cinnamon hair and sparkling eyes and flushed pink cheeks, so different from the portrait of exhaustion he had left—*he had caused*—two hours earlier. Now, with relief, he said, "You napped."

"Oh, yes I did. The window was open, and the breeze was so warm, and so *fragrant*. There are gardenias nearby, aren't there?"

"On the balcony."

"And seabirds, too? And maybe even the lapping of waves? Is that possible? Is the Mediterranean that close?"

"It's that close."

Claire's balcony, shaded, secluded, and abloom with gardenias, overlooked the sea.

"What can I see from my balcony?"

"To the right, and below, is the marina."

"Cluttered with grand yachts?"

"Pretty cluttered," Cole conceded. "And pretty grand. At least two have their own helicopters."

"Can you see the flags?"

"The flags, Claire?"

"Wouldn't each vessel be flying the flag of its country?"

She was doing it again, making him see far more than he ever would have seen. There *were* flags, of course. And as Claire had imagined, in this seaport where the rich and famous came to gamble—and gambol—the yachts hailed from around the world.

"There are flags," Cole said. "All sizes and colors and shapes. We can investigate further, closer up, when we wander to the marina."

Cole told her about the view beyond the marina, the rugged seaside cliffs crowned by a fairy-tale palace, and the landscape beyond that, the villas and high-rises that were nestled, somewhat precariously it seemed, into the lush, steep hillside.

"And everything else, the rest of your view, is sea."

Claire turned to him with a questioning tilt of her sleep-tangled hair and a smile in her sightless eyes. "Is it an aquamarine sea? Or an emerald one? Or is it azure blue?"

The Mediterranean was blue. Blue, dappled gold by the fading rays of the winter sun.

"Blue, but not azure," Cole said. And not indigo, or cobalt, or lapis, or cornflower. Not in fact any of the enchanting colors that he had described and she had named. This blue—this clear, brilliant, joyous blue—had no name . . . until now. "*Claire* blue. The blue of your eyes."

"Oh," she whispered, suddenly breathless. Was it the breath-lessness of panic? That phantom of fear that had stolen so much? *No.* This breathlessness was something else. Something wonderful.

"And there's gold, too," Cole continued, shattering every vow he had made, unable not to, compelled by the wishes of his heart. "Sparkling in the blue. Just like the golden sparkles in your eyes."

"I don't have golden sparkles."

"Oh yes you do. Especially when you're happy. I see them now, Claire, more brilliant than the sun on the sea. And far more beautiful."

"Cole . . ."

His voice had been touching her, a caress more gentle than the balmy breeze, and as he described the splendor of sunbeams on the sea, she truly believed she saw that shimmering gold. And then the bayou girl, that brave and brazen dreamer of im-possible dreams, believed she saw something even more glitter-ing—and quite silver, and brilliant with love, and molten with desire, ablaze in his sensual panther eyes.

Then *he* touched her, and there was a celebration of color, a river of rainbows that flowed warm, *hot*, and vivid in her veins.

And then he kissed her. The lips that seduced the world with songs of love embarked on a slow journey of discovery—her temples, her eyes, her nose, her cheeks—as if it were he who was blind and this was the only way he could learn every inch of her.

But his journey was too slow! Claire's lips trembled for his, hungered for their own song of love. She found his mouth, sur-prising him, and evoking a soft, low sound of pure desire.

"Oh, Claire. *I want you.*"

"I want you, too."

They made love in her bed, caressed by a gardenia-scented breeze, a bridal bouquet, innocent and pure.

"Claire?" They were one. Already. It happened quickly, it had to, for both of them. She had been as hungry as he, as con-fident, and yet . . . "You've never made love before?"

Yes, a thousand times, a million, in my heart, with you. Only with you. "No."

"Are you all right?"

"Oh yes."

The bayou girl could no longer sing with the man she loved. But it did not matter. There was another duet now, a new and glorious harmony. In loving Cole, in this most magnificent sharing of hearts and minds and bodies and souls, she was singing, they were singing, the most perfect love song of all.

Chapter Twenty-Eight

Hyacinth House
Saturday, January Seventh

THE DRIVE FROM SARAH'S PENTHOUSE IN Mayfair to the far reaches of the Cornish coast took a little under six hours. Silent hours, during which, mostly, Sarah was very far away. Remembering the past, Jack decided. And envisioning the future.

Sometimes, however, Sarah would emerge from her trance, startled, worried, and focused quite clearly on the present.

"You still don't see anyone?"

"No one, Sarah," Jack assured. "We're not being followed."

We're not leading a murderer to your daughter. Jack knew it was true. Throughout the journey he had kept a constant vigil of the rearview mirror. He and Sarah were not being followed.

Because Cole Taylor was in Monaco? Perhaps. Or perhaps not. Despite his own surprisingly powerful wishes for the superstar's innocence, Jack had not yet been able to remove Cole's name from his list of suspects.

But there were other names on the master puzzle solver's list, appealing—and haunting—possibilities. None of whom, thankfully, was on the road today to Cornwall.

* * *

When they reached St. Ives, when Hyacinth House was only minutes away, Sarah was trancelike no more. Her entire being was on alert, her expression at once anxious and eager, her fingernails digging deeply into her palms.

"Are you okay?"

"No," she whispered, as her head nodded a brave yes. And then, with a shake of that same head, she offered, "Yes."

Jack smiled. "You couldn't possibly be okay, Sarah."

"No, I suppose not."

"For the record, you *look* more than okay. In fact, you look quite beautiful. I like your hair that way."

The black silk was almost free today, a long, shining flow tied loosely at her nape, captured in a brightly colored scarf, not the ribbons she had worn at Avalon—even though the style was the same. This was the way she had worn her hair for her baby, her daughter.

You think she's going to recognize the loosely bound ponytail? The baby who knew you only from the womb? That's *crazy*, Sarah. You're crazy. Mad, crazy, *still*.

"Sarah?"

"I'm scared, Jack."

"Tell me what scares you the most."

I'm afraid I'll start screaming and never stop. "What if I have to touch her, hold her? What if I go crazy, and grab her, and refuse to let her go?"

"That's not going to happen, Sarah."

"You think I have a firm grasp on my sanity?" *Of course you don't!* her ghosts cackled with malicious glee. If you did, if you had *any* control at all, you would not be suggesting to Jack—of all people—that you might just be a little bit insane. Talk about sheer madness.

"I know you do," Jack said. "Questioning one's sanity is absolute proof that it exists and is intact. You're sane, Sarah Pembroke. It's absolutely normal to be terrified about what you might do."

"But not normal to act out."

"Which you won't. You'll block all the impulses, no matter how strong they are."

"You sound so sure." *Of me.*

"I am sure. If it's any consolation—and, quite selfishly, I hope it is—I'll be with you every step of the way."

She trembled, but she smiled. "It is a consolation. I . . ." *need you, Jack.* "It is."

Oh, how she needed Jack Dalton; because after only a few steps up the winding flagstone pathway to the front porch of the elegant house, everything fell apart.

CLOSED. That was, in essence, the message of the sign on the door. It was written far more graciously than that, and in flowing script. But nothing could soften the blow.

Hyacinth House was closed until April.

"We'll knock anyway," Jack said.

"And say what?" Sarah asked, a quiet plea of despair. "That we can't read? Or that I want to see my daughter?"

Before Jack could reply, their attention was distracted by the sound of a car pulling onto the gravel drive.

"Oh," Sarah whispered as one of the occupants emerged, the only one who mattered. Her baby girl. "Oh, Jack."

He answered with a steadying arm at her waist, which was where the comforting strength remained as Jessica neared. She wore jeans and a parka, and her gait was one of grace and joy. And what of the resemblance between mother and daughter that Enid Duckworth-Parker had claimed was "definitely" there?

It was there, perhaps, in Jessica's elegant cheekbones, and her fine, straight nose, and the shape of her lips. And it was *definitely* there, stunningly, astonishingly, in the luxuriant ponytail that she wore, shining black and silken, and captured loosely, like Sarah's own black silk, by a long bright scarf.

But I never looked like this, Sarah thought. Never this graceful, not as a girl, and never this happy, this safe, this loved. *Not ever.*

Even the driver of the car cared about Jessica Cain's well-being. She was waiting, with her carload of girls, until Jessie was past the strangers who stood on the porch and safely inside her home.

*   *   *

The girls had been ice-skating, Sarah realized, as her daughter drew closer.

Dear Mummy and Daddy, I've been learning to ice-skate. There's a rink near the Academy in Val-d'Isère. When I'm home for the holidays, I'd like to show you what I can do. I hope you'll be proud of me.

"I *know* you!" Jessica exclaimed when she reached the porch. Her voice was pure music, as it had been on the day she was born, and now Sarah saw clearly the color of her eyes, the unique blend of green and blue. Was it an improbable—yet magnificent—gift from a betrayed teenaged girl and her nameless Christmastime rapist? Or did the remarkable harmony of hues come from another source entirely, from Cornwall itself, this mystical place of sapphire sky and emerald sea?

"You know me?"

"You're Lady Pembroke, aren't you?"

"Yes, but . . ." *I'm your mother, your mother!* "Yes, I am. But please call me Sarah."

"And I'm Jack. And you're?"

"Jessie."

"Hello, Jessie."

"Hello." She beamed at both of them. Then realizing that the car from which she had emerged was on the gravel still, its driver waiting to make certain that she was in no peril, she waved. I'm safe with these strangers, her wave proclaimed. *Totally* safe. When the car drove off, she spoke again to Sarah. "Have you come to stay with us?"

Yes, I want to stay with you. Forever.

"That was our plan," Jack said. "But we didn't plan carefully enough. Hyacinth House is closed."

"But not for *you!*" Jessica insisted, still focused on Sarah. "Mummy has helpers in the village, and she can just ring them up, and you can have the corner suite, with views both ways to the sea, and—"

"Jessie?"

Jessica spun from the mother she didn't know to the one she did. "Look who's *here*, Mummy! Lady, I mean Sarah—"

"You mean Lady Pembroke," Emma interjected softly, smiling first at her daughter and then at the woman she had admired for so long.

"I asked Jessie to call me Sarah, if that's all right with you. And this is Jack Dalton."

"And I'm Emma Cain, and I guess I feel as Jessie does, that I know you, that you're family. You're in our house so often, every night now, and from the very beginning of your career Jessie's been one of your most devoted fans."

"Mummy."

"It's true, my love, and I'm sure that Lady—Sarah—won't mind hearing it. Before Jessie could even comprehend the words, she was mesmerized by your voice. She would sit transfixed, just listening, even when your face wasn't on the screen."

That's because she recognizes my voice! For the eight months we were together, when she was a tiny flame of hope within me, I talked to her all the time. And now I need to hold her, love her, never let her go. Help me, Jack! I'm crazy, truly mad, and in another moment—

"It looks like you're a skater, Jessie," Jack said, gesturing to the bright white skates, undoubtedly new as of Christmas.

Jessica nodded, as Emma offered proudly, "Is she *ever*."

"Doesn't it hurt your ankles?" Sarah's voice was quiet, not raving, and her hands were clenched safely at her sides. But she still felt so precarious; especially now, as she recalled her own experiences at the ice rink in Val-d'Isère, the delicate ankles that were black and blue and in constant pain.

Jessica's expression became thoughtful. "There are exercises you can do, should do, that strengthen your ankles." Then she smiled. "After that it doesn't hurt *at all*."

"Did it go well today, love?"

"Really well." By way of explanation to Sarah and Jack, Jessica added, "Mummy couldn't come because she had a wedding cake to make."

"Besides which," Emma embellished, "Jessie's daddy and I aren't exactly *encouraged* to watch her practice."

"Why not?" Sarah asked. Because you get angry when she falls? When she *fails*? Because you demand too much of her? *This is a waste of our time, Sarah! You said that you could skate, and look at you—you're terrible.*

"Because they *worry* too much! Every time I fall they want me to stop skating altogether."

Emma smoothed a tender hand over Jessica's shining black hair. "It's just that the ice is so hard and so cold. About as cold as this wind is becoming. Please come in, won't you? We'd love it if you stayed here tonight. For as long as you want, for that matter. As Jessie said, it's absolutely no trouble."

"It would be just for tonight," Sarah said, the decision made. She hadn't been certain if she would be able to stay at Hyacinth House, to sleep under the same roof as her daughter. But she would keep her hands clutched at her sides, not holding Jessie, not touching her, not smoothing her silken black hair; and she would not scream aloud the wishes of her heart; and what Sarah feared now, most of all, was the specter of tomorrow, of having to say good-bye.

"And as for dinner . . ." Emma frowned.

"Please don't worry about that. I'm sure there are restaurants in the village."

"Actually, you'll have to go to St. Ives."

"You could come with us. Couldn't they, Mummy? With you and me and the grands."

"Jessie and I are having dinner with my parents at the Sloop Inn," Emma translated. "You'd be more than welcome to join us."

"We wouldn't want to intrude—I mean, more than we already have."

"It wouldn't be an intrusion. As I told you, we consider you family. My parents would be positively thrilled to meet you."

"**D**addy won't be coming to dinner with us," Jessica announced as she gave Sarah and Jack a whirlwind tour of her home while

Emma placed calls to her helpers in the village. "He has to work, probably all night. He's going to want to meet you, though."

"And we'd like to meet him."

"We could do it now," Jessie suggested. "He's just outside, in the gardener's cottage, and it's almost four, time for tea. Or, in Daddy's case, hot chocolate."

"Now would be fine," Sarah said, just as Jack knew she would.

If Jessica was going to the gardener's cottage, to take hot chocolate to her father, then that was where Sarah would want to be as well. With Jessie. Because of her daughter, all traces of Sarah Pembroke, lady warrior, had vanished. The war correspondent renowned for her acute powers of observation had utterly disappeared. Sarah was a mother, mesmerized by her child, and oblivious to all else—including the small but enormously foreboding objets d'art that stood atop pedestals in the parlor and adorned the polished hardwood hallways of Hyacinth House.

Jack needed to prepare her, to *warn* her. Which meant finding, or creating, a few seconds of privacy from the gracious little hostess who was Sarah's beloved child.

It was that precious daughter who created the necessary moment. When she disappeared into the pantry, to get the thermos for the hot chocolate, Jack caught Sarah's hand to prevent her from following.

She turned to him, startled.

"You need to be very careful, Sarah."

"What? Oh, Jack, am I being too obvious? Do you think Emma might suspect the truth?"

"No, Sarah, you're doing great, and I'm certain that Emma has absolutely no idea who you are." *You're both mothers, focused on your daughter, oblivious to all else.* "This must be terribly hard for you."

"She's so *lovely*, Jack."

"Like you, Sarah. Just like you. But when we meet . . . him . . . you must be *very* careful."

"Why?"

The moment was over. Jessica had returned.

And soon, very soon, Sarah would discover for herself the answer to her question.

"This is where Mummy and Daddy and I lived when I was little," Jessica said as they neared the cottage. The small building exuded a romantic charm, a quaint coziness, and it enjoyed the towering protectiveness of a stately willow. "Then my grandparents retired to St. Ives, and we moved into the main house, and now the cottage is Daddy's studio."

The flagstone path led to the front door. But just before reaching that entrance, Jessica veered off, leading the way around the cottage, to a less-than-charming aspect that had been concealed by the weeping branches of the mammoth tree.

Clearly a temporary appendage, the uninspired addition was a sturdy creation of plywood, substantially higher than the rest of the cottage, but in overall floor space a virtual twin. There were no windows in the plywood, just a single wide door.

"This is because of Peggy," Jessica explained without explaining, but her sea-green, sky-blue eyes sparkled as she anticipated sharing something quite wonderful with her guests. "You'll see her in a moment. When it's time for her to leave, this will all be torn down." Then, as they reached the door, Jessie's voice dropped to a whisper and her sparkling eyes grew earnest. "I always knock first, very softly, in case he's in the middle of something tricky. Not that he *ever* slips!"

Or turns you away? Sarah wondered, remembering her own attempts at bringing offerings to her father. *Don't bother me now, Sarah. I'm busy. Just put the tea on the table, and leave.*

But the deep male voice that answered Jessie's quiet knock held only love. "Jessie?"

"Hi, Daddy," she replied, smiling at Sarah and Jack as she opened the plywood door. "You'll *never* guess who's with me! Lady Sarah Pembroke and her friend Jack."

Neither Sarah nor Jack had the chance to see Lucas Cain's immediate and unrehearsed reaction to the news. Their view of him was entirely blocked by Peggy, an immense statue of Pegasus sculpted from pure white marble.

Had it been another time—a time without black hearts carved in stone and crimson slashes carved in alabaster flesh— Jack would have marveled at the magnificent winged horse, and at the remarkable coincidence.

Pegasus. That splendid mythologic creature crafted for Jack by his father, as a puzzle, a challenge. But mostly as a gift of love. On the wings of that noble beast the Dalton family had soared from precarious subsistence to vast fortune.

And now that mythical horse, that symbol of so much in the myths and legends of Jack's own life, was here, in this charming cottage in Cornwall. Pegasus was here, and quite alive. The muscled marble flesh fairly rippled with power, and the feathery wings seemed just instants from flight. This mythical creature could fly, *would* fly.

But on this wintry day of black hearts and crimson throats, Jack saw only the stone carver's studio, and the stone carver's tools, the knife-sharp chisels strewn amid chips of marble on the earthen floor.

Jack had known what they would find in the cottage. During their tour of Hyacinth House, when Sarah's eyes had been fixed on her daughter and blind to all else, Jack had seen the statues so proudly displayed. They were small, scarcely larger than the puzzles sold by his family. No puzzle was hidden within the statues carved in stone by Lucas Cain. Only the heart-chilling, heart-stopping clue.

Despite Jack's warning, Sarah was not prepared. She had steeled herself, her heart, for what she already knew about Lucas Cain— that the resemblance between Jessica and her adoptive father was so striking that no one would ever imagine that she wasn't his.

Sarah saw him now, a shadow emerging from behind a snowy white wing. His hair was as black as her own, and his eyes, like hers, were a dark, dark green. His hands were empty, unarmed with a weapon of any kind, but there was such power in those hands, and such fierceness in the stony stillness of his face.

"Hello." His smile was faint, polite yet cool. "I'm Lucas Cain."

"I'm Jack Dalton, and this is Sarah Pembroke. We arrived without reservations, not realizing that you'd be closed, but your wife has graciously offered to put us up for the night."

"And they're coming to dinner with us, too!"

"Oh? How nice." Lucas Cain smiled then, truly smiled, at Jessica.

But the fierceness didn't vanish.

"This is Peggy." Jessica patted the white muzzle of the winged horse as if it was warm velvet, as if the magnificent creature of marble was a beloved family pet. With a wistful sigh that further confirmed her affection for the statue, she added, "She's almost finished. Then she leaves."

"And goes where?" Jack asked.

"To the lobby of Asquith Towers."

Where I will see it—her—every day, Sarah thought. "You must know Timothy."

"He's the one who commissioned this piece."

"There's a black marble Cupid in Timothy's office," Sarah murmured. Then, hearing the echoes of Jack's warning to be *very careful*, she forced cheer into her voice. "It's quite stunning. It must be yours."

"It is."

"And these other pieces?" Jack asked, gesturing to smaller, partially carved statues at the perimeter of the makeshift room.

"Timothy has friends. He's been kind enough to show them my work, and one thing's led to another."

"Daddy's incredibly busy! *Everyone* wants one of his statues. That's why he can't have dinner with us tonight." Jessica's proud smile faded into a worried frown. "I wish you could, though, Daddy. You're working *way* too hard."

"You know what, Jessie?" Lucas asked softly. "I think you're right. Your wish just came true."

"Really?"

"Really."

Chapter Twenty-Nine

"*W*E HAVE TO GET HER OUT OF HERE." Their two-bedroom suite was located on Hyacinth House's third floor, in the wing for guests, far from the rooms where the family lived. Its walls, built by the powerful hands of Lucas Cain, were thick, solid, virtually soundproof.

But still Sarah whispered her urgent plea. "Now, Jack, we need to take her away. *Now*."

Jack's reply was even more quiet. "No, Sarah."

"*No?* But you believe it's *him*, don't you?" she asked. But Jack wasn't going to tell her what he believed, she realized as she gazed with astonishment at his infuriatingly impassive face. "I mean, I *know* you don't jump to conclusions, but he's a *stone carver*. And it's obvious, don't you think, that he knows who I am?"

"Yes. He knows."

"We didn't get to see his reaction that I was here. But I bet he wasn't the least bit surprised. He was *expecting* me, Jack. He probably wrote the letter himself. Enid Duckworth-Parker may not even exist."

"She exists, Sarah. And the handwriting is hers."

"You checked? Why?"

"Because everything has to be pursued. Everything might be a clue."

"*Except* a stone carver? Lucas asked her to write the letter, Jack, so he and I would meet. He undoubtedly offered to carve her something quite lovely in return. A heart maybe, or another Cupid made of black marble."

"Lucas didn't need to contrive a way to meet you, Sarah. He and Emma were at Timothy's party on New Year's Eve."

"You saw them?"

"I noticed them, just before you and I started to dance. And after that, Sarah, I only noticed you."

His dark blue eyes sent an intimate reminder. *We're discussing murder, Sarah, but we're dancers, you and I. Dancers, dancers, not enemies.*

"I'm not saying that Lucas *isn't* the killer, Sarah. But there are obvious questions that need to be answered." *Questions about Lucas, Sarah, but not about us. We are meant to dance, to love.*

"Questions?" she echoed, turning away from him, a graceful twirl, a dance in itself, but *away*. "What questions?"

"Well, for starters, Lucas Cain runs a bed-and-breakfast in England. What's his connection to two of Hollywood's most glamorous actresses?"

"I don't know." Sarah faced the sea, and spoke with quiet passion to that emerald splendor. "But there *is* one. I'm sure of it. We'll find it. *I'll* find it."

And then I'll take my precious daughter far away from here.

In fact, it was Jack who discovered Lucas Cain's link to Hollywood. The revelation came after the dinner in St. Ives, an event that reminded Jack very much of his own family dinners, a circle of love in which children were as important as adults, *more* important.

By the time they returned to Hyacinth House, it was long past Jessica's bedtime. She tore herself away reluctantly—but amiably—leaving her parents and Sarah and Jack in the parlor to enjoy freshly brewed black coffee and grown-up conversation amid the small statues carved in stone.

A dark black storm was brewing outside, fresh and fierce

and gaining momentum in the winter night, a crescendoing fury that occasionally eclipsed, and sometimes merely embellished, the words spoken within the parlor walls. When Jack described the book he was going to write, about Sarah and other war correspondents of the twentieth century, winter-barren forsythia branches tapped lightly against the windowpanes, as if in applause, approval, for his plan; and when they spoke of Sarah's life in the trenches of mortal combat, the heavens hissed and thundered; but they quieted again, permitting more polite applause against the panes, when Emma expressed her relief that Sarah had left that death and danger behind.

It was then, in that moment of almost eerie quiet, that Sarah queried of her gracious hostess, "Now tell us about the two of you, Emma. Where did you meet?"

"In Florence. Lucas was at Stanford and I was at Cambridge, and there was a joint program between the two universities."

"Ashley Alexander was in a similar program."

Emma's eyes widened with surprise. "Ashley was in our group. But how on *earth* did you know that, Jack?"

Because the way I find murderers is by being thorough. That tidbit about Ashley Alexander's academic career had arrived by fax, a single sentence in the volumes that had been forwarded by the private investigator in L.A. The pertinent article had been in *Vanity Fair*, an interview with the famous actress accompanied by imaginative photographs by Annie Leibovitz.

"Since her death, her murder, I've done a little research into her past."

"Are you planning to write a book about her?"

"No. I don't think anyone will until her murder is solved."

"I wish they'd solve it," Emma murmured.

With Emma's words, the wind began to blow again, to *breathe*. The storm had been holding its breath—as, Sarah realized, had she. But now Sarah Pembroke was breathing again, and with astonishing calm. The necessary link between Lucas Cain and the carnage in Tinseltown was there, *almost* there.

"Was Ashley a good friend, Emma?"

After a split second of indecision, Emma's reply was emphatic. "Yes, she was. She was my roommate, and she and Lucas had known each other since their freshman year at Stanford."

"Had you kept in touch over the years?"

"No. But by extraordinary coincidence, Lucas was in Los Angeles last Valentine's Day."

All traces of calm vanished then, both within Sarah and in the storm-tossed world without. It's not a *coincidence*! the wind screamed. Lucas Cain is a *murderer*.

Hush, Sarah commanded her screaming thoughts and the raging wind. Don't let him know that he's been discovered, that the lethal mystery has been solved.

But neither the storm nor her thoughts obeyed her urgent command. Sarah didn't look at Lucas, didn't dare. But she sensed that he was staring at her, and in a moment all would be lost. He would see that she knew the truth about the blackness of his heart and the bloodlust of the gifted hands that turned stone to flesh and flesh to shreds.

Then Sarah heard a voice, *that* voice, and she looked up to blue eyes as calm as ice.

"Did you see Ashley while you were there, Lucas?" Jack asked.

The wind held its breath anew, shocked into silence by the sheer audacity of the question—or perhaps by its unrevealing calm. There was only one storm now, turbulent and fierce, and it raged within Lucas Cain.

"Yes," he answered finally. "Very briefly. The day before she died."

"He knew Ashley, and was *there* when she died. We didn't ask about Paulina—we couldn't, without revealing that we knew— but she and Ashley were friends, so she and Lucas might easily have met. It's *him*, Jack. But . . ."

"But?" Jack echoed. Are you wondering, as I have wondered from the start, and wonder still, how this reverent carver of winged horses, this loving father *and* husband, could be such a vicious beast? "But what, Sarah?"

"I wonder if the killings were impulsive, not as coldly calculated as we'd thought. Maybe Ashley's murder was an act of passion, and then, perhaps because Paulina knew that he was with Ashley, Lucas had to kill her, too. He might have *staged* the romance after the killings. No envelopes were found in either home, you said, which means the letters could have been planted, all three at once, along with the champagne and roses. Do you think that's possible?"

"Yes. It's possible."

"Do you still have questions, Jack? Not about *how* he did it, but that he did it at all?"

After a heartbeat's hesitation he answered without answering. "I guess I'm trying to make sense of the fact that Lucas admitted to seeing Ashley."

"He believes he's safe, *invulnerable*. He doesn't know we're on to him, and he's undoubtedly enjoying this immensely."

"He didn't look like he was enjoying himself. Emma was obviously shaken by the news that he had seen their onetime friend. Why didn't Lucas simply lie about that meeting?"

"Because he's a *monster*. He *wanted* to hurt his wife."

She was so hurt.

"You saw her, Luc?" They were in their bedroom, the place that, since New Year's Eve, had borne witness to ever more daring passion, ever more bold intimacy, between the country girl and the man she loved—and who she trusted to be honest with her, *always*.

"It was Ash who arranged for my trip to L.A. *She* was the so-called art collector. She'd been at the Gemstone Pictures' party in Beverly Hills when Timothy showed photographs of my work. That part was true. But southern belle art aficionado Lenore Buchanan did not exist, just as Daphne never did. I had no idea, Emma, not until Ashley walked into the lobby of my hotel."

"She still wanted you, after all these years. She was still obsessed."

"But *I* wasn't obsessed, Em. In fact, I was furious, and told her as much, in no uncertain terms."

"But you never told me."

"What was the point? She died the next night." *And this betrayal, my love, this omission, is nothing compared with what else I am hiding from you.*

"But—"

"Mummy? Daddy?"

She stood in the doorway, small and precious, the worry in her lovely young face startlingly illuminated by a sudden flash of lightning.

"Yes, darling?"

"The storm is *so loud*, so angry, and it won't stop! Mummy, I'm *afraid*."

So am I, Emma thought. I'm so afraid of what I don't know about the man I love . . . what he hasn't told me . . . the other secrets he has never shared. *Other* secrets? her heart pleaded. Just because Lucas didn't tell you that he had seen Ashley—

There are other secrets. The pronouncement came from deep within, from that package of black, tormented thoughts she had so carefully wrapped in silvery hope on Christmas Day. The wrapping was torn asunder now, ripped to shreds.

"Why don't I sleep with you tonight, Jessie?" Emma didn't look at Lucas, couldn't, no more than she could sleep with him tonight, here, in this room, this *bed*, where there had seemed to be such intimate truths. "If we can't sleep, we'll just spend the night talking. Okay?"

"Okay, Mummy. But will you be all right, Daddy? And what about *Peggy*? What if the willow falls and *crushes* her?"

Oh, my little love, Lucas thought. A shattered creature of white marble is nothing, trivial, compared to what else is shattering on this night.

He managed a smile for Jessie, and for Emma. But Emma's anguished blue eyes would not meet his, nor did she seem to hear him when he assured with a gentleness that was at once fierce and raw, "We'll all be fine."

"No, no, *please!*"

Sarah's frantic cry didn't awaken Jack. He'd been awake all

night. Because of the storm? No. That was a minor, albeit amazingly violent, distraction. It was his own turbulent worries, coupled with the all-important vigil he kept, that precluded any chance of sleep.

Jack spent the night in the living room of their two-bedroom suite. The suite's only entrance was into that central room, a heavy wooden door that was locked, and watched, by him. Not that a killer—especially a clever, artful killer—would commit murder in his own home.

Sarah was safe.

Except that now she was crying out, desperate, frightened, pleading.

But alone. Relief pulsed through him as he bolted into her bedroom. Her assailant lived only in her dreams. A ghostly memory, perhaps, of war. On this night, when the rage of nature mimicked the sounds of battle, it was likely that latent images of witnessed horrors would haunt her mind and stalk her dreams.

Sarah's lips were silent now. But trembling? And her face, ashen amid a cloud of tangled black silk, wore a frown. And as he gently touched her shoulders, Jack discovered that they were warrior-stiff, warrior-wary, on guard even in sleep. His gentle hands discovered something else as well, something far softer. The expensive weave of his own blue shirt.

"Sarah?"

Her eyelids fluttered open with the graceful perfection of two tiny coal-black fans. And the green eyes beneath those exquisite lashes? They were confused—but not frightened.

"Jack."

"Good morning." He smiled, and moved away, allowing her to sit up. "I think you were having a nightmare."

"Oh. Yes, I guess I was." It was more than a guess. Sarah remembered her dream still, knew it well, whether awake or asleep. She had been in that dank, shadowy cellar, being raped, being betrayed, praying that she would bleed until she died.

"Sarah? Are you okay?"

"*Yes.* It is morning, isn't it?"

"Just barely."

"But you're already dressed."

"I spent the night listening to the storm."

"And listening for footsteps?"

"Sure."

"You don't sound sure."

"I admit that the idea of Lucas Cain, brutal murderer, doesn't feel right to me."

"But *Cole* does?"

"No. Not really."

"No?"

"No. But, Sarah, this puzzle is about facts, not feelings."

"I know. And I also know how Jessie feels about Lucas, how much she loves him. Whatever else I want, Jack, I *don't* want my daughter to have to deal with the fact that the father she loves is a killer. But if Lucas *is* a murderer, or if Cole is, then they have to be held accountable." Sarah smiled a wobbly smile. "See how *logical* I can be?"

"I see," Jack said.

Quite suddenly Sarah realized what else Jack saw. Sarah Pembroke, her hair unbound, as it had been in Paris, and tangled with sleep, and spilling onto the pale blue of his shirt, her nightgown, and—*and I'm the girl in the cellar, Jack, that damaged, disposable, disappointing girl.* "I think I'll go for a walk."

"A walk, Sarah?"

"To clear my head, to impose pure logic."

"To search his studio for a stone carving of a heart?"

"No," she answered solemnly. "I promise I won't do that. I'll just go to the cliff, and look at the sea for a while, and then I'll come back. I'll be in plain sight the entire time."

Jessica slept, curled in Emma's arms, far away from the guest suite where Sarah and Jack were staying. She could not have heard Sarah's desperate cry. Still, it was at just that moment that she abruptly awakened.

"Jessie?"

"Mummy."

"Are you all right? You awakened with such a start. Were you having a bad dream?"

Jessica frowned. "I don't know. I don't remember." Her frown vanished as she realized that the bedroom was filled with a pearl-gray light. "Oh! It's *daylight*. And the storm is over, isn't it? I'm going to see if Daddy's all right."

With that, Jessica sprung out of bed and disappeared down the hall, leaving Emma with the echoes of scampering footsteps . . . and with her own buoyant thoughts.

Happy thoughts. Silvery ones. *Yes, my love, the storm is over.*

Emma had spent the night searching for an explanation for Luc's betrayal that could salvage her dying heart. And, at last, she had found one. He had been *furious* with Ashley. Indeed, he had admitted as much. Obviously, given what had happened to Ash, Lucas felt terribly guilty about the cruel words he had hurled at her on the eve of her death. But instead of sharing that guilt, that torment, with Emma, he kept it private; and he kept private as well the truth about what Ashley had done—essentially a betrayal of *her*, a brazen attempt to seduce her husband. By keeping silent, by sparing Emma both the truth and the torment, he had enabled her to mourn the death of the woman who had once been her friend. Her grief had been pure, untarnished and untainted.

There. Lucas had wanted to save her from unnecessary turmoil. That was hardly a betrayal. And as for the *other* secrets? They didn't exist, except in her imagination.

Jessie scampered back then, her eyes as shimmering bright as Emma's own silvery hope. "He's not in your bedroom, but the light's on in the cottage, and the willow is still standing, so Peggy's all right, too!"

"Oh, good," Emma whispered. We're all fine. Just as Luc promised. The storm is over, and we all survived.

"Mummy?"

Jessie was standing at her bedroom window now, frowning, worried. Emma moved swiftly to see what had caused such a dramatic transformation on her daughter's expressive face. "Did the storm do some damage after all, Jessie?"

"No. It's Daddy and Sarah. They seem angry, Mummy. Really *angry*."

The storm was not over. Its true fury, its greatest devastation, was yet to come. Sarah and Lucas were standing on the cliff above the sea, the place where Emma and Lucas had stood on that long-ago day when she had been so bedazzled and he had made such solemn vows. I will be faithful to you, Emma, and honest with you. Always.

Passion. The word, unbidden and laced with anguish, eloquently described the scene on the cliff. Even from this distance one could see the aura that haloed the stunning black-haired silhouettes. Their emotion fairly shimmered against the pearl-gray sky, sparking with heat, threatening to burst into an inferno of flames.

Had that fiery halo of passion ever flamed? *Of course it had.* And the fire was smoldering still, its embers refusing to die, desperately yearning to blaze brightly once more.

Yearning. Desire. Longing. Rage. Those were the emotions Emma had seen in Luc's eyes on New Year's Eve, when he stared at Sarah as she danced with Jack. And just minutes later it was Emma who experienced Lucas Cain's astonishing heat, the fiery magic that burned at the very core of the green-eyed sorcerer.

Emma had been a woman that night, *every* woman for the man she loved. Bride, courtesan, wife . . . and mistress.

Oh, Lucas. When you made love to me, when you needed me as you had never needed me before, I was really just one woman, wasn't I? *I was Sarah.*

"Mummy? Why are they so mad at each other?"

In that instant, Emma grew up. And what of the bedazzled nineteen-year-old whose heart beat within her still? That innocent country girl who had been content to breathe the air Lucas breathed, and who so blindly trusted every word he spoke? *She was gone.*

And now Emma, all grown up, smiled at her worried little girl. "They aren't really mad. They're probably just discussing politics. Come on, my love. Let's get our showers and dress. Then, my Jessie, I'll need your help to make muffins for breakfast."

She did not hear him approach. The wind blew still, the final hisses of the storm, a last chance to punish the sea, the headlands, and the creatures of flesh and blood who dared to wander the rugged cliffs.

"Hello, Sarah."

"*Lucas.*"

"Why are you here?"

"The drama of the sea—"

"You know what I mean, Sarah. You're here because of Jessie, aren't you?"

He was a murderer, and she was supposed to be so very careful with him, to hide her knowledge and her fear. But it wasn't Lucas Cain, cold-blooded killer, whom Sarah saw looming before her on the windswept cliffs. It was merely Lucas Cain, kidnapper, thief. And now Sarah Pembroke, who was an expert on such lesser criminals, lashed out in pure, fearless anger.

"*Yes.* I'm here because of my daughter, my baby."

"The baby you didn't *want*, Lady Pembroke. The baby you gave away, *threw* away. She was a disgrace, remember? The undesirable consequence of a careless—or maybe carefree—week of partying in Gstaad."

It was the same story her parents, or Simon, had told Albert Duckworth-Parker; the tale of a sex-crazed teenaged girl whose virtue had been sabotaged by the wanton mix of three blue-blooded—and hot-blooded—young men, and alcohol, and her own apparently uncontrollable passion. A false story, and yet one that Sarah did not swiftly deny. Indeed, the image of Jessica's conception in the festive, pristine setting of freshly fallen snow was far more appealing than the truth. And that Sarah herself might ever have possessed normal, albeit slightly wild, sexual desires was oddly appealing, too. Sex-crazed, but not crazy. How strange, though, that the story hastily fabricated during the short hours of her labor named alcohol as a conspirator in her fall from innocence. She had not, at that time, ever consumed so much as a drop. But somehow her parents had known just how important to her alcohol would become.

"You didn't want her."

"That's not true! I wanted her *so much*. I loved her. I was going to spend my life loving her. They told me she was *dead*, Lucas. My parents and Simon Beckwith-Jones. They told me she died just moments before she was born."

Sarah had not imagined a dialogue with the killer-thief. They were merely going to rage at one another, madwoman to madman, shouting their own passions, not hearing, not listening, not *caring* about the other's words at all.

But, as if she were a Cupid of sorts, carved from black marble and armed with special arrows that could pierce the marble flesh of the blackest of hearts, her words struck him—and found a home in a heart that was not black, not stone, after all.

Lucas Cain was human, and wounded. But raging still.

"I don't believe you, Sarah."

"It's the *truth*. And that was just the beginning of their cruel deceit, their ghoulish lies. They told me that my dead baby was a boy, a son. They even managed to find a dead little boy for me to hold."

If the sharp arrows of her previous words had proven that he was made of flesh, not of stone, then these words afforded eloquent proof that Lucas Cain could die. Sarah saw his pain— exquisite, excruciating, an anguish that was a mirror image of her own on that August night when she was told her baby had died.

"Oh," she whispered. "He was your son, wasn't he?"

"I never . . . held him." His tormented eyes were unfocused; and yet acutely focused, seeing with vivid clarity the long-ago image he would never forget. "Emma was bleeding, dying too, and after her doctors got my consent to perform an emergency hysterectomy, the only possible chance to save her life, they forced me to leave the delivery room. I didn't want to leave *her*, and I wanted to hold *him*, and I went a little crazy, I suppose. I put up quite a fight."

Crazy. There it was, the word that had haunted Sarah for

years. Was she gazing at a madman now? A compatriot in madness? No. She was gazing at a father, a husband, a man who had watched his entire world fall apart.

"But you never held him."

Lucas pulled himself from his memory of blood, of death, of loss; and such helplessness and fear. "No. They promised me that I would be able to. Later. It was the only way they could get me to leave. But," he said softly, "later was a time of miracles— the news that Em had survived the surgery and that there was a baby girl, just born, who needed a home. Her unwed teenaged mother didn't want her, I was told, by Simon Beckwith-Jones, nor did anyone else in her aristocratic family, except for her grandparents. They opposed the adoption, he said, and would undoubtedly demand proof that their grandchild had died." His jaw muscles rippled. "But there weren't any such grandparents, were there?"

"No." Both sets of grandparents had died by then. And if they had been alive? They would have made the same decision Sarah's parents had made, to dispose of Sarah's baby as they had always wanted to dispose of her. But they had known how much their daughter wanted that baby. So they found a surrogate, safely dead, and put him in her arms. "I held him for a very long time, Lucas. Held him, and kissed him, and told him of my love. He was beautiful . . . and his small face was a portrait of peace . . . and he's been at peace all this time, in a lovely churchyard in Norfolk. Flowers adorn his grave every day of the year, and I visit him still." *And once I tried to warm his cold beloved body with the hot pulses of my own blood.*

With her words Lucas envisioned a scene he had never imagined for that night of death and loss in Penzance. He had given his son to strangers, to the family of an unwed teenager who did not want her healthy baby girl. They had promised to care for his son, to lay him to rest in a peaceful place, but he had been haunted by images too disturbing to name.

But now he saw the scene quite clearly, a wondrous scene— Sarah, cradling the small lifeless body in her arms, loving him, cherishing him, and letting him know, even in death, that he was loved—always.

The scene blurred then, and when Lucas spoke his voice was hoarse.

"Thank you, Sarah," he whispered. *Thank you for loving my son.*

For many moments there was no madness in the world, no murders, no kidnappings, no brutal crimes of the heart. He was a father, and she was a mother, and there was only love for the precious little boy who died before he ever had a chance to live.

The moments could not last. Indeed, like that precious little boy, they never truly had a chance to live. Their warmth was chilled, iced, by a sudden gust of bitter cold wind. And by the truth. Lucas Cain's infant son had died . . . but Jessica was alive. *Alive.*

"She's my daughter, Lucas." Sarah's voice was quiet and strong. "You didn't steal her from me, I know that now. But she *was* stolen. There were never even any adoption papers, were there?"

"No."

Of course not, Sarah thought. *Just the simple exchange of infants—a dead little boy for the girl who had sung such a joyous hello—with falsified birth certificates to match.* Nothing to trace, no paper trail at all, thanks to that clever solicitor Simon Beckwith-Jones.

"It's still not legal."

"Meaning what, Sarah?" The punishing winter wind was balmy compared to his voice. "That you're planning to take this to court?"

"*No.* It shouldn't have to come to that, should it? I'm sure that you and Emma and I—"

"Emma doesn't know."

"I guessed as much." Sarah compelled her voice to *sound* conversational, despite her crescendoing fear. There was no longer anything human about Lucas Cain. He was stone-hard, virtually motionless yet taut with power. "And you figured out my relationship to Jessie when I became Mrs. Simon Beckwith-Jones?"

"Yes."

"Hasn't Emma ever wondered?"

"No. And she never will. *Emma doesn't know.*"

"Doesn't know what, Lucas?" Oh no. *No.* "Emma doesn't know that her baby died and that Jessie is—"

"That's right, Sarah. Emma doesn't know, and she's not going to know. Not ever."

With his warning came ancient, anguished memories of betrayal. Sarah saw the image of her father, vividly clear despite the murky shadows of the cellar where they had been held hostage. Robert Pembroke had made no move to save his daughter. But if the rapists had turned their violent lust to his wife?

Emma doesn't know, and she's not going to know. Not ever.

"All you care about is Emma, isn't it?" Sarah demanded. "You would do *anything* to protect your wife, even if it meant sacrificing Jessie."

"How *dare* you say that to me?" His expression became one Sarah knew so well from men, that special glare of pure contempt reserved just for her. "You obviously know nothing about being a parent, Lady Pembroke. Absolutely nothing. I would *never* choose my wife's happiness over my daughter's. *No father would.* Emma is a grown woman. If this truth comes out, she will survive. But will Jessie survive, Sarah? You may call yourself her mother, but—"

"I *am* her mother. You know that, and so does Jessie. She recognizes my voice. She *remembers.*"

"From before she was born?" Lucas scoffed. "That's madness, Sarah. Your voice and Emma's are virtually identical. It's Emma's voice Jessie recognizes, not yours. Emma is Jessie's mother, and I'm her father. And as her father, I *will not* permit you to hurt her."

"I would never hurt her!"

"That's right, Lucas." The new voice came from a third silhouette in the winter dawn, the tall and powerful shepherd who watched over Sarah, protected Sarah, loved Sarah. "Sarah would never hurt Jessie."

"I take it this means you know everything, Jack?"

"Yes."

"And you're not planning to *write* about it? A poignant little sidebar in your chapter about Sarah?"

"No," Jack and Sarah answered in unison, after which Jack reiterated, "No one wants to hurt Jessica."

"Then leave—and never come back."

"I can't do that!" Sarah cried. "*I love her.* Don't you *understand?*"

"Here's what I understand, Sarah. What you want is for *you*, not for Jessie. And this has to be about her, what's best for her. *Only* her. Not you. Not me. Not Emma. Just Jessie."

Now Lucas Cain was accusing Sarah Pembroke of a significant inheritance from her parents after all. She might not have been the horsewoman that Robert and Geneva wanted her to be, or the skater, or a gourmet when it came to the sensual delights of the flesh. But now Lucas was saying that she was truly theirs, in a most essential and despicable way, quite capable of repeating their selfish crimes, of putting *her* wishes above the best interest of her child.

I am not like them. I can't be. "I can't tell you now, Lucas, not at this moment, that I'll leave and never come back. I *can't*. I need time. I'll give you my private numbers in London, and we can talk again—we need to talk again—and in the meantime I won't do anything rash. I promise. I care about her, too. *I love her too.*"

The conversation that accompanied Emma's freshly baked blueberry muffins was excessively cheerful. As if, Sarah thought, everyone senses that something is terribly amiss, and is trying to compensate. Even lovely Jessie.

Sarah and Jack left before noon, citing the long drive to London and Sarah's need to catch up on the weekend's news. Jack wondered if their journey would be a silent one. But before they even reached St. Ives, Sarah spoke.

"I was wrong about Lucas, Jack. And you were right. He couldn't *possibly* be the killer."

"I didn't say he couldn't possibly be."

"I know. Only that it didn't feel right. And I agree with you.

Lucas Cain would die before letting anyone hurt Jessie. He would lay down his own life to save hers. Don't you think?"

"Yes. And so would Emma." *And so, my lovely Sarah, would you.*

"That's what parents *should* do for their children."

"Yes it is. But the same parent who would die for his child might also kill to protect her. As far as Lucas is concerned, you pose a major threat to Jessie. And maybe Ashley Alexander did, too. Maybe somehow she, too, had discovered the truth."

"But what about his *hand*, Jack? Lucas is right-handed. I'm sure that fact didn't escape you. And there's something *odd* about his left. It's strong, and obviously quite functional, but it's almost as if he has to remind himself to use it. You noticed that, too, didn't you?"

Of course he had noticed. It was subtle, an observation one made only if he were searching for a left-handed murderer. "I noticed."

"And when we were arguing on the cliff, and Lucas was angry—in fact, *enraged*—he gestured a little with his right hand, but not at all with his left. Mostly, as furious as he was, he kept his hands at his sides. Admittedly, in tightly clenched fists. But at his sides. That says something, doesn't it? That even in the heat of anger, his impulse isn't to strike? Lucas is *not* the killer, Jack. I'm sure of it."

"And neither is Cole?"

"That's right," Sarah replied solemnly. "It's someone else." *It has to be.*

Jack thought about the file folders in his office at Scotland Yard—especially the one, in addition to the one on *her*, about which Sarah might be quite displeased. In some ways the revelations of this weekend made the name on that folder even more intriguing.

I'm trying, Sarah. I'm trying to find a murderer whose identity doesn't destroy Claire or Jessie . . . or you.

*C*hapter Thirty

Grosvenor Square
Mayfair
Tuesday, January Tenth

"I T'S LUCAS, SARAH."
"Lucas."

She had known he would call. But not so *soon*, only forty-eight hours since they had stood on the wind-battered cliffs of Cornwall. Sarah had thought of nothing else, of course. And the answer she kept finding terrified her.

Was she truly strong enough, sane enough, to say good-bye forever to her daughter? Yes. Maybe. *Yes*. But not this *soon*.

"I'm coming to London tomorrow. I'd like to see you then, Sarah. Alone. In private. No attorneys. No Jack. Just you and me. Okay?"

"Yes. Okay."

"When and where?"

"My newscast ends at eight, so nine? Here, in my home?"

"I'll be there."

At home, in Harlanville, her memories of love were preserved in tiny snowflakes inside a crystal globe. Now there were new memories of love, and for a while, as those enchanted memories were being made, it seemed as if they would be far too grand, too wondrous, to ever be contained.

But Claire's memories of love had borders now, the white picket fence around the dream, the night-black crepe at the edges of joy. Their love had begun, and flourished, and died in Monte Carlo.

It had to die. Claire had known that even before it began, and Cole had known it, too. But they hadn't spoken that truth. They had merely lived their love.

Yesterday they had bid adieu to Monte Carlo, and to the dream. And as they flew from Nice to London, Cole had withdrawn into brooding silence, and her hummingbird heart, fluttering without respite for their three days of pure joy, rebelled at last, drugging her with such exhaustion that she, too, did not speak.

For those days and nights of splendor, when it seemed impossible that the brilliance of their love could ever fade, the bayou girl had imagined singing again with her panther. But on their return to London, Claire had forsaken even the *charade* of such courage. She missed Monday night's rehearsal, pleading fatigue, and in so doing avoided the issue of singing—her inability to sing—for the rest of the week.

One of Gemstone Pictures' top directors was in town, to plan the new Cole Taylor music videos, a project that would monopolize the daylight hours of the entire week. Indeed, on this Tuesday morning, Cole, Sydney, David, and Mick were at Asquith Towers, attending a "creative" meeting that included Timothy Asquith himself.

Claire had declined Cole's invitation to participate in the planning sessions for the videos. A slight cold, she had murmured, perhaps even the beginnings of the flu. Was Cole disappointed? She didn't know. But in his quiet voice Claire wondered if she heard the truth—that the focus of this week would be *visual* . . . and therefore no more a place for a blind woman than a recording studio was for the bayou girl who could no longer sing.

Claire was in her bedroom in her happy pink suite at the Drake, not in the executive conference room at Asquith Towers, and she was remembering their weekend of love, containing the memories, preserving them, and shrinking them until they were the size of miniature snowflakes, those small perfect crystals that danced within the smooth confines of her glassy globe.

I had my time with him, Aunt Augusta. My days of love. And do I regret it? Never. But my period began today—which means, like you, I will always regret that our loving did not leave me with his child.

The phone trilled then, for the second time already this morning.

"Hi, Claire. It's Sydney. How are you feeling?"

"Fine, thank you, Syd. Much better."

"Good. Well, rest assured that you're not missing a *thing* over here. Artistic differences would be putting it mildly. Not to mention the fact that Timothy is so preoccupied that he might as well not even be present, and Mick is his usual charming morning self, and David is mute as always. We're taking a necessary break, a few minutes between rounds. However, the guys don't seem to understand that *I* need a break from *them*, too. Mick? David? A little privacy, *por favor*? Thank you. Cole wants to talk to you when I'm through. But at least *he* has the grace to wait outside." When Sydney spoke again, the gaiety in her voice, her despairing but cheery recounting of the day's events, had vanished—along with her audience of David and Mick. "What's wrong with Cole, Claire? Do you know?"

"Wrong?" *Nothing. He's wonderful.* "Nothing. Why?"

"He's not ill? He doesn't have some fatal illness?"

"Sydney! You're scaring me."

"Well, I'm scared, too. About an hour ago, Cole got a call from a doctor in New Orleans. He insisted on taking it, which annoyed everyone but the already distracted Timothy, and when Cole returned to the conference room he looked *awful*, like death itself. Like he had just been told he was going to die. I thought maybe when he was in Louisiana last month, visiting you, he'd seen a doctor in New Orleans, and that the results just came back. Did he see a doctor, Claire? Do you know?"

"No. I don't know. But Cole seems so healthy." *We made love, an infinity of times, just as he promised in the moonlit gazebo at Belle Rêve. An infinity of times, each one perfect, and his passion was strong, yet gentle, and so powerful.* "He *is* healthy, Syd."

"And what about you, Claire? *You're* not ill, are you? I know how fatigued you sometimes get."

"No. I'm not ill, Sydney." *I'm only blind. And my fatigue? That was love. But that's better now. All cured. My heart isn't even fluttering anymore.*

Claire was fine—except that now, in the exhausted body where the hummingbird heart fluttered no more, she felt a frisson of pure fear. The dream was over. The memories of love had been crystallized into tiny perfect flakes of snow. But were even those glass-encased memories now in great peril? Was she on the verge of learning something that would actually shatter the glass itself, spilling its precious contents, destroying even the small lovely memories that had always seemed so safe?

"Did you happen to hear the name of the doctor Cole spoke to? If he's a prominent New Orleans specialist, perhaps I'd recognize it. Or I could call my friend Millicent and have her check."

"I heard it, and it's pretty memorable. First of all, he's a *she.* Dr. Angelica Gabriel, to be precise. The Angel Gabriel. Have you heard of her, Claire?"

Oh, yes. She was my doctor, the neuro-ophthalmologist who would have been willing to operate, to try to save my vision, but perhaps not my life.

Claire felt the glass begin to shatter, its lovely memories lost, only to be instantly replaced by ones so mammoth, so monstrous, that they could never be contained. She imagined Cole's telephone call to Andrew at Belle Rêve. *I know you were probably driving the car on your wedding night, Andrew, and that you, not Claire, are to blame for the accident. But don't worry, that's not why I'm calling. You had your political career to think of, after all, and if Claire forgives you, then so do I. I can also forgive your demand that Claire have the surgery. I understand, all too well, your preference of a dead wife to a blind one. I feel that way now, too. Maybe you're my long-lost* brother, Andrew. I wonder. Anyway, I need the name of Claire's doctor. I want to find out just how dangerous the surgery would be if done today. I like Claire, I really do. But she's just a little too blind for my taste.

"Claire?"

"Yes. I've heard of her. And you don't need to worry about Cole, Sydney. He's fine."

"You're sure?"

"I'm positive. Dr. Gabriel's specialty has nothing to do with him." *And Dr. Gabriel has nothing to offer him, either.* The chance of reversing my blindness is long gone.

"But—oh, Timothy, hello. I'll be right there."

"It sounds as if you're about to reconvene."

"We are, and from the looks of it we may actually have the attention of a rather happy Timothy Asquith. He, too, must have just gotten some very good news. I wonder what it was. Oh, well. We're still on for dinner tomorrow night, aren't we? The director, who is as pompous as they come, is taking us on a field trip tonight, to check out castles. But we should be back, hopefully without having killed one another, by early tomorrow evening. Okay?"

"Yes. Although it will only be the two of us, Syd. Sarah called just before you did, to cancel again. I'd still like to go, though, if you would. In fact, there are some things I'd like to discuss with you."

"Then it's a date. You're *sure* you're all right?"

"Absolutely." Never better. The dream is over. My course is clear. And, with your help, Sydney, my mission will be accomplished.

"Terrific. Oh, here's Cole, reaching for the phone. I'll see you tomorrow, Claire."

Wait, Sydney! I don't want to talk to Cole, not ever! I don't want to hear the pity in his voice!

But there was no pity, only tenderness.

"You're feeling all right?"

"Yes."

"Well enough to come with us tonight? We'll be going to

Cadbury Castle in Somerset. It's considered by many to be Camelot, so I thought, given how much you always loved that musical, that you'd enjoy visiting."

The precious memories, the tiny perfect snowflakes, had not spilled and died after all. They were still there, small and brave, and determined to dance still in their miniature world of joy. And now Claire saw one of those twirling memories: a boy and girl, so innocent and pure, singing the love song from *Camelot*. How to handle a woman? Just love her, love her, *love*—

"Thank you, Cole. But no, I think I'll stay here." I have some things to do, you see. I need to pack my bags, and to plan very carefully what I'm going to say to Sydney. And I also have to make reservations for a flight tomorrow night. A red-eye, I think such flights are called. Red, like the blood clot I chose not to have removed, because I wanted to live—for Aunt Augusta *and for myself*—despite this great flaw. I need to take that red-eye, to get to Harlanville as soon as I can, to hold the glass globe in my hands and cherish the small lovely memories that are mine.

"Thank you for coming, Jack," Sarah greeted when he arrived at her penthouse at nine-thirty Tuesday night.

"My pleasure. Have you heard from Lucas, Sarah? Is this a dress rehearsal?"

Alone. In private. No Jack. As Sarah led the way to the starkness of her black and bone living room, she answered vaguely, "I just need to talk, Jack. Or maybe I need to listen. I'm trying to be *logical*, to find the right answer."

"There may not be a right answer. Not with something as emotional as this."

Sarah looked up at him. "But if I keep Jessie in mind, *only* Jessie and what's best for her . . ."

"That's what you've been doing, though, isn't it, Sarah? And the answer still isn't clear."

"Well, *mostly* it is clear. *Mostly* I agree with Lucas. She's happy. Safe, loved, secure. What more could a mother wish for her child? And as far as blood being thicker than water, I imagine you've deduced that my own parents didn't always have my best interests at heart. In fact, I spent much of my childhood fantasizing about escaping from them. If I could just get to Harlanville, I decided, then Claire would become my sister and Aunt Augusta my mother and it's *clear*, isn't it, Jack? I have to let her go, to vanish from her life. Forever."

She was a portrait of courage, and love, and hope, a mother aching inside and yet aglow—because she *was* a mother, willing to give her own heart for the happiness of her child.

Jack should have smiled at her, so very proud of her courage, her generosity, *her*.

But Jack could not smile, could not agree that Sarah's decision was right or best. *Could not lie.* Yes, there had been lies, and yes, betrayals. But those had been necessary, and hopefully forgivable, in the name of keeping her safe until the puzzle of death had been solved.

And after that there would be no more lies. After that . . . when he and Sarah spent the rest of their lives loving each other? Jack hoped so, prayed so. But whether or not he and Sarah were destined to dance forever, Jack could not lie to her now. Not about this. Such a monumental betrayal could truly not be forgiven.

"What happens, Sarah, when Jessie discovers the truth?"

"But she'll never discover the truth, Jack," Sarah countered, her hopefulness clouding with surprise, and worry. "Lucas won't tell her, nor will you or I, and I can't imagine Mrs. Duckworth-Parker approaching her—but I could forestall that by speaking with her myself—and virtually everyone else who knows what happened in that hospital in Penzance . . ." *is dead.* "No one's going to tell her, Jack, and there are no legal documents that she might accidentally find."

"But she could still find out." *I'm sorry, Sarah.* I must tell you this truth. Even though it feels like a betrayal, *you need to know.* "What if, for her science project in school, she's required to sketch her family pedigree? Hair or eye color would pose no problem, and maybe blood type wouldn't either. But maybe it would."

"Why are you doing this, Jack? Why are you making me doubt my decision?"

"Because, Sarah, I *know* how it feels to discover that the parents—and sisters—you believed to be your flesh and blood aren't related to you after all."

"You're adopted?"

"*Given.* It *was* a gift. Especially for me. I could not have been raised with more love. But still, as much as I loved them, learning the truth was quite difficult for me. I felt disconnected, displaced. For a while I even withdrew from them, not in anger, just confusion. Eventually, in desperation I suppose, my father made the Pegasus for me, to remind me of our history together, all the years of caring and of love."

"And in return you gave them the company."

Jack followed her gaze to the mantelpiece, to the small, glittering community of shapes. "It wasn't a conscious decision. But in retrospect, I guess that's true. I wanted to bind us together, as a family, always. It was also my way of thanking them for saving me."

"Saving you?"

"I came from an abusive home. At least my father was abusive. I know nothing about my mother, except that it wasn't she who rescued me from his abuse."

"Who did?"

"A neighbor boy."

A neighbor boy. In Texas, at a truck stop, on a moonlit December night. Sam had been doing carpentry work in Corpus Christi, and was driving home, straight through, to be with his wife and twin daughters for Christmas, and . . .

. . . and it was only when Jack finished his brief recounting of what he had been told about that night that he looked from the statues to her—and saw her ashen skin and bewildered yet oddly brilliant green eyes.

"Sarah?"

"There's something I need to tell you."

"Okay." *Good,* he amended silently as he looked from her ashen face to her pale, delicate hands. They were clasped together, in a way that enabled her slender fingers to encircle her wrists, the places of flesh that bore the thick scars of her secret anguish. *Tell me about your scars, my love. Trust me with that pain.* "You can tell me anything, Sarah. Anything."

"I hope so, Jack."

"I know so."

"I have to get something, from the dresser in my bedroom. I'll be right back."

She insisted that he sit on the couch, while she remained standing before him. She was an actress onstage, a one-woman show, and he was her audience.

Sarah clutched her script, the thick, ancient envelope; but she didn't refer to it, didn't open it, didn't need to.

Her first question caught him completely by surprise.

"Did you ever try to find your biological family?"

"Yes." When it seemed that she was waiting, wanting to hear more, he elaborated, "Although my parents forewarned me that it would be futile. They'd already conducted their own search, when my father first brought me home. They'd gotten copies of local newspapers, to make certain that what the neighbor boy had said was true—or at least that there was no evidence that I'd been stolen from a loving family. They'd expected *something*, even a one-sentence notice of the accidental drowning death of a two-year-old. But there was nothing at all, as if my biological father either couldn't be bothered, or had been reluctant, to report my death. Either way, it confirmed the essential truth of what the boy had said. Still, fourteen years later, when I learned about that December night, we all drove to Texas, even Marcy and Krys. The truck stop was still there, and this time we checked with funeral parlors and the bureau of vital statistics. But again, nothing. And there was nothing, either, about my older brother."

"Your older brother?"

"He died, was killed, by my father—although he apparently managed to convince the police that it was accidental. Which may explain why he was reluctant to report yet another accidental death of a son. Years later, when I became a consultant to the FBI, I returned to Texas to talk to the police. They opened their files for me. But still nothing. Some puzzles, it seems, aren't destined to be solved."

"But you obviously tried very hard to solve this one. Despite what you knew about your father, you wanted to find him, to meet him."

"I didn't give a damn about my father. Who I wanted to meet was the neighbor boy, to thank him for what he had done."

Oh, Jack. You will have your chance. I only pray that you still want it when you know.

"Sarah? You look so upset. Let's stop talking about me and start talking about you."

"But this *is* about you, Jack." She could have handed him the letter, to read for himself the astonishing—and devastating?—truth. But instead she clutched it even tighter. "This letter is from Claire, written twelve years ago, on the night Cole's father died. Jed Taylor's death, and its impact on Cole, are extensively described, and it's important that you read them. But first I have to tell you what Cole told Claire the night before Jed died. Oh, Jack, it's Cole. *He's* the boy."

"What boy?"

"The one who gave you away. There was a rusty wagon. He pulled you in that. And he covered you with a tattered patchwork quilt. Cole told Claire about the images sewn onto that quilt. He *remembered* them, even after all those years. And I remember them, too, because I re-read this letter just ten days ago. There was a calico kitten, and a bouquet of tulips . . ."

And a gingham train, and a smiling sun, and a tiny sailboat gliding across a rippling blue sea. How well Jack knew that quilt, its faded—yet brilliant—images of joy.

For almost two years the bright but silent boy who had been rescued by the Daltons kept his beloved quilt nearby, held protectively, and sometimes desperately, in his young embrace. It was only when he broke his silence that Jack truly relinquished the quilt. It was stored in a cedar chest after that, and it was there still, in his parents' bedroom in Denver, the solitary clue to the one puzzle in Jack's life that he had tried—and failed—to solve.

"He sang to you that night, a favorite lullaby. I don't know what song it was. He didn't tell Claire. Jack?"

"It was Cole? He was my neighbor?" The boy who protected me, and sang to me, and loved me, and saved me?

"No," Sarah answered softly. "Cole wasn't your neighbor, Jack. He was your brother. He *is* your brother."

He roamed the night-black streets of London as he searched the night-black shadows of his mind. Somewhere, in that dense and foggy darkness, were memories . . . and light. No moon shined down on this English winter night. No moonbeams guided Jack on his journey to the past. But there had been moonbeams once, on that night, golden shafts of light that beckoned to his brother as he trudged across the West Texas fields.

His *brother*. And a killer?

No. *No.* Just a brother. *His* brother.

His *frère*.

Frère. Frère. Frère Jacques.

There was no moon, but suddenly there was the most brilliant light, and the cold night air was warmed by the remembered strains of that beloved lullaby, and by the truth.

We spoke French. That was our secret language. And in Denver, for those first two years when I spoke just one word, which they all heard as *Jack*, I was really saying *Jacques, Jacques, Jacques*.

The memories flooded then, a kaleidoscope of images, like glimpses of dreams; and they were draped in emotions as delicate, as lacy, as garlands of Spanish moss. Jack saw the bayou, and the lush foliage along its banks, and two boys, walking hand in hand, and speaking French, and laughing with joy. And he felt? Safe. And happy. And loved.

Jack needed no moon to guide him to the shadowy memories

of his past—because the memories themselves were pure gold, a brilliant beacon of light shimmering in the darkness.

No moon tonight. We'll just have to *imagine moonlight*, won't we, bitch? What a *prescient* title that turned out to be, wouldn't you say? I would definitely recommend that you imagine moonlight tonight, on this, the final night before your death.

Yes, yes, *yes*. I am quite aware that February fourteenth is still weeks away. But one has to be flexible in matters of murder. I miscalculated last time, too. But I adjusted beautifully, as I am doing now. You'll see, bitch.

Well, you'll *know*.

Chapter Thirty-One

Hyacinth House
Wednesday, January Eleventh

"I'M GOING TO LONDON TODAY, EMMA. I'LL be there overnight."

She didn't turn to him. She simply nodded in reply, a resigned bob that nonetheless caused a dance of curls, an unwitting burst of joy from the tangle of gold that was so blissfully unaware of the pall that had shrouded Hyacinth House since Sunday.

"Are we ever going to talk, Em? I'll tell you every word Ashley and I said to each other, if that's what you want, if that will help. They were very angry words. I was furious that she'd tricked me—tricked *us*—and she was furious that I wasn't thrilled with her little surprise. But that's *all* that happened, Emma. That's it."

Emma turned to him then, straightening as she did, lifting her shoulders against the invisible weight of her sadness and lifting her chin as she met his dark green eyes.

"But that's *not* all, Luc. And yes, we are going to talk. We have to, because this is killing me, and I think Jessie's beginning to worry, too. I *know* why you're going to London. It's to see Sarah, isn't it?"

Please say no! Even if it's a lie. And then somehow, please, convince me that it's the truth. It won't be hard. I want to believe in you again, to be deceived . . . and bedazzled.

356

But Lucas Cain did not lie to his wife.

"Yes. I'm going to see Sarah. How did you know?"

"I saw the two of you on the cliff Sunday morning. I saw the emotion, Lucas, the *passion*." A soft shake of her head caused another unwitting dance of joy from the oblivious curls. "I'm such an *idiot*, aren't I? Naive little Emma. You were staring at Sarah on New Year's Eve with such fierceness, such longing, and right after that we made love as we'd never made love before, and yet I didn't put it together. And would you care to hear my foolish interpretation of the dark circles I saw whenever you returned from a trip to London? I imagined that you had difficulty sleeping in a strange bed. It never occurred to me that you weren't *trying* to sleep, and that the bed where you spent your nights in London wasn't strange to you at all."

"You think that Sarah and I are *lovers*?"

"I *know* you are."

"Oh, Em, you couldn't be more wrong. I've been faithful to you, as I promised I would be, *as I've wanted to be*. The beds in London are strange to me, and far too empty without you."

This was what she wanted, wasn't it? The lie told with such conviction that she could believe it was the truth and could yield yet again to the sorcerer's magic spell? Yes, and no. Because even then, even at nineteen, that innocent country girl had wanted more than sex, had wanted *love*. "You're *lying* to me, Lucas."

"I wish I were lying, Em. I wish the passion you'd witnessed between Sarah and me *was* simply a lovers' quarrel."

"*Simply?* Meaning you don't consider infidelity a monumental betrayal?"

"Not compared to the secret I've kept from you all these years."

"The secret? Oh, was there really a Daphne, after all? A fiancée you loved with all—"

"I've never loved anyone but you."

His words, and the intensity with which he spoke them, stole her breath. *He was not lying*. And now that glorious silvery truth illuminated the world.

Lucas *loved* her, loved *her*. And yet there was some secret, some long-ago betrayal that he believed to be far greater than a betrayal of the flesh. A betrayal of the heart, then? But how could that be, when he had just told her of his love?

"What secret, Luc? Please tell me." *Before this shimmering silver fades to gray.*

"It's about Jessie, Em."

"*Jessie?* Oh, Luc, is she ill?"

"No, she's fine. But our son . . ."

"Our son, Luc?" *No, please. I don't want to know this.* "Our *son?*"

"From the beginning you knew our baby was a boy. And he was, Emma. He was a precious little boy who died before he was even born."

She felt it then, the same terrifying feeling she had experienced on that August night when she awakened in a pool of blood, the grim certainty that all was lost. Her baby was dying, and she was dying. Her baby, her son, had died. And now it was Emma's turn.

But now as then, as she swirled into darkness, a swift descent to death, she heard a voice, his voice. So strong, so tender, as he fought to hide his own heart-stopping fear.

"As our son was dying, Em, a little girl was being born. Her mother was only sixteen and didn't want her. At least that's what I was told. But it wasn't true. Sarah Pembroke wanted her daughter." *And wants her still.*

His voice was tender. But his words, the truth at last, were so harsh.

Emma's head dropped, weighted by despair, and even the dancing curls were still. And those curls remained motionless, frozen with shock and grief, when she looked up at him anew.

"Why didn't you tell me, Luc?"

"I couldn't tell you then, not that night. I just . . . couldn't."

Why? On a storm-ravaged night Emma had found an answer to another *why,* an answer that enabled her to survive the revelation that Lucas had seen Ashley on the eve of her death. And now?

Now Emma Cain found a way to survive yet again.

"Because I was so weak from the surgery, and then so very

happy when I held Jessie in my arms. You wanted to spare me the sadness, didn't you? You wanted to protect me."

His lovely Emma was letting him off the hook. But his secret, unshadowed now, must be fully revealed.

"That was part of it, Em, especially that night. But there was more, something far less noble."

"What more could there be, Luc?" *I don't want there to be more*. I can live with this secret. I *am* living with it. But please, no *more*. "You truly believed that Jessie wasn't wanted, that she *needed* us." *You didn't steal her. I know you didn't.*

"Yes." His voice was very soft. "Jessie needed us, and *I* needed Jessie. I didn't think about the selfishness of my decision that night. I wasn't thinking *at all* that night. I was just feeling." *Such loss, such fear . . . such fear of losing everything.*

"I don't understand. What could possibly have been selfish about your decision?"

"The decision itself was selfish. I had no right to make it for both of us. For you. We married because of your pregnancy, because of our baby, our son. And when he died, you could have resumed the life you always planned, graduating from Cambridge, meeting someone else—"

"You could have, too, Luc."

"Yes. But, Emma, I already knew where I wanted to spend my life, and with whom. With you."

"Oh, *Luc*," she whispered, and then frowned. Because, perhaps, the silvery brightness was now nearly blinding? Or because of something else?

"What, Em?" Was my betrayal too great? Am I going to lose you after all?

"You *couldn't* have told me then, Luc. Not then, and not in so many of the years that followed. I never would have believed you. In my heart I would have believed that it had been a decision of guilt, not of love—that you were staying with me, and creating a family, because when I lost your baby I lost my chance to have more children." *And you knew that*, she thought. You knew how much I loved you, how infatuated I was . . . and yet how uncertain, how young. Your secret, the truth, would have tainted all my happiness with doubt. You knew that, and you chose to protect me, and whether you believe it or not, you *are* noble. "I would never have believed that you wanted *me*, loved *me*."

"But I do love you, Emma. Then. Now. Always. Do you believe that now?"

In the shimmering silver mist Emma saw what she had never been able to see before. *He* was bedazzled, too. He was her sorcerer, and she was his fairy enchantress, and . . .

"Yes," she whispered as the golden curls that framed her face danced anew, with untarnished—and triumphant—joy. "I believe you. And I love you, too. Then. Now. Always."

For a very long time, they simply held each other. It was the embrace he had wanted for so long, an embrace so close that there could be no room for secrets. And when at last Lucas spoke, he made a promise of love.

"I'm going to make this right, Em. I'm going to convince Sarah to leave our daughter alone."

Emma drew away from him then, not out of his arms completely, just enough to see clearly the fierce solemnity of his handsome face. She touched that beloved face, gently tracing the lines that had been etched over the years, lines of love, and of worry. Then she wove her slender fingers into his night-black hair. One day that hair would glitter with threads of silver, as shimmering bright as her hope; and she would be with him on that day, touching him, loving him—and trusting him, always.

"Before you go, Luc, there's something I need to say."

No attorneys. No Jack. Just the two of us. Alone. In private.

Sarah had not told Jack about her impending rendezvous with Lucas. Not last night, of course, and not today, when she had called to see how he was, and he had shared with her his memories of two small boys speaking French as they wandered hand in hand beside the bayou.

Jack had shared as well his plan to talk to Cole, perhaps this evening. It was a disclosure that afforded Sarah an ideal opportunity to reveal her own plans for this Wednesday night. Indeed, in the silence that followed his words, Sarah sensed a tension, a tautness, as if, somehow, Jack already knew that she would be seeing Lucas.

And was waiting for her to tell him, to keep her promise to notify Scotland Yard, or him, or both, whenever *anyone* came to visit.

Lucas Cain posed absolutely no threat to her. He was a father, not a killer. Sarah was sure of it. But . . . *I wonder if we're ever going to trust each other?* Jack had demanded of a glowering gray sky. *Yes!* the shadow woman had bravely proclaimed. *Mais oui*, Jacques.

It was that bold phantom who now dialed the phone number, reserved just for her, to Jack's room at the Drake.

Midway through the fourth ring an electronic voice offered her the chance to leave a message on the hotel's voice-mail system. Which she did.

"Hello, Jack. It's Sarah. I have a confession to make. It's nothing to worry about, just a promise to keep. I'm going to see Lucas tonight. He's coming here—I'm at home—in about fifteen minutes. Anyway, I wanted to let you know, even at this late date. Maybe you're meeting with Cole. I hope so. I hope it goes well."

He was so much taller than Sarah remembered. Taller, more powerful, more menacing, without Jack nearby.

But Lucas Cain is a father, not a killer, Sarah reminded herself. There is *not* a bottle of Cristale in that small, dark bag he's carrying, and not, either, a jagged-edged hunting knife or an elegant heart carved in stone. And even though there would be room, there are no crystal champagne flutes, and absolutely no wilting blood-red roses.

There aren't. There *can't* be.

He can't be.

And if he is? I'm *strong*, Jack! she had announced with such daring, and foolish, defiance. Her strength could not begin to rival that of Lucas Cain. *Fine*. But I will be armed, with knowledge, and wariness, and, of course, my can of pepper spray.

That weapon was nearby, in her purse in her bedroom. But Sarah didn't need the pepper spray now—*I won't need it ever!*—because Lucas had already put a safe distance between them, having crossed her spacious living room to examine at close range the Pegasus statues.

He was gazing at them, apparently quite absorbed. Or perhaps it was a sightless gaze, a chance merely to collect his emotions and his thoughts.

It was Sarah who broke the silence.

"I've made a decision, Lucas."

He turned from the statues to her. "Have you?"

"Yes. I've decided that you're right, that it would be best—for Jessie—to never know anything about me. And she *won't*. I promise. I'll leave her, and you and Emma, alone."

That was her speech, the almost impossible words she had prepared for a father, not to placate a killer. Sarah expected relief from that father, perhaps even gratitude. But his already grave expression only became more solemn.

"No."

"No?" *That's not enough? You want to insure my silence?*

"Emma thinks we should tell Jessie everything."

"Emma?"

"She saw us arguing on the cliff and decided that we were lovers. I told her the truth, including my plan to stay right here until I convinced you to make the decision that you've already made. A few hours ago I would have given anything to hear you say those words, and even now I think it would be for the best."

"But Emma doesn't agree."

"She knows—as I do, Sarah—that Jessie's always been fascinated by you. As impossible as it seems, maybe she really does recognize your voice. It's not mysticism that makes Em feel so strongly about this, though. It's her sense of fairness, of honesty; and she also worries about the betrayal Jessie might feel if, at some later date, she discovers the truth. If she hadn't already met you, and if you hadn't wanted to keep her from the start, Emma's decision might be quite different. But Jessie *has* met you, and we all know that, in essence, she was stolen from you, and even though I'm not as certain about this as Emma is—in fact, not certain at all—I promised to convey her feelings to you. They aren't whimsical feelings, Sarah. Emma believes with all her heart that Jessie should be told. Soon."

"And you're willing to defer to Emma's judgment?"

"Yes," he said quietly, not saying the rest, not even beginning to.

But Sarah knew the unspoken words. The relationship between Lucas and Jessie was wonderful, a tender, loving, extraordinary bond. But Emma *was Jessie's mother*. That most intimate of bonds.

Now, to Jessica Cain's *other* mother, the one who had already concluded that it would be best if her daughter never learned the truth, Lucas said, "It's up to you, Sarah. You cast the deciding vote."

For the past three and a half days Sarah had said good-bye to Jessie. *For* Jessie, she had believed. Now she was being given a reprieve, not a stay of execution but a full pardon, a chance for her heart to truly be free.

Emma—Jessie's mother—believed that Jessie should be told. *As did Jack.*

Sarah gazed at the statues on the mantelpiece beside Lucas, the glittering symbols of Jack's struggle with, and triumph over, the revelation of his own parentage. Although it had been difficult for him at first, disruptive and disorienting, his deep love for the Daltons had ultimately been affirmed; and had Jack never known the truth, he would not, perhaps at this very moment, have been reunited with his brother.

For Jack, the revelation had been for the best, far more triumphant than disturbing—

Sarah's train of thought was abruptly, and quite harshly, severed. Lucas was holding one of the statues now, the white marble Pegasus itself. And what was so troubling about that? Once correctly assembled, the puzzles would not shatter.

But . . . *but* Lucas Cain was holding the Pegasus with grace, with strength, and *with his left hand*.

"I thought you were right-handed."

Lucas looked from the winged marble statue to her. "Did you say something, Sarah?"

She had whispered, she realized. A whisper of fear? Of horror? When she spoke again, she was Sarah Pembroke, the woman-warrior who projected pure calm even in the madness of war. "This past weekend, at Hyacinth House, I noticed that you used your right hand almost exclusively. I don't know why I noticed, my journalist's eye for detail, I suppose."

"You're very observant. I don't use my left hand much. Except when I carve. . . ."

"Come in, Jack."

"Thank you."

Cole waited to speak again until they both were seated in the living room of his hotel suite. "You said it was important that we talk."

"Yes. I want to tell you who I am. I'm not a writer, Cole." *I'm your brother, the one you loved enough to give away, the one who—because of you—was spared the kind of brutal childhood that transforms young human hearts into the stone-hard ones of monsters.* "I'm a consultant to the FBI. I help solve cases involving murder."

Cole Taylor's stone-gray gaze did not waver. "And you're here because of Ashley and Paulina."

"And Sarah."

Cole's gaze was unwavering still, but definitely worried. "Sarah?"

He's worried *about* Sarah, Jack decided. About *her* welfare. Not his. "She's the killer's next victim."

"How do you know?"

"I'll get to that. If you don't mind, though, I'd like to ask you some questions first."

"I didn't kill them."

Stone eyes. Stone voice. And a stone heart? No. *No.* "Then you won't mind my questions."

"Not at all."

"Good. I'd like to start at the beginning. You were born in Breaux Bridge, Louisiana—"

"On February fourteenth. I didn't kill them, Jack. Not even as a birthday present to myself."

"You must be fluent in French."

Something sparked deep in the granite eyes, a tiny flame from a smoldering ember. Of love? Perhaps. Although it was definitely not love that Jack heard when Cole spoke again.

"No. I'm not."

The denial was harsh, punishing. *And a lie. It had to be. The two boys, the two brothers, had spoken French beside the bayou.* "Isn't Breaux Bridge in the heart of French Louisiana?"

"Yes. But that geography didn't matter to my father. He believed rather strongly that Americans should speak English. Only. So, Jack, if you're looking for a murderer who seduces his victims in French . . ." Cole's shrug, although slight, was eloquently dismissive. "But I've already told you I'm not the killer."

"Yes you have. Now please tell me about your family."

"*What?*"

"According to the Bureau of Vital Statistics in Breaux Bridge, it was a family of four. Two parents, two sons."

Jack Dalton's queries were intrusive, painful, and irrelevant. So why, Cole wondered, was he permitting such an invasion? And why, now, was he actually going to *answer?*

Was it because he felt respect for Jack, admiration for the man who was so centered, so whole, that under no circumstances would he have permitted a death—even the accidental death of a monster—when such a death was destined to destroy his dreams? Or was it something else entirely? Was it because, astonishingly, Jack seemed a little uncertain now, not so centered after all, and searching—as if there were actually dreams that had eluded him as well?

Don't look to me for answers about lost dreams, Jack.

Yet that was precisely where Jack was looking. And Cole

Taylor, expert on lost dreams—on losing them, not saving them—offered a quiet reply.

"I had a younger brother. He drowned when he was two."

With the confession, the fingers of Cole's right hand moved slightly, as if the memory of that long-ago Texas night lived within the crippled flesh. His hand had been whole then, on the night he bid farewell to his brother. But when he had reached to touch that beloved brother's cheek, his fingers had felt numb, and then on fire. They had recoiled then, suddenly seared, and they were recoiling now, clenching as much as they could, seared by the foolishness of the notion that Jack had *needed* that emotional truth from him.

Jack Dalton is a murder maven, and I am quite obviously his prime suspect. "My mother left after that, and my father and I drifted from town to town, finally ending up in Harlanville, where we lived until the night I killed him with a hunting knife. That's where this interrogation is going, isn't it, Jack?"

"According to Harlanville's chief of police, your father's death was self-defense." *And the girl who loved you believed it was an accident.*

"But you're wondering if it was murder? If I killed the bastard in cold blood? You want me to just casually confess to first-degree murder? So that I can be put on trial for killing Jed Taylor because you can't tie me to the more recent deaths?"

"No. I just . . ." *want to know.*

There it was again. That odd look, as if Jack Dalton were searching for something, needing something, *from Cole.* Something quite distinct from a confession to murder.

"It was an accident, Jack. Don't get me wrong. If anyone ever deserved to die, it was my father. But it mattered very much to me *not* to kill him, even by accident. I was trying to subdue him, to hold him until the police arrived, when he fell onto a splintered guitar. As he twisted in surprise, the knife plunged into his heart." *I know, even though you seem less than confident now, that such a mishap would never have befallen you. And I can see that you wish it hadn't happened to me—as if you understand that it shattered my dreams.* "I didn't murder my father.

And I didn't murder Paulina. And I didn't murder Ashley." Cole paused, then added quietly, "And I would never hurt Sarah."

"I believe you."

"You do?" There was life in the granite now, *emotion*, a spark of surprise, and of hope?

"Yes. I do." *Of course I do.* "I would like to ask a few questions about the two actresses, though. Since you knew them both, you might, without even knowing it, have insight into the identity of their killer."

"Feel free. No one wants to find him more than I."

"Good. Were you involved with both of them?"

"If you mean sexually involved, only with Paulina. Ashley and I were friends. In fact, Ash and I were closer than Paulina and I ever were."

"Did you want more with Ashley?"

"No. She was obsessed, I suppose that's the right word, with a man she had known in college. He was married, but she still fantasized about getting back with him." *We both had fantasies about past loves that could not be.* "Ashley and I were good for each other, tough with one another. We forced each other to face reality. But I wasn't there for her when she really needed me, on the night she faced the most grim reality of all."

"Was the man's name Lucas?"

"How in the world do you know that?"

"Coincidence." *Destiny?* "Did you know that he was in L.A. last Valentine's Day?"

"What? *No.* But if that's *true*, Jack, then he's your killer." The panther was on alert now, eager for the kill, intent on accompanying Jack when he apprehended Lucas Cain. "When Lucas and Ashley were in college she told some lies, fairly significant ones, in an attempt to sever his relationship with the woman he eventually married. When Lucas found out what Ash had done, he confronted her. In a rage, she said. In fact, she truly believed he was going to kill her. . . ."

"You carve with your left hand, Lucas?"

"Always. I was born left-handed, yet another trait inherited from the father my mother despised. She and her many boy-friends made a special point of ridding me of that undesirable inheritance. I was punished if I used my left hand, if I so much as gestured with it. I became right-handed—in public, that is. In private, when I carved, which I did from the time I was quite young, I always used my left. I had no choice. Whatever talent I have exists only in that hand. Sarah? You seem upset by this. *Why?*"

Because a son whose mother enlisted the help of her many boyfriends to punish him for using his left hand might well become a man who takes great pleasure in carving, *with that same harshly punished hand*, the bodies and throats of women.

"Sarah?" Lucas replaced the white marble Pegasus on the mantelpiece and began to walk toward her. "What's *wrong*?"

Nothing. Everything is just fine. While you're unpacking the champagne and roses, I'll get the pepper spray from my purse, and when the time is right, when I'm certain that *I'm* right, I'll stun you—and flee. I'll take the stairs, and even with your long, powerful legs you won't be able to catch me. I'm an athlete now, as my parents always wanted me to be, and I'll be able to escape, and then Jessie and I—

You think a little pepper spray is really going to deter a mad-man? Or that you can actually run faster than he? Or that even when his eyes are stingingly blind he won't be able to carve, to slash, to kill?

"Sarah?"

It doesn't matter if I can't escape. My Jessie will be safe. Jack will save her. He'll get my message, later tonight, after I'm dead. He'll know that Lucas was here, and Jack Dalton, who overlooks nothing, will find the fingerprints that Lucas forgot to wipe off the marble Pegasus, and *this* is the reason I lived un-til now, *to save my daughter.*

Suddenly Sarah felt calm, at peace. She even smiled. "Noth-ing's wrong, Lucas. What's in the bag? Something for me?"

Lucas frowned at the sudden transformation from obvious apprehension to almost flirtatious nonchalance. "Yes."

"I have something for you as well. It's in my purse in my bedroom. Why don't I get it while you unpack?"

While you fill the champagne flutes with Cristale, and arrange the long-stemmed roses, and conceal the jagged-edged hunting knife beneath a cushion on the death-black sofa . . .

. . . but Sarah did not return to a scene of romance that was a prelude to murder. On the black lacquer table, where there should have been honey-gold champagne and blood-red roses, was a bouquet of photo albums in soft shades of pink and cream.

"We thought you'd like to see photographs of Jessie, from the time she was a baby."

"Lucas . . ."

"We have negatives, and will make copies of every one if you like. But Emma thought I should bring these with me tonight. Unless you'd rather not look at them?"

"No, Lucas." Her hands were already touching the light pink album designed to hold the first pictures of a baby girl. "I *want* to."

"Which means you've made your decision, doesn't it? You want us to tell her."

Sarah's hands didn't leave the album. But she looked up, focused on him, and answered, "Yes. I'm sorry. I know it's not what you think is best."

"No, it's not. But I told you that I'd defer to Emma, and to you." His smile was slight, and as authentic as it could be in the face of his lingering misgivings. "Em thinks we should tell her this week, while she's still out of school. We could tell her tomorrow, and you could plan to return to Cornwall for the weekend . . . except that you're frowning. Do you have a conflict, Sarah? A prior engagement?"

No conflict in the world could prevent Sarah from seeing her daughter. But she *did* have a prior engagement, a rendezvous with death, and even though Jack was never going to let that murder happen, what if it did? What if she put herself in harm's way, as she might have done tonight, letting Jack know of her plans when it was too late for him to intervene?

Perhaps it was unfair to tell Jessie the truth. Ever. Or perhaps, *please*, it was not. But no one would dispute the unfairness of telling an eleven-year-old girl about the existence of a mother she had never known just a month before that mother was stabbed to death.

"I'd like to wait until after Valentine's Day, if that's all right with you."

"All right," Lucas concurred, but with obvious surprise. "Whenever you prefer."

"Thank you—except now it's you who's frowning."

"There's a favor I'd like to ask of you."

Sarah's heart trembled. She was *so close* to a reunion with her daughter, and his expression was so solemn. A favor? You mean you'd like me to pretend that I'm a *friend* of Jessie's birth mother? A mother who died but whose deathbed wish was that I meet her daughter, just once? "What favor, Lucas?"

"Emma and I would like to visit the grave of our son." *Our.* His voice included them all. Our son. Our daughter.

"That's not a favor."

"No. The favor is that I was wondering about his gravestone."

"You mean, should he have a new one? Carved in marble by his father? Yes, Lucas. He should."

For a while only their thoughts filled the silence, thoughts about two infants who had been born on that August night in Penzance. Eventually there was a slight sound, as Sarah opened the album that had been resting beneath her hands.

Then she was lost in the wonder of Jessie, in a photograph taken just hours after her birth, just hours after she had greeted the world—and her mother—with a melodic hello.

Sarah did not notice as Lucas moved away.

And if he was moving behind her? To slash her throat? To splatter the newborn image of joy with crimson droplets of her mother's blood?

It could happen. The warrior was totally disarmed, vulnerable to attack; vigilant, wary, no more. She was a mother, a *mother*, lost in the splendor of seeing her baby for the very first time.

"I don't believe that Lucas is the killer," Jack said quietly. *Jessica's father is not a cold-blooded murderer any more than you are. He can't be.* "I want to show you something, Cole. This symbol was sent by the killer to his victims. I need to know if you've ever seen it before."

And you have, Jack realized as he watched his brother's reaction to the stylish black heart. Not guilt, just recognition. And concern.

"You recognize it, don't you?"

"I recognize the *concept*, not the symbol itself."

"The concept?"

"Of a heart carved in stone and imprinted in black ink. It was something we discussed."

"*We?*"

Cole paused as he retrieved the memory. When it came it was crystal-clear. They were in Hong Kong, in the green and white marble lobby of the Jade Palace, talking about acquiring chops—their names, in Chinese, carved in stone—as they waited to be transported by Rolls-Royce limousine to dinner on a floating restaurant in Aberdeen Harbour; and waiting, as well, for Lillith.

"Me, Sydney, Mick, David, and Timothy."

Jack had files on all of them, of course. But two of them loomed at the very top of his private list of suspects. One was eminently logical. Indeed, he came as if presented on a silver platter, complete with a set of coincidences and clues that were as striking as the ones that had accompanied Cole. The other name was illogical, implausible. And yet, despite a search that, to date, had yielded no hard data to support his concerns, it endured, haunting and powerful.

Jack pursued the eminently logical name first.

"I've been wondering about Timothy."

"As a potential killer?"

"Yes."

"No," Cole said decisively. "It couldn't be Timothy."

But it could, Jack mused. At least, so far, he had been unable to find anything that could conclusively clear the billionaire, and there was that long list of beckoning clues. Timothy owned Gemstone Pictures, the studio for which Ashley Alexander had won an Academy award and with which, shortly before her death, Paulina Bliss had been signed to a two-picture deal. Timothy also owned Global News, and it was he who had commanded Sarah to leave the blood-soaked trenches of war and return to London. And as for Timothy Asquith the man, the aristocratic patron of the arts who had commissioned Lucas Cain to carve a Cupid from black marble? There was something tormented about Timothy, some deep, gnawing hunger. And . . .

"I haven't yet been able to place him in L.A. last February fourteenth. But his private jet was on the ground in New York from the tenth to the twenty-first."

"That's right. Timothy was in New York the night Ash and Paulina were murdered. He was at Sloan-Kettering, in his wife's hospital room. Lillith had just been diagnosed with breast cancer and was undergoing chemotherapy." Cole frowned. "That's been a closely guarded secret, although she's done very well. Yesterday, in fact, Timothy learned that her most recent tests show that the tumor is still in remission."

"A closely guarded secret that Timothy shared with you."

"He knew I was worried about Lillith when we were all in Hong Kong, that I'd noticed how fatigued she was. And maybe Timothy needed someone, aside from Lillith, with whom to discuss her illness. Not surprisingly, it's been very upsetting to him."

The black-hearted killer's most grisly signature was the imprint of the heart, in the victim's own blood, on the silken flesh of the left breast. Was that the side on which Lillith Asquith's tumor had been diagnosed? Did Timothy harbor a lunatic rage against young women whose breasts were intact and cancer-free?

Cole obviously respected Timothy. As did Sarah, who had conspicuously omitted him from her long list of men who would happily see her dead. Quietly, and with a note of apology, Jack persevered.

"Timothy could have flown to L.A. on the fourteenth, a quick round trip, just long enough to commit the murders."

"He could have," Cole conceded. "But he didn't. I'm his alibi, Jack. Timothy was the first person I notified when the police found Paulina's body. She was going to be Gemstone Pictures' newest star. When Timothy didn't answer his phone at the hotel, I tried the hospital. He was there, in the middle of the night, fours hours after Paulina's murder, and just two hours after Ash was killed. He's not your killer, Jack."

Which means, Cole thought, unless the conversation about the heart carved in stone is just coincidence, one of the band members is.

Jack had a similar—although far more specific—thought. And it came gift-wrapped in a haunting memory. But before he could utter the troubling name, Cole spoke, replaying for him the salient features of the monumental conversation that had taken place in Hong Kong.

"It was Sydney who suggested that instead of carving my name in Chinese, I should get a symbol. A heart, she said, because of the love songs I sing. That I should dip it in black ink was Mick's idea, although any of them might have said it. The notion of my stone-cold obsidian-black heart had been bandied about for years. David was silent, as always. David *is* silent, and Mick is overtly hostile. In fact, Mick—"

"It's Sydney who worries me most, Cole." *It's Sydney who I saw onstage on New Year's Eve.*

Cole hadn't seen her, of course. She was behind him, in the shadows, her arms slender but so strong—and equally agile—as she played her drums. There had been a moment, that haunting moment, when the spotlight had followed Cole across the stage, illuminating Sydney's face and creating a macabre dance of light and shadows. Her face had gleamed in that eerie light, as stark and white as a vampire's; and her amethyst eyes had been on fire, aglow with a searing rage.

It was the most fleeting of glimpses, and when the spotlight found her again, she was smiling, lost in the music, loving it, and the swift, flickering portrait of evil seemed merely a fanciful mirage.

But its memory had lingered, and haunted, and now—as Jack confessed to Cole his worries about Sydney—something haunted Cole as well.

"What is it, Cole?"

"I was remembering last February fourteenth. It was early evening. Both Ash and Paulina were still alive. Sydney dropped by, to wish me happy birthday, and happy Valentine's Day. She was euphoric, mysterious, and *smug*, as if she had a secret." Cole took a breath and inhaled pure fear. "And tonight, right now, she's having dinner with Sarah and Claire."

Not with Sarah, Cole. The woman I love is perfectly safe. And the woman who is loved by the brother who saved my life? "Nothing's going to happen tonight, Cole. Nothing's going to happen until Valentine's Day, by which time—"

"*No*, Jack. You don't understand. The way Sydney was this afternoon was exactly the way she was last Valentine's Day. *She's going to act tonight.*"

"Okay." Jack's voice was quiet, calm, despite the racing urgency he felt. The woman you love will be safe, too. *She will be.* "We'll find them, Cole. We have all of Scotland Yard at our disposal. Do you know where they were planning to go?"

"No. I asked, but . . ." *Sydney was euphoric, mysterious, and smug.*

With a minimum of words, the Taylor brothers sprang into action. While Jack used one line to call Scotland Yard, to instigate a search for the famous Elle Syd and her blind, copper-haired companion, Cole compelled hotel security to enter each woman's room.

The rooms were quite empty, quite free of carnage. Indeed, Sydney and Claire had been seen leaving the hotel at least an hour before. On foot, the bellman reported, recalling as well Sydney's cheery announcement that they wouldn't need a taxi because they were *tubing* it tonight.

The women were somewhere in London. One was a maniac,

and the other was in mortal danger, and the bayou panther and his brother were caged in Cole's spacious suite, imprisoned and pacing.

"I can't stay here," Cole said finally, a hoarse but quiet explosion of emotion. "I can't just stay here waiting for the phone to ring."

"Why don't we go to the lobby, then? I'll be notified by Scotland Yard the moment they're found."

Jack's pager sounded during the swift elevator ride to the lobby. After looking at the number illuminated on the display, he met his brother's eyes—and was forced to dash the sudden hope in the worried gray.

"It's not about Claire." *It's about the woman I love, the one who is safe.* "But I do need to answer it."

"He's gone, Jack."

"And?"

"There were some very tense moments, for her as well as for us. We *knew* he didn't have a weapon. Still, when he admitted that he carves with his left hand—"

"*What?*"

"He's right-handed—except when he uses a knife."

Jack swore, softly, lavishly. "Is she all right?"

"She's fine. If he *had* been the killer . . . well, we're pretty sure that she was planning to do something heroic. We could almost *hear* her thoughts. We would have intervened, of course. Hell, we almost went in right then. But she didn't know that. She believed she was flying solo. Courageous lady."

"Yes she is."

"Anyway, it ended well. They decided to tell Jessie everything after all, after Valentine's Day."

"They may not need to wait that long."

"You have something?"

"I think so. Which means that your night's work may be just beginning." *Because our killer murders in pairs, women who are friends.*

After explaining the situation, and giving specific instructions about what was to be done, Jack returned to the lobby, to Cole, *who was not there.*

But who had been seen leaving the hotel, a panther on the prowl . . . a panther who suddenly knew precisely where to find his prey.

Where, Cole? Jack demanded—a silent query that was answered with amazing clarity. Jack told the concierge to contact Scotland Yard, and precisely where to send an army of police.

Then he followed his brother's heartprints into the night.

Chapter Thirty-Two

Gemstone Recording Studio
Waverton Street

A SINGLE LIGHT, A PORTABLE SPOT, SHONE brightly on the two women. It was a small moon, and it haloed them in a mist of gold. They sat in the center of the studio, in straight-backed chairs, facing each other across a low wooden table adorned with crystal champagne flutes, blood-red roses, and a piece of lavender jade that was hand-carved with the symbol of a heart. It was a moonlit scene of romance, and of murder—a jagged-edged hunting knife adorned the table, too, its silvery blade gleaming brightly in the golden mist.

There was clutter as well, beneath the small glowing moon. This was a recording studio, after all, and all manner of musical instruments, including the drums of the famous Elle Syd, were strewn about, and the floor itself was a tangle of electrical cords, snakelike links to microphones, amplifiers, keyboards, and guitars. There was an alien, however, amid the sinister black coils. A slender white cane, delicate and pristine, had been thrown into the snake's nest by a murderess—far away from the slender, delicate, snowy white hands of Claire.

"Cole!" Sydney greeted gaily, a most gracious hostess at this romantic party of death. "I'm *so* glad you're here. My conversation with Claire has, well, *deteriorated.* We're drinking sparkling cider, since she's a teetotaler just like you. But this cider is unique, laced with a few drops—a few too many, I'm afraid—of each of my favorite drugs. *Hallucinogens*, mostly. You've taken your fair share of drugs, Cole, so what do you think? What would hallucinogens do for someone who is *blind*? Claire is definitely somewhere else, outer *outer* space. But is she *seeing* things?"

"What are you doing, Sydney?"

"I think you know. At least, except for your obvious—and disgusting—concern for little miss space cadet here, you don't seem terribly shocked. *Interesting*. I suppose this means that Sarah showed the heart to someone. That gorgeous Jack, maybe? I never really believed he was as advertised. An authentic biographer would have been after you. *Us*. Cole Taylor *and* Amethyst."

"It's over, Syd."

"Over? Oh, no, Cole. It's *just* beginning. Speaking of which—beginnings—would you care to hear my master plan, from the very start?"

"Sure." *Just keep talking, Syd.*

"*You* were supposed to be blamed, of course. The black heart, the killer who didn't drink champagne. Those were just *teasers*, too little for an arrest but enough to point the police in the right direction, where they would have found two of your shirts, covered with the victims' blood—you'll notice I'm wearing one of your shirts even now—and, naturally, the murder weapon. I was going to plant those incriminating items at your house, discreetly hidden, and you were going to languish on death row. I would have had you all to myself then, and you would have seen how loyal I was, Cole, how very much I loved you. When you and I weren't recording duets of love from behind bars, I would have been visiting with the governor, pleading for your life. But I didn't plant the evidence. Do you know why? Because you called me that night, right after you called Timothy. You reached out to *me*, Cole. And for a while, everything was fine. Almost perfect. You didn't sleep with me, *and you were supposed to*, but at least there wasn't anyone else. I truly believed that, given time, you would see the light. But you're as blind as Claire, you bastard. Then came that fateful day in Denver. We were backstage, and the television was on, and there was Sarah Pembroke, telling us about the awful state of affairs in Goražde. The way you *looked* at her, Cole. It was the way you were supposed to look at me—with longing, with *love*. But the look wasn't really for Sarah, was it? It was for her friend, her pen*mate*, Claire."

Cole's solemn gray gaze was on Sydney, feigning absolute attentiveness to her. As long as she kept talking, and was wholly focused on him, Claire would be safe.

Claire *was* safe, at this moment. But, both literally and figuratively, she was terribly far away. Her cinnamon head was tilted in thoughtful contemplation; and it seemed as if her sightless blue eyes might truly be seeing some phantom created by chemicals that were so foreign to her—and had been administered in such overzealous amounts—that her reaction was extreme; and it was possible that in her faraway world Claire was hearing voices as well. She was definitely not hearing *their* voices; of that, Cole was quite sure. Claire was deaf to Sydney's confessions of murder . . . as she would be to the words of love—and escape—that Cole longed to speak.

Cole was still too far from Sydney to make his move. She could still get to the knife, and to Claire, before he could subdue her. But he was moving closer, slowly, carefully, a stealthy prowl.

If Claire, that courageous bayou girl, had not been drugged, she would have become his most able accomplice. At the precise moment when he lunged at Sydney, Cole would have commanded *Run, Claire*, and she would have scampered over the black serpents as fleetly—and as fearlessly and sightlessly—as once she had scampered over the thick vines that lay on the lush green carpet of their wooded paradise.

But Cole's fleet-footed elf-angel would not hear his command. Which meant that Cole had to be even closer to Sydney, and absolutely confident of his success, before making his move. At the moment there was no urgency. Claire was far away from both the truth and the terror. And Sydney seemed quite content to tell him—with obvious pleasure and such stunning madness—of her evil.

"It *was* Claire you were seeing, wasn't it, Cole? Claire who you wanted, or *believed* you did. But you didn't know then what had happened to your precious Claire. You had no in*sight*, as it were, to the deal breaker, her unfortunate—and unaccept-able—blindness. Your heart really *is* black, Cole. In fact, you're the real villain of the piece, the true murderer. I merely put your victims out of their misery. The coup de grâce, so to speak. Both Paulina and Ashley were positively miserable. Although, admit-tedly, as I discovered a bit too late, Ashley's misery wasn't your fault. She wasn't secretly lusting after you after all."

Sydney frowned, an expression that was more theatrical than real, an advance indication that whatever it was that had given her pause was not of great consequence. "I suppose I should have plied both Paulina and Ash with champagne *before* mak-ing the decision to kill them. Neither was nearly the threat I be-lieved her to be. It didn't matter for Paulina, of course. The outcome would have been the same. You weren't in love with her, but you were *sleeping* with her, and for that, she had to die. And as for Ashley? Well. I couldn't very well arrive at her place with champagne and roses, shortly after killing Paulina using the same props, and then just *leave*, could I? Besides, the two of you were friends, and might have become lovers after Paulina's unfortunate death. Anyway, I did Ashley a *favor* by killing her. She was suffering that night, truly suffering, terribly hurt by a man she referred to as *cool man Luc*. Good old Ash. She *was* funny, wasn't she, even when she was in pain? I have to admit that Luc sounded like quite a bastard. A small-time one, however, compared to you, Cole. You *live* to make women miserable, don't you? Me. Paulina. A thousand others. Even sweet little Claire."

Even sweet little Claire? Cole didn't speak, it was far too dangerous, and for a moment even his prowl came to a halt. Sydney was staring at him, searching his face for the truth she *must not see*—how much he loved Claire, how it tormented him that he had ever hurt her. Even his surprise that Claire had shared with Sydney his cruel crimes of the past must remain concealed.

It wasn't cruelties of long ago that Sydney recounted, but new ones.

"Claire made a few confessions before vanishing into never, never land. There was some *deep dark secret* about you, something for which she needed my help—that she never quite got to. Maybe you'll tell me that secret, Cole? I hope so. But first, I want to tell you the confession Claire did make, so you'll know how much she was suffering and how very lucky she is to have an angel of mercy such as myself. The theme is angels, Cole. The Angel of Mercy, yours truly, and the Angel Gabriel. Claire *knows* you called the good doctor, knows you couldn't stand her blindness and wanted it fixed. Even if it killed her. You wanted Claire to die for you, didn't you, to be willing to die? And she *will* die, Cole, thanks to *my* knife, not Dr. Gabriel's. It's too late for lethal surgery. That's what you found out, wasn't it? Claire is blind—forever—and that's just not good enough for you." The Angel of Mercy was on the warpath now, accusing the true murderer, the man who left in his wake hearts that were so badly wounded that death was a blessing. "*Is it*, you bastard?"

Please don't hear my words, Claire. Not these words. *Not these lies.*

He had called Dr. Angelica Gabriel with a single purpose: to offer his eyes, his darkness, in exchange for Claire's. He would willingly live in the blackness that had always filled him with such terror—for Claire; and, if she would have him, with Claire . . . for his darkness would not be so terrifying with her at his side.

And if Claire did not want him? He would live, in darkness, all alone. *But Claire would see.*

Cole had imagined that medical advances might have been made in the past six years. Indeed, he had spent the entire journey home from Monte Carlo willing there to be; willing it, wishing it, so intent on compelling it to be true that the journey was made in silence. There *would be* advances, and they would be eminently safe. A simple transplant of gray eyes for blue. But this *lesion*—Dr. Gabriel's word—was far deeper, an optic nerve that had been crushed, and eventually destroyed, by the blood clot Claire refused to have removed.

That was the truth. Cole Taylor had been prepared to live the rest of his life in darkness, for Claire. But now, to Sydney, he spoke the necessary lie.

"That's right, Syd. Blindness isn't good enough. I feel sorry for her. I pity her. But I don't want her, *can't* want her."

So let her go.

Sydney's sighted eyes flashed with savage rage. "But you *slept* with her, didn't you, Cole? In Monte Carlo? She didn't admit it. I asked before the drugs were working their magic and our little southern lady actually blushed. But I *know* you did."

"It was a mistake, Syd. A disappointment." *The most wondrous weekend of my life, Claire. A dream. Our dream. I'll tell you that—all the truths—soon. I'm almost there, Claire, almost close enough to imprison Sydney in my arms until the police arrive. They will be here, I know they will. Jack will have figured this out and—*

"That's far enough, Cole!" With the command, and with catlike quickness, Sydney grabbed the hunting knife, moved behind Claire, and pressed the jagged-edged blade to her throat. Claire's brow furrowed slightly at the sudden pressure, but there was none of the terror that Cole had seen on that long-ago night when Jed Taylor had held a knife to Annabelle Prentice's throat in a hauntingly identical way. Identical . . . until Sydney moved again, a swift sleight of hand. "Oops. I need to do this left-handed, don't I? I'm not *ready* to do this yet, Cole, to make my merciful slice. And I won't. Unless you force me to. Are you going to force me?"

"No."

"Good." Sydney rewarded him with a brilliant smile, the radiant California girl, sun caressed—and totally mad. Then, still smiling, and with the knife still at Claire's throat, she grasped the black cord that connected the spotlight to its socket and pulled, casting the studio in pitch-blackness. "Now we have an even playing field, wouldn't you say? We're all blind. Except, perhaps, little miss space cadet. I guess we'll just have to *imagine moonlight*, won't we, Cole? You wrote that for her, didn't you? For our sweet blind little Claire. You didn't realize she was blind then, did you? Just as you still haven't realized the truth about the song. You wrote it as a duet, you *bastard*. A duet to sing with Claire. But why don't *we* sing it now, Cole? You and I. Oh, I *know* you don't sing duets. How well I know. Except, of course, with Claire. But this is a special circumstance, wouldn't you say? Did I mention that I'm recording our session? Making my own album of my *favorite* hits? Paulina. Ashley. Claire. And us, Cole. *Us.* Go ahead. The first line of 'Imagine Moonlight' is yours."

It's so dark, Claire, and I feel the serpents at my feet. But I'm still walking toward you , toward Sydney's voice . . . but really, my love, to you.

"*Sing*, Cole."

As Cole obeyed Sydney's instruction, he realized that what she said was true. He had written "Imagine Moonlight," his heart had written it, as a duet to sing with Claire. Sung alone, it was a song of loss, of farewell, a tormented good-bye. But as a duet? It was a joyous hello, a celebration of a forever love.

Cole finished his lyric of love, and it was time for Sydney to serenade her reply, but suddenly there were two voices. Sydney's *and Claire's*. Oblivious until now, Claire had been awakened by his song of love—for her.

"Claire. *Don't sing.*"

She did not heed his urgent command. His bayou girl was singing now, singing again at last, a soprano of pure joy.

"It's okay, Cole." Sydney spoke from the blackness. "Why don't you sing 'Imagine Moonlight' first with Claire, and then with me? You'll see—unless you're as blind as Claire—that you and I were meant to sing together, to *be* together. Admittedly, it's a revelation that comes a bit too late. But . . . it's your turn again, Cole, your lyric, and the next line you sing together."

As Cole and Claire sang in the darkness this most glorious song of love, he walked toward her still. And did this man, who had always had such terror of a world without light, stumble on the black serpents coiled at his feet? He did not. He was a panther still, surefooted and stealthy, and guided now by the voice of his angel.

Cole floated toward Claire, envisioning her throat, the knife, Sydney's hand—and knowing that he had to subdue Sydney before the song ended . . . because he knew, a terror far greater than any phantoms of darkness, that the moment he and Claire finished their duet of love, his beloved Claire would die.

But Cole was wrong.

There were still more words to sing, more love, more joy, more forever hello. But now there was a new sound in the studio, not music really, just a rhythmic thumping, like a metronome; and there was a new sensation in Cole's chest, hot and sharp, but not painful. No pain was greater than the fear of losing Claire, and nothing mattered more than traversing the night-black field of snakes to get to her.

But now something was blocking Cole's path, an obstacle that was responsible not only for the rhythmic noise but for the heat, the sharpness, in his chest.

The realization came vaguely, already he had lost so much blood, and his mind was focused on Claire, not on himself. But vaguely, Cole realized that the obstacle was Sydney. She was stabbing him, again and again, a methodical slaughter that would end, with a flourish, when her jagged-edged blade impaled his heart.

It was at just that moment that the studio door flung open, casting in silvery light the brutal carnage and filling the air with yet another new sound, the scream of sirens nearby.

Then there was a closer sound, the desperate shout of one brother to another, as the younger one saw with stunning clarity the blood-slick knife held high above the madwoman's platinum head, clutched in both of her hands in savage anticipation of the final, lethal plunge . . . and the ashen statue, his *brother*, stark white except for the bloodied chest that was crimson proof of his passive acceptance of Sydney's vicious assault . . . and now that dying brother's smile, faint and ghostly, as Cole realized that, with Jack's arrival, Claire would be safe.

"Cole!"

Chapter Thirty-Three

SARAH HEARD THE SIRENS WAILING IN THE night, just as twelve years before Claire had heard similar strident cries. Then as now, the sirens were a discordant and confusing counterpoint to moments of sheer joy.

As the wails came ever closer, Sarah drew her gaze from the smiling face of her daughter as a toddler and listened to the distressing shrillness; and like Claire, all those years before, comforted herself with a defiant thought. *My loved ones are safe.*

Lucas was on his way to Cornwall, where Emma and Jessie were awaiting his return in the cozy comfort of Hyacinth House; and Claire and Sydney were dining in candlelit elegance; and Cole and Jack were sharing quiet conversation, in French perhaps—

Sarah's phone rang then, another harsh intrusion on this night that should have been so gentle.

"Sarah? It's Frances."

"Frances," Sarah murmured vaguely, still lost in thoughts of reunions of the heart, of mothers and daughters and brothers and friends.

"Your *secretary*, Sarah. I'm calling because my boyfriend

works at Scotland Yard, he's a dispatcher, and something terrible has just happened at the Gemstone recording studio on Waverton. That's very near you, isn't it?"

Sarah was lost, disoriented, no more. "Something terrible, Frances?"

"A stabbing. The details are sketchy, but both Cole Taylor and Jack Dalton are somehow involved. I thought you'd want to—"

"Yes. Thank you, Frances."

Within seconds Sarah was dashing across the granite floors of the penthouse foyer, a swift sprint toward the stairs.

"Lady Pembroke!"

The voice was male, distinctly American, and as she spun toward it, Sarah saw two men, tall and powerful, and emerging from the *other* penthouse. The one she owned, and kept empty.

"Who are you?"

"I'm Peter, and this is Doug. We're . . . Jack asked us to keep an eye on you, to make sure that you were safe."

"Jack?"

"He didn't want you to know about us. But we heard the phone call from Frances, and, well, we all want to get to him, don't we?" Peter saw the answer on her worried face. "So let's go."

He gestured toward the elevator, so notoriously slow in its vertical journeys from floor to floor that Sarah had not considered waiting for it now. But the elevator was awaiting *her*, its gleaming brass doors flung wide open.

"We added some circuitry to the system," Peter explained. "In case of emergency. The elevator comes when we call it, bypassing all the other floors."

"We have other gadgets as well," Doug offered as the elevator began its nonstop descent. "Metal detectors, among other things. We knew that Lucas didn't have a knife—any weapon at all—and wished we'd been able to let you know, *especially* when he revealed that he always carves with his left hand."

"You heard everything," Sarah murmured.

"We heard, and will forget. Jack didn't want to invade your privacy, Lady Pembroke. In fact, he *hated* it. But your safety mattered to him most of all. We never listened when you were alone, or when Jack was with you."

Jack. This conversation was really about him. Jack . . . who might be bleeding, dying, stabbed to death by his brother—or perhaps even worse, might himself have plunged a knife into that brother's murderous heart. Jack . . . for whom Peter and Doug felt such great admiration that they were justifying his actions—his invasion of her privacy—in the name of nobility. Jack . . . who was her shepherd, her very own knight in shining armor.

Peter and Doug were, in essence, delivering Jack Dalton's eulogy.

No. Jack will be all right, and so will Cole, and—

But even as Sarah was issuing that defiant protest, she heard herself speak. "I called Jack, just before Lucas arrived, to let him know that we were meeting tonight." *To tell him what he already knew, but had been waiting, so patiently, for me to confess. I kept my promise, Jack!*

"We told him about your message," Peter assured her just as the elevator doors opened to the building's marbled lobby. "He knows."

Peter and Doug had parked their van, with its portable version of their state-of-the-art surveillance equipment, on Upper Brooke. But Sarah led the way, on foot, across Grosvenor Square. Waverton was a mere five blocks away, and all of them were fit, her two shepherds—surrogates for the most beloved shepherd of all—and the graceful warrior, the fleet-footed gazelle.

On another night, a happier night, Sarah had bounded across Place Vendôme with Jack. Now she was running toward him, and now Waverton was just ahead, aglow with flashing red lights and cluttered with police.

Sarah wove through the crowd, relentless in her determination to get to Jack. The studio door was open wide, as if gaping in horror at the scene within, the bloody aftermath of what Jack had witnessed as he flung open that same door, casting a silver beam of light onto the carnage. . . .

"Cole!"

The frantic cry was a duet. The deep voice of a brother and the soft soprano of a bayou girl.

Sydney heard both voices and realized that the end was near. Cole stood before her—was somehow still standing—a silvery white statue cloaked in bright crimson. How she *wanted* the lethal stab to his faithless heart, to feel transmitted through the jagged blade the final, desperate, dying beats.

But there wasn't time for that bloody luxury, that delicious pleasure. Cole was virtually dead. In the next few moments his wounds would weep their final tears. And maybe this was better after all. Cole's wounds would weep, *and he would weep*, as he witnessed the death of his cinnamon-haired angel.

"I loved you," Sydney hissed at Cole's ashen face.

But even in death Cole would give her *nothing*. He was looking at Claire, loving Claire, dying for Claire, and his expression was so calm now, at peace, not fighting his death but embracing it. He saw the knife poised above Sydney's head, and the gleam of sheer madness, sheer pleasure, as she anticipated its final plunge. And, his calm expression said, he would permit that lethal plunge, *would welcome it*, because as he died Jack would rescue Claire.

You're wrong, you bastard. Watch this.

Sydney spun, a pirouette *en pointe*. Her arms remained above her platinum head, a ballerina's graceful pose—except for the weapon clutched tightly in her hands.

Claire was a few steps away, standing now, and moving toward her. Not a space cadet anymore, Sydney mused. And not even, it seemed, a blind woman. Claire was looking up, as if she could actually *see* the gleaming blade, and the arms stretched out before her seemed more purposeful than groping, as if she actually planned to wrest the knife from Sydney's hands, and then there was that face, so innocent, so angelic, so fearless.

"*Bitch*," Sydney snarled, enraged by the need for haste and furious that Jack, that gorgeous, *traitorous* Jack, was so perilously close. She had time only for a single stab—to Claire's heart—but how she wished for more. How lovely it would be to pierce those sightless blue eyes, until they were no more, and to hear Claire's cries of pain, and then to slash the throat of the woman chosen by Cole to sing duets of love.

But there was no time. In fact, she had to hurry. Two quick steps and she would be there. Two quick steps, all the while glaring into the eyes that could not see—and yet were *pretending* that they could.

The black serpents, stretched and coiled at her feet, posed no problem for Sydney Quinn. Indeed, in this silvery Eden, the snakes were accomplices to her evil. But there was that alien creature among the snakes, that pristine symbol of blindness that Sydney had thrown far away from Claire . . .

. . . and it was on that delicate snow-white cane that Sydney tripped, just as she made her lethal lunge. Tripped, and fell, and because she clutched the knife with such resolve, so intent, still, on plunging the blade into Claire's angelic heart, her hands did not free themselves to break her fall, to soften the blow of her temple against the low wooden table.

Her head struck just so, at the most vulnerable place in her model-perfect skull, splintering the bone and severing the artery that pulsed just below. Death came swiftly for the famous Elle Syd, on the floor amid black serpents and an innocent white cane. Vestiges of romance floated down to her from the table above, a honeyed river of sparkling, drug-laced cider and the fragrant petals of blood-red roses.

"*Claire.*"

The voice came from the ashen statue.

"Cole," she whispered as she rushed to his loving, dying voice.

The black serpentine coils were no more obstacles for Claire than Cole had imagined they would be, no greater menace than the thick vines over which she had danced with her eyes closed in their forest beside the bayou. Then she was in his arms, and she felt such heat, a liquid fire that spilled from him to her. Blood, *his* blood, flowing as if it would never stop and searing her with pure fear.

Once before, in Cole's arms, Claire had been stained with blood. Jed's blood, and Cole's. On that night Cole had driven her away with the cruelty of his words—and on this night there were different words, loving but so urgent, pleading for them to part.

"Claire, it's Jack. Cole is losing blood, losing consciousness. He needs to lie down, Claire, *now.*"

Claire obeyed Jack's urgent plea, and met resistance. Cole did not want to let her go, not this time. Or maybe it was just Cole's body, sensing its imminent death and clinging instinctively to the life in hers, to the strength of her heartbeats as his own weakened and died.

"Jack," Sarah whispered with unsurpassed relief as she bolted through the studio door.

She saw him clearly. Every light in the studio was illuminated, glaring with the brightness of an autopsy suite. She saw Jack, and the circle of medics and police. They knelt on the floor, and their expressions were all so grave, and at the center of that circle . . . oh, no. *No.*

There, in the midst of that sober circle, was the corpse, naked to his waist, his chest awash with blood. But that blood was *still* spilling, *still* spouting, from the deep gashes in his eerily white skin.

Still bleeding, still *alive.* Barely.

That ominous truth was carved on every face save one, the famous cover girl who was already quite dead, adorned with rose petals and honey-gold tears. There was a smile on Sydney's face, and her amethyst eyes, open still, seemed triumphant.

Cole is *not* going to die. That determined pronouncement, too, could be read on the grave faces that encircled Cole. Determined—but helpless. There was no way to stem the flow of blood, not here, in this recording studio that looked far too much like a dissection room. The arteries that had been pierced and sliced by the rhythmic slashes of Sydney's knife were deep beneath the muscled flesh of Cole's bone-white chest. He needed another knife now, a surgeon's scalpel.

Sarah knew it, from her years spent at war. And the police and medics knew it, too, because now they were carrying Cole's motionless body toward the studio door, toward her, and the ambulance that was waiting just outside the door.

They. One of the men transporting Cole's bloodied body, swiftly—and yet with the reverence of a pallbearer—was Jack. He was alive, but dying, too, with his brother. His dark blue eyes were clouded with anguish, but there was a slight flicker, the faintest glimmer of light, when he saw her.

"Jack," she whispered, touching him, because they needed to touch, and his hands were filled with his precious cargo. "He'll be all right. He *will* be."

Jack answered with a nod, a defiant gesture of hope in the face of despair. "I'm going with him in the ambulance, Sarah. *Take care of Claire.*"

Claire? Sarah had not even seen her friend in the autopsy suite garnished with serpents and rose petals and the grim circle of solemn-faced men.

But now those men were gone, and Claire was on the bloodied floor, quite near the place where Cole had lain. Her legs were tucked beneath her, concealed by the billowing skirt of her dress, and she was crumpled, a copper-haired rag doll who had been carelessly discarded. But *not* carelessly, of course. In the name of care, for Cole, the blind woman had been brushed aside; or perhaps she had moved aside of her own accord.

Now, in this too bright room, Claire was huddled in her private darkness. *But not alone.* Two shepherds stood guard over the small, desolate doll, fiercely protective but clearly uncertain—and immensely relieved to see Sarah.

"Sydney gave her drugs," Doug said so quietly that even if fully alert, Claire would not have heard his words. "Hallucinogens. From the looks of it, a pretty potent mix."

"How do you know?"

"The police told us. Everything was recorded. Apparently Claire was quite lucid earlier, but now . . . she'll probably be floating in and out of reality for a while."

Which may be all for the best, Sarah thought as she knelt on the floor beside her friend. "Claire? It's Sarah."

The crumpled body moved, and its head lifted. "Sarah?"

Sarah had prepared herself for glassy blue eyes, and a face ravaged by confusion. Or, perhaps, no response at all. But what Sarah saw was the staggering proof of Cole's loss of blood. A thick coat of crimson painted Claire's coppery hair, and her cheeks, and her throat, and her *entire* torso.

Cole Taylor's blood had once been searing hot, heated from within by smoldering flames and molten steel. But now, away from the burning core of the powerful panther, the blood had chilled—and now it was chilling Claire, an iciness that was enhanced by the rushes of cold night air through the open door.

Claire's lips, what could be glimpsed beneath the layers of Cole's dying blood, were blue; and her teeth were chattering.

"We need to go to your hotel room, Claire. You're cold, and you need a nice hot shower. Okay?"

"I'm cold, Sarah?"

"Yes."

"Why?"

Claire was obviously confused. But *how* confused? Sarah wondered. How befuddled by drugs and by shock? She would find out, by providing Claire with the most simplistic answers possible, hoping that they would satisfy. She would not, under any circumstances, plant in her friend's mind the terrifying worries—or memories—with which, for the moment, Claire clearly could not cope.

"Because, Claire, it's a cold, wet night." When Claire responded with a frown, but without a demand for more clarity, Sarah continued, "I'm sure that someone—" a police officer "—can give us a ride to the hotel."

"And in the meantime Doug and I will get the van," Peter

added quietly. "After which we'll wait for you in the lobby of the Drake. In case you want to go anywhere else, later."

"*Frère Jacques, Frère Jacques, dormez-vous . . .*"

He wasn't a singer. At least he never had been. That talent belonged to his older brother.

But now, as the ambulance screamed through the rain-slick streets of London, Jack sang to Cole, just to Cole, a hoarse whisper of emotion, a private plea for remembrance sung in their secret language of love.

"Don't stop," one of the ambulance attendants commanded as he checked yet again his patient's precarious blood pressure. "Whatever it is you're saying to him, Mr. Dalton, it seems to be helping."

So Jack sang, and although it didn't matter, couldn't matter less, on this night, for his brother, Jack carried a perfect tune.

Chapter Thirty-Four

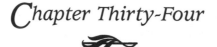

CRIMSON. CARDINAL. SCARLET. RUBY.

As she stood beneath the hot flow of the shower, the words flowed through Claire's mind, words that she and Cole had shared, exotic and enchanting names for the wonderful colors of London as seen through the palette of memories of their bayou home.

And *vermilion*, don't forget that rich, lush hue. The roses on Aunt Augusta's verandah then. The hibiscus blooms in the Asian Garden now.

The lovely names flowed, and floated, recalling wondrous memories and bringing their dazzling colors with them to paint her blackness.

Red.

Blood red.

Those two words, that color, caused a sharp, piercing pain. *Why?* Because her period had just started? Because there would be no baby? Claire hadn't seen the blood-red tears wept by her womb, but she had known when those tears had begun to flow.

But there was something more, blood red, too, and much worse, a source of far greater pain. What? *What?*

The memory eluded her, spinning away, just beyond the reach of her floating mind. Then a new memory began to dance, close enough to touch, to hear, *to see.*

Claire heard the memory first, a duet of moonlight, of love, sung with Cole. Then she saw the remembered image of a silver moon. She wanted the memory to stop there, *there*, forever. But her mind was groping through the dense fog of drugs; and there was beginning to be a little clarity; and now she heard the memory of another sound, unspeakably horrible, rhythmic and thumping; and then, before her eyes—*her* eyes?—the silver moon changed shape, from a glowing ball to something quite pointed and sharp, a lightning bolt, it seemed, frozen in a night-black sky.

In her awakening memory, the lightning bolt began to beckon to her, compelling her to walk toward it, and she was doing that, and she was even going to touch that swordlike shaft of light; but then there was thunder, and then Cole's voice, and then ... oh, then she believed she saw his silvery eyes, as glowing as her imaginary moon, and then she felt the steel and fire of his body, and—

"*Sarah!*"

"I'm right here, Claire."

Sarah had been pacing in Claire's bedroom, listening to the sounds of shower water splashing onto her friend's bloodied body, ready to offer Claire a warm plush towel the moment the sounds stopped. Claire already had that towel, had reached for it herself, with an arm that was snow-white, as *all* of Claire was snow-white now.

But there was evidence of carnage still. Claire's dress, bright red with Cole's blood, was neatly folded, reverently folded, as if Claire intended to take it with her, to pack it along with the rest of her recently packed clothes.

"What is it, Claire?"

"What happened to Cole? Was he *stabbed*, Sarah?"

"Yes. Cole was stabbed. He's at the hospital now. I called to check while you were showering. He's already in surgery."

"I have to get to him!"

"We'll go to the hospital, Claire. Soon."

"He's going to be all right, isn't he, Sarah? He's going to be fine?"

The drugs were wearing off, releasing their strangle hold on Claire's mind. But, Sarah realized, they weren't yet gone. Undrugged, and fully in possession of her memory, Claire would know that Cole's prognosis was far from good, and would be able to deal with the grimness of that truth.

But now, to her confused and desperate friend, Sarah reassured, "Yes. Absolutely."

"Oh, *good.*"

Soon, Sarah knew, Claire would have more questions, more worries and more doubts. But for now could her friend be distracted? Were the drugs, in a way, still a blessing?

"Claire? While I was waiting in your bedroom I noticed your suitcases, that they're all packed."

Claire's frown deepened with surprise. But the drugs were still permitting her thoughts to float away, even the thoughts she wanted to keep, so she shifted, floated, to this new topic of conversation. "Oh. Yes, Sarah. That's right. I'm on a seven A.M. flight for Harlanville. Well, New Orleans by way of New York. I was going to take the red-eye, but that seemed too rushed. I wanted time to meet with Sydney, and then call you, and—" A memory appeared from the fog. "*Sydney.* She's a *murderer*, isn't she?"

"Yes. And she's dead now, Claire."

"And Cole is all right?"

"*Yes.* But what I cannot understand, Claire, and I'd really like your help with this, is why you're planning to return to Harlanville."

"I *have* to, Sarah. It's what Cole wants."

"I can't believe that."

"Oh, but it's true." *Blindness isn't good enough. I pity her. But I don't want her, can't want her.* There was no fog around the memory of Cole's words. Not even a gentle wisp of mist. There was only pain. "I *have* to go home, Sarah. But . . ."

"But what, Claire?"

You don't love me, Cole. But I love you. Still. Always. And I came here with a purpose, a dream—for you. "But what about Cole's brother? I was planning to ask Sydney to make the announcement for me. *Sydney.* But maybe now Mick could, or David, or Timothy. Or you, Sarah?"

"I would have, Claire. But I don't need to, not anymore. He's been found. Cole's brother has been found. It was something *I* was going to tell *you,* as soon as Cole had been told. As soon as Jack told him. Jack is Cole's brother, Claire. Jack is the brother Cole gave away on that December night."

For the past few moments Claire had seemed quite lucid. Deceptively lucid, Sarah realized as her astonishing revelation, the extraordinary coincidence, caused a response that was so subdued, and so utterly unsurprised, that Sarah wondered if Claire had even heard her words.

She had, apparently, because now there was a lovely smile, and her blue eyes were brilliantly clear. But the drugs were obviously still playing havoc with Claire's thoughts, because when she spoke her words made no sense.

"Jack, yes, *of course.*"

"Of course, Claire?"

"Yes. I should have *known,* from the way they walk."

But you've never *seen* them walk, Claire, Sarah thought. Not both of them. Just as you've never seen Jack's face.

The similarities between the Taylor brothers were striking, but virtually invisible. Likenesses of essence, of strength and character and nobility and grace. But Cole and Jack did not look alike. And as for the way the two powerful men roamed the earth?

"I should have known," Claire repeated, smiling still, deceptively lucid still. "At Timothy's party on New Year's Eve, I thought I heard Cole approaching—I was so sure! But it was Jack, and the sound was . . . identical." *The sound of bayou panthers on the prowl.* But were those brothers, those panthers, prowling, searching still? Or had their restlessness found peace? "Cole must be so pleased. Is he, Sarah?"

"I don't know. I'm not sure that Jack has told him yet." *Or if Cole will die before Jack ever has that chance.*

"I won't mention it then, when I talk to him."

"To whom, Claire?"

"To Cole. I'd like to say good-bye to him before I leave for Harlanville. I have time, don't I? It's still Wednesday night?"

"Yes. It's just about midnight." *But, Claire, you don't understand.*

"Then I *do* have time. I suppose I should check out of the hotel first, and leave my luggage with the bellman, and I'm rambling, aren't I?" Claire frowned. "It must be the drugs. Sydney gave me drugs, didn't she? I'm still a little jumbled, aren't I?"

A little jumbled, Sarah thought, *but so blissfully unaware . . .*

. . . or so Sarah believed. But just before leaving for the hospital, and leaving her hotel room forever, Claire silently packed one final item—her blood-soaked dress, neatly folded and placed into one of the Drake's jade-and-alabaster laundry bags.

Cole Taylor's heart was not black, nor was it made of stone. Indeed, Cole's heart would most certainly have died had it been struck directly by a jagged-edged knife. But because Jack arrived in time, and the murderess turned her savage fury toward Claire, that lethal blow had never been delivered.

Which meant that as the thoracic surgeons probed the knife wounds in Cole's chest, extending those wounds until they could see, and repair, the severed arteries beneath, they had an ally in Cole's heart. They caught glimpses of it through the windows they created in his chest wall, the openings that gaped through sliced muscles and shattered ribs. The surgeons could not see the secrets of Cole's heart, or its shadows. But they saw clearly its power, the strong, steady heatbeats that did not falter, did not stumble—but merely sang.

Lub-dub. Frère Jacques. Lub-dub.
Frère
Jacques.

At five A.M. the chief surgeon, exhausted but jubilant, appeared in the waiting room.

"He made it."

"He's going to survive?"

"Yes. Already he's survived the greatest peril." The surgeon allowed himself a wry smile. "Cole may not agree, however, because for him the most difficult part lies ahead. For a while every breath he takes will cause intense pain, and it gets worse, because we're not going to permit him to take the breaths *he* wants. They would be far too shallow. We're going to do his breathing for him, with a ventilator. Deep breaths." His voice softened as he spoke to Claire's sightless, worried eyes. "But *necessary* ones. The complications of inadequate ventilation can be significant, and if we do this correctly now, despite the near-term discomfort, his complete recovery will be more certain and more swift."

"But you can give him something for the pain, can't you?"

"Yes. In fact, we've already begun. He came out of anesthesia surprisingly quickly, and the moment he realized he had a tube in his throat, he began to fight it. Rather dramatically. He was conscious, and absolutely alert, and there's no doubt that he understood our explanations. But he fought still, grabbing for the endotracheal tube and bucking against the efforts of the ventilator. We've sedated him, quite heavily. We had no choice. We've even had to restrain his hands. This is how it will have to be, I'm afraid, for several days at least. But please believe me, it's absolutely necessary."

"Can he hear if we talk to him? Can he understand?"

"Hear, yes. Understand, maybe. Or maybe not. But in a few days—"

"I'm returning to the States today. I just wanted to say good-bye."

"All right, then. Just give the nurses a few minutes to get him settled in the ICU."

"You don't *have* to leave today, Claire."

"Yes, Sarah, I do. I know that you were worried about me earlier, and I know why. I was still feeling the effects of the drugs, in my hotel room and for a while after we got here. But those effects are gone now, completely gone."

Yes they are, Sarah thought.

She had watched the drugs release their hold on her friend, watched Claire's crescendoing fear as she became ever more aware that Cole might not survive. Claire was Claire again, *clear* again—and determined.

"I know the drugs are gone. But still, Claire, that doesn't mean that *you* have to go."

"Yes, Sarah. I do. Really. And the timing is perfect, isn't it? I'll just say a few words to Cole, and then call a cab."

"We're not just going to put you in a cab for the airport, Claire."

"Really, Jack, it's—"

"Not a chance. In fact, maybe Sarah and I should fly with you to Harlanville."

"You need to be with Cole, Jack! I know you won't tell him anything until he's fully awake, and the tube is out of his throat. But you need to be with Cole, and Sarah needs to be with you, and it's important to me, truly it is, to make this journey on my own."

And I *can* make this journey on my own. All I have to do is follow the trail of tiny snowflakes that leads to my small glassy globe of love.

"It's Claire, Cole. You're in the hospital, but you're going to be *fine*, just fine—although your chest will hurt for a while. The tube in your throat is necessary, Cole. It's only for a few days, and I know you must hate it, but the doctors are giving you medications to make it more tolerable." *Just as Sydney gave me drugs to ease my pain.* But my pain was not eased. I heard you admit how you feel about my blindness. I will *always* hear those words. But in Harlanville I believe I can make them more quiet, can smother them with other memories. "I'm going home today, Cole. To Harlanville. I came to London—to you—with a purpose, and amazingly, even before my plan could be put in place, that purpose was accomplished. Something *wonderful* has happened, Cole. Truly wonderful. I can't tell you what it is. I promised not to. And I don't even know if you're hearing my words, or will remember them."

But you will remember them, Cole, just as I have remembered yours, even though I was drugged when you spoke them. The drugs wear off. But the memories don't. *I pity her. But I don't want her, can't want her.* "Anyway, it's wonderful, Cole. You'll see. Please think of that during these next few days, when your chest hurts so much and you can't even speak. At the end of these days there will be great happiness for you. Well . . . I need to go now. Good-bye, Cole."

His arms were imprisoned, tied at his sides, and his powerful legs were pinioned, too, and his throat was filled with plastic, and they had given him something that made his muscles so weak that he could scarcely move.

But he heard her, *and he saw her.* And his eyes, the stone shadows she could not see, spoke volumes. Unshadowed now, they blazed with the intensity of molten steel.

What I said to Sydney, I had to say, Claire. To save you. Something wonderful? No. Not if you leave. Not ever. Don't leave me, Claire. Please. I love—

Cole watched her leave through eyes that were open wide and bright with pain. Those eyes were open still when the cinnamon beacon of her hair vanished from his sight. And then, with his eyes wide open still, Cole Taylor's entire world turned black.

Chapter Thirty-Five

"IT'S OVER, SARAH."

Yes, she mused. *The puzzle of death has been solved. The black-hearted murderess is no more. Claire is on her way home to Harlanville, and Cole's savage wounds will heal, and even though it's still early Thursday morning and most Londoners are just greeting this cold and dreary January day, for us it's* over.

"Over," she echoed. "Yes. Thank—"

"So now we can begin," Jack interjected softly. "Can't we, Sarah? Can't we begin, now, to tell each other the truth? To trust each other?" *To love each other?* "I lied to you, Sarah. I promised I wouldn't have you watched. But I did. I *had* to."

"I know. You were just doing your job, Jack. You were here to catch a killer."

There it was, that rush of wild fury that only Sarah Pembroke could evoke. Jack allowed just a whisper of its immense power to touch his voice. "Is that *really* what you believe, Sarah? That all I cared about was catching the killer?"

"No," she confessed. "But there are things—*truths*—you don't know about me." *I once was quite mad, and so terribly disliked, and so utterly disposable . . . and I'm so very damaged still.*

"Tell me, Sarah. Trust me."

He needs to know, before this fantasy of love goes any further, before he discovers for himself—*in the flesh*—just how damaged and disappointing you are. Tell him now. And then it *will* be over.

"There's something I want you to read. It's a letter I wrote, but never sent, to Claire. It explains everything. I'll give it to you, and you can take it with you to read, and . . ." *Then you'll know the truth, we both will, because I will learn just how disposable I am. Still.* "It's in my bedroom. I'll just go get it."

"No." Jack caught her by the wrists, a gentle imprisonment. "Let me tell you what the letter says."

"You've already read it?"

She was asking him if he had betrayed her even more than he had already confessed, if he had let himself into her penthouse, her bedroom, and read the letter that was her most private diary. And yet . . . her query seemed hopeful, not accusatory, as if she wished he *had* betrayed her so completely, knew every secret shame, and wanted her still.

For a moment Jack was tempted to make a bargain with destiny. *Allow me just this one last lie.* Let me tell her that I've read the letter, and know everything, *everything*, and we can begin our love—now.

But there were to be no more lies in the love of Sarah and Jack.

"No, Sarah, I haven't read the letter. I'll read it later, if that's what you want. But right now, will you let me tell you what I believe it says? And will you tell me when I'm wrong?"

You're going to watch as he learns the truth. You'll see the tenderness disappear, and disgust and disappointment take its place. But that's for the best, isn't it? Even the shadow woman won't dare to fantasize after that.

"Yes, Jack, I'll tell you."

"Okay." Lifting her gently imprisoned wrists to his lips, he kissed her scars and whispered, between kisses, "You tried to kill yourself."

"Yes." *Oui!* the shadow woman cried with joy. You already know that proof of my madness, and still I see such love.

"And you very nearly succeeded, *wanted* to succeed."

"Yes." It was a punishing whisper, a confession meant to drive away the most brazen of shadows and the most tender of love.

But neither the shadow nor the tenderness vanished.

"When, Sarah?"

"Eleven years ago, on December twenty-third, four months after I was told that my baby had died."

"December twenty-third?"

Quite suddenly, Sarah saw torment, a ferocious storm of worry, and anger, on his handsome face. Why? Because the day she had tried to kill herself marked the one-year anniversary of Jed Taylor's death? Because even the mention of that date—and the reminder of his vicious father—evoked turbulent emotions?

"Jack?" Her wrists were still imprisoned by his hands, and held so tenderly against his lips; but now she reached for him, uncurling her fingers until they lay with love, with care, on the rippling hardness of his cheeks. "Are you thinking about Jed?"

"No." His voice was a storm in itself. But at its center, in the eye of the hurricane, was gentleness—for her. "I was thinking about you, Sarah. I never believed that Jessie was conceived during a week of wanton sex in Gstaad. I'd decided that Simon was her biological father, and that he raped you. But even that's wrong, isn't it? You became pregnant on December twenty-third, didn't you? During those hours when you and your parents were held by kidnappers."

That was the anniversary that filled him with such fury. The anniversary of her own descent into madness. Sarah's fingers curled anew, and her nails dug without mercy in the flesh of her palms, and when she sought freedom from the gentle imprisonment of his hands, she was granted it.

"You knew about the kidnapping?"

"I asked Scotland Yard for whatever could be found about your childhood. It was necessary, Sarah, a search for even remote links between you and Ashley and Paulina. The report about the kidnapping was brief, and reassuring. It said that you and your parents emerged from the ordeal unharmed." Jack gazed at the woman who stood apart from him now, close still, *but so very far away.* "But you were harmed, weren't you? Terribly, horribly harmed."

No lies, Sarah. *Tell him* how unworthy you were of being loved, how disposable. Tell him that your parents didn't have any qualms whatsoever about sacrificing you. "The kidnappers wanted me. And my parents . . . well, they didn't offer the slightest protest, not a gesture, not a word."

She was a warrior now, facing a firing squad with great dignity, steeled for the bullets that would irrevocably shatter her heart.

"Sarah," he whispered, extending a single hand, to cherish, not to kill, to hold, not to imprison, to love, not to cast away.

He was imploring her to meet him halfway, to entwine her hand with his, to choose him as he chose her—still. But Sarah's hands remained in tight fists at her sides, and her nails dug even deeper. There's *more*, Jack. More. Too much.

"Did Scotland Yard have a record of my stay at Avalon?"

"No." After a moment Jack's hand fell from the place in midair, that special place where the lovers were to meet, and trust, and love. It fell of its own accord, and then curled into a fist, hard and tight; but which could not begin to contain the powerful emotions that churned within. "Is that where you were during your pregnancy?"

"Yes. But it wasn't because I was pregnant that I was sent there. No one, except me, even knew about my pregnancy until I went into labor. Avalon is an insane asylum, Jack. And I was their prized inmate. As crazy as they come."

"Oh, Sarah," he said softly. "Not crazy. Never crazy. Just so hurt, so terribly betrayed. And the betrayal on that December twenty-third was just the beginning, wasn't it? Eight months later you were told that your baby had died, and less than six months later you married the man who had given Jessie away. Why, Sarah? Why did you marry him?"

Not crazy. Never crazy.

But crazy still, because now her foolish, damaged heart was beginning to pound with hope.

"I was *mad*, Jack. Certifiably insane. And my madness only

became more profound when I believed that my son had died. I began drinking then, every minute of every day—except when I could be with him, beside his grave. I needed to be there, talking to him, and eventually I made the decision to be with him. Always." *And I was almost there.* My blood was melting the tiny crystals of frost, seeping down to him, to warm him. "But Simon arrived just in time, and later, when he proposed marriage, I accepted his offer, because he promised that we would have children. But Simon Beckwith-Jones could not *have* children. He knew it, *made sure of it.* Simon did not want the babies of a madwoman. He only wanted her body."

"I wish they were still alive."

Sarah hadn't been looking at him. She had been staring at the black porcelain lamp instead, staring but not seeing, and hearing only vaguely her own confession of madness. And now she heard, only vaguely, Jack's words. But she heard with great clarity his tone. Quiet, yet fierce. Controlled, yet impassioned with fury.

She turned to him. "What did you say, Jack?"

"I wish they were still alive. Not the kidnappers. They were minor players, merely henchmen. But your parents, Sarah, and Simon. And do you know why?"

Sarah did *not* know why Jack would wish such a thing. But she was frightened. For herself? Because of his fury, the rage that gleamed with such terrifying power in his indigo eyes? No. Sarah did not fear for herself—just for him.

"No, Jack. Why?"

His lips answered first, a slight wry smile; and when those lips spoke, Sarah heard the bitter edge of pain. "Because, Sarah, I would like the great pleasure of killing them. One by one. With my bare hands. I really *am* Jed Taylor's son, aren't I? I feel it now, the seething violence Cole feared so much. But you know the truly interesting part? I'm not afraid of the violence. Not at all. I would welcome it, *welcome* it, if only they were alive."

"Oh, Jack, you're not a violent man."

"I think I am."

"*No.* You're not a violent man, Jack Dalton. You're just a wonderful one."

Sarah moved to him then, meeting him far more than halfway. She uncurled his clenched fists with her delicate—yet empowered—fingers, then slipped her fragile hands into his, trusting him not to crush her, *showing* him her trust.

And in so doing Sarah Pembroke discovered an extraordinary truth. She had something to give this wonderful man. Her *love.* That worthless, disposable, crazy thing? *Yes,* because it wasn't so worthless after all. Not worthless, just powerful. Because now, with her touch, with her love, Jack's torment was vanishing before her eyes, its mammoth fury replaced by something even more immense. *His* love for *her.*

The shadow woman was urging courageous words now, monumental confessions to be spoken, in French, to Jacques. And did Sarah banish the gossamer phantom who had survived so long on sheer folly, on the mad and glorious fantasies of love?

No. She merely embraced her. You are part of me, shadow woman. You always have been. And now we are one.

Softly, boldly, and in the Queen's English, Sarah asked of Jack, "Will you dance with me?"

They danced, in her stark and spacious living room. But the room wasn't stark now, it was filled with love, and there was color, where once there had been none. On the black lacquer table, like a perfect bouquet of pastel roses, lay the photo albums, where Sarah had left them when she had run to the studio to be with Jack.

And there was music, too. Not the distant sounds of London, of a city waking up; but music within. Their hearts sang a love song of joy, and were there truly carolers in the room as well? A tiny choir of crystal and silver and gold that encircled a winged horse of white marble?

Perhaps, after all, the eclectic community of glittering shapes had not huddled together merely to escape the stark frigidity of Sarah's penthouse. Perhaps they were *meant* to be together, assembled just so—so that on this day they could serenade the dancers with this crystal-pure, crystal-clear celebration of destiny . . . and of love.

Marry me, Sarah. Jack would say those words, when he could speak. And there would be more words, promises of love to the woman who had been raped but had never made love, and who had needed champagne to endure his touch. We'll dance, my love, and when our bodies demand rest, we'll sleep, just sleep, trusting each other with that chaste yet extraordinary intimacy. And sometime, when you're truly ready, when your lovely eyes don't fill with terror, we'll make love. And if that time never comes, cannot come? I love you, Sarah, always, no matter—

"Make love to me, Jack."

Her green eyes were glowing, clear and bright and gloriously unafraid. But still . . .

"There's no rush, Sarah. We have our entire lives."

"Don't you want to make love?"

Jack smiled. "You know I do." And then became solemn. "But, my love, you've been known to drink, to need to drink, to permit my touch, because you were so frightened."

"Yes. But it wasn't *remembered* fear, Jack. It was new fear. When you touched me in Paris . . . I'd never felt that way before, that wanting, that need. I believed those wondrous feelings could not be real, not for me. And what I feared most of all was my madness. But now . . ."

"But now, Sarah Pembroke, you are loved, and wanted and desired. Forever. And the only madness is not making love, right now, if that's what you want."

She had nothing to fear, his warrior who was a woman. He loved her carefully, a slow dance of love, a leisurely waltz of wonder. And as they held each other after, dancing still, always, Sarah's thoughts floated one last time to the shadow woman, that Parisian phantom who had been almost free.

Sarah and her shadow *were* free now. Wholly free. Whole. And free. And—

"Jack?"

She moved to see his face, searching it with such intensity that he frowned. "What is it, Sarah?"

"There's something I want you to know. You're not a violent man, Jack Dalton. But you *are* a murderer. You killed them. My parents and Simon Beckwith-Jones. They *were* alive still—their ghosts were—but now they're gone."

It was a daring pronouncement. But was it true? Or after a few seconds of stunned silence would she hear the familiar cackling of those malicious ghosts?

But Sarah heard nary a cackle, only his strong, steady heartbeat kissing hers; and then his whispered words of love; and then, in the distance, something joyous and faintly musical . . . the fluttering wings, perhaps, of a tiny marble horse.

Chapter Thirty-Six

THURSDAY FLOATED BY ON A FLEECY CLOUD of love and farewell. Of loving Jack, and saying good-bye—*au revoir*—to Claire, and bidding a forever *adieu* to a black-hearted murderess.

Now it was Friday, and Sarah was in her office at Asquith Towers, and already her direct line was trilling. Timothy, per-haps, admonishing her to take at least one more day before re-turning to work. Or Jack, loving her despite his own worries, and missing her, as she missed him, because an hour apart seemed far too long.

"I wasn't sure you'd be at work today."

"Lucas."

"Now I know why you wanted to wait until after Valentine's Day."

"You know?"

"You haven't seen this morning's papers."

No, not yet. But it was hardly surprising that during her own floating day of love and farewell, journalists here and in L.A. had been hard at work uncovering the grisly details of Sydney Quinn's transatlantic crime spree.

"Jessie was *always* safe, Lucas. Jack and I weren't followed to Cornwall. We made sure of it. I would never have put Jessie in jeopardy of any kind."

"I know that, Sarah. Emma and I both know. But now that it's over, and Jessie's still out of school, we're wondering if we should tell her."

"Today?"

Yes, today, this morning, *soon*. Sarah's hand touched the receiver long after her conversation with Lucas ended, not wanting to sever the link to Cornwall, to Jessica, to love. The invisible bond would linger, become even stronger, when she used that same receiver to speak to Jack, to let him know what Lucas had said. She would make that call soon.

Or would she? Would she share with Jack her hopes, and her worries, on this day when his own were already so immense? Today, at least, there *was* hope. Yesterday, on that floating day of love, there had been only such anguished worry.

Just moments after Claire had said to Cole her private good-bye, Jack stood beside his brother's bed in the ICU, making certain it was safe to leave him, just long enough to take Claire to Heathrow. Cole's eyes were closed, and his muscles were flaccid not fighting, and the ventilator puffed breaths into his chest, expanding it without resistance—or pain?—and a slow and steady beeping sound signaled the rhythmic beating of Cole's heart.

Cole was that way still, healing and at peace, when they returned from the airport. It was then that Jack took Sarah home, and they danced, and they loved. But had Cole truly been at peace? Or was that portrait of tranquillity, the panther tamed and docile, a surrender not to drugs . . . but to death?

If it had been a surrender to death, a willful acceptance of that ultimate fate, by midday the panther had changed his mind. He was fighting again, a ferocious battle despite ever-increasing doses of drugs. Jack and Sarah were there, at his bedside, helplessly bearing witness to his destructive torment. Cole was a caged beast, and the sight of his imprisonment was horrifying enough.

But it was made worse by the fact that the frantic fight for freedom came at the expense of what precious reserves he had, the energy necessary to heal the massive wounds of his flesh.

Cole was a wild beast, and a blind one. His gray eyes were wide open, and black with rage, but unseeing. Blind to their anxious faces, and deaf to their worried pleas, and if he didn't stop fighting, he would exhaust himself to death, or the drugs—ever-increasing doses, astonishing ones—would finally be too much, an overdose that would vanquish even the will of the panther.

Finally, as night fell over London, Cole's gray eyes focused. On Jack. It was a beseeching gaze, and a commanding one. Just as he had done when they met in the lobby of the Drake, Cole silently compelled his brother to look at his hand. On that night, it had been the right hand, the crippled hand, that Cole had wanted Jack to see. But on this night it was the left, the hand Cole had so painstakingly trained to do all manners of things, including to write.

That was what he wanted to do now, a task that required at least partial release of the restraints that were like chains to the panther. But Cole's doctors complied. It was imperative that they find a way to communicate with this patient who was killing himself.

Help me, Jack, Cole wrote. *I can breathe without the tube. I will. Tell them to let me try. Please.*

It wasn't the tube that was breathing for him, of course, but the ventilator. But in the name of compliance, to show their patient—who seemed quite lucid now—how terribly weak he was, how very far from being able to breathe on his own, the doctors conducted a test. The tube remained in his throat, but was temporarily detached from the ventilator, and Cole was told to breathe.

It wasn't a fair test. Cole was a living pharmacy of drugs designed to make him weak, to impede his urge to breathe on his own and to compel him to yield to the mandates of the ventilator. But still the panther breathed. Deep breaths. He's inhaling pure fire, Sarah thought as she watched. But he doesn't care. The pain doesn't matter.

But the weakness did. The drugs did. A few deep breaths were not enough to convince Cole's doctors to remove the tube. Not now, late at night, when his fatigue, not to mention the cumulative effect of all the drugs, could cause a sudden respiratory arrest, and when there wasn't an anesthesiologist nearby to rescue him.

They reached a compromise, however, a deal brokered by Jack. No more drugs would be given, and by morning, when Cole was virtually drug-free, they would conduct the test again. Cole would discover then what the fire truly felt like, unnumbed by narcotics; and the doctors would be able to assess the unencumbered strength of his muscles, and his will; and then, if it seemed safe, and was what Cole wanted still, in the light of day they would remove the tube.

When Jack and Sarah left the hospital at midnight, Cole was truly calm. He would surrender to the breaths of the ventilator overnight, and even to sleep, and in the morning his rested body would secure its freedom. And as for the panther's younger brother? He was tormented still.

It was not a night to make love, to be so free when his brother was so bound. And was it a night to sleep, to share that most vulnerable intimacy? That was the plan, what Jack wished *for her*. But wouldn't his own tossing and turning keep her awake? No . . . because he lay absolutely still, on his back, his hands at his sides, as if he, too, were chained.

But Sarah did not sleep. This is the man I love, she thought as she felt his silent torment. This wonderful man. And I have gifts to give him.

She reached for him, for one of the hands invisibly bound, and they spent the night talking, in the darkness, sharing *that* most vulnerable intimacy.

Two nights without sleep, but with such trust, such love.

Jack was at the hospital now, waiting to witness today's "test"—and the removal of the tube that he, although not Cole's doctors, was convinced would surely follow. The extubation itself was not without risk, the potentially lethal spasm of the larynx. For that reason, an anesthesiologist would be present, just in case. And afterward, if the time seemed right,

Jack would show Cole the package that had arrived from Denver, and—

And should she really try to reach Jack now, to tell him that for her as well this would be a day of risk and revelation? On this day when he had his own burden of worry, and of hope, should she add hers to his?

Yes. Because there was such trust . . . and such love.

"No!" Her cry of despair was identical to that of her mother, eleven and a half years ago, when Sarah was told that her precious baby had died. *"You're* my mummy. Aren't you? I don't *want* her to be my mummy." It seemed impossible that Jessica's despair could become even greater, but it did. "But you don't *want* me, do you? Daddy's known the truth from the time I was born, but you didn't know, and now that you do—"

"Oh, my love," Emma whispered, her own despair a halo of grief around her trembling body. "You're my *daughter*, Jessie. My baby, my miracle. I love you with my entire heart. You *know* that." *Please know that.*

"No I don't! If you did, you wouldn't be telling me this. *Daddy* didn't want me to know. That's why he was arguing with Sarah on the cliff. He doesn't want me to leave. But *you* do!"

"Stop this, Jessica." Lucas Cain's voice was more stern than his daughter had ever heard it, although his harshness was for himself, not for her. He was the one who had kept the secret all these years, but now it was Emma who was suffering for his secrecy. In Jessie's mind, *his* love was unquestioned. He had known from the first, indeed had *chosen* her. But Emma . . . "I'm sorry if I sounded cross, Jessie, but please don't do this to Mummy. Do you know how much she loves you? And how very brave she is? She was willing to risk losing the thing that mattered most to her in the entire world—*you*, Jessie—because she believed that telling you was honest, and right, and fair."

"Lose me?" Jessie looked from the father whose love was unquestioned to the mother she had doubted. And she saw such pain. "Oh, *Mummy*, I would never leave *you*."

Then she was in Emma's arms, being rocked so gently. "I'm so sorry, my Jessie, my precious love. *I was wrong.*"

Jessica pulled away from the embrace, just enough to see her mother's glistening eyes and to touch her mother's tear-damp cheeks. "No, Mummy, you *weren't* wrong. It was honest to tell me, and right and fair. But . . ."

"But?" Emma asked as she gazed at her daughter's lovely earnest face. "But what, my love?"

"Could we just pretend this never happened? Could we just be like we've always been?"

"Of course," Emma answered, praying that it could be so, but fearing that it could not. "Just you and me and Daddy. *Always.*"

Jessie looked to her father then, and when his dark green eyes—and were they glistening too?—made the same solemn vow, she asked, "Could you call Sarah, Daddy? Now? Could you just tell her . . ." Jessie's words faltered as images of Sarah—not her phantom mother, but *Sarah*—filled her mind; and then were banished. "Could you just tell her that we're fine, the way we are? Please?"

He found her on the roof, her private sanctuary atop the shining silver glass of Asquith Towers. She wasn't standing in her usual place, the vantage point from which to gaze at the Thames below and Westminster beyond. Instead she stood at the building's westernmost edge, facing the gusting winter wind . . . and Cornwall.

Her hair, which had abandoned its sleek knot, that austere punishment, a week ago, had now escaped even the loose confines of its colorful scarf. The black silk swirled about her head, at once dancing and lashing, and as he neared her, it seemed as if her body swayed, away from him, toward the windswept Cornish coast. And if she chose, if that was the decision she made, long before he reached her she could take the single step toward her daughter—and to the eternity that beckoned forty floors below.

"*Sarah!*"

"Jack?" She heard his heartstopping fear, and as she rushed to meet him, and the gusting wind swept away the blur of her tears, she saw the full measure of that fear. "Oh, Jack, has something happened to Cole?"

"No. No, Cole's fine."

"Then what is it, Jack? You look so worried."

"I'm worried about you."

About us. Sarah saw that truth quite clearly in the dark shadows of his dark blue eyes. Jack had obviously discovered that she had heard from Lucas, and believed that Sarah had chosen not to share her sadness with him. But that wasn't true.

"I *called* you," she pleaded softly. "You were in Cole's room, and the doctors were there, too, and I told the receptionist not to disturb you, that I would call back. I asked her not to tell you that I'd called."

"But she did tell me."

"She did?" *Then why do you look so betrayed?*

"Yes. And when I called your office, Frances told me how upset you seemed. You heard from Lucas again, didn't you? After he told Jessie about you?"

"Yes."

"He didn't waste much time, did he?" Jack's voice was edged with anger now, anger toward Lucas, and toward himself. *He* should have called Lucas, to be certain that if the news for Sarah from Hyacinth House was a rejection from her daughter, Lucas would let him know first, so that he could be with Sarah, so that she wouldn't rush up here, by herself, to this most dangerous place.

"Lucas didn't *enjoy* making the call. Even though he'd opposed the idea of telling Jessie, once that decision was made, he wanted it to go well—for Jessie, and Emma, and, I think, even for me. Quite obviously, it didn't go well. Although Lucas didn't really elaborate. He was apologetic, and very gentle, and he offered the hope that perhaps in time . . ."

"Were you going to give it time, Sarah?"

"No. I mean, I can't let myself dwell on some future that may never—" she stopped abruptly.

His eyes were so bleak, so *haunted,* as if plagued by some

sinister ghost from the past. And now they weren't even looking at her, but at the place where she had been standing, the
building's very edge. And, at last, she knew.

Yesterday, with his love, with his loving, Jack Dalton had
murdered the menacing ghosts of her parents and Simon Beckwith-Jones. But there was still that *other* ghost, the one that
only she could kill. And what of that phantom of her madness?
The one that had compelled her to slash her wrists to the bone
the last time she believed that her child was lost to her forever?

Was that demon of despair truly dead?

Yes. Oh yes. Sarah knew it. And now she touched the ice-
cold cheeks of the man she loved, framing his face with hands
that bore the gravestones of her once desperate madness.

"Oh, Jack," she whispered. "What happened makes me terribly sad. You know how hopeful I was. But I wasn't going to
jump. I didn't even think about it. And I never would. Never
again."

The ghost of my madness is dead.

The enormously valuable throat of the world's most famous
singer of love songs did not go into spasm when the plastic tube
was removed. Indeed, Cole did not even cough, an impulse
blocked by the powerful muscles of his neck and the certain
knowledge that such turbulence would cause even more fire
from the flames that seared his entire chest.

He spoke, because the doctors insisted that he do so, and after they left, he spoke again, to Jack, a hoarse whisper of fear.
"Has something happened to Claire?"

"No. She's fine. She called last night from New Orleans."

"New Orleans? Not Harlanville?"

"She decided to spend the night in New Orleans. A friend,
someone named Millicent, was with her. They're returning to
Harlanville today."

Cole's mind might have drifted then to Claire, relief that she
was safe and anguish that she was gone. But Cole knew that
anguish all too well, and Jack Dalton stood beside his bed, as
he had for much of yesterday, and his expression was the one

Cole had seen before—a look that said Jack needed something from *him*, as if the man who was so centered and so whole truly believed that Cole had answers to give him.

Answers? To *what*?

"Why are you here, Jack?" *Why did you seek my freedom last night as if it were your own? And why did the pain I was feeling seem to be shared by you?*

"Because of this," Jack answered quietly as he handed Cole the contents of the package that had been shipped with astonished urgency from his parents in Denver.

Cole's hands, unbound now, but trembling, touched the tattered quilt. It was smaller than he remembered, just barely large enough to wrap a battered boy, to protect a beloved brother from the chill of a December night and to cover his small, bruised face from peering eyes.

Cole looked from the tattered quilt to the powerful man who stood beside him. But who once had been a battered boy? And who had walked hand in hand with him along the banks of the bayou? And who, two nights ago, had sung to him their favorite lullaby?

"You're . . . ?"

"I'm your brother, Cole. I'm the little boy you saved."

Something wonderful, Claire had promised. A promise that seemed as impossible as their love. But Claire, the cinnamon-haired angel who believed in all dreams, had been right.

"You *did* save me, Cole," Jack said softly, shaken by the wonder he saw in Cole's eyes but wanting to say the words he had longed to speak for so many years. "My childhood was happy, filled with love."

Cole nodded. But he could not speak. Not yet. His throat, empty of that foreign tube, was filling again, with something just as foreign—emotion, and love.

"We spoke French, didn't we?"

"Yes." Cole could speak now. And the emotion? His voice sliced right through it, a vicious slash made by the knife-sharp edge of bitterness. "I taught you to speak French. It was our secret language. You were very verbal, fluent in English as well, and so smart. You knew never to speak French in front of our father. But that night, you didn't realize he was home. Neither of us did. That's why he hit you, Jack. It was my fault. I'm the one who defied him by teaching you French. But he hit you." *To punish me.*

"It wasn't your fault," Jack countered quietly. "You *saved* me."

Jack had no memories of the trauma inflicted on him on that December night, no glimpses of the nightmare in which his father's fist had savaged his small head. But two nights ago, during his phone call to Denver, Jack learned that his father's violence had indeed left a mark. He had always imagined, because his childhood memories were such happy ones, that despite his unwillingness to speak other words, he had cheerfully, and constantly, uttered, "Jacques, Jacques, Jacques."

But that wasn't true. He had *whispered* that forbidden word, his remembered—yet not remembered—fear overcome by his need to speak aloud that precious reminder of a secret lullaby sung by a beloved brother.

For Jack, all his life, French had been a language of love. And now he touched the brother who had taught him that special language, had given him that gift. And so much more.

It was Cole's crippled hand that Jack touched, the hand that had been ravaged by their father but which once had been so strong . . . and had once led a little brother on wondrous journeys through verdant forests beside a languid blue bayou . . . and had awakened that brother so gently on the night they said good-bye . . . and had touched that brother's cheek, had needed to, just one last time, for courage, and strength.

And now, with his brother's hand in his, Cole felt strength once again. *Strength* in that hopelessly crippled hand, as if it were healing, as if *he* were healing.

And when Jack whispered the same words, the last words, that Cole had whispered to him on that moonlit December night—*Je t'aime, je t'aime*—Cole Taylor felt almost whole . . . almost home.

Chapter Thirty-Seven

I T WASN'T A USUAL DAY AT HYACINTH HOUSE.
How could it be? But it was a day of love, of being together,
all three of them, all the time. They went to the cottage, to pat
Peggy; but Lucas put no chisels in his hands. On this day his
gifted hands were devoted to his daughter, and his wife.

They talked about going to the rink, for a demonstration of
Jessie's newest spin; but such separation, her on the ice and
them in the stands, seemed far too great. They played Scrabble
in front of a chattering fire, and they chattered themselves, and
Lucas shared with his "girls" his plans to take them both to
Italy in the spring.

And when Jessie faltered? When, suddenly, her face became
bewildered and she looked so lost? Their arms went around
her, creating a perfect circle of love, a ring so complete unto itself that it could not be broken.

And after dinner, they sat in the parlor and talked about the
gondolas of Venice. And was the television on, as usual? So
that Sarah Pembroke could tell them the news of the world, as
she had done, a most welcome guest, for the past two weeks?
No. It was not.

Until Jessie turned it on.

And four hours later, as Emma and Lucas stood in the doorway of her bedroom, Jessie's voice spoke to them from the darkness.

"She looked so sad. I don't *want* her to be sad."

"Sarah? It's Emma. We're at the Drake. Jessie would like to see you. She wanted to make the drive late last night, but we left at dawn instead."

And, Sarah thought, you didn't call in advance . . . because somewhere between the enchanted land of King Arthur and the rain-slick streets of Londontown, lovely Jessie might have changed her mind.

But Jessica Cain had not changed her mind, and in less than an hour she and Sarah were approaching each other in the Asian Garden at the Drake, and moments after quiet hellos—identically hopeful and shy—they were strolling amid gardenias and fan palms, gazing at the polished jade-green stones beneath their feet, their twin ponytails swaying in perfect harmony.

"I didn't want you to be sad."

"That's so nice of you, Jessie. But please don't worry about me. The most important thing is for *you* not to be sad."

"I'm not."

"I'm glad."

During the short journey from her penthouse to the Drake, Sarah had rehearsed a thousand things to say. How much she would have loved her, had loved her, *did* love her; but how very lucky Jessie was to have the parents, the mother *and* father, that she did. And the grandparents. And if Jessie wanted to see her just once a year, or perhaps even just write, that would be fine, *anything* would be fine.

Her words were far too presumptuous. Sarah knew that. Because what if what Jessie wanted most, still, was nothing? Besides, from the first quiet hello, Sarah sensed that Jessie had rehearsed words as well.

And Jessie's words, Jessie's wishes, were the only ones that mattered. *Even if she had come to say good-bye.*

Now her lovely daughter had told her not to be sad, and that was a glorious gift. But as they wandered beneath an arcade of bright yellow plumeria trees toward a massive flock of birds of paradise, there seemed to be even more that Jessie wanted to say.

Sarah waited, her heart racing with hope and fear, yet luxuriating in the sheer joy of being in this fragrant garden with her daughter.

"You're not going back to war, are you?"

Sarah smiled, her entire being smiled. "No. I'm not. Jack's already forbidden it. Not that I would *want* to go, of course."

"Are you and Jack . . . ?"

"We're going to be married, Jessie."

"Oh, *good*. I like Jack." The young voice was decisive, then curious. "When?"

"We thought Valentine's Day."

Jessica stopped walking then, stopped staring down at the polished jade-green stones. She looked at Sarah instead, her earnest biue-green eyes matching the solemn sincerity of her voice. "I wonder . . ."

Her unfinished query faded into a frown.

What do you wonder, my love? If Jack and I are planning to have children? Yes, we are, we were, but if it matters, if it would make you sad, we can wait until you're older. "What do you wonder, Jessie?"

"Well, Mummy makes—" She gasped. "I mean . . ."

"You mean Mummy," Sarah said softly. "It's all right, Jessie." *Anything is all right, my Jessie, no matter how my heart weeps.* "She's your mummy, and I'm Sarah. Okay?"

"Okay."

"Now, tell me what she makes."

"Wedding cakes. *Beautiful* ones. And Hyacinth House would be a very pretty place to be married, although in February the ceremony would have to be inside, and the flowers wouldn't be in bloom. But . . . oh, *no*. You're *crying*!"

The delicate fingers that, just yesterday, had touched the tears that dampened her mother's cheeks touched *these* tears now, the warm drops that spilled from her other mother's eyes.

"But I'm not sad, Jessie. In fact, I've never been so happy."

The panther fled England at midnight. It was a solitary journey, but not an unassisted one. After a loving, impassioned—but ultimately futile—attempt to convince him to stay, to heal, just a little longer, his younger brother became his accomplice. Indeed, it was Jack who convinced the doctors that, even if ill-advised, and perhaps dangerous, this journey was *necessary* to Cole's very survival.

Timothy provided the jet, and hence the privacy, and by midnight the lights of London were far below. And if only the searing fire in his chest did not melt the trail of tiny snowflakes, Cole, too, was on his way home.

He found her at dawn, beneath a pastel sky in their forest beside the bayou. The water was as still as glass, and a color he knew to be sapphire, and on this morning their bayou was a reflecting pond, mirroring perfectly the gossamer veils of Spanish moss and the snow-white birds that soared above.

His angel was singing, as she had been singing on that first, long-ago day.

"Amazing Grace, how sweet the sound—"

"That saved a wretch like me."

It was his lyric, and Cole sang it, and it didn't matter that his chest screamed with pain or that his voice, that multimillion-dollar voice, was still hoarse from the unyielding pressure of a plastic tube.

All that mattered was that she turned to him, and that her Claire-blue eyes were aglow.

The next lyric was his as well, in this duet that he and Claire had never sung. "I once was lost, but now am found—"

"*Cole,*" she whispered, stopping him, *needing* him to stop. "What are you doing here?"

I've come to see an angel. And I see her. But, despite her glowing blue eyes, she's such a troubled angel.

"We should have gotten married in Monte Carlo, Claire, before we ever made love. That was a promise I made to myself, for us, long ago. It's a promise I should have kept."

His voice heated the cool dawn air with the warmth of love. So why wasn't her hummingbird heart soaring with joy? Why was it so oddly, so ominously, still? "You've spoken to Dr. Gabriel, haven't you?"

Cole frowned. She *knew* he had, although she did not know the truth of that conversation. And now her expression was so grim, so sad, that surely she was remembering the words, the lies, he had spoken to Sydney. So why was Claire asking if he'd had a conversation with Angelica Gabriel *at all?*

"Yes. I thought you knew. I spoke with her the day after we returned from Monte Carlo."

"But not since then? Not since my visit to her office on Friday?"

"No."

"No?" *Then why are you here?*

"Did Dr. Gabriel tell you why I called her, Claire?"

"No. But I *know* why, Cole." *Because of that unfortunate deal breaker, that unacceptable flaw, the blindness that is just a bit too extreme for your taste.*

There was such pain in her lovely sightless eyes . . . a pain so great that even the golden flecks from her own inner sun had ceased to shine.

Softly, urgently, Cole spoke to that valiant—and vanishing—golden glow. "No, Claire, you *don't* know why. Not if Dr. Gabriel didn't tell you. I called to ask her about surgery, a transplant of my eyes for yours. My eyes were more than willing, Claire. They would have seen so much more with your heart guiding them. And I was more than willing, too. But I was going to ask a favor in return, a monumental one. I was going to ask if you would guide me through my darkness. Always. I'm asking that now. Will you marry me, Claire? I love you. *I have always loved you.*"

He didn't know, and his voice, so gentle and so raw, spoke with brilliant clarity of his love and his need.

Claire walked toward him then, across the thick vines that lay on the plush mossy carpet. It was a journey of shadows, not of darkness, a journey that one day, according to Dr. Gabriel, would be bright and clear.

The regeneration of her crushed optic nerve had begun long before Cole's Christmastime return to Harlanville. But until that night of snow, with him, she had not noticed the shimmering sparkles of color, the tingles of life from the slowly healing nerve.

Would she *ever* have noticed, without him? Or, without him, would her world have remained forever dark?

She stood before him now, and looked up to the beloved face she would one day see. "Yes, Cole. I will marry you. I love you, too. I have always loved you—too."

Claire believed she saw his eyes then, the brightest of silver glistening with tears of joy. Or perhaps she did not.

But Claire Chamberlain Taylor *would* see such joyous tears in the eyes of her panther, and clearly, in sixteen months, when Cole cradled in his arms their Augusta, their copper-haired baby girl, their precious Gussie.

But now it was Claire who was cradled in Cole's arms, in the sanctuary of his heat and of his love, and as they swayed to the music of the bayou, their hearts sang the final lyric of their duet . . . the lyric that was the most magnificent truth, for both of them.

Was blind, but now I see.

ABOUT THE AUTHOR

Katherine Stone is the bestselling author of eleven novels, which include *Happy Endings*, *Illusions*, *Promises*, *Rainbows*, and *Pearl Moon*. A physician who now writes full time, Katherine Stone lives near Seattle with her husband, novelist Jack Chase.